Before I Loved You

a love story by

Ashley Elizabeth

Before Series: Book Three

To my Lily,

the best niece and goddaughter I could have ever wished for.

Please don't read this book until you are much older.

Or your mom will never forgive me.

Love, Ashee.

AUTHOR'S NOTE

Before I Loved You takes place during the same time frame as *Before I Saw You*. There are some scenes depicted in both books, giving you a different character's perspective.
Although it is highly recommended that you read the Before series in chronological order to fully appreciate the story, it is not a requirement.

Book 1 – *Before I Tell You*
Book 2 – *Before I Saw You*
Book 3 – *Before I Loved You*

CONTENT WARNINGS

This book contains references to blackmail, gun violence, losing a parent (years prior), panic attacks, sexually explicit scenes, unknowingly being filmed during sex, and topics that may be sensitive to some readers.

Reading is an escape for many of us, so if you feel that the mention of any of the above will upset you, please put this book down.

I present to you Sarah and Paul's love story.

Xoxo, Ashley Elizabeth

Prologue

SARAH

God, I need a fucking distraction.

Hmm. Come to think of it, a *fucking* could be just the kind of distraction I need.

The bartender slides a second drink my way, winking, while I thank him with my best attempt at a flirty smile. Bringing the glass to my lips, I let my eyes gaze around the dimly lit room, searching for the one who will spend tonight making me forget everything.

And maybe if I'm lucky, he'll make me forget what day it is, too.

Let's see…

Too preppy.

Too old.

Too not my type.

Just my luck, I think, letting out a defeated sigh. Taking a sip of my drink, I close my eyes, enjoying the burn coating my throat, but when my eyes blink open, I see *him.*

My stomach flutters, my core instinctively pulses, and my lips part just from the mere sight of him.

He's the one—my *distraction.*

Inhaling deeply, I remind myself that I'll be the one in control tonight.

Not him.

Me.

Throwing back the rest of the liquid in my clear glass, I let my eyes drift over him from head to toe, and I can't help but wonder how freaking tall this man is as he ducks down under the arch of the entryway inside the bar.

God, he's gorgeous. From his muscular biceps, short dark hair that's faded on the sides, light brown skin, perfectly hypnotizing smile, and tall, lean frame, reminding me of an Olympic god, he seems to be the whole damn package, ready to be my...one-night distraction.

Yeah, I like the sound of that.

One-night distraction.

Nothing more than that.

Three guys surround him, tall too, but nowhere near as tall as him, and head toward the back of the bar for an empty booth.

But for whatever reason, the mystery man doesn't go with them. Instead, his eyes wander around the space. And as though he can read my every thought pertaining to him and the wild, sweaty night I have planned for us, his eyes land on me. They subtly glance up and down my body as I rest against the counter and purposefully stick out my ass, hoping to gain his interest.

And it works like a charm.

He saunters over to me—all ten feet of him. Okay, maybe he's not ten feet tall, but the closer he gets to me, the more my eyes have to look up, and my head has to tilt back.

"Hi," he says smoothly, leaning his hip against the counter.

He keeps a comfortable distance between us, which I appreciate. Still, at the same time, I find myself wishing he was closer.

My index finger glides around the edge of my glass as I smile at him. "Hi."

His eyes glimpse down at the empty glass in front of me. "Let me buy you a drink."

"Well, it's the least you can do, seeing that it's my birthday," I tease.

He smiles, and I swear I'm about to pass out.

Either that or jump on him, wrapping my legs around that torso that I'm certain contains a perfectly sculpted six-pack.

"Your birthday, huh?" He signals to the bartender, who begins fixing us drinks.

"Yup." Not a day that I very much care for, and honestly, I don't even know why I admitted that to him so easily. No one knows when my birthday is. And I keep it that way on purpose. I brazenly take a step closer to him, feeling his warmth radiate over me, and inhale his masculine scent.

It might be the two drinks talking, but this man feels like he was made for me. Even if just for one night only.

"Is it the big twenty-one?" he asks.

"Mm-hmm."

He glances around the room before his eyes land back on me where I want them to stay. "Are you celebrating with anyone?"

I shake my head.

"Well, happy birthday…"

He waits for me to say my name, but I won't.

Giving names will only make things complicated. Messy. But this can only happen once.

"Nope." I shake my head. "No names."

"No names? You on the run or something? Should I alert the authorities?" he asks, grinning.

I laugh, and it feels unfamiliar but pleasant. It makes me realize I can't remember the last time I genuinely laughed.

Pathetic.

I shrug. "You can. But then that would probably spoil my plans for tonight."

He licks his thick bottom lip, and I clench my thighs together in response.

I'm the one in control. Not him.

"And what would those plans have you doing?" he asks.

"You," I say very matter-of-factly.

The bartender slides two drinks towards us, and I reach for mine without a second thought, gulping down the liquid courage.

His eyes watch me, darkening with each sip I take. As I place my glass back on the counter, I purposefully stick my finger in my mouth, sucking off the contents that spilled on my skin.

"Fuck," he whispers, giving me satisfaction in knowing how much I'm affecting him.

"As a matter of fact, that's exactly what I hope we'll be doing tonight."

He takes a single step, closing all of the distance between us. "Don't you at least want to know my name?" He leans into me, his lips lightly brushing over my ear. "You know, before I give you your birthday present."

My birthday present.

No one has given me a birthday present in years. Granted, what he'll give me won't be wrapped in fancy paper and tied with a big, pretty bow. But somehow, I think it will be the best birthday present I've ever received.

I smile but shake my head. "No. It's better this way."

"Better for whom?" he asks softly. His large hand splays over my hip, his thumb gently stroking my bare skin, which is not covered by my black crop top, emitting a pleasurable surge throughout my body.

I was worried I wouldn't be able to do this. I was worried his touch would make me feel suffocated. Make my skin crawl. Make my body cringe and my feet want to run.

It's what has happened every time I've tried doing this with a man since *that* night.

But all I know right now, in my tipsy haze, is that I want this man more than I've wanted anything in my entire life.

But just for tonight.

One night only.

I look straight into his chocolate brown eyes when I say, "For me."

He nods, gently pulling me closer to his body. "And what else can I do for you?" he asks, searching my face for an answer he'll never get. At least not the honest answer, anyway.

"Make me forget."

One

SARAH

ONE MONTH LATER

"Shit."

I stare at the two vibrant pink lines, hoping that the longer I do, the greater the chance that one of them will disappear and I'll wake up from this living nightmare.

My fingers grip the white stick, bringing it to my eyes for a closer inspection. Unfortunately, both lines are displayed smugly, mocking me, with no intentions of going anywhere. I drop the stick onto the bathroom counter and pick up the box, flipping it over for directions, which I quickly scan.

How complicated is it to pee on a stick?

My eyes dart back and forth until I get to the part I'm looking for, and my fear is confirmed.

One line: not pregnant.

Two lines: pregnant.

Shit. Shit. Shit.

Absently, I drop the box in the trash and push the stick off the counter and into the small metal barrel, seeing that staring at it won't change the results.

A rush of anxiety sweeps through me, and I quickly sit on the edge of the bathtub, gripping the porcelain tile with shaky fingers as the seriousness of the situation hits me like a ton of bricks.

And then it dawns on me.

I don't even know who the father is.

Oh. My. God.

I mean, I know who the father is. He's the only guy I've slept with since *that* night, but what I don't know is his goddamn name.

A high-pitched laugh bubbles out of me at the insanity of that statement. *Oh great.* I'm not just pregnant, but I'm also officially losing my mind.

How could this happen?

We used a condom. I know we used a condom. I rolled it on his huge dick, for God's sake!

Did it break?

How am I going to be able to afford a baby?

How do you even take care of a baby?

Are they like pets that can care for themselves while you go to work and school?

Can I do this alone?

What am I going to do?

I pinch the bridge of my nose, a throbbing headache forming with each question assaulting me one after the other, and I can't make them stop.

Deep breath. You'll figure this out. You always do.

I stand and turn to the side, looking in the mirror. So far, there's no baby bump. At this stage, not a soul would even know I'm pregnant, but I wonder how long I have until a bump does show because I need time to figure everything out.

My hand rests on my flat stomach, hoping to feel something that will give me a sign, but even I know it's too early.

I let my hand fall to my side as I make my way out of the bathroom and into my bedroom. My textbooks are stacked on my desk, ready for my first day of classes as a junior next week at Linrey University. My new paints remain bagged in the corner of my room, waiting for inspiration to find me. And the terrifying pile of bills on my dresser makes my stomach plummet. But maybe that's just the pregnancy and not the impending doom looming over me.

Up until this point, I've been able to get by financially. *Get by* meaning I have a roof over my head and food in my belly. I have a decent apartment thanks to my small trust fund, I received academic scholarships that covered most of my school expenses, and I've worked for as long as I can remember to cover any and all necessities, never needing much.

But my trust fund is almost depleted, and getting by isn't going to be enough with a baby on the way.

There's diapers and formula and bottles and toys and a crib and...

Breathe!

I rest my hands on my chest, the intense spike of my heartbeat concerning me as I take a deep breath, trying to figure out what step one should be.

As long as I make a game plan and don't let anything mess with this plan, then everything will be fine.

Everything will be fine.

Sitting on the edge of my bed, I reach for Teddy, hugging him tightly against my chest. The poor guy has seen better days. His once bright beige sherpa fabric has dulled out with several little stains. One of his eyes hangs on by a thread. *Literally.* And the pink bow around his neck has a few splits at the end, the fabric fraying. He's not much to look at, but he's my teddy bear.

My teddy bear that has been with me through the good and the bad of the past twelve years.

Even if the bad days have outweighed the good ones.

He's always been here for me.

And yes, I know he's an inanimate object, but...he's all I have.

Placing Teddy back in his spot in the center of my bed, I straighten my shoulders and take a deep breath.

I guess step one should be to make an appointment at a doctor's office to confirm whether I am pregnant or not. Maybe that stupid stick was lying to me, and I'm worrying over nothing.

Quickly, I take my phone out of my pocket and call to make an appointment nearby. The receptionist informs me that they'll be able to see me in an hour, which is great. *The sooner, the better.* And then I'm sure they'll tell me I'm not pregnant, and everything will go back to normal.

But what if they do tell me I'm pregnant?

Then what?

I chew on my black-painted thumbnail, contemplating this.

It will be so embarrassing to admit to people that I don't even know who the father is.

He was just some guy at the right place at the right time.

Some guy who was the perfect distraction.

Some guy I haven't been able to stop thinking about for the past month.

And some guy who gave me the best sex of my life.

The best night of my life, if I'm being honest.

I look up at the ceiling toward the "Big Man" upstairs.

"Well played, sir. You got me. Lesson learned. No more one-night stands for me."

I throw my hands in the air, jutting out my middle fingers in frustration before turning to my closet to grab a black T-shirt to wear over my black lace bra. I reach for a pair of denim shorts on the floor and throw those on, too, before sliding my feet into a pair of black sneakers. Throwing my long, dark hair in a pony, I take one final look in the mirror and then make my way out of my apartment, ready to end this little nightmare.

Because there is no way that I'm pregnant.

* * *

"You're pregnant," Dr. Martin, the obstetrician, says matter-of-factly, looking over the test results in her hands.

"Are you sure there's no way it could be wrong?" I ask, praying for a sliver of a chance it could be negative. "Aren't there like false positives all the time?"

"Afraid not," she responds. "Your blood work shows a high level of hCG, the hormone produced during pregnancy."

"But we used a condom," I complain as though it's her fault I'm in this predicament.

"I'm afraid condoms are only ninety-eight percent effective when not used with another form of contraception like the pill or an IUD. And when not used correctly, the effectiveness drops to eighty-five percent." She places her clipboard on the counter, crossing her arms over her chest.

"Well, they should put that in a big, bold font on the front of the box," I mumble, anxiously biting my bottom lip.

Dr. Martin pushes her glasses to the top of her head over her short, auburn hair and gives me a sympathetic smile. "I'm going to take a wild guess and say this wasn't planned?"

"Gee, what gave it away?" I ask with sarcasm dripping from my voice. I sigh and lean back on the awkward table with stirrups at one end, planting the palms of my hands into my eyes. "Sorry. No. This was definitely not planned."

She rolls her little stool closer to me and takes a seat. "And the father?"

I drop my hands to my sides and let out a long breath, shaking my head.

It's my own fault.

"Any family?" she asks.

My throat tightens as I shake my head again.

It's just me.

There's no way I'm discussing my family or lack thereof right now. All it will get me is a look of pity, and I don't think I can handle one of *those* looks at the moment.

"You know, there are options for you." She opens a drawer, digs around, and then extends her arm toward me, handing me a few brochures. The top one reads, *Adoption. Is it for me?* My stomach immediately coils into tight, guilty knots. She then pushes a thick packet into my hands titled *Hello, New Mom,* containing all the essential information needed to have a baby. "Why don't you take these home and do some research? Think about what feels best for you and the baby."

I give her a tight lip smile, trying to rein in the overwhelming urge to cry.

"Call us when you're ready to schedule your next appointment, and we'll take it one step at a time. I know it might feel like you're alone, but there's a whole team of amazing doctors here who will do everything they can to help you through this." She smiles warmly, like a loving mother, and my heart constricts.

"Thank you," I choke out, holding in the tears.

She stands and walks out, giving me the room to myself. And that's when the tears rain down, cascading over my cheeks. I look down at the floral tattoo pattern covering my left arm as my finger traces the lily located right over the inside of my wrist.

My mom's favorite flower.

I take a deep breath and look out the far window, noting the ominous grey clouds producing big rain droplets, mirroring my tears.

How am I going to be a good mother when I barely had enough time with my own?

Two

PAUL

"**O**h my God! Are you Paul Weston?"

Stopping dead in my tracks, I spin around on the balls of my feet, longing to see those angelic emerald-green eyes I've been dreaming about for the past month.

The ones I see every single damn time I have my hand wrapped around my cock with my eyes closed, savoring my delicious memory from the night with the girl of my dreams.

The girl with no name.

Or, as I've been referring to her in my head, *She-Who-Must-Not-Be-Named.*

But as my eyes land on the girl before me with long, straight blonde hair and dull brown eyes that widen in my presence, I let out a disappointed sigh.

No, she is most definitely not the girl from my dreams.

Her red-headed friend beside her grips her shoulder in excitement. You would think this would be something I'd be used to by now, but I'm not.

And it hasn't seemed to get any easier over time.

If anything, it makes me feel more isolated and alone.

Sometimes, I feel like an animal in a zoo, biding my time in an enclosure behind a glass wall for everyone to gawk at, purely because of the last name on my basketball jersey.

But they don't know me.

Not the real me.

I plaster on a fake smile, knowing these girls are fans and it's not their fault I feel like this.

This is a *me* problem.

"Yes, I am." I hitch my sports bag over my shoulder, rolling my neck.

"Could I... I mean, can you sign something for me?" the blonde girl asks nervously.

"Of course. What did you want me to sign?"

She opens her purse, digging through it, and then quickly pulls out a Sharpie.

"Can you sign my shirt?" She turns around, moving her blonde hair over her shoulder. It takes me a second to realize she's wearing my jersey.

Taking the Sharpie from her, I lean down to sign her back.

This girl's not too short, probably just over five feet tall. But being six foot nine can make most average-sized people appear small compared to me.

Something I'm very used to.

Of course, it didn't deter *She-Who-Must-Not-Be-Named*. If anything, she loved it. Proven when she climbed me like her own personal ladder, wrapping her luscious thighs around my waist as I fu—

"Thank you!" the girl squeals in excitement, taking the Sharpie from my hand.

"Anytime," I respond, internally shaking my head to rid myself of thoughts of that night.

Not something I've easily been able to do.

The two girls walk away giggling as I turn and continue into the locker room, finding my teammates prepping for practice.

"Look who it is. The legend himself!" Glen, my friend from grade school and now my teammate on the Linrey University basketball team, broadcasts as I make my way over to my locker. He jumps up, trying to tap me on the head, but, like always, comes up too short.

A few guys from the team pat me on the shoulder or fist bump me as I sit on the bench, dropping my bag to the floor.

"Coach Rivers wants to see you," Tony, one of our shooting guards, informs me.

"Do you know what he wants?" The zipper on my bag snags as I yank it back, revealing my essentials for practice: headband, sports drink, protein bar, and basketball shoes.

He shakes his head and then shifts it toward the coach's office. "All I know is that Greyson is in there too."

Greyson Black, the captain of the Linrey University basketball team.

I've never liked the guy.

Something has just always felt off about him, so I make sure to keep my distance. And he usually does the same to me.

"Thanks." Quickly, I change into my practice uniform and throw my bag into my locker before walking to Coach Rivers' door. My hand wraps around the silver handle as I hesitantly push it open, unsure what to expect. "You wanted to see me, Coach?"

"Yes, Paul, please take a seat." He motions toward the chair in front of his desk, placed beside Greyson.

Greyson doesn't look at me as I approach, taking a seat. Nor does he show any emotion on his face besides a clenched jaw as he stares straight ahead, his fists tightened by his sides.

"I was just discussing logistics for this year with Greyson," Coach deadpans.

"Logistics?" I ask.

He nods, sitting back in his seat as he places his right ankle over his left knee. "Yes. I'll cut straight to the point. We want to offer you a place as a captain for your senior year."

And now, I know why Greyson looks ready to murder me.

"But Greyson is the captain," I counter.

"Yes. Yes. Well, we were looking to have you both be co-captains of sorts. Having the two of you as head figures for the other team members to look up to will be motivational."

Motivational?

I wish he would just say the real reason.

They want me to be captain because of my last name.

Weston.

Just like the famous Steve Weston.

Aka my dad.

Making me captain will guarantee more publicity for the team, which the organization wants and needs.

I sigh, rubbing at my chest. "Sir, I would be honored, but..." I glance at Greyson. "This doesn't feel right. I only joined the team in the spring after transferring here, and Greyson has been here for three years now."

"Greyson doesn't mind. Do you?" Coach Rivers directs his sight on Greyson as his fingers steeple in front of him, waiting for Greyson to respond.

Greyson turns his head toward me, an unpleasant grin appearing. "Not at all. It would be an honor to share the spotlight with Paul *Weston*."

The smug way he enunciates my last name goes right over the coach's head.

"Good." Coach nods, sitting up. "Paul, there's also a couple of scouts out there to watch you today. I'll make the announcement at the beginning of practice so they're all aware of what's going on."

Squeezing the back of my neck, I nod. "Sounds great, Coach."

No, it doesn't. It sounds fucking horrible.

He stands from his desk, grabs some folders, and prepares to leave. "Well, see you boys out there."

The moment the door closes behind him, I feel Greyson's beady blue eyes latch onto me.

The tension in the room could be cut with a knife.

A big fat fucking steak knife.

Greyson shakes his head and gets up, walking toward the door when I stop him.

"Wait, Greyson." I grab his shoulder. "I didn't want this. I can tell them I won't accept if that's what you want. I understand if—"

He laughs, shoving my hand off of his shoulder.

Eyeing me up and down with a condescending scowl, he sneers, "Better keep both eyes open out there." While walking out of the room, his fist connects with a locker, denting the metal. As he passes through the space, the heads of every nearby player turn to gape.

Glen walks up beside me, his eyes on Greyson's back as he walks out the door. "What the fuck was that about?"

I scratch the back of my head, exhaling deeply. "I think I just ended up on Greyson's shit list."

Glen lets out a low whistle. "You're so fucked, man."

Wiser words have never been spoken.

* * *

The wind whips at my face as splashes of saltwater caress my warm, sun-beaten skin. It's the last summer weekend before school resumes, and I plan to do what I do best.

Relax.

"Don't get too comfortable. I'm going to need your help eventually," Nate announces as we come to a dead stop, surrounded by ocean water for as far as the eye can see.

Nate Thomas, my closest friend, is one of the main reasons I transferred to Linrey University, conveniently centered in my favorite city, Boston.

My family home is only about thirty minutes from campus, so when I first went off to college after high school, I thought I needed some distance and ended up in New Hampshire.

But by the beginning of my junior year, I realized that distance was the last thing I needed from my family and decided to come home.

It was one of the best decisions I've ever made.

"Yeah. Yeah." I cross one arm behind my head, closing my eyes as I lie back on the cushioned bench seat. My larger-than-life legs dangle off the boat.

I hear the familiar crack of a beer can and peek my eyes open to find Nate handing me one.

Sitting up, I take it. "Thanks."

The cold liquid flowing down my throat is refreshing and just what I need after spending all morning in the gym with my team.

The news of me becoming a co-captain with Greyson went as well as expected.

The scouts were all overly eager to talk to me. My teammates gave me a congratulatory slap on the back. And Greyson spent the rest of the practice scowling at me from across the room.

I run a hand down my face.

This is going to be one fucking long season.

"Why so down?" Nate sits on the captain's chair, crossing his ankles before him.

I shrug it off. "Just a long day."

"What's going on, man? You haven't been yourself for the past month." He crosses his arms over his chest, brows furrowing. "Do you regret transferring to Linrey?"

"No." I adamantly shake my head. "It's not that."

He arches a brow, waiting for me to continue, but I don't know if I can.

Because what I'm about to admit is going to make me sound like a prepubescent teenage boy.

Pinching the bridge of my nose, I close my eyes.

Let's get this over with.

"There's a girl…"

"Aha! I knew it." He chuckles, turning his baseball hat backward. "Who is it?"

"Well, that's the thing." I let out a resigned sigh. "I don't actually know."

His face scrunches in confusion. "You've lost me."

I rest my elbows on my knees, staring at the vinyl flooring. "About a month ago, some guys from my team and I went to On The Rocks, the bar near campus under a hotel. I honestly didn't even want to be there, but…" I shake my head. "The second I walked in, my eyes locked onto this girl." The memory of her pops into my mind, fresh and vibrant. Her long, silky black strands of hair smelled of apple and honey. Her iridescent green eyes sparkled under the bar lights. That damn beautiful smile and those delicate floral tattoos on her pale thighs and arms I traced with my tongue. "My legs walked over to her on their own accord. It was like she was some damn magnet, and I couldn't pull away from her even if I wanted to. There was something about her. It was as though I knew her, but I didn't." I look off at the sea. "I knew she was there, looking for someone to leave with. So I made sure that someone was me. We left the bar to get a room, and we…" I wave my hand around dismissively. "Well, you get the picture."

Nate laughs, shaking his head.

"It was the best night of my life," I say matter-of-factly. "I haven't been able to stop thinking about her. And it's driving me fucking crazy."

"Then why don't you just call her?" he asks, tilting his head.

"I can't."

"Why not?"

"Because I don't even fucking know who she is," I say, sounding as exasperated as I feel.

Nate's brows raise, clearly needing me to explain.

"We never exchanged numbers. And we never exchanged names. She didn't want to make things complicated. She just wanted one night, and that's what I gave her. One night."

There's pity on Nate's face. "But Paul, you're not a one-night stand kind of guy."

I let out a humorless laugh. "Yeah. I know that." I finish the rest of my drink and toss it beside me. "She had no idea who I was. No care about my last name or how much money sits on my future NBA contract. And yet, she wanted me. Do you know how refreshing that was?"

Nate nods, taking in my words.

He's the only one I've talked to about this.

The weight that crushes my shoulders, knowing what people expect from me because of the last name on my jersey.

Because once a girl finds out who I am, or more accurately, my last name, that's all they care about.

Not me, but a front-row seat in the spotlight that shines too bright for my liking.

They know I'm the NBA's most sought-after player, expected to be the number-one draft pick next year, and all they see in their pretty eyes are those flashing neon dollar bill signs.

"There must be a way to find her," Nate insists, removing his hat to run his fingers through his dark brown hair.

"I've tried. I've tried absolutely everything." My fingers grip the side of the boat as I lean back, gazing up at the clear sky. "I've gone back to the bar several times. I've searched aimlessly through campus. I've even gone through the campus website, searching for her damn eyes when I don't even know if she's a student here." My eyes pinch shut. "I've looked for her every night since then, but I think it's time for me to accept defeat at this point."

"Every night?" Nate questions.

"Every. Damn. Night."

"Last call!" the bartender shouts as he flicks the lights on.

I swirl the remaining amber liquid in my glass before finishing it off, relishing the burn that travels down my throat. Every taste reminds me of that night—of her.

"You're sure you haven't seen anyone that resembles the description I just gave you? Long, black hair. Perfect green eyes. Floral tattoos covering her arms." I tilt my head toward the bartender, waiting for his response.

He sighs, shaking his head. "Like I've told you almost every night for the past month, I've seen thousands of girls coming in and out of this place. At this point, they all look the same to me." The bartender wipes down the counter before throwing the rag over his shoulder. "You're a good-looking guy. I'm sure the ladies must love your height, so trust me when I say there's someone else out there for you. Stop wasting your time on finding some girl." He lifts a container of dishes from the sink and disappears into the back room.

Sighing heavily, I pull a couple of bills out of my wallet and place them on the counter before turning to leave. I've lost count of how many times I've escaped here, searching for her. The girl with no name.

And every night, I leave here with a dull, hopeless ache in the center of my chest.

Maybe the bartender was right. Maybe I should just give up.

But I've never been a quitter. And I won't start that shit now.

"I'll be back tomorrow," I yell over my shoulder, knowing he can't hear me but not giving a damn.

I'm not giving up on finding her.

Because how can you give up on finding the one person in a world of over seven billion people who somehow makes you feel not so alone anymore?

You can't.

"I'm sorry, man." Nate nudges my hand, bringing me out of my memory with another cold can of beer that I gladly take. "Maybe she'll turn up when you least expect it."

"Yeah. Maybe." I know she won't. I don't have that kind of luck. "I just... For a fleeting moment, I thought I might have what you and Natalie have."

Nate and Natalie.

The couple of all couples.

Nate shakes his head. "You will, Paul," he says adamantly. "I know you will."

I tug on the silver chain dangling against my chest, twisting it around my finger. "Maybe it's the beer talking, but I guess I've just been feeling lonely. You've got Natalie. Jason's got Vanessa."

Nate's brows shoot up to his hairline.

"Don't kid yourself. Jason and Vanessa will be together before the end of the semester, mark my words."

It's no secret that Jason, Natalie's younger brother, is in love with her best friend, Vanessa.

But the only one who doesn't know that yet is Jason.

Nate chuckles, clutching the brim of his hat. "Yeah, you're probably right."

"And then there's me." I lie back on the bench, staring at two seagulls flying over us, closely together. Even the damn birds have found love. "And for one night, being with that girl didn't make me feel so alone anymore. I felt...whole."

For one night, I felt like I had found my person.

And I know that sounds ridiculous, especially when I had never believed in love at first sight.

Never even believed in finding my happily ever after.

Until that night, that is.

When those green eyes embedded themselves not just in my mind but in my heart too.

And now...

Now, I don't know what to believe.

Three

SARAH

I spin on my black cushioned leather office chair in front of my new espresso brown desk, feeling so damn proud of myself.

I did it.

I freaking did it!

After spending a mundane year doing my time as the coffee girl at a bank close to school, making minimum wage, I scored myself a paid internship at a corporate office for one of the biggest banks in the world, LH United. Not only is it just a quick car ride from my apartment to its location in the financial district, but it's also a position that allows flexibility with my schedule while attending school. It's perfect.

My end goal of becoming a financial analyst is becoming closer and closer with each day.

I can feel it.

And no, my dream out of life was never to be a financial analyst. In fact, the thought of working in a corporate office for the rest of my life makes me want to gouge my eyes out and eat oysters.

Yeah, I really don't like oysters.

But it's a good, stable job. A job that will bring in a decent salary and allow me to continue taking care of myself like I always have. Money is tight enough as it is in this economy. Never mind adding a baby to the mix.

Even if I'm not entirely sure what I'm going to do about that yet…

Anyway, the point is that everything depends on me doing well in this internship, especially when I no longer have the option of failing.

"Hi, Sarah." A beautiful, tall brunette approaches my desk, extending her slender hand. "I'm Gianna. It's so nice to meet you."

"Nice to meet you." I smile as I stand, extending my arm toward her, currently covered in my black cardigan. I didn't think my floral arm tattoos would fit in a place like this and would most definitely guarantee a judgmental look from each stuck-up person here, so I opted for a boring cardigan to be safe.

I'll say it. Banking people aren't my cup of tea. But again, I'm here to bring home a steady paycheck. And it helps that I'm pretty good with numbers.

Scratch that. I'm really damn good with numbers.

"I'm the financial service administrator and sit just down the hall over there." She points her French-manicured finger toward her desk, and I suddenly wonder if it's acceptable that mine are black. Shit, I didn't think about that. "It's so nice having another woman in the office, so if you ever want to grab a coffee or lunch and save me from all the boredom, just let me know."

"I will definitely take you up on that."

She smiles and then walks away, leaving me to turn on my computer and start my day. After a few hours, my stomach rumbles, so I reach inside my purse for one of my protein bars to hold me over, and just as I take a rather large bite of the bar, my phone rings.

I pick it up without looking at it like an idiot. "Hello," I murmur through a mouthful of food.

"Hi, Sarah, this is Sabrina, Mr. Black's secretary. He asked for you to see him now."

I gulp down my bar. Mr. Black. The big boss. The head of this corporate office wants me to see him. "Of course! I'm on my way." I jump out of my seat, straighten my dress, ensure my cardigan is buttoned, and smooth out my hair before letting out a deep breath. My heels click on the glossy floor with each step I take, getting closer and closer to his office.

As I approach, I see who I assume is Sabrina sitting at a desk outside his office. She looks at me, smiling, and tells me to go inside.

My fingers tremble as I carefully open the frosted glass door.

"Mr. Black. You wanted to see me, sir?" I ask, cautiously making my way inside.

"Ah, yes. Sarah. I'm so sorry." He stands from his seat and walks toward me, extending his hand. "I hoped to meet you this morning, but the day has been quite hectic."

The man looks like Santa Claus in a black suit, which makes me smile. There's something so warm and welcoming about him. Although his eyes hold a familiar deep blue hue that I can't quite place.

"No worries, sir. Everyone here has been very welcoming," I assure him, clasping my hand around his in a handshake. Not too firm. And not weak. But just right. I might have practiced a few times this morning with myself. I internally cringe at how pathetic I sound.

"Good. Good. I'm glad to hear that." He motions for me to sit on the chair closest to me, putting my back to the door as he takes the seat opposite me.

"I have to say we were quite impressed with your resume—a perfect 4.0 GPA. You're clearly a very diligent worker, and we're excited to help you become a financial analyst," he says.

"It would be a dream, sir," I lie. Maybe someone else's dream. Not mine, though. But this probably isn't the best time to mention my dream, which entails me sitting in a private art studio that overlooks water and wildlife. Painting until I can't feel my fingers.

We'll save that conversation for another time.

"Well, we're delighted to hear that." He smiles. "Unfortunately, I won't be here for the next few months to help mentor you, but my son—"

Knock. Knock. Knock.

"Ah, perfect timing." His smile grows as he stands, motioning for the person to enter. I hear the door open behind me, followed by a shuffle of feet. "Son, this is our newest intern and someone I see having real potential with our company."

I stand and turn with a friendly smile until, suddenly, the air in my lungs all at once leaves me. My eyes widen, and my smile falters as a familiar pair of deep blue eyes narrow in on me, sending an instant wave of nausea throughout my entire body.

No. No. No. No.

"Greyson, this is Sarah." Mr. Black looks between me and his son. "Sarah, this is my son. He will be here to assist you with your transition."

Greyson smirks, extending his hand for me to take. "It's nice to meet you, Sarah. I'm looking forward to working closely with you," the smug bastard says, knowing damn well who I am.

I do everything I can to show no ounce of fear as my hand briefly touches his in an uncomfortable shake. "Likewise."

"Someday," Mr. Black starts, "Greyson will be taking over for me, making his old man proud." Greyson subtly nods, but my eyes catch on his fist, tightening close to his side. "If I'm correct, you both attend the same school, Linrey University." Mr. Black squeezes his son's shoulder.

"That's correct, sir," I add, my pulse beating rapidly beneath my chest.

"My son here is the captain—" Greyson gives him a slight scowl, cutting off his words. "Or I mean, he's one of the captains of the basketball team." He smiles proudly, and I instantly feel bad for this man who has no idea how evil his son is. "So he is quite busy, but in his downtime, he'll be here watching over the office while I'm away for business. He'll also be here to help you with whatever you need."

I nod, displaying a fake smile as I fight the urge to vomit in the middle of his office. I'm quite sure that would warrant me getting fired on my first day.

"Well, I didn't mean to keep you, Sarah, but again, we're thrilled to have you here, and we hope you feel the same," Mr. Black notes.

"I am. Thank you," I confirm, shaking his hand again before I walk past him, avoiding the beady eyes drilling holes in the side of my head from his son.

The second I'm out of his office, I book it to the bathroom, no longer able to keep down the protein bar in my stomach. I push the bathroom door open, relieved to find no one else inside and enter one of the stalls to empty my stomach.

I wipe my mouth with a piece of toilet paper and flush, leaning against the wall as I stare at the ceiling, fighting back tears that want to escape.

This can't be happening.

I hear the door open and straighten my spine while smoothing my hair. I unlock the stall and walk toward the sink to wash my hands, keeping my gaze straight ahead. The freezing water on my skin is comforting as my heart continues racing erratically.

Calm down. Just breathe. Everything is fine.

"Not happy to see me, Sarah?"

Every muscle in my body tenses, fear crescendoing throughout me.

The cruelty in his voice sends a shiver down my spine, and I grip the edge of the sink so I don't fall straight to the floor. Glaring in the mirror, I find Greyson leaning against the door with his arms crossed, watching me maliciously.

"What the fuck are you doing here?" I demand, relieved my voice doesn't give away to the panic inside me.

He makes a *tsk* sound of disapproval before standing straight, locking the door, and walking toward me. "Now, that's no way to talk to the boss's son. Is it?"

I remain silent as he approaches, feeling every part of my body ready to turn on flight mode. But as he stands directly behind me, looking in the mirror at me, I calmly say, "What do you want?"

He looks me over, making me feel like a cheap used car up for auction. "I haven't decided yet. But when I do, you'll be the first to know." His eyes catch mine in the mirror.

"I won't do anything for you."

"Oh, but you will." He leans down, brushing his lips over my ear. "You see, I can be quite convincing when necessary."

"You don't own me," I grit out.

His smile grows, his eyes glinting with cruel intent. "I think you'll find that I do." His hand grips a piece of my hair, twirling it around his finger. He brings it up to his nose, deeply inhaling. "Apple and honey?"

"Don't touch me." I step to the side, pushing away from him, but in mere seconds, he has me pinned to the wall with his hands wrapped around my neck.

"Don't piss me off, Sarah, when you know what I have on you." His fingers dig into my neck as I fight for breath under his hold. My hands claw at his, digging my nails into his skin, but it's futile.

"You're disgusting," I manage to spit out.

"I just know how to get what I want. It's not personal. Just business." He releases me, and I clutch my neck, gasping in as much air as I can.

"See you around, Sarah. Oh, and don't be late. The boss is a real stickler for that." He chuckles and then taps my nose before he walks out the door as though he didn't just try to strangle me in the bathroom.

I slide down against the cold wall, letting tears run fervently down my cheeks.

What am I going to do?

I worked so hard to be here, and I need this money. It's too late in the year to try to find a new internship, and even if I do, it won't be comparable to this.

He's going to destroy me.

I could see it in his cold eyes.

Even though I never did anything to him to make him feel this way toward me. He's just hated me since the night he chose me as his personal pawn.

The night I'll never be able to escape.

After finishing my work for the day, acting as though the boss's son didn't attack me in the bathroom, I stop at the grocery store on the way home, starving for food but feeling too emotionally exhausted to make anything. Not to mention, I only have twenty dollars in my wallet. So I leave with a pint of Ben and Jerry's, a tub of peanut butter, and a jar of dill pickles.

Opening the door to my apartment, I've never been so relieved to be home. As I lock up behind me, I rest my forehead against the smooth surface and let out a long, deep breath that has been waiting for this moment to make an appearance.

I'm home.

I'm safe.

I kick off my heels, toss my cardigan to the floor, and unzip my dress, leaving me in nothing but my black panties and bra. I place the bag on the coffee table, go to my room, take off my bra, and throw on an oversized T-shirt. Grabbing the brochures on my nightstand, the ones I have refused to look at for the past week that the doctor left me with, I walk out to the living room and set everything up.

The pickles, ice cream, and peanut butter line the edge of the table as I sit back on the sofa and start glancing through each pamphlet with a blanket wrapped around me.

Reaching for the pen and paper nearby, I'm ready to start creating a pros and cons list, but after only a few minutes of looking at each brochure, I toss the papers to the floor and lie back, fisting my hands at my side, frustration seeping out of me.

How am I supposed to make a decision when I still don't even know who the father is?

I even went to the bar a few days ago, hoping that, by some miracle, I would run into him. The bartender was clearly annoyed with me as I sat there ordering water. And maybe me repeatedly asking him if he knew of anyone matching my mystery man's description was his final straw and why he finally stopped coming to my side of the bar, but whatever.

I rub my throbbing temple, closing my eyes. *I'll never be able to find him. And the only person to blame for that is myself.*

He could be a married businessman living in another state for all I know, who just happened to stop in that damn bar the same night as me, looking for the same thing.

A distraction.

And because I made the stupid decision of not exchanging names, I'm never going to know who the father of my baby is.

My baby.

I sit up, eyes widening.

My baby.

This is the first time I've thought of those two words together.

And as if a light bulb turned on above me, I know what I'm going to do. I stand up and pick up the brochures, throwing out all but one.

I'm Ready to Be a Mom stares back at me. A woman on the cover is smiling, holding her stomach proudly, and I wonder if I'll ever feel like that.

Maybe this isn't the typical pregnancy per se, but I firmly believe that everything happens for a reason.

So maybe there's a reason I can't find this man.

Maybe I'm meant to do this myself.

And that's okay.

I've managed to take care of myself perfectly well for this long, so how hard could it be to add a baby to the equation?

* * *

After waking up at the crack of dawn with a stiff neck, immediately regretting falling asleep on the couch, I throw back my prenatal vitamins while turning on my computer to look at the Excel document I spent the whole night creating, preparing to be a mom.

There's tab after tab of everything I need to know in order to take care of a baby. One tab consists of different baby foods organized by the overall consumer rating. There's a tab with everything I should be taking now, like vitamins and supplements to keep me and the baby healthy. A tab of everything I need for a nursery.

That's the tab that has me stressed out the most because of the cost of each item.

Financially, it's going to be tight. *Very tight.* I reviewed the numbers three times, and even with my salary from my internship, the cost of caring for a baby will eat over half of my income, which doesn't leave a lot left over for rent, bills, and essential items like food. A baby crib alone averages around five hundred dollars that I haven't saved up. And when I researched the cost of diapers, it stated to add one hundred dollars a month to my expenses—one hundred dollars just for something that gets shit on and thrown away.

Baffling.

But I suppose this would qualify as a time I am justified to use my emergency credit card, which I got when I first came to school and haven't touched since it arrived.

I'll spend the afternoon trying to find as many items as possible and make the best of the last weekend before my classes start. Guess I never really imagined myself shopping for baby supplies while still in college, but here we are.

Life throws things at us when we least expect them, or maybe it's when we need something thrown into our lives the most that it happens.

Change.

I've never been a fan of it, but as someone who has experienced enough change to last a lifetime, I can handle one more curveball thrown my way.

As I lock my door behind me, my ears perk up to recognizable voices down the hall. I walk toward the apartment with the door left wide open and see my neighbor, Natalie Spencer, standing inside, causing a sudden burst of warmth to fill me. I haven't seen her since the beginning of the summer, but I'm sure glad to see her familiar face, especially with everything new going on in my life.

Although, I'm going to hold off on telling anyone I'm pregnant for as long as I can. I don't need people's pity as I explain to them that I have no idea who the father is.

I internally shake my head, putting that thought to the back of my mind for the moment.

Everything happens for a reason.

I knock on the side of the doorframe and smile, looking over at Natalie as she turns to face me, beaming. I'm assuming this is her new apartment because she told me that her best friend, Vanessa, was going to be rooming with her, and they needed a bigger space, so they took the vacant unit in the same hall, and her brother, Jason, took her old one.

"Sarah!" Natalie's beautiful grey eyes widen. "Perfect timing. We were just about to have some pizza. Did you want some?" Her long, blonde hair falls over her slender shoulders as she wraps her arms around me.

Being hugged, even just for a quick moment, suddenly makes me feel emotional. And I don't get emotional in front of people.

Ever.

"Oh, that's so nice of you! But I was just on my way out and wanted to say hi." I smile, holding in tears, and wave at everyone in the room before my eyes falter over a very tall guy standing in the kitchen with his back to everybody, placing food on the counter, appearing oblivious to me being here as Natalie continues the introductions.

But as my eyes scan over his body from head to toe, my gut clenches.

No...it can't be. Can it?

"Let me introduce you to the gang." Natalie takes a step away, and I turn my head to see her pull on a girl's arm, standing near her. From the beautiful chestnut strands and big brown eyes I've seen in pictures on Natalie's phone, there's only one person this could be. "This is my best friend, Vanessa."

Vanessa gives a slight wave, and I walk over to her, squeezing her in an embrace.

"I am so glad to finally meet you!" I exclaim.

"You are?" Vanessa breathes out.

I unwrap my arms from around her. "Yes! I knew the moment I met Natalie that something was missing from her life. And"—I peek over at Nate—"no offense, Nate"—my eyes move back to Vanessa—"but it was you."

"None taken," Nate responds, reaching into the fridge to pull out a cold beer.

Vanessa's cheeks turn the slightest shade of pink.

"And you know Nate, of course," Natalie continues. "And you met Jason last time he was here."

"Hey," Jason adds with a quick nod. I smile, but knowing there's only one person left for Natalie to introduce me to causes my heart to thump wildly.

Stay calm, Sarah. Maybe it's not him. It's just some random guy who looks exactly like the father of your baby from behind.

But as he turns toward me, locking his dark chocolate brown eyes onto mine, everything around me blurs.

It's him.

Natalie looks over her shoulder at the man who is now raking his eyes over my body, seeming like maybe he's been thinking about that night as much as I have.

"And Sarah, this is—"

"Paul," Paul says, walking over to me, reaching his hand out for me to take, acting as though we didn't fuck each other's brains out five weeks ago. But maybe to him, that's a typical Saturday night. His large hand wraps around mine, sending a swoosh of tingles to my core, bringing me right back to that night we spent together.

My heart gallops in my chest, and I pray he doesn't notice the effect he has on me.

"Paul," I repeat back to him, playing along with the whole "not knowing each other" act as I process the turn of events today.

Five minutes ago, I didn't have a name for this man, and now I have the whole delicious package standing in front of me.

I realize we've been holding each other's hands for too long and pull back, taking a step away. "Well, it was really nice to finally meet the rest of you, but I better be going." I turn to leave and can't help but take one last glance over my shoulder at Paul, who hasn't been able to take his eyes off of me.

Walking down the hall toward the elevator, I realize, with a bit of hope in my heart, that I may not have to do this alone anymore.

Four

PAUL

S*arah.*

I was beginning to think this girl was a figment of my imagination and that the whole damn night between us was just a dream.

A really good dream, if I say so myself.

But the moment my eyes locked on her Disney Princess emerald-green eyes just now, I knew it was her. The girl I haven't been able to get out of my fucking head because she was too busy invading every waking thought and wet dream.

As my hand enveloped her small one, I had to rein in the caveman inside me so I wouldn't throw her over my shoulder and scream, "I found her!" in front of everyone.

I wonder if—

"What the hell was that?" Nate asks, breaking my trance.

"What was what?" I emerge from my daze and step toward the fridge, reaching inside for a drink.

"That!" Nate waves his hands between me and the now vacant entry-way.

"I don't know what you're talking about," I respond before guzzling the soda in my hand. Even though Nate knows I've been searching for my mysterious one-night stand, this does not feel like the appropriate time to tell him that it was her. I place the cold can against my burning cheek. "Natalie, is the heat on in here? It feels like I'm in a sauna."

She smiles knowingly. "Nope. I think it's just you, TB."

"Oh Jesus, you gave him a nickname?" Nate pinches the bridge of his nose.

"Of course, I gave him a nickname."

"What does TB stand for?" Jason asks.

Nate sighs and then rolls his eyes. "Teddy Bear."

I burst out laughing. "Oh, Natalie. You are definitely my favorite."

"You think you're so funny, don't you?" Nate stands behind Natalie, his arms surrounding her waist.

"I know I am." Her face tilts toward him, and she reaches up, pressing a kiss to his cheek.

The way the two of them look at each other is sickening.

But damn, I wish I had someone who looked at me that way.

Like their hearts are whole because they have each other.

And the word *lonely* never crosses their minds like it frequently does in mine.

"All right. Everyone, dig in," Vanessa announces as she organizes the food on the marble island in the kitchen.

Jason grabs a pizza box and makes himself comfortable on the couch, so I grab one as well and sit on one of the counter stools. Nate and Natalie sit beside me, and I realize there's no seat left for Vanessa.

"Hey, Vanessa, take my seat." I start to get up, but she shakes her head.

"It's okay." She looks over at the couch where Jason is sitting. "I'll go sit over there." She lets out a breath, straightens her shoulders, and takes her salad with her as she strides toward the couch.

I chuckle, shaking my head, before taking a bite of my pizza. I worked up an appetite today, helping everyone move into their apartments. We spent the day moving Natalie and Vanessa into their new apartment and bringing Jason's things into his, which was Natalie's apartment last year.

I worked muscles I hadn't used, even on the basketball court. Which is why I'm glad that Nate and I moved into our place at the beginning of the summer, so when I leave here, I can take a refreshingly cold shower and crash for the night.

It's not like I have anything else to do.

Or maybe I do…

After asking Jason to hang something in Vanessa's room, Natalie walks back into the kitchen to sit on her stool.

Why didn't she ask the tallest guy in the room? No idea.

"So Natalie…" I clear my throat. "Have you and Sarah been friends long?"

She swallows what's in her mouth before saying, "We met last year when I moved in. She's a junior at LU and lives down the hall across Jason now."

She lives in this building…

Just down the hall…

Is this a sick joke?

I rub a hand up and down my face, not letting Natalie see me internally berating myself because apparently, I wasn't looking hard enough for Sarah if she's been living in this building the whole damn time I've been searching for her.

I finish the slice of pizza in my hand and get up from my seat. "Well, I better get going. I've got to be up early for basketball tomorrow. I'll see you at the house," I say to Nate as I pat Natalie on the top of her head.

Walking into the hallway, I start to make my way for the elevator, but before I know what I'm doing, my feet take me in the opposite direction, heading down the hall straight for the apartment door across from Jason's.

My feet stop right before the threshold as I bring my hand up to knock, but I stop myself.

What am I doing?

This girl probably hasn't even thought about that night.

She only wanted one night.

One fucking night.

I shake my head, squeezing the back of my neck, and take a deep breath, pinching my eyes shut before opening them and looking directly at her door.

I'm not a coward.

I am Paul fucking Weston.

And I will knock on this door if it's the last thing I do.

I tap my knuckles against the door and step back, not wanting to crowd her if she does open the door. I know some people find my height intimidating, and that's the last thing I want to do: intimidate her.

Of course, she didn't seem intimidated by my height that night...

I wait a minute and another and another before I start to feel discouraged.

She's not here.

Well, that or she sees me through the peephole, and she's choosing not to answer.

I'll go with the first option for the sake of my pride.

My shoulders drop as I spin on my heels and stride toward the awaiting elevator, mocking me with its silver doors wide open for me.

An hour later, I'm home, showered, and lying in bed, resuming my solo *Star Wars* marathon.

Yes, I'm a nerd.

I'm also a twenty-two-year-old guy who should be out enjoying his senior year of college, but I'm an old soul. Or at least that's what my mom always calls me. I prefer the comfort of close friends and nostalgic "nerdy" movies to going to unfamiliar places and meeting new people.

And because of that, I've always felt like something was wrong with me.

Maybe I'm being a bit dramatic, but it's hard not to think that way when you've spent half your life feeling like an outsider. I've always been the person people want to know on a surface level, but when it comes down to knowing me personally, people seem to lose interest.

Because they don't truly care about the man in the jersey.

They only care about the status my last name brings with it.

A loud thrumming noise echoes near my ear as the light from my phone screen awakens. Grabbing my phone off my nightstand, I see my agent's name, Dan, flash across the screen. My finger hovers over the red button before pressing it, sending him straight to voicemail, and then flipping my phone over.

I'm in no mood to hash over my future tonight, and I certainly don't give two shits about numbers on a piece of paper.

Especially when it means nothing if I don't have someone to share it all with.

With a frustrated sigh, I throw the covers back and hop out of bed, taking a few steps toward my computer.

Aka, the one thing I use to distract myself with when nothing else seems to work.

I rotate my blue gaming chair and sit, facing the monitor. Adjusting the headset over my ears, I position the microphone away from my mouth, not wanting to talk to anyone tonight. I slide the cover over the camera situated on top and power on the desktop. The screen fills with bright colors as the futuristic scene appears, my standard avatar waiting for me to begin.

I spend the next half hour making it only one level ahead before getting my ass kicked by a twelve-year-old in New Zealand.

Pathetic.

God, if people knew the real me behind the highly recognizable last name, the one I only show to my closest friends, they'd probably think I was weird.

I let out a laugh, leaning back in my chair as I scrape a hand over my face.

But come to think of it, Sarah didn't know who I was that night, and she didn't choose me because of the last name on my jersey.

She chose me because she wanted...me.

The girl clearly had a lot on her mind that night, searching for a distraction in a bar. And maybe that's what I was doing, too.

I didn't want to go out with Glen and the guys that night.

I wanted to stay home and read a book or rewatch an episode or two of *Game of Thrones*.

But there was also a tiny part of me that thought I could find someone out there to *distract* me.

To make me not feel so alone anymore.

At least just for one night.

And I did.

And goddamn, I've lost count of the nights I've spent thinking about her. About how good her curves felt in my hands. About her soft moans and whimpers that escaped her as I pounded into her, making her forget, just like she asked me to do.

And as I fell asleep with Sarah snuggled up in my arms, I envisioned myself doing this every night with her. I had never felt a connection like that before with someone, so I was optimistic that there might not be an expiration date on our one-night stand.

Maybe it never had to end.

But waking up in the morning to find an empty spot on the bed beside me ultimately hindered those dreams.

And just as swiftly as the loneliness left me, it returned.

Shutting my game off, I throw my headset to the side and make my way to my bed and under my covers. Closing my eyes, I bring the blanket to my waist, enjoying the slight breeze from the open window near my head, stretching out on my extra-long bed. As I turn on my side to look out the window toward the bright moon shining high above, feeling that extra thick memory foam contour to my body, I wonder what Sarah is doing right now.

* * *

My fingers grip the familiar orange leather, looking to my left and right for an open teammate but finding them all guarded, leaving me with no option but to handle business myself.

Seeing that it's just a practice, everyone on the court is my teammate. But you wouldn't know that from the way Greyson is covering me.

He's been on me like bees to honey.

When I move, he moves.

If I shoot, he blocks.

If I fall to the ground, it's because the son of a bitch shoved me while no one was looking.

Yeah, the whole co-captain thing is going really well.

And I've just about had enough of his fucking attitude.

His eyes narrow in on me like a rabid dog, watching every move I make. Anticipating every play and every step I take.

But it's not going to work this time.

I subtly move my body toward the right without shifting my feet, my eyes focusing on Glen, who is completely covered and unavailable for assistance. But Greyson doesn't know this because Greyson only has his beady eyes plastered on me. So, as I shift the ball in front of me, appearing as though I'm about to dribble to my right side, I fake him out, pivoting on my left foot, bypassing him with a not-so-gentle elbow nudge.

Taking Greyson by surprise, he doesn't react fast enough as I dribble from the arc to the basket, dunking the ball in the hoop.

Victory has never tasted so sweet.

"That was a fucking foul," Greyson bites out, advancing toward me.

"Excuse me?" I place my hands on my hips, my chest rising steadily from each huff of air I release, my lungs burning from the over-exertion of hustling on the court nonstop for hours.

My teammates watch, not saying a word.

"You pushed me," Greyson accuses. "So that basket doesn't count."

"Oh, you mean like what you've been doing to me all night," I challenge, cocking my head to the side.

Greyson gets right up in my face, or at least as close as he can, seeing that he's half a foot shorter than me. "You better watch yourself."

"Are you threatening me?" My brows furrow as I step into his space, bumping into his chest.

"I'm simply warning you to—"

The piercing ring of a whistle blows nearby, causing us both to whip our heads to the side and take a step away from each other.

"Paul." Coach Rivers motions for me to join him on the sidelines.

Before heading his way, I look down at Greyson, narrowing my eyes. "We have a whole season to get through together. So calm the fuck down."

Just as I turn, Greyson ensures he has the last word. "Too bad your daddy's not here to see you riding his name."

I clench my fists at my side.

Glancing over my shoulder, I see Glen, who mouths, *He's not worth it*. And he's right. I know he is. Greyson's egging me on, trying to do anything he can to provoke me into losing my shit in front of the coach. Bringing up my dad was a low blow. But I refuse to be a pawn in Greyson's game, giving him what he wants, so I walk away with my head held high before I give myself a chance to let his words soak into my skin.

"You wanted to see me, sir?" I swipe at the sweat dripping down my temple.

A tall, slender man with salt and pepper hair stands beside him, smiling, as he pushes his wire-rimmed glasses up his nose.

"Yes, Paul, this is Peter Green." Coach shifts his stance, crossing his arms in front of his chest. "He's a scout for the Boston Celtics and wanted to introduce himself to you before he left."

Holy shit.

Peter sticks his hand out. "It's a pleasure to meet you."

"The pleasure is all mine," I respond, happily taking his hand.

"I remember watching your dad play like it was yesterday." His smile falters as he says, "I was really sorry to hear about what happened to him. Terrible tragedy."

I swallow the lump in my throat.

Even after all of these years, the pain hasn't dissipated at the mention of him.

Although, does the pain of losing a parent ever get easier over time?

If it does, I have yet to experience it.

"It was," I respond solemnly.

He nods. "Well, it's no secret that you're anticipated to be the number-one draft pick next summer. And I can tell you, just from the little I've observed today, Boston would be lucky to have you."

"Thank you, sir." I run a hand over the top of my head.

"Have you ever considered playing for Boston?" he asks, shocking me into silence.

Being drafted to play for Boston is everything I've ever wanted.

It's the city I grew up in.

It's the city where my family lives.

And it's the city where my dad spent his whole career playing.

But if Boston drafts me, is it only because of my last name?

The words that Greyson taunted me with earlier flash before me.

"Too bad your daddy's not here to see you riding his name."

My eyes meet Peter's. "I'd like to play for a team that chooses me because of what I bring to the team and not because of the name I wear on my jersey."

Peter squeezes my shoulder. "I'm not going to lie to you and say if you come to Boston, you won't have some big shoes to fill because you will. People will expect everything from you that your father gave them over the years, if not more. But it's up to you to show them who you are." He lets his hand drop, peering around me. "Plenty of great basketball players are out there, waiting for a chance to be recruited into the NBA. But there's a difference between being a great basketball player and being one of the greats. And you, my friend, are well on your way to being one of the greats." He shrugs. "You may have the same last name as your father. But it's one you should be proud to wear as you continue his legacy, making your own path and choices." His eyebrows raise. "So, tell me. Do you think you can fill those shoes?"

I take in his words, letting them absorb within me.

Am I able to fill my dad's shoes? To dribble down the same courts my dad played in regularly, clinching championship wins year after year?

"I don't think there's a right answer to this question, sir." I lift a shoulder and let it drop. "But I know it's not something I take lightly. My dad was the best man I know. He's the reason I'm standing here today. I hope I can be half the man he was someday, especially on a basketball court. And I think it would be a dream come true and an honor to my father's legacy to play for Boston if the opportunity was presented to me."

Peter smiles widely. "That's the kind of answer I was hoping to hear." He looks at Coach Rivers and then back at me. "I have your agent's information and will be in touch. Take care, Paul. Let's do what we can to get those green and white colors on you."

I smile, watching as he walks away.

Boston wants me.

They want...*me*.

Five

SARAH

Sitting my ass on the grass and leaning my back against the enormous maple tree, I stare off at the water before me, also known as the Charles River. It glistens and gleams as the sun appears ready to set, but don't let that pretty exterior fool you.

You won't catch me jumping in that water anytime soon.

A slight breeze cascades over my arms, making me wish I had brought my jacket.

You never can keep up with the weather in New England this time of year.

I reach for my sketchbook and a charcoal pencil in my bag and place the pad against the top of my thighs, now positioned like a makeshift easel. My eyes wait for the sun to hit just the right spot over the distant buildings across the water, and when it finally does, my hand begins to move fluidly across the page in a rampant state, hoping to beat the light before it dissipates into darkness.

This is the moment that I refer to as getting in the zone.

It's when everything around me dims into nothing more than a shadowed mist, and all I see is the image before me that I replicate on the paper.

I do this to shut off my brain when things are slightly overwhelming and uncertain, and it all begins to feel like too much.

Like when you find out you're pregnant and have no idea who the father is, but then find out who he is and spend the next week trying to think of how you're going to tell him. You had to use most of the available balance on your emergency credit card to order all the necessary items for a nursery because your checking account is inching closer to the negative. And on top of all that, your boss's son plans to make your life a living hell, and you have no idea how to escape his cruel grasp.

As I mentioned...*overwhelming*.

"Is this seat taken?"

I let out a quiet gasp, abruptly drop my pencil and sketchbook, and slap my hand to my chest as my eyes look up at...Paul.

The man I was searching for stands before my very eyes for the second time in a matter of days as though being handed to me on a silver platter.

The world certainly has a cruel sense of humor.

"Sorry, I didn't mean to scare you." He throws his hands in the air defensively, displaying an adorable yet apologetic grin.

Paul's deep voice resonates in my mind, bringing back delicious memories of words whispered in my ears...

I internally shake my head, blinking a few times to escape my thoughts. "Sorry. Just caught me off guard." I smile and pat the space beside me. "It's all yours."

He appears relieved and sits, stretching out his longer-than-life legs, making my usually long legs appear short.

"So you're Sarah," he says with a charming smile.

"And you're Paul," I add, playfully nudging the side of his arm with my shoulder. "I have to say, you were pretty smooth at our introduction."

He laughs, dragging the palm of his large hand over his stubble. "Yeah, well, I didn't think everyone should know we already *technically* met."

My cheeks heat up as my eyes linger on his hand. His fingers are so long and thick, powerful and skilled. The memory alone of what those fingers are capable of has me clamping my thighs together, repressing the dull ache in my core.

His eyes glance over at my sketchbook, thankfully unaware of the obscene images floating across my mind. "What are you drawing?"

"Oh." I pick it up, showing him the sunset I was in the middle of shading. It's nothing impressive. The shadows seem a bit off, and I should have—

"You drew that? Just now?" he asks, with widened eyes.

"Well, yeah. I know the shading isn't accurate, but I just—"

"It's perfect." He cuts me off, appearing mesmerized by the sketch in my hands. "May I?" He holds out his hand, and I hesitantly give him the sketchbook. His eyes look from the paper to the sunset before us. "It's identical to the real thing. You even got the trees just right. This is amazing." He gives it back to me, and I place it on my other side, hiding it from view, suddenly feeling self-conscious of my work.

"Thanks," I say, twirling a piece of my hair.

"But can I ask you something?"

"Go for it."

"Why draw a sunset with a grey pencil?"

I shrug, looking across the water. "Sometimes it's easier to see the world in black and white. Too many colors can make things..."

"Overwhelming?" he offers as though reading my mind.

"Yeah." I look out at the sun, which is still slowly setting. It won't be much longer until it completely disappears, welcoming darkness.

"So, are you a professional artist?" he asks.

"Me? Oh no." I scoff at the idea. "I wish, but unfortunately, art doesn't pay the bills unless you've made it big." I shake my head. "No, I'm a finance major. I just started an internship over at the financial district at LH United, hoping to work my way up to being a financial analyst."

"Well, that sounds—"

"Boring," I answer for him, knowing it's what everyone thinks.

"I was going to say safe," he replies, the corners of his lips tugging up.

"*Safe*. I guess you're right." I pluck a red leaf that fell from the branch above me onto my dark denim jeans. But I guess having a safe job is the only suitable option when you've lived a life like mine. "And what do you do?"

He looks at me curiously, his brows furrowing. "You really don't know who I am, do you?"

"Am I supposed to?" I ask, raising a brow. "Are you offended I don't?"

He chuckles. "No. Not at all. It's refreshing."

His eyes settle on me, and his smile instantly trickles warmth over every square inch of me.

The longer we stare at each other, the more I feel my cheeks redden. Pushing my hair back, I say, "Well, are you going to leave me in suspense or..."

"Right. Sorry." He shakes his head. "I'm a basketball player. I'll most likely be playing in the NBA next year."

"Basketball." I nod, pursing my lips, not knowing a damn thing about the sport. "So I take it you're good if you're going into the NBA?"

He hesitates before admitting, "I'm okay."

"Hmm," I ponder.

"What?"

I look up at him with a teasing smile. "Just thought you would have been more of a hockey player."

He chuckles. "Nah. I'd look like a giraffe on skates."

"But a sexy giraffe," I offer, stifling a laugh.

"You think so?"

"Oh, definitely." I bite my bottom lip, tilting my head. "Let me guess. You're the guy who puts the ball in the net."

"How'd you know?" His lips curve up. "What, are you stalking me now?" His arm playfully bumps into mine.

"Ha. That would have been pretty hard to do when I didn't have your name or anything to work off of. Even the bartender from that night was no help with me finding your—"

Shit. I cover my mouth with my hands. I've said too much.

Paul's brows raise, and his smile widens. "Oh, so you were stalking me?"

Heat spreads from my face down my chest. I move my hands to the top of my thighs, rubbing back and forth, looking anywhere but at him. "No. Umm, I didn't mean—"

"Sarah?"

"Yeah?" I hesitantly look up at him, biting my bottom lip.

"I'm just messing with you."

I smack the top of his bicep, the very muscular and solid bicep, making him laugh. "Don't do that to me. I have enough on my plate."

He leans back, crossing his arms over his chest, eyeing the water before us when he asks, "Do you ever think about that night?"

My throat goes dry as my lips part, but no words come out. Paul looks down as I look up, his beautiful, deep chocolate brown eyes locking with mine, desire flashing in them. Memories of that night unfurl in my mind as though playing on a screen in front of us, generating a guttural need between my legs.

Suddenly, all I want is to repeat that night. I want to feel his hands caress my skin, grazing over every curve. I want to hear his voice whispering sinfully delightful words in my ear. I want his lips on mine, stealing my screams as I cry out in pleasure.

I want him—all of him.

Clearing my throat, I say, "I think about—"

"Paul!" someone nearby shouts, breaking our trance. "Coach wants to see you."

Paul looks to his side and yells, "Be right there!"

He looks back at me, pausing before saying, "Come to my game on Friday."

"What?" I ask, surprised.

He cocks his head to the side, grinning. "Come to my game. Well, it's not an official game, more of a scrimmage before the season officially starts, but they still treat it like a real game. And then we can get dinner after."

"I...umm..." I momentarily look away, taken aback. Would this be considered a date? Did he just ask me out on a date?

"Please?" he adds.

His eyes pierce mine, pleading with me to say yes.

And I want to. I really do.

Not to mention, it might be the perfect time to tell him we're having a baby.

Although, considering the circumstances, I doubt there is a perfect time for that.

I bite the inside of my cheek, mulling over the request as I glance around. But the second my eyes meet his, I know my answer. "Yeah." A smile breaks free. "Yeah. Okay."

His body relaxes beside mine. "Great." He reaches into his pocket and pulls out his phone, giving it to me. "Put your number in it, and I can send you the info."

I do, typing out my full name and then handing it back to him, feeling like a schoolgirl who just got asked out for the first time.

Because technically this is my first time getting asked out.

He types out a quick message and texts my phone, so I have his number, too.

"Well, I'll see you Friday, Sarah."

Before I comprehend what is happening, he leans down and brushes his lips across my cheek, kissing my skin softly, sending shivers up and down my spine. He jumps up and flashes a smile before turning around and jogging toward the gym.

Is this what being on cloud nine feels like?

My hand presses against the cheek he just kissed.

I guess I'm going to his basketball game, and then—

Wait...

Basketball.

As in the same sports team that Greyson plays for.

Paul's teammates with Greyson.

They're probably friends.

Or maybe they're not?

I don't think Paul seems like the type that would fall for Greyson's act.

But then again, most people don't know the real Greyson.

I bend my legs and place my arms on my knees, resting my head as I watch the sun vanish.

Maybe I shouldn't go.

But as a soft rumble reverberates throughout my stomach, I realize there's one crucial reason I need to go no matter what.

My phone vibrates, reminding me I have an unopened text.

Gazing at the screen, my heart turns to mush.

Unknown Number

I missed those beautiful green eyes.

Guess I'm going to a basketball game, I think with a sigh.

* * *

"You're very talented."

"Huh?" I twist in my seat, finding my art professor, Mrs. Blossom, behind me, eyeing my easel. "Oh, I was just playing with the textures."

"Don't diminish your work." She shakes her head, her red curls bouncing around her face. Pushing her glasses higher on her nose, she approaches for a closer inspection. "I asked the class to create an image of what the word *family* means to them. Peter has sketched a family portrait, and Shelby has painted a picture of her family's home, but you painted a field of flowers. Why?"

I swallow nervously. I've never liked discussing my art with others or even showing it, for that matter.

Putting my art out there for others to judge and critique is what has stopped me from putting my art in shows in the past, even after all of the compliments I've received from professors over the years. Their words meant little to me when the only person I wanted to show my art to was no longer here to see it.

But after seeing Paul's reaction—his genuine adoration for a simple sunset sketch I created, I've started to question my motives behind not showing my art to the world in the first place.

"I don't know." I put down my brush, wiping my hands across my apron.

"Yes, you do." She smiles, her eyebrows raising, waiting for me to continue.

"Well, I guess it's because of my mom." I absentmindedly rub at the lily tattoo on my wrist. "Her favorite flower was the lily. My dad brought her a new bouquet almost every week." I smile, remembering all the moments my dad walked through the front door with a fresh bouquet in his hands and a smile on his face. "She painted flowers every chance she got. She's why I love art so much; I guess I can attribute everything to her. So when I see this flower, I see her and my dad. And in essence, I see my family."

"And that is what we call art." She removes her glasses, letting them dangle on a chain over her chest. "But can I ask why you created the image in black and white? Why not use color?"

It's the second time I've been asked this question in a matter of days, but my answer has yet to change.

"It's easier for me to see the world in black and white."

Her lips purse to the side as she nods in understanding. "Well, I hope someday soon, color comes back into your life."

I look back at my easel.

Is it so wrong to live a colorless life?

"Ah!" She reaches for something inside her apron pocket. "During winter break, there is an art show in the city featuring up-and-coming artists. I think you should consider it." She takes out a small folded-up piece of paper and hands it to me, detailing all the information for the show.

"Oh." I quickly scan the paper. "I'm not a real artist. I only create for fun. I've never sold anything or had any professional lessons."

She looks sternly at me, placing her hand on her hip while waving the other in the air. "Is a person not an author because they've self-published? Is a person not a singer because they've only sung in front of the mirror? Is a person not a baker because they've only baked for friends and family?" She looks back at my work before saying, "Think about that." And then she walks away.

Staring at the paper in my hand, I wonder if I have what it takes to be a part of something like this. My eyes glance over at the image I created.

It's simple. Basic. Plain.

But maybe all it needs is a little color.

Hesitantly, I reach for the bottle of red acrylic paint near me and mix a few drops with the white paint on my palette.

After researching the safest paints to use while pregnant, I discovered watercolors and acrylics as options and have prioritized sitting alone in the back of the classroom next to an open window. I won't take any chances when it comes to my baby's safety.

Not loving the shade of pink I created, I grab the yellow bottle and let a few dollops fall into the mix—my brush swirls and twirls, combining the colors until a soft shade of orange appears.

I can work with this.

I can do this.

With shaking fingers, I lift my brush before the easel and take a deep breath.

It's just a little color.

I shouldn't be this scared to paint with color.

But as my hand moves closer to the canvas, I drop the brush and quickly step back, knocking the paint bottles onto the floor, red paint splattering all over my clothes.

I freeze, taking in the mess I've created.

It's too much. It's all just too goddamn much.

Sucking in my trembling bottom lip, I close my eyes, caging in the unshed tears.

I can't do this.

My heart thuds in my chest, sadly knowing there's more meaning behind those four words than I will ever admit aloud.

Six

PAUL

"Paul, are you...crying?" Natalie asks.

Fuck.

"No, I am not crying, Natalie. I just got something in my eye." I wipe haphazardly at my face, removing all evidence of any tears.

"It's okay if you're crying, Paul. Girls like a guy who isn't afraid to show their emotions." Natalie displays a sympathetic smile.

"I'm not crying." I sniffle, wiping at my nose. "It's just..." I point at the TV screen; the sight of Joyce and Hopper reuniting for the first time in a year punches me right in the gut.

Maybe it's because it's what I wish I had.

Someone to come home to after a game.

Someone to spend my Friday nights with.

Someone who sees me for me.

Goddamn, *Stranger Things*...putting me in my feels right now.

"Keep it together, big guy." Jason pats my back, clearly stifling a laugh.

I should have known these four idiots wouldn't appreciate this masterpiece. Scratch that; Natalie can do no wrong in my book, and Vanessa is sound asleep on the other side of the couch, so she's also excused.

I'm never going to live this down.

As the episode winds down, Natalie lets out a yawn. "I'm so tired."

"Yeah," Nate adds, looking at me. "You want to make the couch your bed tonight? Or you know there is a neighbor down the hall... I could always see if she has a spare room." An obnoxious grin spreads over his face.

I still haven't told this fucker that Sarah's the girl I've been searching for.

And now, I think I'll continue holding on to this secret for a little longer.

"The couch is fine," I grit out, stretching my legs.

"Suit yourself." Nate lifts Natalie in his arms and walks her toward her room. "Night, everyone."

I reach for a blanket off the ottoman and position a pillow beside me.

"Guess I'll bring her to her room," Jason murmurs, regarding Vanessa.

Oh, this is going to be fun.

I can't help myself when I ask, "Do you need help?"

"Nope. I'll take it from here," he spits out, clenching his jaw.

I internally shake my head, laughing at this idiot who won't admit his feelings for her.

My lips curve up as I watch him lift Vanessa, holding her against his chest, appearing so tiny in his massive arms as he shuffles toward her bedroom door and disappears inside her room.

I lie back on the sofa, placing a pillow under my head. The blanket barely covers my body, and as expected, my legs hang over the end. And knowing how much back pain I'll be experiencing tomorrow makes me groan in frustration as I turn on my side.

My eyes blink a few times as I stare at the front door.

The door that opens to the hallway.

The door that's down the hall from...

Sarah.

Maybe I should...

No, I definitely shouldn't.

But I could. I mean, I did bring the jersey with me.

But what if—

Fuck it.

Jumping up from the sofa, I reach into my gym bag on the floor and pull out the new jersey I picked up today from the campus store.

Quietly, I open the door, sneaking out like a kid trying not to get caught by his parents. I reach Sarah's door and hold my fist up, ready to knock when I stop myself.

What am I doing?

It's way too late to be knocking on her door. She's probably asleep, and I'll end up scaring the shit out of her if she thinks I'm a burglar.

But would a burglar knock?

I look at the ceiling and mutter, "I'm an idiot."

"Paul?"

Shit. I glance to my side, finding Sarah in the hallway. She's got a smile on her face that she's trying but failing to hide as she tilts her head to the side, observing me with those big green eyes. Her long, black hair is in a messy bun on the top of her head, except for a few loose strands that have escaped, framing her face.

"Were you just going to spend the night staring at my door?" she asks, taking a few steps toward me.

I shake my head. "No. Sorry." Running a hand over the top of my head, I explain, "I was just over at Natalie's with Nate, and everyone was crashing for the night, so I thought I'd head over here to..." Why was I heading over here? Oh right. The jersey. "I was going to knock, but then I realized how late it was." I take in her outfit, my eyes scanning up and down. Fitted jeans with a black top, both pieces covered in a red substance. "Please tell me that's paint."

She laughs, suddenly peering down at herself. "Yeah. I just came from the art studio on campus." She runs the back of her arm over her forehead, pushing back the loose strands of hair. "I probably look like a mess."

I shake my head. "Not at all." I reach for a piece of her dark hair that refuses to stay in place and tuck it behind her ear. "You look beautiful."

Her eyes catch mine as my hand cups her cheek, my thumb swiping softly over her creamy, pale skin. I pull my hand away, showing her my thumb, now covered in red paint. "You missed a spot."

She grins, but suddenly, her head tilts to the side as her eyes glimpse down at my hand, narrowing in on what I'm holding. "What's that?"

"Oh." I lift the jersey, handing it to her. "I got you my jersey so you could wear it to the game tomorrow night. You don't have to if you don't want to. I just thought you might need something to wear and—"

"Thank you." She smiles, taking the jersey from me. "Weston," she says with amusement as her eyes dance over each embroidered letter. Her fingers hold the jersey from the top, letting the material dangle in front of her.

And that's when I realized I fucked up because it's going to be ridiculously huge on her.

"Shit. I didn't know what size to get you." I start to reach for it. "I can take it back and get you a different size."

She clutches it to her chest. "It's perfect. I'll just tie it up on the sides."

"Are you sure?"

She nods adamantly. "Yeah."

"Okay." I nod, trying to think of anything to say. "When you get to the stadium, you just need to go to the ticket booth by the entrance and tell them your name. They'll be holding a ticket for you." My brows furrow. "Or do you want me to meet you out front? Because I can if—"

"I'll be fine, Paul. I'm a big girl. I think I can manage getting my ticket and finding my seat." She chuckles.

"Yeah. Sorry. I just...want to make sure everything goes smoothly for you." Clearing my throat, I confess, "I've never asked anyone to come watch my game before."

"No?" she asks, her eyes slightly widening at my admission.

I shake my head. "The only people who usually come to watch me are my family, and Nate and Natalie have, too, a few times."

She bites her bottom lip, looking anywhere but at me. Did I say too much?

Be bold, Paul.

I reach out, lightly gripping her chin between my fingers, angling her face so our eyes meet. "So, I'll see you tomorrow then?"

She licks her lips, her chest heaving the slightest bit. "I'll be there."

A thousand thoughts are dancing across her eyes—a story I want to read over and over again.

Her lips part as she looks up at me under those damn long eyelashes, her green eyes sparkling under the dimly lit hallway light. My hand slides down her jaw to her neck, where I feel her pulse beating as fast as mine. My fingers slide to the back of her neck, tilting her head ever so slightly as I lean down. Her eyelids flutter closed as she lets out a whoosh of air, anticipation building between us. I let my lips brush across hers but don't press down. Not yet. Not until—

A door nearby opens, breaking the spell as I drop my hand and step back. We both swivel our heads, finding Jason walking out of Natalie's apartment with something crumpled in his fist, muttering to himself. He smacks his forehead, shaking his head, clearly upset about something. When he finally looks up, and his eyes spot us, observing the closeness of our bodies, he momentarily freezes, his eyes darting between Sarah and me.

His lips open and close. Open and close. Until finally, he says, "I'll just..." He points to his door and quickly moves around us, heading inside his apartment with a slam of his door.

I scratch the back of my head. I don't know how I'm going to explain this to him...

"He seemed pissed about something," Sarah murmurs, staring at his door.

"Yeah." I lift a shoulder. "I'm sure it has something to do with Vanessa."

"Are they...?"

I shake my head. "I don't think so. Not yet, anyway. But from that little show, I would say it won't be much longer," I note with amusement.

Sarah laughs, and it sends a ripple of tenderness through me.

"Good for them," she says, folding the jersey. She takes a step toward me, filling the space. "Good night, Paul." She curls her finger, motioning for me to lean down toward her. Standing on her tiptoes, she rests her free hand against my chest and presses her lips on my cheek.

I stand straight as she smiles and turns, a whiff of her alluring apple and honey aroma filling my nostrils as she enters her apartment.

"Good night, Sarah."

Seven

SARAH

"You're Sarah Fleur? Paul's girl?" The older man with salt and pepper hair behind the counter asks with a big, warm smile.

"I...umm, what?" I ask, confused.

"Paul told me he had a ticket on hold for a girl, but he's never had one put aside for a girl before, so I figured you must be pretty important to him," he muses, reaching for an envelope.

"Oh. No. I'm just...a friend."

Baby mama.

Friend.

Either way.

The man hands me my ticket, chuckling. "Well, enjoy the game, Paul's *friend.*"

I smile, take the ticket, and head toward the court entrance.

I spent the entire day rehearsing my speech, preparing to give Paul news that would inevitably change his life forever. I had thought the more I repeated the words, "I'm pregnant" and "You're the father," the more I would feel ready for what I needed to do. Instead, I feel nauseous and unsure.

I'm overthinking everything.

But I'm prepared to give Paul a choice. He can be a part of our baby's life or not. It's up to him. Either way, I know what I want, and if I need to do it alone, then so be it.

As I walk through the hall and into the arena, my mouth falls open in shock. This place is enormous and vastly impressive. I marvel at everything. The lights. The crowd. The atmosphere, which is buzzing with excitement. No wonder why so many people flock here for home games.

Even if, like Paul had mentioned, this isn't a real game. It still feels like one, though, making me wonder how insane a real game must be.

"Do you need help finding your seat, Miss?" A petite older woman with reddish-brown hair looks up at me as I look down at her.

"Actually, yeah." I flip over my ticket, revealing my seat number.

"Ah, you're in the friends and family section. Follow me," she instructs, turning around and leading us in the right direction.

I follow close behind her, walking on the edge of the court. The teams aren't out yet, but the game should be starting soon.

"Here you are." She points to a black leather cushioned seat in the front row directly opposite the home team's bench. "Enjoy the game."

"Thank you," I say as I sit, and she turns, making her way to help the next lost-looking soul.

Wow. This is amazing.

A couple of people walk by me, and my eyes immediately zero in on the last name on their jersey.

Weston.

I laugh, tucking in the backside of my jersey beneath my black leather jacket. When I put it on at home, it draped to my knees, but I was adamant about making it work. It was the first gift I had received in years and well, it means a lot to me. So, with the help of some safety pins and a rubber band, I made it appear like a perfect fit...as long as you don't look at the back of it. Hence, the leather jacket.

Two guys take their seats beside me, fisting a drink in each hand.

"Can you believe they made him co-captain? I think this will be his best year yet!" one of them says.

"Have you seen his stats? Paul's anticipated to be the number-one draft pick next summer," the other responds before guzzling his drink.

Seems to me that Paul's better than just "okay" at basketball like he had told me he was.

The one closest to me stands, removing his jacket, and I spot the name Weston out of the corner of my eye.

Hmm. Another fan.

I guess I didn't realize how popular he is.

A group of girls walk by me, appearing more ready to walk a runway show than attend a basketball game.

"Can you believe he signed my shirt for me? God, he's even cuter in person." The blonde girl flicks her hair over her shoulder, displaying a signature for her friend to see.

"I still can't believe you ran into Paul. Lucky bitch," the friend murmurs.

"I'd definitely do him," the third girl says, causing them all to laugh.

My teeth grind together as I hold back my tongue from saying something I'll regret. Paul and I aren't even together. I have no reason to feel jealous.

And I'm definitely not jealous.

But as I spot another Weston jersey in my periphery, I wonder...

Turning my body, I face the rest of the fans in the stands, spotting jersey after jersey with the last name Weston on them.

Holy shit.

"You think he'll break his dad's record for most wins?" the guy beside me asks his friend, piquing my interest. The nosy part of me gets the better of me, so I saddle up closer to the man.

"Who knows? He has a good chance. Maybe someday he'll even—"

Suddenly, the lights dim drastically as a spotlight illuminates the floor, and a deep bass reverberates throughout the arena. Music starts playing, and an announcer begins rattling off players on the opposing team who come out one after the other.

More boos than cheers are heard for them, exposing more hometown fans tonight.

"And let's hear it for Linrey University!"

The home team starts jogging out onto the court, and the whole place erupts in a victorious roar, going absolutely feral. The energy in the place is palpable, to say the least.

"Give it up for our first co-captain, Paul Weston!"

Paul strides out looking...well, fuck me; he looks like sex on a stick. His uniform molds perfectly to his sculpted chest and thick thigh muscles. He walks toward the center, appearing serious and focused, but so mouthwatering delicious, just like that first night we met. And just like that first night, his eyes catch on me, eliciting the most beautiful smile I've ever seen on his face.

I smile back and then melt like butter when he winks at me.

"And for your second co-captain, Greyson Black!"

My smile immediately falls as Greyson walks out on the court, appearing smug and cocky as he pounds his chest and yells at the crowd, riling everyone up even more. A shiver runs through me as I cross my arms over my chest and sit back, trying not to stick out like a sore thumb to this man. But unfortunately, as he gets closer to Paul, his eyes move in my direction, landing right on me.

I feel like the canary, which is about to be eaten alive by the cat.

Greyson appears like a giant fucking Siberian tiger, eyeing me like I'm tonight's dinner, making my skin crawl and a flash of sweat form on the back of my neck.

I look away, pretending to be distracted by something on my phone, scrolling aimlessly.

Thankfully, it doesn't take long for the rest of the team to be brought out and for the game to start.

Throughout the night, my eyes remain glued to Paul as he dribbles down the court, owning the game. I may not know his position or any of the rules, but I know with confidence that Paul is the best player on his team.

The evidence that he'll be playing in the NBA next year is right in front of my eyes. It's like watching art as he moves across the floor with the ball in his fingers. It's absolutely breathtaking.

God, he looks so happy out there in his element.

And it makes me feel overjoyed to know that he'll be living his life, doing something that gives him that much satisfaction...

Guilt hits me like a ton of damn bricks.

Maybe telling Paul I'm pregnant isn't a good idea...

I don't want to be the reason he doesn't follow his dream.

Don't go down that road, Sarah. You have nothing to feel guilty about. It takes two to tango. Besides, you're giving him a choice.

I internally shake my head, gripping the edge of my seat. *I know. I know.*

It doesn't take long for me to notice that when Paul is on the court playing, Greyson isn't, and vice versa. And as much as I love watching Paul play, I prefer when he's on the bench because that means Greyson isn't staring at me like he has been every time he's been benched. It has me considering leaving early, but because of where I'm sitting, Paul would notice if I left, and I don't want to be rude, so I ride out the inevitable glares from Greyson, keeping my focus solely on Paul.

Right before halftime, the cheerleaders stand by my section, preparing to perform their routine.

"Have you seen Paul tonight?"

My ears perk up at the mention of his name, and I glance slightly to my side to see a petite little blonde girl with way too much glitter on her body talking to a brunette with boobs that put mine to shame.

And I'm pretty proud of my perky C's.

"How could I miss him? That man is delicious. I just want to lick him from head to toe," the brunette declares.

"God, you're bad. Have you slept with him yet? I wonder what he's packing under those shorts." The blonde girl tilts her head as though she's envisioning Paul's cock, and I'm this close to getting up and poking her eyes out.

"Not yet. But I'm sure it will be any day now." The brunette flips her hair and raises her skirt, which is already showing too much of her ass. "That man can slam dunk in me anytime he wants."

"Oh my God. You're so bad."

They both cackle like drunk hyenas, sending my blood pressure into overdrive as my hands tighten into fists on my lap.

Who does this little whore think—

No. He's not mine. Why am I getting territorial all of a sudden? I don't do that.

As halftime begins, the players march to their locker rooms while the cheerleaders run out to the center of the court with their short skirts and pom poms, performing some upbeat, scandalous dance. After watching them for what feels like an eternity, the buzzer sounds, and the players walk out from their locker rooms as the cheerleaders return to the sidelines. When I look over at the bench, Paul stops in his tracks and winks at me before sitting lax on the bench with his legs parted, squirting water in his mouth.

Fuck me.

The sight alone makes me tighten my thighs together, anticipation building between my legs.

It should be a crime to look that good in basketball shorts.

Maybe tonight we'll have a repeat of our first night together...

"Did you see that? He winked at you!" the blonde girl shrieks with excitement, jumping up and down with her friend before heading to their prospective places.

Oh, please.

The second half goes by just as fast, with Greyson's beady eyes on me while my eyes remain on Paul. I'm counting down the seconds when the buzzer finally sounds, and we win by twelve points.

Standing awkwardly to the side, I watch everyone around me jump up and down, celebrating as the team congregates in a congratulatory huddle.

Zipping my jacket, I take a few steps away from my seat when a hand grips my elbow.

My eyes whip to my side to find Paul towering over me.

"You came." God, why did those have to be his two words to me? I bite my lower lip as my eyes rake over him. His chest heaves, sweat glistening all over his body. How his eyes narrow in on me, or more accurately, on the jersey I'm wearing, makes my head dizzy. His fingers push back the opening of my jacket, revealing more of the jersey. "Fuck," he murmurs softly, shaking his head.

He releases my arm, and I tuck a loose piece of hair behind my ear, feeling...nervous. Why the fuck is my heart beating so fast? "You were amazing out there," I confess.

"You think?" I assume he must be joking, but he's looking at me as though he's really wondering if I thought he played well.

"Yeah. I've never seen anything like that before. It was incredible. The game. The crowd. The energy in here." I shake my head, laughing. "Clearly, I don't get out much, but I'm really glad you asked me to come...here. Come here."

Fucking hell, get your mind out of the damn gutter, Sarah!

He shyly smiles as though knowing what I'm thinking and runs his hand across his forehead, wiping away the sweat. "Sorry, I'm so gross."

I shrug one shoulder. "I think it's kind of sexy."

"You know—"

"Paul! Coach wants everyone in the locker room!" someone behind Paul yells.

He sighs. "I have to talk to the team, but it shouldn't be long. Then I'll just take a quick shower, and we can grab dinner if you still want to?"

I smile. "I'd like that."

"Okay. Great. So—"

"Paul!"

"I'm coming!" Paul shouts over his shoulder, shaking his head. "I'll meet you outside the locker room as soon as I'm done." He steps toward his teammates but then pivots back for me, leans down, and presses a quick kiss to my cheek before turning and jogging to the locker room.

A blush spreads over my face. And as I notice the two cheerleaders from earlier staring at me with mouths agape, I flip my hair over my shoulder and make my way off the court, feeling like a goddamn queen.

I walk out to the locker room area and wait in the hall, leaning against the wall. Player after player exits the room, but not Paul. After twenty minutes, I'm tempted to text Paul asking to reschedule because my stomach is starting to eat itself, but I remind myself that the conversation I've rehearsed repeatedly can't wait any longer.

It's happening tonight.

Suddenly, the door swings open. Looking up, smiling, I expect to see Paul. Instead, it's the last person I'd ever want to see.

Greyson.

"Well, what a pleasant surprise," he surmises, approaching me.

"Don't come near me," I warn as I take an ample step away from him.

"Relax. There are cameras here. Wouldn't risk doing anything to get kicked off the team." An evil smirk appears. "You're well aware how cameras can change a person's life, aren't you, Sarah?"

"Fuck you," I lash out.

Fear grips me in place as he approaches, leaving no room between us. He leans down, ghosting his lips over my ear, my whole body shivering. "Is that what you want? For me to fuck you again?" His fingers dance across the top of my jeans, plaguing me with terror. "You took me so well that night. Like the good little slut you are. Sometimes, I just watch it on repeat, listening to your sweet moans."

My stomach churns. "G-get away from me." I place my hands on his chest, trying to shove him away, but it's futile.

He steps back, glaring at me with anger in his eyes. "I saw the way you were looking at Paul all night. Disgusting."

"You mean while you sat on the bench, and he played better than you ever will?" I counter, signing my own death certificate.

His nostrils flare as his eyes narrow down on me. Silence fills the space between us until a sinister grin spreads over his face, and he says the words I've feared for so long.

"I know how I plan on using *it* now."

Terror suffocates me.

No. No. No.

He nods. "You're going to stay the fuck away from Paul."

"Excuse me?" I blurt out, taken aback by his request.

"You're done with him. And if I find out that you two have anything to do with each other, your little five minutes of fame will be released for the entire world to see."

I open my mouth to speak, but he stops me.

"Oh, and with a simple hack, I'll make it appear like Paul released it in a jealous rage. Ruining any chance of a career in the NBA. Heck, it'll probably even ruin his life." His eyes turn cold, fury dancing across his irises. "You wouldn't want to be responsible for doing that to him, right?"

My equilibrium vanishes as everything around me spins. He's backed me into an ominous dark corner, one I will never be able to crawl out of, no matter how hard I claw and bite my way to the surface.

I shake my head, trembling. "You...you can't do that."

"I think you'll find that I can." He shrugs his shoulders nonchalantly.

But I need to talk to Paul.

I need to tell him I'm pregnant.

"But you don't understand—"

"Listen, I don't care what's going on between the two of you. I really don't. But Paul took something from me, so now I'm taking something from him. Just teaching him a little lesson." He pats me on the top of the head like an obedient puppy. "It's not personal. You just got caught in the crosshairs."

He turns and exits the building, leaving me on shaking legs with tears streaming down both cheeks.

I don't think. I just run. I run as fast as I can from the building to my car, and as I unlock the door, I feel my phone vibrate.

Paul

Hey, where are you?

I hit delete and throw my phone onto the passenger seat. My fingers tremble as I turn the key in the ignition and press my foot on the gas. *I need to get the fuck out of here.* Tears blur my vision as I finally reach my parking spot near my apartment and shut off my car, resting my head against the side window.

What the hell am I going to do?

Eight

PAUL

My feet dangle off the end of the couch as I lie back, tossing a basketball in the air. We won tonight's scrimmage against a nearby school, and you'd think that would make me happy. Even if just a little bit. But I'm not. In fact, I'm far from it.

It's been a week since Sarah stood me up after my game, and not knowing what I did wrong to make her leave is killing me.

Why would she go through the effort of coming to my game to then disappear right after, ignoring my texts and calls?

I don't get it.

Not one fucking bit.

"Aw, poor Sarah," Natalie murmurs, sitting on the love seat beside the couch.

"What?" I sit up in a panic, tossing the ball to the floor. Was I talking out loud?

She narrows her eyes at me suspiciously. "Are you okay?"

I mold into the leather couch, sliding a hand over my face. "Yeah, sorry. Just tired." I rest my feet on the ottoman, trying to appear casual. "What was that you were saying about Sarah?"

She looks down at her phone in her hands. "We were supposed to go out tonight, but she just canceled. Said she's not feeling well."

Sarah's sick?

And alone.

I don't like this.

But why don't I like this?

People get sick all the time.

But what if she's so sick she can't get out of bed? Or what if she caught one of those rare flesh-eating bacteria? Just last week, I saw a story on the news about a guy who tried on a new shirt at the mall and then lost both of his arms a week later. Oh God. This isn't good.

"Maybe I should bring her some soup," Natalie ponders, tapping her chin.

I straighten, gripping the edge of my seat. "I was heading out anyway. I can stop by with some soup." Natalie's eyes focus on me, her brows pinching together. She's on to me. "If you want," I add, shrugging my shoulders to feign indifference.

"You wouldn't mind?" she asks.

"No." I stand abruptly, not giving her a chance to make more out of this than it is, which is just a guy bringing a girl soup. "I'll go to that little deli nearby and grab some chicken noodle soup," I say over my shoulder as my fingers grab my keys on the entryway table, and my legs book it out of there.

After picking up some soup, it occurs to me that I don't actually know what Sarah is sick with. And after convincing myself that it's not a flesh-eating bacteria and probably just the common-day cold, I stop by the pharmacy and get a bit of everything: tissues, a thermometer, pain reliever, cough suppressants, vitamin C, and a bag of chocolate candies.

Because, obviously, chocolate makes everything better.

Thirty minutes later, I tap my knuckles against her door, which soon opens, revealing Sarah in nothing but an oversized T-shirt, looking extremely surprised to see me.

Can't say I blame her.

"Umm, Paul. What are you doing here?" She wipes her hand across her damp forehead and pushes her hair out of her face. Her normally iridescent eyes appear slightly bloodshot and puffy like she's been crying.

A wave of fierce protectiveness washes over me.

"I was at my house when Natalie was there and said you weren't feeling well. I was heading out anyway, so I thought I'd pick you up some soup." I reach inside the bag to pull out the warm container.

"You...you went out to get soup for me?"she asks, confused.

"Yeah." I shrug. "You should smell this. I don't know what they put in it, but the aroma is mouthwatering. Had me salivating the whole drive here." I chuckle. "My mom always makes me this kind of soup when I'm not feeling well."

Her face softens, and a half smile appears.

I peel back the lid and bring it close to her face so the fragrance surrounds her.

Suddenly, her eyes widen in horror as her hand clamps down over her mouth. She quickly sprints toward the back of her apartment to, I assume, the bathroom.

Shit. Good job, Paul. Guess it's not the common-day cold.

I walk inside, shutting the door behind me as the ever-familiar heaving sound fills the apartment. Quickly, I place the bag and the soup on the counter and then head to her bathroom, where I find her kneeling, praying to the porcelain god.

Her back hunches as she grabs the toilet seat and once again heaves out whatever is inside her. I stand behind her and pull her hair away from her face, keeping it in one hand as my other hand gently rubs her back. She stays like this for a minute or two before her body finally relaxes, and I reach over her to flush the toilet.

"Please go away, Paul. You don't want to see this," she mumbles, placing her cheek on the toilet seat.

"I'm not going anywhere," I assure her.

I see a bottle of mouth rinse and a washcloth on the counter beside it. Obtaining a cap full of the mouth rinse, I hold it out for her to take. She looks at it hesitantly before grabbing it from me with a shaking hand, throwing it back, gurgling, and finally spitting it in the toilet. I then hold the washcloth under cold water before wringing it out. When I look back at Sarah, her eyes are closed, as though she is about to fall asleep with her head on the toilet seat, which won't do.

"Okay, you're not sleeping here." I reach down, placing one arm under Sarah's knees and another around her waist, pulling her up against my chest. She doesn't fight it like I thought she would and instead nuzzles her head into the crook of my neck.

"Why are you such a nice guy? You're making this so much harder for me," she murmurs, the scent of her minty breath wafting into my face.

"Being nice is making things hard for you?" I ask, confused.

She remains silent, clutching onto the center of my shirt as I walk into her bedroom.

It's different than I would have imagined. Her bedding is all white with a black throw and black accent pillows. Her white curtains are draped to the side, revealing her view of the city all lit up. And it looks like a collection of new art supplies is in the corner of her room, left alone and in their original wrappings. The pristine white walls are bare and vacant from any photos or decorations. Overall, it's very plain. Some may even say it's depressing.

For an artist, I thought there would have been more color in her room—more life. But instead, it feels a bit desolate, reminiscent of a blank canvas. It's as though all the life and color drained from the space within these four walls.

"Sometimes it's easier to see the world in black and white."

I ponder her words. It might be easier, but it sure as hell isn't a life worth living, and I'll be damned if I let her continue living like this for another second.

I lay her body on the bed, bring a blanket up to her chest, and then lightly press the folded washcloth on her forehead as I sit beside her, my knuckles stroking her jaw. I don't know if the damp cloth is needed, but again, it's just one of those things my mom always did for me.

Without warning, my eyes spot the ugliest damn thing I've ever seen in my life on the side of the bed beside her. I pick it up, examining it as I hold it between two fingers, not letting it any closer in fear of catching a disease.

This right here is what they would call *Patient One.*

"What in God's name is this?" One of the eyes is hanging by a thread, and the rest of its fur looks matted and worn.

Sarah's eyes pop open, and she quickly snags the little gremlin from my hands. "Don't touch Teddy."

"You named your teddy bear...Teddy?" I ask, my lips curving up. "I'm disappointed." I *tsk.* "I took you as someone a little more creative than that."

"I was nine when I got him." She closes her eyes. "My creativity hadn't flourished yet." Her hands clutch it to her chest, holding on to it for dear life like it's the most valuable thing in her life.

And maybe it is, even if it looks like it would be happier living at the bottom of the trash barrel.

I watch her taking gradual, deep breaths, rubbing her stomach.

"How are you feeling?" I cup her cheek, checking for any sign of a fever, but thankfully, she's as cool as a cucumber.

Her eyes flutter open. "I'm fine." She releases a rush of air. "I must have eaten something that didn't agree with me."

I nod. "Sorry about the soup."

She lets out a weak laugh. "It's okay. Don't worry about it."

"I will. Probably won't be able to sleep tonight because of it," I joke, but it's true.

Her smile wavers as she watches me. She bites her bottom lip and closes her eyes, an internal war raging inside her head. Right before opening her eyes, she whispers, "You should stay here then."

I catch her eyes, wishing I could hear every thought inside her head. "You want me to?"

She nods. "I'm just having one of those days where I don't want to be alone." She looks at the ceiling before returning her sight to me. "Do you ever have days like that?"

I don't hesitate when I say, "All the damn time."

She moves her teddy bear to the other side of the bed and lifts the blanket, motioning for me to slide in beside her, which I do, positioning myself on my back. Turning on her side, she removes the washcloth from her forehead and throws it on the nightstand before she rests her head on my chest and melts against me as my arm wraps around her waist, my hand brushing her bare skin where her T-shirt has ridden up.

Her hand rests on the lower half of my torso, her fingers tangling around the fabric, and her leg swings over mine, clinging to me.

We're cuddling. And it doesn't feel forced or weird. It feels natural, like something we should be doing all the time.

"You're good at this," she says softly.

"Good at what?"

Looking up at me, under those dark lashes, she says, "Cuddling." The corners of her lips curve up as she moves herself on top of me, her chin now resting right on my chest. "Thank you for taking care of me. No one has done that in... Well, thank you."

I slide my hands under her shirt on her back, applying a soothing pressure. "Of course." I lean up, kissing the top of her head, her raven-black hair cascading over her bare shoulder. "Can I ask you something?"

"Sure." She pierces me with those damn beautiful emerald-green eyes, momentarily distracting me.

Removing one of my hands from her back, I watch as she subtly frowns until I place it on her cheek, my thumb gliding across her smooth skin. "Why did you leave after my game?"

Her whole body tenses in my arms as she pales, looking like she might get sick again.

"I...umm," she starts to say.

"I texted and called you, but nothing. I left the arena searching the parking lot for you, worried something might have happened." Her lips part, her eyes glimmering against the translucent moonlight entering her window. "You don't seem like the type who would just up and ghost someone. So why?"

Her eyes avert me, her bottom lip trembling before she sucks on it. "I'm sorry for worrying you, but...I don't do relationships, Paul," she admits with a shaky breath. "I'm not that kind of girl, and I didn't want you to get the wrong impression of me if I went out with you after your game."

My eyes flick up at the ceiling, her words leaving an unpleasant taste in my mouth, but only momentarily. Because the bigger part of me, the part that witnessed her light up when I asked her out, doesn't believe a damn word she just said.

She came to my game.

She wore my jersey.

She wanted to be there.

So what made her leave?

"It was just supposed to be one night," she whispers, tucking her chin down.

The impact of those words stabs me right in the center of my chest, but I ignore it because she's right. It was supposed to be just one night, but now, I want more.

I want all of her nights...if she'll let me.

"Yeah. You're right. I knew that," I say, hiding the pain of not feeling good enough to be more than one night for her.

"I'm sorry, Paul." She looks up at me with glistening eyes, blinking fast to keep her tears at bay.

"It's okay, Sarah." I slowly swipe my thumb across her bottom lip, trying my best to give her a small smile.

"If you want to leave, I understand."

I hold her tighter, savoring the feeling of her body against mine. "I'm afraid you're stuck with me for one more night."

"Promise?"

"Promise," I reply, pulling the blanket up around us as she closes her eyes and, soon after, drifts off to sleep.

Why did I fall for the one girl in the world who wants nothing to do with me?

I don't know, but what I do know is I'll do whatever it takes to prove to her that I'm worth it.

And I sure as hell am not going to give up on her.

Or *us*.

The only sound comes from the raindrops hitting the windowpane steadily, providing a relaxing white noise that eventually lulls me to sleep with the girl of my dreams in my arms.

Nine

SARAH

Sitting my ass onto my office chair with an unladylike groan, I feel like death. I scoot closer to my computer screen to get a better view of my reflection, and I realize death is a word that is too kind to describe the way I look right now.

Bags under my eyes the size of Texas barely remain hidden under the three layers of concealer I put on, and my hair has certainly seen better days. Reaching into my purse, I grab my trusted concealer and start working on a fourth layer before throwing my hair up in a bun and wiping a sheen coat of gloss across my lips.

Whoever came up with the term "morning sickness" clearly has never experienced it before, seeing as I've been vomiting at all hours of the day and night. Thankfully, my last episode was around one this morning, and I haven't felt the need to sprint to the bathroom yet.

And according to everything I've been reading online, this should hopefully improve by my second trimester.

Fingers crossed.

"Hey, Sarah. Everything okay?" Gianna approaches my desk; her well-polished ensemble of a black pencil skirt, white blouse, and perfectly coifed hair only makes me feel worse about my own appearance.

"Hey, Gianna." I throw on a smile while trying to smooth out a couple of wrinkles on the front of my dress. "Yeah. Just a bit tired."

After spending all weekend rotating between resting my head on the toilet seat and bawling my eyes out because of Greyson's threat looming over me and not being able to tell Paul that I'm pregnant, I had to force myself out of bed this morning to meet with my advisor about trying to graduate early.

Finding out I can was fan-fucking-tastic. But finding out that would mean I need to double up my courses next semester was downright dreadful.

But I don't see how I have a choice in the matter.

I need to do what's best for the baby, which means not taking classes while working and raising a child simultaneously.

Especially alone.

Even Wonder Woman would have to draw the line in the sand somewhere.

I then went straight to my doctor's office, worried over how often I had been getting sick, but she assured me it was normal and told me to pick up some ginger gummies and electrolytes, which I did on my way here.

So yeah, I'm fucking exhausted.

Gianna regards me with sympathy in her hazel eyes. "Well, if you need anything, just let me know. Okay?"

I nod. "Of course. Thank you."

She smiles and turns, heading toward her desk. As I spin in my seat to face my computer, I see a familiar reflection on my screen and turn around in a panic.

"Paul? What are you doing here?" I look around nervously, praying Greyson isn't in today. I haven't seen him yet, but that doesn't mean he isn't watching the security cameras like the creep that he is.

Lord knows he loves his cameras.

"I just wanted to make sure you're doing okay after the other night. I would have stopped by sooner, but we had an away game, and I just got back today. Natalie mentioned you were working." He smiles but tilts his head, noticing my hesitation. "Don't take this the wrong way, but you don't look so great." His hand reaches out to cup my cheek, and I find myself melting into his warm touch, my eyes closing. "Are you still not feeling well?"

I internally shake my head, opening my eyes. "I'm fine. I promise. I've just been busy today."

He drops his hand and takes a step away. "I brought you some things, just in case." He lifts a small bag in his hands. "Some saltines and ginger ale. No soup this time." He laughs nervously.

"That was so...thoughtful," I murmur, still glancing around the office tensely. I glimpse toward Greyson's office but notice the door is closed. Maybe he isn't here today.

Still, I can't take any chances.

Because if Greyson sees Paul here visiting me, it's game over. And both me and Paul will lose.

"But like I said the other night..." I straighten my shoulders, hating what I'm about to say. "I don't do relationships, Paul, and this feels like something a boyfriend would do, so I really wish you hadn't done this."

I don't do relationships. Words I previously rushed out to him the other night as he held me in his arms. My mind had raced for any excuse to use as to why we couldn't be together, and it was the only one I thought he might believe.

Because telling him the truth is not an option.

At least for now, until I figure a way out of Greyson's grasp.

And until then, I'm left with only one option.

I must lie in order to protect us—all of us.

He looks taken aback, and it instantly crushes any and all of the tough persona I'm trying to exhibit.

Not to mention, it fucking breaks the stupid beating thing beneath my chest.

"Yeah. I know." He places the bag on my desk, rolling his lips deep in thought. "Sorry, I didn't mean to bother you during work. I'll go." He turns to walk away, and I should let him keep walking.

I try to at least.

But before I know what I'm doing, I'm jumping out of my seat and chasing after him in my heels.

"Wait, Paul." I grab his elbow, stopping him. He spins around to face me, hurt flashing across his big brown eyes, and it guts me. "I'm sorry. It's just been a stressful day. It was really sweet of you to bring me those things." I throw myself into his body, wrapping my arms around his torso. His long arms enfold tightly around my waist, and his hand that presses against my lower back, splaying out as he pulls me against him, feels perfect.

Like a tether to his body that makes me feel...safe.

"Of course," he says softly, kissing the top of my head. I want to melt into his arms and tell him to take me away from here. Tell him everything. But I don't because I can't.

Not yet.

Frustration bubbles inside me at the situation I've found myself in, so I hesitantly step away from him, putting just the tiniest bit of distance between us.

"Well, well, well. Paul, what are you doing here?"

My heart thuds erratically as fear invades every morsel of me, spewing to the brink of an eruption.

Shit. Shit. Shit.

I feel Greyson's presence behind me and immediately turn to face him, cowering closer to Paul. My whole body feels weak as shivers run over me.

Paul being here is the last thing I need right now.

I should have let him go.

"Greyson. I had no idea you work here," Paul says coldly, his voice on the cusp of sounding ominous.

"My dad is the head of this bank," he states matter-of-factly, looking between us.

Paul discreetly tugs on the back of my dress, pulling me closer to him, leaving no space between us. His solid body becomes a support for mine to lean against.

"Interesting," Paul remarks. His fingers rub against my lower back, and there's no way he doesn't notice my body shaking.

My heart is beating rapidly as the thick tension between these two can be felt pulsing in the air, cascading all around us.

Greyson's eyes narrow in on him. "But as far as I'm aware, you don't work here. So what are you doing here?"

"Was in the neighborhood, so I thought I'd stop by to get some advice on my stocks," Paul says plainly.

Greyson laughs. "You probably have more money in your account than half the population. I think your stocks are doing fine."

Wait...Paul's rich?

"Can never be too sure, which is why I like to always keep an eye on things to avoid any unexpected issues," Paul warns, and for whatever reason, I feel like there's a hidden meaning to his words.

"That's very smart of you," Greyson adds. "But sometimes, it's best to step back. Sometimes, being too involved can get you into trouble." Greyson crosses his bulky arms over his chest, his chin lifted defiantly.

I peek over my shoulder at Paul, who shrugs his shoulders. "I've never shied away from trouble to keep things I care about safe."

The two stare at each other, like soldiers from opposing sides, ready to conquer the other. And it's scaring the shit out of me.

"Well..." I clear my throat. "I have a lot of paperwork to complete today. And Paul was just leaving." I step to the side, away from both of them. Paul's hands drop from my dress, leaving me cold from the loss of his touch.

It takes Paul a moment before he finally nods in agreement. "Yeah. I'm leaving." He looks down, his eyes focusing on the slight tremble in my body as my heart races uncontrollably. "You're good?"

I know his question has a double meaning, but now is not the time to tell him I'm not good. And it's definitely not the right time to tell him that Greyson is blackmailing me to stay away from him when all I want to do is tell him I'm pregnant with a baby.

His baby.

So instead, I say, "Yeah. I'm good here. As soon as I finish my paperwork, I'll be heading home."

Paul squeezes the back of his neck, scanning around the office. His eyes focus on each employee nearby. Is he making sure there are people around me?

It seems to practically kill him to say his next words. "All right. I'll see you then."

"See you around, Paul," Greyson haughtily interjects, waving an arrogant hand.

Paul hesitates, narrowing his eyes on him, before finally turning and leaving the office.

As much as I know he had to, a part of me wishes he weren't walking out those doors right now.

I quickly face Greyson to find him glaring at me with his familiar cold blue eyes.

"I thought I told you—"

"I didn't know he was coming here," I cut him off, panicking. "We have nothing to do with each other. I swear," I insist, my voice shaking with the fear and realization of what he might do.

Of what he might show the world.

He sighs, running his fingers through his short, blonde hair. "Okay." He looks at the door Paul just walked out of and, before stepping away from me, says, "Be sure it doesn't happen again. That's your one and only warning."

I faintly nod, my shoulders hunching in. "It won't happen again."

A few hours later, I slump through my apartment door and lock it behind me. Kicking off my heels, I unzip my dress and let it fall to the floor. I toss my bag on the coffee table and begin to open the first piece of mail in my hand, scanning the information.

Oh lovely. A bill from the doctor's office.

Since I'm only an intern at LH United, I don't have a fantastic health insurance plan. Not until they hopefully offer me a full-time position with better benefits at the end of the semester, which means this pregnancy is probably going to cause me to file bankruptcy.

Gotta love the American healthcare system.

The total of seven hundred and thirty-three dollars stares back at me, mocking me. An expense I never even thought about or planned for and will have to pay eventually. But for now, I'll add it to my ever-growing bills, previously piled in my bedroom but now moved to the kitchen island because they insisted on tormenting me before sleep rescued me.

I collapse on my couch, staring at the ceiling, trying not to let the impending doom of having no money and a baby growing inside my belly get to me, but it's pretty much impossible.

My eyes blur as tears threaten to spill out, and my hand rubs my stomach softly in soothing circles. "We'll be okay. I'll figure everything out. I promise I will."

My phone vibrates inside my bag, so I pull it out.

Natalie

Hey, Sarah! Tomorrow night, a few of us are going to the new bar that opened near campus. Please come!

I stare at the screen, feeling unsure.

It's not like I have money to spend. But I guess water won't break the bank.

And I really could use a night out with some friends.

But what if Paul's there?

You know, the man who rubbed your back as you hurled your dinner in the toilet the other night and then proceeded to stay the night, holding you tucked into his arms, making you feel a warmth you'd never experienced. And the same man who then went out of his way to pick up things for you in case you still weren't feeling great.

Why does this man have to be so nice to me?

It's not something I'm used to, and it's making it harder and harder for me to stay away from him when I know it's risking messing everything up...

And I won't be responsible for ruining Paul's career when he deserves the whole goddamn world.

I won't do it.

Rereading Natalie's text, I chew on my thumbnail, weighing my options. The odds of Greyson being at the same bar as me in this city, with thousands of bars to choose from, are minuscule and practically impossible.

And if I'm being honest with myself...I want to see Paul.

I want the overwhelming, comforting feeling of safety that surrounds me like a warm blanket when I'm in his presence.

My throat burns as the tip of my nose tingles.

I fucking need him, and I wish I could tell him that. I wish I could tell him everything.

Pinching the bridge of my nose, I take a deep breath.

I'm so tired of feeling alone all the damn time.

My fingers hover over the screen, hoping I won't regret my decision.

Sarah

Count me in!

* * *

I'm squished between Jason and Vanessa when we pull up to the bar in Nate's car, seeing a line forming outside the entrance, which we eagerly join.

"There he is," Nate announces, looking over my head.

I cautiously turn, already knowing who *he* is referring to.

A part of me feels nervous that Greyson will show up at this exact moment, causing me to glance around warily, but there's no sign of him, so I tell myself for the hundredth time tonight not to worry.

Everything will be okay.

"Hey, man," Paul says, walking up to Nate, looking like utter perfection in a pair of dark jeans and a white fitted T-shirt, showcasing his muscular biceps. A few silver chains hang around his neck, swinging with each step he takes. His eyes move over everyone as he smiles until he sees me. Those deep chocolate eyes lock onto mine, and I can't help but feel disappointed when his smile falters. "Hey, Sarah."

"Hey," I say softly, pulling nervously at the hem of my dress. Heat flares up inside me, feeling his gaze on me, but I look away, wiping away at an imaginary piece of lint on my stomach.

"Next," the bouncer calls for us, and Natalie grabs my hand, pulling me inside with her.

As we enter the bar, Nate says, "I'll go grab the booth in the back." Natalie and Jason walk with him while Vanessa makes her way over to the bar.

Leaving me and Paul to decide which way to go.

The booth or the bar?

I feel Paul's presence behind me. It's intimidating, but in the best way because I know what this man can do. I was lucky enough to experience it firsthand on a night I wish I could live over and over again.

But I can't.

Even if I want to.

And I really want to…

But maybe one dance wouldn't cause any harm.

So, instead of choosing the booth or the bar, I make my way to the dance floor, squeezing through the crowd of people until I find a free space to move around. The DJ changes the song to something upbeat and stimulating, and I let my body sway with the beat, closing my eyes and allowing myself to get lost, even if just for a moment.

It doesn't take long for a solid body to attach itself to mine as Paul's large hands slide over my waist and hips possessively.

And God, it feels so damn intoxicating.

"Why does it feel like you're hiding something from me?" he asks, his lips brushing against the shell of my ear.

I momentarily freeze from his question before regaining my composure, pressing my ass harder into the front of his jeans, feeling the firsthand effect I have over him. His body molds together with mine perfectly, his hips moving sensually in sync with my own.

"I don't know what you're talking about." My hands glide over his, interlacing our fingers and bringing them lower on my hips, where his fingers dig into the noticeably short hem of my dress.

"I think you do know, but you won't say." His fingers scrunch the fabric into his fists as he presses his lips across my neck.

I lean my head against him, loving the feeling of his body supporting me upright.

I could fall at any second, and this man would catch me like it was his only mission in life.

And somehow, knowing this, I feel free.

Free to fall.

At this moment, I don't think about the fact that I'm being blackmailed into staying away from him, keeping me from telling him I'm pregnant with our baby.

I just feel him.

And it feels really fucking good.

"Tell me what you want, Sarah," he whispers, his voice low and sultry.

A subtle mist of smoke fills the dance floor as a fog machine in the corner turns on, covering the floor in a thick cloud.

"I want..." No. *Want* isn't the right word to use. I peek around, seeing people nearby, but notice everyone is in their own little bubble. No one is looking at us. "I need you," I admit, taking his hand in mine and gliding it between my legs.

The second his finger traces the center of my thong, I fold into his chest as my knees buckle.

"You're soaking wet," he groans in approval. "Do you have any idea how much I've missed this pretty pussy?" His hand cups me firmly, making me moan out a sound that is, thankfully, lost in the music surrounding us. "How much my cock has missed being inside you, making you come over and over again as I watched you fall apart in my arms, looking so goddamn beautiful?"

I feel wetness building between my legs, the anticipation of knowing what his hand is capable of doing driving me absolutely senseless.

"Please, Paul..."

His fingers shove the fabric aside, and then he plunges two fingers inside me at once. I bite my bottom lip as my eyes pinch shut, and my hands grip his powerful forearms.

"Have you missed my cock?" he asks, thrusting his fingers inside me at a maddening pace. "When you're getting fucked by someone else, is it my cock you think of?"

I shake my head, feeling weak all over as pleasure builds in my core.

"Words, Sarah," he demands.

"I-I haven't been with anyone since... Oh God... You," I manage to get out. He lets out a groan as his fingers pump harder, his teeth grazing the side of my neck. "Please don't stop," I beg, gripping his forearm harder in encouragement. The familiar buildup of an orgasm starts looming inside me, one as strong as a tidal wave ready to destroy me, and I'll gladly let it.

"I just need you to tell me what you're hiding," Paul whispers into my ear.

"I can't..." I breathe, lost in a haze of lust.

"So there is something," Paul murmurs, his fingers curling inside me, hitting that special spot. "Tell me, Sarah," he coaxes.

I shake my head, riding his hand wildly. "N-no."

His hard cock straining behind the fabric of his pants pushes into my back, sliding over my ass cheeks.

Oh God.

It's too much.

It's not enough.

Every nerve ending in my body is on fire, and I need more.

But suddenly, it all stops.

Paul removes his fingers from my pulsing wet pussy, taking a step back.

"What...what are...you doing?" I stammer, the orgasm inside me rolling away, no longer in reach. I'm left on edge, feeling like a shaken can of soda ready to combust at any moment.

Paul quickly fixes the bottom of my dress by pulling it down. He straightens his posture, towering over me. "I'll give you what you need when you talk to me and tell me what's going on."

My lips part and then close. My eyelashes flutter furiously.

The audacity of this man.

I'm only lying to him to keep us all safe until the time is right for me to tell him everything.

And here he is, pushing my buttons by withholding an orgasm.

Punishing me.

I shake my head, fisting my hands at my side in frustration. "There's nothing for me to tell you."

He grips my chin between his thumb and forefinger, tilting my head back so that my eyes have no choice but to latch onto his.

"You're lying to me, baby girl. And that won't do."

Baby girl.

He hasn't called me that since…

Shaking my head, I pinch my eyes shut, holding in the words he wants to hear.

His thumb runs smoothly across my bottom lip before he walks away, leaving me panting, flushed, and hornier than I've ever been in my damn life.

"Hey, Sarah!" Natalie bounces over to me, grabbing my hand. "Are you okay? You look a little run-down."

"Just from all the dancing." I fan myself with my hand, hoping she won't see past my lie.

She smiles. "Let's go find Vanessa."

I glance over my shoulder, toward the back, seeing Paul watching me with darkened eyes and his arms crossed over his chest, daring me to come over and tell him everything.

He has no idea how badly I wish I could.

"Yeah. Let's go," I respond, fighting the sudden ache behind my chest.

Ten

PAUL

"*There's nothing for me to tell you.*"

I slide a frustrated hand over my face, approaching the table that Nate sits at.

I know Sarah's hiding something from me.

I'm not a damn mind reader, but I could see it in her eyes. Those beautiful, vulnerable eyes that told me *yes* when her lips said *no*. There's something she's not telling me, something keeping her from me as she builds a giant wall between us, brick by brick.

But mark my words, I will knock down that damn wall and find out her secret if it's the last thing I do.

"Rough night?" Nate asks, cocking his head to the side as I drop onto the booth opposite of him.

I let out a defeated sigh, rolling my neck. "There's something I need to tell you, and it has to stay between us. I love Natalie like a sister, but I need to know I can count on you to keep this between you and me."

Nate straightens his shoulder. "You know I won't lie to Natalie."

"I'm not asking you to lie. I'm asking you not to tell anyone what I'm about to say."

Nate's eyes wander over to the dance floor, probably spotting Natalie, before he looks at me, subtly nodding.

"Sarah is the girl I was looking for."

His eyes widen. "Come again?"

I squeeze my neck, looking up at the pitch-black tiled ceiling. "The girl I met at the bar near campus about a month before school started was Sarah."

I peek over at Nate to see his mouth parted in shock before the corners of his lips slowly turn into a grin. "So, the girl who refused to exchange names with you, who you spent every night for a month looking for, has been living in the same apartment building, the same floor, as Natalie? She's been right under your nose this whole time?"

"Yeah, the irony is not lost on me."

"Does she know you were looking for her?"

I purse my lips, shaking my head. "She told me she doesn't do relationships," I admit with a shrug.

Nate straightens. "That's usually just an excuse." He pushes a beer toward me, which I gladly take. "So what are you going to do?"

"What can I do?" I gulp the liquid, enjoying its icy coating on my parched throat.

"You were looking for her that whole time. She at least deserves to know that."

I place the bottle on the table. "Maybe. I don't want to scare her away, though." I rub the condensation off the glass with my thumb. "I've never had this problem before."

"Leave it to you to find the one girl who doesn't want to be tied down."

I scowl, running the pad of my thumb over the bottleneck. "The thing is, it feels like she's keeping something from me."

"Keeping something from you?" Nate raises a brow. "Like what?"

"I don't know. It's just this feeling I'm getting, and when I tried to talk to her about it..." I shake my head, bringing the glass bottle back to my lips.

Nate's eyes drift over to the dance floor, locking on Natalie. "Your gut instinct is usually right." He turns his attention to me. "Just make sure she knows that you're there for her and that she can talk to you. That's all you can do. Sometimes, there are things that aren't easy to talk about. Things that haunt them."

If anyone would know what that would be like, it's Nate.

"Move over," Jason grunts to Nate, sliding on the seat beside him.

"And where were you?" Nate asks. The two of them sharing a booth look like two full-grown-ass adults trying to fit on a kid-sized bench.

Jason shrugs, bringing his drink to his lips. "Just dancing."

I glimpse at Nate, and we both exchange a knowing smirk. *Vanessa.*

"By yourself?" Nate asks with an arrogant grin.

Jason glares at him, finishing off his beer, not saying a damn word.

"Not to make things worse for you"—Nate looks back at me—"but you have fans coming this way."

I sit up, seeing a group of overzealous girls approaching.

Not what I need right now.

"Oh my God. I can't believe it's him," one of the girls squeals.

Somebody save me.

"Hi, ladies," I say, showing a tight smile.

"Wow. You're even better looking in person," the one closest to me affirms as she tries to shove her cleavage in my face.

My cheeks heat up in embarrassment. I've always hated this kind of attention. The kind that comes from ogling and inappropriate comments. I'm just praying no one asks me to sign their boobs tonight.

Yeah, it's happened before, and it's pretty damn awkward when your mom is standing beside you.

"Are these seats taken?" another one asks.

I look to Nate for backup, who picks up the water beside him, guzzling it.

"They are." Sarah squeezes around the girls and slides on the seat beside me. There's not much room, so her body grazes up against mine, and her hand lands firmly on my thigh, staking her claim. After she smiles triumphantly at them, the girls sulk, walking away disappointed.

"Remind me to never mess with you." Nate chuckles.

She smiles, but then, remembering she's touching me and, more importantly, that she's mad at me, she instantly separates herself from me, leaving an inch between us. We sit like this for an hour, her presence beside me like a comfort my body has been craving. Just being close to her without even touching her does something to me.

The waitress drops a few drinks on the table, and Sarah reaches for the glass closest to her, taking a sip before promptly spitting it out.

"Shit," she hisses. "I thought it was water."

My brows furrow. "Don't like vodka?"

She grabs a napkin, patting down the liquid on the table. "I-I have to be up early for work."

I reach out, brushing my thumb over a drop of liquid on her chin. She tenses beside me, but as my hand remains on her, I feel her face soften, almost pressing into me for support as her eyes close.

Natalie pulls Vanessa beside the table and asks, "Is everyone ready to go?"

Nate laughs, shaking his head and pushing Jason out of the booth to get to his girl.

Wrapping his arms around Natalie's waist, he kisses the top of her head and says, "Let's go, baby." He looks at me with a sly smirk. "Paul, do you mind taking Sarah home? I know there wasn't a lot of room in the back of my car for everyone."

Sarah's hands clench on her lap, appearing unhappy by this new arrangement.

"Is that okay?" I ask loud enough so that only she can hear me.

Her head turns, facing me. "It's fine," she says reluctantly.

* * *

The ride to Sarah's apartment is quiet. Her arms are crossed over her chest, and her eyes have been glued to the window beside her the whole time. I'm pretty sure she's still mad at me for withholding the orgasm from her, and I don't blame her, but I'm determined to knock down this brick wall between us, even if I have to do it one block at a damn time.

"Sarah, about earlier..."

"It's fine, Paul." She doesn't look my way.

This isn't how we are going to solve this.

I put my blinker on and pull into a nearby deserted parking lot, stopping by a line of trees in the back.

"What are you doing?" she asks, looking around nervously.

"I just want to talk."

She sighs and leans back in her chair, staring forward.

It's a slight improvement.

"There's nothing to talk about." Her chin trembles as she takes a deep breath.

I twist in my seat and reach over, gently grabbing her chin and facing her toward me.

Here goes nothing.

"I haven't been able to stop thinking about that night," I confess. My hand glides down her neck, and my thumb rests on her pulse point, which is beating rapidly under my touch.

She looks down when she whispers, "Me neither."

I brush a strand of her raven-black hair behind her ear. "Then why does it feel like you're purposely pushing me away?"

Her eyes meet mine, and it feels like she's trying to tell me so much in one look, but I can't understand the confusion and sorrow in her eyes.

She shakes her head. "Because, like I said, I don't do relationships—"

"That's bullshit."

"Excuse me?"

"You heard me. I'm calling bullshit on your sorry ass of an excuse."

"It's not an excuse—"

"I was looking for you."

Her brows furrow in confusion. "When? Tonight?"

I shake my head. "Every night for a month after our night together until the very moment you walked into Natalie's apartment. The moment I saw those big green eyes staring back at me was when I felt a weight lift from my chest because I finally found you."

She shakes her head, scrunching her face in confusion, her bottom lip slightly trembling. "I don't understand. Why would you look for me? I'm no one important. You're the guy going into the NBA. You can have any girl you want."

I let out a humorless laugh. "Clearly, I can't."

She gazes down, biting her bottom lip as a tear slides down her porcelain cheek. "If any part of you truly cares for me, even the tiniest bit, then you would stay away from me. You would look for some other girl to keep your bed warm." Tears rain down her cheeks as she wipes them away. "Because it's not me."

My fingers gently brush her tears away. "Why are you fighting this? I know it wasn't just me that night who felt something, so why are you trying so hard to push me away?"

"You don't understand!" she snaps, her chest heaving from releasing those words.

"Then tell me, Sarah," I coax softly. "I'm here now. Tell me what is holding you back. Tell me why you've put up a damn wall between us."

She throws her hands over her face as a sob overtakes her. "I can't." With shaking fingers, she unbuckles her seat belt. "I can't do this." And then she bolts out of the passenger door faster than I can comprehend what the fuck is going on.

"Shit!" I struggle with my seat belt before flinging it off. "Sarah, wait!"

I jump out of my car and follow her into the woods, where I find her holding her heels in one hand and bracing her other hand against a tree as she bends down, breathing erratically, gasping for air.

"Please...leave me...alone, Paul," she pants.

I immediately know what's happening, and I'm not going anywhere.

"You're having a panic attack," I say calmly, taking small steps toward her.

"No. I'm not," she bites out, dropping her shoes to the ground. Both of her hands press into her chest.

I shake my head—*this woman.*

"You are. I know you are...because I have them, too," I admit, hoping that opening up to her might be enough to put a crack in that wall.

She looks up at me with glossy eyes and mascara running down her face. "You do?"

"Yes." I sit on the ground, lean against the rough tree bark behind me, and carefully pull her onto my lap. Her shoulder rests against my chest, and her long, gorgeous legs drape across my thighs.

"I can't...I can't breathe," she pants, and the tears streaming down her cheeks instantly break my heart.

"You can, baby girl. I'm right here. Everything is going to be okay." I rub my hand up and down her back and take her shaking hand in my other one, placing it firmly against my chest. "Feel the movement of my chest, Sarah. With every breath I take, I want you to take one too. Can you do that for me?"

She slightly nods.

I inhale slowly, holding it in for a few seconds, and then slowly exhale. She mirrors my breathing the whole time.

"You're doing so good, Sarah. Let's do it a couple more times, okay?"

She nods again, and eventually, after a few more times following my breaths, her breathing begins to even out, and her body relaxes in my hold.

I push the hair away from her face, looking into my favorite green eyes. "Are you okay?" My thumb wipes at the remaining tears and smeared mascara under her eyes.

She curls her fingers into my shirt. "Yeah. I'm sorry. That's never happened to me before. I don't ever cry in front of people. Like ever."

"It's okay to cry. It doesn't mean I think less of you. If anything, it just lets me know how you're feeling. And right now, it seems you have a lot going on upstairs." I tap the top of her head. "Maybe too much for one person to manage."

She tilts her chin down and suddenly buries her head in my chest. "I think you're right."

I wrap one arm around her back, holding her small body firmly against me, keeping her safe.

"What's going on, Sarah?"

"I can't…"

I take my free hand, placing it on her cheek. Something is stopping her from telling me what's bothering her, and I wish I knew what it was.

But I'm not pushing her any more tonight.

Because now, it's time to take down that top layer of bricks.

"One of the things I liked about you when we first met was that you had no idea who I was. Or who my father is…was…I should say." Her face tilts up the tiniest bit. "My dad was one of the best NBA players in the league, Steve Weston." I feel her hand gently grip the center of my shirt, getting comfortable. "He broke record after record and brought his team to the championship year after year. He was unstoppable. Until he wasn't." I heave a sigh. "When I was ten years old, he died. He had just returned to the airport after being on the road, and instead of taking the bus with the team to the arena, he opted to rent a car to head straight home. He was eager to see my mom. They were so in love. As a kid, I thought it was gross." I let out a little laugh. "But now, when I think about it, I find it beautiful. They were soul mates in every way. But on his way home, a drunk driver hit him, running straight through a stop sign. He died on impact. It was only a few days after Christmas."

My eyes begin to blur as the memory plays out before me. The twinkling Christmas lights and decorations were still up. There was a knock at the door, and my mom smiled wide, telling me to answer it because she assumed it was my dad. But as I opened the door to find two police officers standing there, confusion hit me. I asked them where my dad was, and they looked at each other as my mom approached me, pulling me behind her. That's when they gave her the grim news.

My dad was dead.

"I never grieved properly. I just threw myself into...basketball." I let out a lungful of air. "The apple didn't fall very far from the tree with basketball. People compare me to my father all of the time. They tell me I'll be just like him, if not better. I have NBA teams fighting over me when I haven't even graduated yet, and sometimes, it just feels like too much. It's just so fucking—"

"Overwhelming," she whispers.

I brush my fingers against her arm, eyeing her tattoos that somehow help calm me. "Yeah. Overwhelming. And sometimes so overwhelming that I panic. I panic I'll never be good enough to be compared to him. I panic over letting everyone down, including my dad. I panic that I'm not worthy of that last name on my jersey. And I panic that I don't even know who I am anymore. The only people at school who know I get panic attacks are Nate and my buddy Glen because they've both witnessed them happening to me. But you're the only person I've ever admitted any of this to."

She looks up at me with fresh tears cascading down her cheeks. "I'm so sorry, Paul."

"Don't cry, Sarah. It breaks my heart to see you cry," I whisper, tightening my arms around her.

"I don't know what's happening to me." She wipes away her tears, her mascara smudging under her eyes.

"You're letting go. And I bet tomorrow morning, you'll feel a lot better for doing so."

She presses her hand to my cheek. "I'm so sorry you went through all of that as a child. Losing a father at such a young age...it's not fair."

Her eyes close momentarily before opening and looking intently at me. "When I look at you, I only see you, not the name on your jersey. I see a man who is kind and smart. Strong and giving. I see someone who puts others before himself and has only ever...only ever cared for me even when I don't deserve it." Her voice cracks at the end as she looks away.

I cup her cheek and brush my thumb across her bottom lip. "You deserve everything."

She shakes her head softly. "I've made mistakes that I can't...well, what I mean is..." Her eyes pierce mine. "I see you, Paul Weston. All ten feet of you." She smiles, and it's the most beautiful smile I've ever seen because it's real. I lean in, sweeping my lips against hers. "Even if you don't see yourself for who you truly are, I do. And I like what I see."

Her words lift an invisible weight from crushing my chest.

She leans in, softly brushing her lips against mine before pressing down.

It's soft and slow.

Sensual and sweet.

It's everything we both need right now.

"Sarah?"

"Yes," she breathes against my lips.

"Do you remember those three words you said to me at the bar that night? What you asked me to do for you?" My hand slides behind her neck, savoring the warmth of her soft skin under the palm of my hand.

She hesitates before nodding.

"Make me forget."

Those three words that I took to heart, doing exactly what she asked of me.

And without me saying anything, she knows. She knows it's what I'm asking of her now.

Her soft lips crash hard on mine as her hands cling around my neck, pulling me closer. My hands grip her waist as she twists her body, straddling my lap. She bites my bottom lip hard, sucking it between hers before sliding her tongue into my mouth.

I push up my hips, letting her feel how badly I want her and need her.

"Please," she whimpers, desperately grinding her greedy pussy over my length. "Please make me come."

Those four words send me over the edge.

In one swift motion, I remove my thick jacket and wrap it around her back, noting how it swallows her whole.

"I'm not cold," she protests.

"It's not for the cold, baby girl. It's so the bark doesn't scratch that pretty body."

Her eyes go wide as understanding registers in her bright green irises.

One minute, we're sitting on the cold, hard ground, and in the next, I stand up with Sarah in my arms, turning her so her back presses against the tree. The thick coat protects her from the hard bark, as her legs wrap tightly around my waist. I separate our mouths for only a moment to admire her in my arms.

"You look like a goddamn fantasy." I nibble eagerly on her neck before quickly licking over the mark, soothing her skin.

"Do that again," she demands.

I grin, repeating the motion.

"You going to be a good girl for me and let me fuck you in the middle of the woods against this tree?" I breathe against her ear, scraping my teeth down the side of her neck.

She nods her head impatiently, pulling me closer to her. "And don't even think about telling me to be quiet."

A deep laugh rumbles in my chest. "Wasn't planning on it." Her hands fumble with my zipper, quickly shoving down my pants. "Be as loud as you want, baby girl, because no one will hear you scream."

She moans, reaching inside my boxers and then fisting my cock with excitement. Her soft hands feel so good wrapped around me, her grip firm, eliciting a form of pleasure I haven't felt since I was last with her.

Knowing I'm not going to last much longer if she keeps touching me like this, I reach into my coat pocket on her body and pull out a condom from my wallet, quickly sliding it over my length. I shove her panties aside, gliding a finger back and forth through her wet center. "Always so wet for me." Abruptly, I push two fingers inside her and watch as her back arches against the tree and her eyes pinch shut while her lips part, sensations overtaking her.

"Show me how badly you want my cock."

She opens her eyes, mischievousness floating across them as she rides my fingers, taking whatever she needs from me.

"Such a good girl," I praise, my palm grinding against her clit.

"It feels so good." She grips my shoulders for support and continues her up-and-down motions.

I feel her begin to clench around my fingers and immediately pull out because she's not coming on my fingers tonight.

She's coming on my hard cock that's throbbing to be inside her again.

She whimpers at the loss of pressure but is instantly met with satisfaction as I thrust my cock inside her in one go. A savory moan leaves her lips as a ravenous groan leaves mine. Her luscious lips form a perfect O as her eyes flutter closed and her nails dig into my shoulders.

After giving her a moment to adjust, she finally opens her eyes, biting her bottom lip.

"I forgot how big you are."

Goddamn.

"Well, let me remind you." I slowly start moving inside her, savoring the feeling of her needing me at this moment as much as I need her.

She moans with each thrust, the heels of her bare feet digging into my ass.

"More," she pants. "Please, Paul. I want it harder."

My lips curve up as I slam into her, harder and faster, watching her as she's about to unravel with me. Her whole body tenses just as I move my hand between us and press down on her clit.

"Scream for me, Sarah."

And she does, free-falling before me as an orgasm takes over both of us. I hold her tighter to me as I wait for the tidal wave of pleasure to roll through us, leaving us both panting and spent.

"I've got you, baby girl. I've always got you."

As I stare into her beautiful, glossed eyes, I only think about how I'm not ready to let her go and how I don't think I'll ever be.

Eleven

SARAH

My face snuggles into my pillow, a manly, musky, familiar smell emitting into the air, eliciting a grin as I burrow into the mattress, cocooned in blankets that are...

Wait a minute.

My pillows don't smell manly.

They smell like apples and honey, my go-to shampoo and conditioner.

Slowly, I turn my face to the side and let my eyelids flutter open, taking in my surroundings. Panic engulfs me. I twist, clutching the blankets to my body, my chest heaving steadily with each terrified breath I take.

Stay calm. Stay calm.

There's a bookcase on one side, shelving books and trophies, a TV in the corner, and a desk on the side of the room with...a computer. A computer with a camera attached to the top of it pointed directly at me. Dread fills me as I swallow nervously, my mouth going dry.

This can't be happening. Not again.

A bead of sweat rolls down my forehead as the once comforting layer of blankets on top of me now feels suffocating.

I throw them off of me, relieved to find that I'm fully dressed in the same clothes from last night. But my eyes dart to the camera, my chest tightens, and my breathing becomes erratic.

What the fuck happened?

I remember going to the bar with everyone. I remember Paul driving me home. I remember running out of Paul's car and talking in the woods...amongst other things, and then... Did I fall asleep in Paul's car?

I was so exhausted.

Mentally. Physically. Emotionally.

But how the hell could I have let this happen?

I would never voluntarily sleep in another man's bed.

Not after what happened last time.

A horrifying flashback fills my head.

"I own you" appeared on my phone from an unknown number, followed by a video. My trembling finger clicked play, fear permeating every pore in my body, knowing what I was about to watch.

Bile rises in my throat.

I jump out of the bed on shaking legs, wrapping one of the blankets around me. Tears teeter on the edge, threatening to spill out.

No. No. No.

A soft knock causes my eyes to jump to the door right before it opens. "You're up." Paul's wide smile falters as he looks at me, instantly observing my distress. "What's wrong?'

"W-why am I here?" I demand.

He takes a step inside, seeming confused. "You fell asleep in my car. I didn't want to leave you alone after your panic attack, so I brought you here to sleep in my bed. I slept downstairs on the couch."

"No. No. No. Not again." I run my fingers through my hair, shaking my head.

"Sarah, breathe." He reaches out for me, but I instinctively flinch, stepping back. His eyebrows pinch together as pain flashes across his face. "What's wrong?" he asks again.

I point a shaking finger toward the computer, the source of the problem. "That!"

He looks at the computer and then at me. "What about it?"

"Did you film me in bed?" Tears stream down my face. The rational part of me knows that we didn't have sex in his bed last night and knows that Paul would never film me, but the part of me right now that is stuck back in time, living through the same nightmare every single day, isn't being rational.

She's fearful. She's scared. And she's so fucking tired of having this video hanging over her head like a goddamn storm cloud ready to un- leash terror upon her.

"What?" he asks, bewildered by my accusation.

"Di-did you film me?" I let out a shaky breath, closing my eyes.

He hesitates before asking, "Why would you think I would do that to you?"

"It's facing me!" I scream, opening my blurry eyes. The palms of my hands brace the sides of my head, dropping the blanket as my fingers dig into my scalp.

He walks over to his computer and examines it. "Everything is off, Sarah." His voice is calm as he removes the camera piece sitting on the top. "This isn't even plugged in. It's for gaming." He picks up a pair of thick headphones and a controller lying on the desk. "See?"

I shake my head; my whole body is a trembling mess. "I have to go."

I move for the door, but he blocks me, holding my shoulders in place so I can't run.

He looks up at the ceiling, clenching his jaw. When his eyes fall back onto me, they're void of all emotion except rage. "Did someone film you?" he asks, cautiously as though knowing my secret when it's imper- ative that he never finds out.

Because if I tell him the truth, he'll try to take care of the problem for me, and there's no fixing this. It's already too late. I'm already risking enough just being here right now.

"I need to go!" I say forcefully, yanking my shoulder out of his grip.

"Sarah, talk to me!" His voice is rough and enraged.

"Let me go," I plead through a sob. "I want...I want nothing to do with you. I lied to you. That night, it meant nothing to me. I barely remember it. You were just one of many. So just let me fucking go." I bang the palm of my hands against his chest, my fingers shaking, giving away every ounce of fear within me, but not of Paul. Never of Paul. But only fear that the longer I stay here, the greater the chance of me slipping up any second and telling him what he wants to hear—the truth. "P-please," I beg, my voice quivers.

He looks down at me, and there's so much fury reflected in his eyes, but I know it's not aimed at me when his grip on my shoulders loosens and he steps away, letting me run out the door and down the stairs, feeling a tightness in my chest like I've never experienced before.

* * *

It's been days since I ran out of Paul's room like the world was set on fire. And my heart hasn't felt the same.

Staring at the blank canvas, I feel utterly ashamed.

I came to the art studio to escape my own thoughts.

The cruel words I lashed out at him have played over and over again in my mind like a broken record, and no matter what I do, I can't make them stop. I can't push the pain away.

And after sitting here for hours, the only thing I've accomplished is mixing black and white paint, forming an ominous grey, representing my mood.

How could I say those words to Paul?

How could I look him in the eyes and hurt him like that?

Because I had no choice.

I won't let Greyson ruin Paul's career.

I can't do it.

With a defeated sigh, I drop my paintbrush in its holder and remove my smock. There's no point in creating art tonight when I feel like this.

Walking the path back to my apartment, I look up at the bright, prominent moon above me, fighting with everything inside me to keep the tears at bay.

I'm depleted. Both mentally and physically, and I don't know how much more of this I can take.

The second I enter my bedroom, I make my way over to my bed, slide under the covers, still wearing my clothes, and cuddle up into the center of the bed with Teddy, closing my eyes and searching for an escape from reality.

Just as I'm about to fall asleep, my phone vibrates on my nightstand, making me jump. Rubbing a hand down my face, I reach for it and bring it right before my eyes, which bolt open when I see Paul's name flash across the screen.

Should I answer it?

It's one in the morning.

He's probably drunk.

But what if something's wrong?

Pinching the bridge of my nose with one hand, I press the green button with my other, waiting to hear his voice.

"S-Sarah?" Paul slurs.

"Paul? Is everything okay?"

"I just don't feel great. I didn't know who else to call."

I sit up straight. "What do you mean? Where are you?" Suddenly, shrill voices and deafening music float through the phone. "Are you at a party?"

"Yeah. I just needed a...distraction."

My chest squeezes, remembering how he was the perfect distraction for me, and here I am, running away from him when he needs the same.

"Let...let me be your distraction, Paul," I say softly, gripping my phone.

"No. It's too dangerous for you here."

I panic. "What do you mean? Where are you? I'll come and get you. Just please tell me where you are."

"The Kappa Alpha house," he gets out.

My chest pounds as I rub at my throbbing temple. Returning to that house fills me with dread of epic proportions.

Fuck. Fuck. Fuck.

"Okay." I press my hand to my chest, trying to calm myself as Paul taught me. Deep breath in. Deep breath out. "Just stay where you are. I'll be there in fifteen minutes."

"Sarah?"

"Yeah?" I jump out of bed, pressing my phone between my shoulder and ear, while I find a hoodie on the floor to throw over myself.

"I'm sorry."

"For what?" I ask, coming to a halt.

"For thinking there was something between us when there wasn't." He pauses before saying, "I guess it was only me who felt it."

My eyes sting with unshed tears as my heart cracks, my chest tightening to the point of unbearable pain.

"No, Paul. Please forget everything I said to you the other day. Okay? I didn't mean it. I was just...not in the right headspace. But please stay where you are. I'm leaving now."

Fifteen minutes later, I park in front of the frat house with a horrible feeling in my gut. Cars are lined up and down the street on both sides, and people are filing in and out as music blares from the large house. I hadn't been to this house in a few years and had planned on never returning.

But I'm here for Paul. That's it. Nothing bad will happen this time.

I'm in control.

Just as I'm about to leave my car, I realize I might need assistance, so I grab my phone.

Walking inside the house, I'm immediately assaulted with anxiety. This was the house that changed me. And not for the better.

People crowd every square inch of this place, shoving past me as I make my way inside, with drinks in their hands that conveniently dribble onto me.

"Back the fuck off," I shout at one guy who walks right into me, too drunk to realize I'm standing in front of him.

He leers down at me before side-stepping around me, eventually swaying into the wall.

Shaking my head, I walk farther into the house until, after what feels like forever, relief fills me as I spot Paul sitting on a chair in the corner of the large room. That relief quickly dissipates as I notice his head lolled to the side, a nearly empty bottle of vodka in his hand, and...a girl sitting on his lap.

What the actual fuck?

Fury radiates through me as I approach them, never letting my eyes look elsewhere. But the closer I get to Paul, the more I notice the subtle hints of how incapacitated he is. His eyes are red and glossy, his eyelids are barely open, and his tongue keeps poking through his lips, appearing as though he can't feel it at all.

"What the fuck do you think you're doing?" I place both hands on my hips, sneering at the girl who looks way too comfortable on Paul's lap as her hand rubs over his chest. Her bright pink dress does nothing to contain her store-bought boobs.

"Who the fuck are you?" the girl questions, appearing pissed off at my interruption.

"Sarah," Paul slurs, trying to sit up but barely able to move.

"I'm here for him," I respond, my nails digging into the palms of my hands. "So I suggest you remove yourself before I do it for you."

The girl laughs.

She. Fucking. Laughs.

"Paul doesn't seem like he wants me to go. In fact, he seems pretty content with me staying right here." She pats his chest and places the side of her head on his shoulder, a smug smile creeping on her face.

"He's clearly not in his right mind." The anger inside me boils beneath my skin as my body shakes with adrenaline. "This is your final warning. Remove yourself before I have to do it for you."

"Umm...I don't think so." Her hand slides dangerously low on Paul's chest. "I think we're going to move this private party upstairs to one of the bed—"

I don't think.

All I see is a haze of red when I grab her by her hair, dig my nails into her scalp, and pull her off of Paul, watching with satisfaction as she stumbles to the floor on all fours.

Her bleach-blonde extensions, now ripped from her head, remain in my iron-clad grip.

She looks up, scowling at me. But that dreadful grimace falters as her eyes widen, noticing what I have in my hand. Her hands repeatedly tap the top of her head, and a horrified scream slips from her lips as she jumps up on her feet. "You fucking bitch!"

"I warned you to get off of him." Standing in front of Paul, preventing this piece of trash from getting near him, I shrug, dropping the extensions to the floor.

She screams and suddenly throws herself at me, but just as I lift my arms to block my stomach, I witness Nate step between us and reach for the girl's arm, taking her by surprise as he turns her around in one swift motion, pinning her arm to her back.

"Don't fucking touch her," he seethes. People begin to whisper and stare as he guides the girl toward the front of the house. "If I ever see you near them again, you will regret it. Do you understand me?"

The girl nods, and Nate releases her arm, letting her scurry off into the crowd.

"What happened to him?" Nate asks, his eyes roving over a barely conscious Paul.

"I don't know." To think of what that girl might have done to him if I didn't get here in time makes my insides boil. "He called me to say he wasn't feeling well."

Nate takes the almost empty bottle of vodka from his hands, tossing it to the side before running an exasperated hand over his face. "I'd say from the amount of alcohol in him, he's not going to be feeling well tomorrow either." He sighs, reaching behind Paul, trying to help him to his feet, but it's pointless. The man can barely utter a complete sentence, let alone walk. Nate stands and looks at me. "Do you think if I take one side, you can take the other?"

I nod, stretching out my arms before me. "This will be fun."

An hour later, we make it to the bottom of the stairs in Nate and Paul's house. I look up, count how many steps we need to take, and mentally prepare myself.

"I know it's not my place," Nate starts, "but I think you should know how good of a guy Paul is."

"I know—"

"No." He shakes his head as we reach the fifth step. "I don't think you do. As much as it pisses me off, there's a reason why Natalie refers to him as a goddamn teddy bear."

We reach the top step just as Paul chuckles and then slurs, "Teddyyyyy bearrrrrr."

Nate grins, opening Paul's bedroom door. "This guy takes care of the people he cares about. And he deserves someone who would do the same for him. He's been off this past week, keeping to himself. I wasn't really sure why, but I think now I'm starting to." He pins me with a look, but it's not judgmental. If anything, it's understanding. "So, all I'm trying to say is, please don't hurt him, Sarah."

I nod, swallowing the large lump in my throat. The last thing I want to do is hurt Paul, but I'm unintentionally doing it every day by not telling him my secret—*our secret*.

We push Paul onto his bed, and Nate rolls him toward the center so he doesn't fall off. "Jesus. That was a workout." He wipes his forehead with his forearm.

As Nate steps away, I move toward the bed to remove Paul's shoes and pull the blanket up around him.

"Sarah?" Paul murmurs, his eyes fluttering open the tiniest bit.

"Yeah, Paul?" I stroke my hand over his cheek.

"Can you stay?"

"I...umm..." I glance over at Nate, leaning against the doorframe. He nods in understanding, closing the door behind him.

My eyes move around Paul's room, immediately spotting the camera on his computer, causing me to stiffen. But I know Paul would never take advantage of me, so as I take off my hoodie, I say, "Just for a few minutes. Okay?"

A sleepy smile appears on his face as I crawl under the covers beside him. I try to create space between us, but Paul's arm suddenly wraps around my waist, bringing me up against his chest.

I sigh, giving up as I let myself enjoy this feeling of contentment from being in his arms. If I'm honest with myself, it's the best feeling in the world.

It's where I feel the safest I've ever felt.

"I always feel better when we're like this," he mumbles. "You and me." He brushes his lips against my neck, and it takes everything in me not to turn to face him.

Not to admit that I feel the same damn way.

"Good night, Paul," I whisper, my heart slowly breaking, knowing I will never end up with someone as good as him.

He responds by pressing his lips against my neck before slumping his head on his pillow, soft snores filling his room.

Twelve

PAUL

RIP Paul Weston.

An animalistic groan leaves me as I stretch out on my bed, slowly blinking open my eyes, carefully avoiding the sun peeking through the partially closed blinds. I twist to my side when I'm hit with a familiar scent. Honey and apples. My eyes bolt open.

I smother my nose into the pillow beside me, inhaling that familiar scent: Sarah's scent.

But why am I smelling her on my pillow?

And why am I still in my clothes from the night before?

Slowly, I sit up, rubbing my pounding head with the palm of my hand, fighting the nausea invading my stomach.

What the fuck happened last night?

Knock. Knock.

Fucking hell. I grip the side of my head as the knocking sound reverberates back and forth inside my skull like there's a goddamn tennis match going on in there.

"Come in," I say gruffly, my throat hoarse and raw. Maybe Nate can clue me in as to what the hell happened to me last night. But it's not Nate who pokes his head inside my room.

"Hey." Sarah grins, walking toward me. I think I'm too stunned to speak or completely forgot how to because I'm sitting here like a silent idiot. "I brought you something for the headache I'm sure you have."

She holds out a couple of pills with a bottle of water.

"Thanks." I take the pills and eagerly swallow them down, hoping for a reprieve from my headache.

She sits on the edge of my bed beside me, rubbing her thighs nervously. "How are you feeling?"

I sit up straighter, rolling my neck side to side. "To be honest, I'm not sure."

"Do you remember what happened?" she asks.

Do I?

I had been in such a funk for the past few days that when I heard the Kappa house was having a party, I decided to go, even though I'm not usually a frat house party kind of guy. Scratch that; I'm never a frat house party kind of guy. But my head had been so overwhelmed, playing Sarah's words to me repeatedly on an endless loop, that I just needed a break, an escape from my own head.

Maybe I tried to escape a little too hard.

"I remember going to the party, but the rest is a little hazy." I squeeze the back of my neck, feeling ashamed to admit that. "I don't think I've ever drunk that much in my life."

Just the thought of alcohol has my stomach churning.

She nods, looking down at the comforter where her index finger traces a circle. "You called me," she says matter-of-factly.

"I did?" Why don't I remember this?

"You told me you weren't feeling well and that...you didn't know who else to call." She bites her lower lip, dropping her shoulders. "I went to get you and texted Nate for help. And when I got there..." She pauses, her hand suddenly clenching into a fist beside her. "A girl was sitting on your lap."

I sit up in a flash. "I don't remember that. Sarah, I swear—"

"I know," she says reassuringly. "She was taking advantage of you in the state you were in, and it made me so fucking mad." She shakes her head, her whole body slightly trembling. "I told her to get off you, but she wouldn't listen. So I kind of...threw her off of you and ended up pulling out her hair extensions in the process."

My eyes widen. "You did what?"

"I had no choice," she quickly spits out. "I'm not a violent person, but I couldn't let her..." She blows out a deep breath. "Well, obviously, the bitch wasn't happy with that, and she went to hit me, but Nate showed up right in time to stop her." She finally looks at me with a little smirk. "Don't ask us how we got you out of that house and into your bed. Let's just say you owe Nate big time." She lets out a little chuckle. "I stayed here with you for a few minutes because you asked me to, but when you fully passed out, I left to give you some space."

Doesn't she know that space is the last thing I want from her?

I let out a rush of air, scrubbing a hand over my face. "Jesus, Sarah. I'm so sorry I put you through that." I reach for her hand, letting my thumb rub her soft skin gently back and forth.

"No." She shakes her head. "I know why you were there. Nate talked to me. He said you weren't yourself this past week, and I know...I know..." Suddenly, a tear rolls down her cheek. "It was my fault that you were there. I was horrible to you."

"No, baby girl." I wrap my arm around her waist, pulling her toward me, bringing her between my legs, her side molding against my chest. "I'm a grown-ass adult. It was my fault for drinking that much. I was having a tough week. I needed a..."

"Distraction," she whispers.

I nod. "Yeah. But it wasn't your fault."

"Paul?"

I place two fingers under her chin, tilting her face closer to mine.

"I didn't mean anything I said to you before I ran out of your room that morning like a coward. I just..." Her eyes move from mine, locking on the camera on my computer. "I panicked. And I lashed out at you. I'm sorry. I know you would never...take advantage of me."

Her eyes pinch shut, and I wrap her up in my arms, bringing the blanket around the both of us.

"I know you're not ready to talk about whatever is haunting you, but can you give me a yes or no answer?" She opens her eyes, staring right at me when I ask, "Did someone take advantage of you?"

Her bottom lip trembles, and her eyes glisten as she quietly breathes, "Yes."

My worst fear is confirmed in that one word.

I kiss her temple as she nuzzles against my chest, letting her tears fall down her cheeks and onto my shirt.

"I've got you. Let it all out, Sarah."

Maybe this is what she's been keeping from me.

The cause of her putting a wall between us.

Her fingers clutch onto my shirt for support. "I've never felt this before."

"Felt what?"

"Safe. Cared for. All of it. It's just a lot to process."

"Baby girl, you are safe with me. I will never let anything happen to you. Do you understand me?"

She nods, relaxing against my body as I stroke my hand over her back. We sit here in silence for a few minutes, neither of us moving as I savor the feel of her body against mine when an idea pops into my head.

"Will you do something for me?" I ask.

"Anything."

"Go on a date with me."

Her eyes widen, her lips parting in shock. "A date?"

"Just one date to prove I'm not like the others."

"I already know you aren't."

"Then what's stopping you?"

"I...umm..." She hesitantly peers up at me, the look of defeat crossing her features as she gives in. "Just one?"

"Just one," I confirm.

"Okay."

"Okay?" I ask, sounding a little too eager.

The corners of her lips lift as she nods.

It's fucking adorable.

"This is going to be the best date you've ever been on," I tell her, confidence laced in each word.

"I've...never actually been on a date before," she admits.

What kind of fucking guys has she been involved with?

"Then I promise this date will put all future dates to shame." I push a loose strand of hair behind her ear, my finger falling to her arm, tracing one of the many tattoo flowers I love so much, noting a tiny shiver running through her. "Are you sure you'll be able to handle all of this?"

She laughs, patting my chest. "I can handle you just fine, big guy."

"Big guy, huh?" I smile. "I love it when you call me that. It lets me know you appreciate *all* of me."

She playfully smacks my arm. "Don't let your ego get the best of you."

I shake my head, laughing. "My ego's been out of control ever since I saw those big green eyes watching me in the bar like I was the only man you've ever had eyes for."

A blush spreads over her cheeks as she looks down. "You wanted me just as badly. Admit it."

I tip her chin up, our eyes connecting. "I wanted you more than I've wanted anything in my entire life. The second I saw you, I was a goner."

She looks pleased with my answer, resting her head against my chest. "It was my ass, right?"

I laugh. "Yeah, baby girl. That was it."

She sighs. "It was a good night, wasn't it?"

"It was the best night," I respond, kissing her hair and inhaling my favorite scent.

She has no idea how much that night means to me.

We sit in a comfortable silence, enjoying each other's company, but after a few minutes, she lets out a little yawn, appearing ready to fall asleep.

"How about we get under these covers and take a nap?" I suggest, lifting the blanket beside me.

She appears intrigued by the idea, her body relaxing until her eyes jump to my computer, and she stiffens. Before she can say anything, I slide out from behind her and walk over to my desk. I remove the camera, put it inside one of the desk drawers, and unplug every piece of the computer before facing her, waiting for her rebuttal.

But to my surprise, she slides back on the bed and then, hesitantly, lies down so her head rests on the pillow, silently giving me her answer.

I quickly remove my shirt, watching as Sarah's eyes roam down my chest in appreciation.

"Like what you see?"

She blushes, ignoring my comment by turning to her other side.

I slip in behind her, wrap my arm over her torso, my hand splayed out over her stomach, and place my other arm under her head. She presses her back against my chest and takes me aback, intertwining our fingers. Her body relaxes against mine at the same moment she lets out a deep exhale. My thumb gently rubs over the back of her hand as I brush my lips across her neck.

"I've got you, baby girl. Don't ever forget that."

* * *

Silence.

As fans scream, coaches yell, music wafts throughout the arena, and teammates' feet scuffle past me on the wood floor, positioning for a pass, all I hear is complete silence.

It's just me and the ball.

My fingers grip the leather basketball before letting it fall to the floor as I dribble with precision outside the three-point line, watching and observing everything around me—the bright lights shadow most of the fans in the stands, focusing on only the players.

Neon lights from the scoreboard flash, displaying the score. Sixty-five to sixty-five. Tied.

The clock ticks down in warning...

Twenty... Nineteen... Eighteen... Seventeen...

"Paul!"

My eyes catch on Glen jumping up and down behind his opponent, blocking him from a clear pass. He tries to perform a back door cut toward the basket, but the fucker defending him is double his size, making it impossible for him to break free.

My own opponent doesn't touch me when it comes to height, but he's fast. Probably the quickest guy on the floor tonight, which is why he was assigned to cover me. When I shift to my left, he shifts to his right. When I shift to my right, he shifts to his left. It's how it's been all fucking night.

And I'm over it.

I dribble between my legs, quickly gazing up at the timer.

Ten... Nine... Eight...

With my feet kept shoulder-length apart, knees bent, and back straight, I leap in the air, giving it everything I have. My eyes focus on the basket as I release the ball with a quick extension of my elbow and a flick of my wrist and fingers. The ball soars through the air with just the right amount of backspin before bouncing off the backboard and directly into the basket, the perfect bank shot.

The place erupts in cheers as the buzzer blares in the stadium.

"Weston! Weston! Weston!"

I look up at the scoreboard seeing the final score.

Sixty-eight to sixty-five.

"Hell yeah!"

"Fuck yeah, Paul!

"We won our first home game!"

The guys gather around me, celebrating by jumping on each other and patting my back.

I smile proudly, scanning the crowd.

Natalie and Nate stand, cheering in one spot.

A few family members celebrate three rows below them.

And the seat where Sarah sat last time is empty. Empty because I was too chicken shit scared to ask her to come to my first game after what happened the last time she was here, so I let the ticket sit in an envelope, wasting away behind the ticket booth with Will.

I didn't want to mess up the subtle progress we seemed to be making.

Especially with a lot on the line, like a first date. Possibly the only date to prove to her that I'm worth it. And I'm not going to fuck this up. After leaving here tonight, I plan on making some finishing touches to prepare everything for tomorrow.

Everything has to be perfect.

"Paul!" Spinning on my heels, I notice the scout from Boston, Peter Green, walking my way. "That was one heck of a game you played out there."

Straightening my spine, I say, "Thank you, sir."

He claps my back. "You've got instinct, kid. You knew exactly what to do to get that win, and you didn't hesitate to take that shot. That's what we like to see. Instincts."

I wipe the sweat from my brow with the back of my arm. "I try."

"Your father would be damn proud of you." He crosses his arms over his chest. "Damn proud."

Tightness spreads through my chest as I nod. "I hope so."

He waggles his finger at me. "We'll be in touch, Paul. Reach out if anything comes up." He clasps my shoulder before walking away.

"I will, sir. Thank you."

Suddenly, I'm tackled as a person jumps on top of me, rubbing his fist into the top of my head. "Look at you getting your ass kissed by a scout." Glen chuckles as I fling him off me.

"Fuck off," I tease, adjusting my headband before running the palms of my hands over the tight fade. "I just had this cut."

"Mwahhhhh," Glen mimics a kissing sound. "I could hear that ass-kissing all the way from the other side of the court." He shakes his head, smiling. "But speaking of ass-kissing..." His eyes rove over to the empty seat nearby. "Where's your girl?"

"What girl?" I feign indifferently.

"Don't play that." He rests his hands on his hips. "The fine-as-hell girl who had her eyes glued to you the whole night during our first scrimmage game." He scrunches his face. "It was disgusting. Don't know what she sees in you when I'm right here."

Fine as hell. I shake my head, my fists clenching at my sides. He's lucky we're friends. "I don't know who you're talking about, but if I did know, then you should be smart and not talk about her like that again."

His hands fly up in surrender. "Chill, man." A knowing grin appears. "So, she is *your* girl."

I shake my head and turn, walking toward my family. "You're an idiot," I mutter over my shoulder.

"Are we still playing Fortnite at your house later?" he shouts.

I roll my eyes. "Yeah. I'll text you when to head over."

Because first, I have a date to prepare for.

One that will hopefully secure me a second date.

And a third date.

And a fourth date.

And...every date.

Because I want them fucking all with Sarah.

And only Sarah.

Thirteen

SARAH

My eyes dance over the mirror one last time, my hands smoothing out my black dress over my thighs as I twist, ensuring I'm still clear of a noticeable baby bump.

My arms drop to my sides as I gaze upon myself.

What am I doing?

Why did I agree to go on this date?

Because you really fucking like Paul.

But we can't be together. At least not right now.

Because if Greyson finds out...

Pinching the bridge of my nose, I shake my head.

This was a mistake.

Agreeing to this date was a fucking mistake.

Picking up my phone to text Paul and cancel, I stop when a knock sounds at my door.

It's too late.

Sighing, I grab my purse and jacket and reach the front door, wrapping my hand around the handle.

Everything will be fine.

It's just one date.

After tonight, you will go back to pretending you don't like him.

You have to.

You have no choice.

Throwing on a smile, I open the door to find…

Holy hell.

My mouth hangs wide open at the sight before me.

Paul is leaning against the doorframe, his burly arms crossed over his chest, covered in a white button-down tucked into a pair of black slacks accentuating his muscular thighs. When my eyes make their way back up to his, I find him observing me with amusement.

"I'd ask how I look, but I think I already know the answer." His eyebrows raise as he smirks knowingly.

My cheeks heat up at being caught gawking at him like a teenage girl.

"Pshh." I toss my hair over my shoulder, shoving my way around him. "Get over yourself. I had something in my eye."

He grabs my forearm, spinning me into his chest. My breaths quicken from our proximity, his familiar masculine smell engulfing me, sending my hormones straight to the center of my core, pulsing madly.

His lips brush across mine gently, barely touching me. "You look unbelievably beautiful." His hand runs down my hair before pausing and stepping away. Clearing his throat, he says, "I promised you a real date, which means no kissing until the end." I sulk with a slight pout, making him laugh. Every part of my body is left tingling in frustration. "Come on." He reaches his hand out for me. "We've got places to be, baby girl."

* * *

"Where are we?"

I'm awestruck as I take in the small but quaint restaurant resembling a greenhouse. There's an assortment of flowers in almost every color in the room. Vines hang from a pure glass ceiling, allowing patrons the privilege of seeing the picturesque night sky above while they eat.

"It's called Il Fiore. They opened a few weeks ago. I was walking by one day, and when I saw it, well, I hoped you might like it, seeing that you love flowers." His eyes glance appreciatively at my floral tattoos, and his hand reaches out, tracing the images.

The feeling is intimate, creating an instant throb in my core.

I clear my throat, clenching my thighs together. "You would be right. This place looks like the perfect backdrop to a fairy tale." Even the tables we sit at have an acrylic top, displaying crushed flowers underneath.

"You look..." He stops before saying, "You look happy."

I roll my lips together, thinking. "I guess that's because I feel it." Picking at the piece of bread before me, I say, "Thank you for tonight."

"We haven't even had dinner yet, and you're thanking me?" he muses, laughing. "Maybe if the night goes well, you'll let me take you on a second date."

Dread fills me, knowing we can't.

We only have tonight.

I twist the napkin on my lap, guilt bubbling inside me.

How can I do this to him?

How can I sit here and pretend everything is okay when it's far from it?

How can I not just blurt out that I'm pregnant with his baby?

Looking down at the table, I squeeze the napkin in my hand. "Paul, there's something—"

"You're done with him. And if I find out that you two have anything to do with each other, your little five minutes of fame will be released for the entire world to see... Oh, and with a simple hack, I'll make it appear like Paul released it in a jealous rage. Ruining any chance of a career in the NBA. Heck, it'll probably even ruin his life. You wouldn't want to be responsible for doing that to him, right?"

I drop the napkin, placing my hands on the table before me.

"What is it?" His fingers lightly grip my chin, angling my face toward him.

I hold his eyes, praying he won't see what lies beneath my beating heart. The truth. "It just feels like a night I'll never forget."

His hand drops to the table, intertwining our fingers. "Me too."

His eyes sparkle with things I can't give him, like hope. Hope for the two of us. A ripple of sadness surrounds me, knowing I can't give him what he wants. I can't give myself to him because I won't risk Greyson destroying his career.

A young waiter approaches, clearing his throat. "Good evening, and welcome to Il Fiore. May I start you off with a drink or appetizer?"

I hesitate before saying, "Water for me, please."

Paul squeezes my hand. "We'll also have a bottle of your finest red tonight. And an order of the bruschetta, crab cakes, stuffed mushrooms, the lobster mac and cheese bites, and..." He looks at me. "Am I missing anything?"

I shake my head with wide eyes.

"We'll start with that then. Thank you."

Start?

The waiter lowers his chin before walking away.

"Paul, I...umm..." There's no way I can afford to split this bill with him. I don't even want to know what a bottle of the "finest red" costs. Pulling my hand away, I whisper so no one nearby can hear, "I can't afford this."

My cheeks heat from embarrassment.

Paul frowns, reaching for my hand again, which I let him take.

"And why would that matter?"

"Well, because when the bill comes, I don't think—"

"This is a date, Sarah. A date that I asked you on. That means I take care of the bill. Besides, to be completely honest with you, I'm fucking starving, and those items were the only things under the appetizer section that I recognized. It was a safe bet." He laughs, and I feel my shoulders relax from his words.

"Okay." I nod, biting my bottom lip, suddenly feeling self-conscious, knowing Paul has money and I don't.

The waiter brings a bottle of wine, pours each of us a glass, and then leaves the bottle on the table for us. Paul lifts his glass toward me.

Shit.

I lift my glass, mirroring him.

"To a first date with the most beautiful woman I've ever laid eyes on."

I look down for only a moment, blushing. "And to the guy who twisted my arm to do this. Thank you."

He smiles as our glasses clink. Bringing my glass to my lips, I pretend to take a sip before quickly putting it back on the table.

"So, have you created any new art pieces recently?" He places his glass on the table, leaning forward.

I break off another piece of bread. "I'm trying to. My art professor mentioned that there's a show in the city during winter break, and she felt I should exhibit some pieces, so I've been working on it by painting in the studio on campus. I'm not sure my pieces will be good enough for it or if anyone will even like them, but I—"

"Will you let me see them?"

"I...umm..." Tucking a loose strand of hair behind my ear, I ask, "You want to?"

"Of course. After seeing the quick sketch you drew, I can only imagine how beautiful one of your paintings would be."

A small smile pulls at my lips. "Okay."

His hand reaches for mine, his thumb running across the back, sending a shiver over my entire body.

The rest of the dinner goes by quickly with good food and even better conversation.

It's like a dream I never want to end.

After Paul signs the bill, he stands, retrieving my coat from the coat check, and takes my hand.

"This was the best date I've ever been on. Even if I have nothing to compare it to." I nudge his shoulder playfully.

"Who said it was over?"

I raise my brows, realizing that he's not leading us outside toward his car but, instead, down a hallway.

"Where are we going?"

Paul keeps walking ahead, bringing me with him as he pushes open a large door, leading us to a set of stairs.

"After you, baby girl."

I narrow my eyes at him but continue walking until we get to...

"Is this...an art studio?"

"It is," he answers, leading us through another door in the corner of the room, which reveals a dark room lit only by twinkling lights outlining the ceiling.

Dropping my hand, he walks toward the corner where two pristine white coveralls hang. He grabs both of them, handing me one to take. "You might want to put this on. I would hate to see that pretty dress get ruined."

Looking around, I notice giant white canvases standing close together and varieties of bright neon shades of paint all over the room.

"And whose studio is this?"

"A family member's," he answers vaguely, already zipping up his jumpsuit.

Removing my heels, I step into the oversized jumpsuit, bunching up my dress to my hips so it doesn't get caught in the zipper.

"Let me help you." Paul stands before me, taller beside me without my heels on, and it fucking does something to me.

Goddamn, who knew a man's height would be my kryptonite?

As I hold my dress to my sides, just barely covering the front of my panties, Paul slowly zips the jumpsuit in place. Once he reaches my hips, I drop the fabric and slide my hands into the sleeves before he continues his sensually slow glide up with the zipper, going even slower over my breasts until eventually getting to the top.

"Knew you'd look sexy in this," he states, his eyes darkening.

I peek down at myself, extending my arms wide. "I look like a marshmallow."

He shrugs. "But a sexy marshmallow."

He hands me a pair of goggles, a thick pair of gloves, and a pair of new white sneakers that I take hesitantly before putting on to complete the outfit.

"You did all of this for me?"

"I knew if I was only getting one date with you, then I had to make it count." He gives a playful wink, appearing hopeful for tonight.

My heart breaks from his words.

Why would he do all of this for someone like me?

Someone who keeps trying and failing to push him away.

If only he knew how badly I wanted to fall into his arms and tell him everything.

But I can't.

Displaying a forced smile, I gaze around the room. "Now what?"

Fourteen

PAUL

"**N**ow, we fuck shit up."

The bewildered look on Sarah's face has me bent over laughing, my hands clutching my stomach.

"Excuse me?" She pulls the goggles up on her forehead, pushing her dark hair back, her green princess eyes widening under her long lashes.

God, she's perfect.

I walk to the closet, reach for the baseball bat, and carry it over my shoulder. I then pick up some clear sugar glass globes from the basket I filled with paint last night and place one on the top of the baseball batting tee.

I hold the baseball bat out for her and say, "Hit it."

She looks from me to the baseball bat and then back to me again, blinking rapidly. "Hit what?"

Nudging the bat toward her, she hesitantly takes it. "Hit that globe."

"Why?" She cocks her head to the side, appearing confused.

Sexy, but confused.

"Just trust me," I respond.

She purses her lips and confidently struts over to the tee like a baseball player up to bat. Lining up her swing, she hits the globe on her first try and is stunned as neon pink paint splatters across the giant easel before us.

Her mouth goes wide, quickly forming into a beautiful smile. "That felt so fucking good."

I chuckle, pulling out another globe and depositing it on the tee. "It's called rage painting. Not only do you create something cool in the process, but it also helps with letting off some steam."

Stepping away, I watch as she swings again, revealing a neon blue color that transforms into purple when blended with the pink paint.

She looks at me with a twinkle in her wide eyes. "I love this!"

"I thought you might."

After several more hits, she wipes her forearm across her forehead, laughing as she hands me the bat and places a globe on the tee. "This is the most fun I've had in so long."

Lining the bat up, I smack it against the globe and watch as bright splatters of green scatter across the wall.

"Damn." I hear Sarah mutter and turn around to find her tilting her head, watching me with lustful eyes. "How do you look so hot while also looking like a member of the Ghostbusters team?"

Bending down, giving her a good view, I reach for another ball and place it on the tee. "Baby girl, you should know by now that I make anything look good." *Smack.* The bat lands hard across the globe, sending the color black all over the easel.

Handing the bat over to her, I notice her chest heaving hard. Her cheeks are flushed, and her eyes are glossed, giving away desires running rampant within her right now.

My girl is horny.

And I plan on taking care of that.

Discreetly reaching for a brush, I dip it into a nearby jar and turn, facing her back as she lines up to swing. "You got some paint on you."

She pauses, rotating around to look down at herself, covered in splatters of paint. "What do you mean? There's paint all over—"

Her words cut off as my brush softly glides across her cheek.

"Oops…" I state, fully knowing this was no accident.

Her mouth parts in shock. Her gloved fingers reach up to wipe off a line of the paint. When she brings her fingers before her eyes, she finds neon pink staring right back at her. Dropping the bat to the ground, she laughs. "You have no idea what you just did."

"Give me your best." I wink.

Reaching for a bottle of yellow paint, she quickly uncaps the top. She turns and takes slow, leisurely steps toward me. Her hand extends for my zipper, and I watch in amusement as she slowly begins to unzip my jumpsuit before squirting the yellow mustard color across my white shirt while I make no motion to stop her.

"Oops." She stands there, batting her thick lashes at me.

Without hesitating, I remove my arms from the jumper and unbutton my shirt, tossing it to the side. When my head swivels toward her, I find her licking her bottom lip, her eyes half-hooded.

"You might want to wipe off the drool on your chin." My thumb brushes across the corner of her lip.

She sucks in her bottom lip, enjoyment evident on her face, but all of a sudden, she brings a paintbrush to my chest, creating a sizeable green zigzag along my torso, circling both of my nipples.

"Picasso would be proud." She smirks, placing her hand on her hip, admiring her handiwork.

I shake my head, rubbing the stubble over my face. "Now, you've done it."

In one swift go, I unzip her jumpsuit and tug her body to mine, rubbing the paint onto her as I tightly wrap her in a bear hug.

She squeals, laughter echoing in the room. "You're getting paint on me!"

"Should have thought about that before you made me your next art project."

Suddenly, she snakes out of her jumpsuit and gloves, leaving her in just her black dress, now featuring splashes of green paint. She steps away from me with a giant, satisfied grin.

With every step I take toward her, she takes one back until she finds herself backed against the easel.

"Looks like you got yourself trapped, baby girl. What are you going to do about it?" I remove my gloves and place my hands in the paint on the easel beside her head, caging her in. My hardened cock rubs against her stomach, eliciting a whimper between those luscious lips. Her warm, quick breaths caress my skin just below my collarbone as she tilts her face up, meeting my eyes.

"Let's make art," she says breathlessly.

And fuck me if those words don't make me painfully hard.

Grabbing the bottom of her dress, I lift the fabric slowly over her body, admiring every square inch of her that is about to be turned into a palette of infinite colors.

Tossing her dress to the ground, I watch as she confidently removes her bra and then places her hands above her head, waiting for me to take her.

Devour her.

Which is exactly what I do.

Our lips crash as I hold her wrists in place, pressing my body into hers. Our tongues collide, and our bodies mold together, becoming one. Releasing her hands, I grip the back of her thighs, lifting her in my arms and holding her against the canvas as I lower my lips across her jawline, down her neck, and toward her breasts, finding her hardened nipples with my tongue.

"Oh God," she moans, clutching my shoulders as I twirl my tongue around one nipple before ravenously sucking on it.

My eyes skim over her body, admiring the different paint colors on her porcelain skin.

She begins to grind her pussy against my stomach, searching for the friction she so desperately needs.

"Do you need something?" I ask, amused.

"Touch me," she begs, panting uncontrollably. "Please."

Wiping my fingers against the jumpsuit still hanging off my hips, I ensure all of the paint is removed before I bring them between us and glide them across the center of her panties, finding her soaking wet for me.

Her head rolls back, and a beautiful moan surrounds me.

"You're so wet, baby girl." I push the fabric to the side, running two fingers back and forth. "So deliciously wet."

Her fingers fumble with the button and zipper on my pants, not stopping until she reaches inside and takes out what she wants: my hard cock.

"Back pocket," I tell her.

She quickly reaches behind me, pulls out a condom from my pocket, and then puts it on me at record speed.

Gradually, her hand fists me up and down, making me groan in pleasure as I push two fingers inside her, drawing a sensual moan from between her lips.

The grip she has on me, both literally and figuratively, is irrevocable.

"Please, Paul." Her eyes pierce mine, begging me to give her what she desires. "I need you."

I graze my lips across hers. "You beg like such a good girl." With one of my hands, I grip her wrists, placing both over her head, holding her captive beneath me. She arches her back, pressing her breasts into my chest, rubbing them across my skin, her whole body aching to be touched. "Are you ready to come all over my cock?" I slide my nose across her cheek, a variety of colors spreading over her skin.

The fact that we're both covered in paint right now ignites a primal need in me to ravage my girl. Hard and fast.

Just the way I know she likes it.

She nods as I remove my fingers from inside her, lining my cock up at her entrance.

"Good." I thrust inside her, feeling her walls clench instinctively around me. "Fuck, Sarah."

She moans, tightening her legs around my torso as her head rolls back against the canvas, spreading paint all over her hair.

"More," she pants.

I start slow at first, giving her body time to adjust, but the second I feel the heels of her feet dig into my ass, I pick up speed, pounding into her like there's no tomorrow.

"Fuck yes!" she screams.

"You like that baby girl?"

"Yes!"

Keeping one hand under her thigh, I bring my other hand flat on the wall for support as my thrusts become all-consuming, giving her exactly what she needs from me.

She moves her hands to my shoulders, digging her nails into my skin. "Harder," she begs.

Her whole body begins trembling in my arms, waiting for the final touch to send her over the edge. Gliding my hand down to her pussy, I grind my palm over her clit, rough and fast.

"Paul... I'm going to..."

"Come for me, Sarah."

She screams my name, gripping onto me as I continue hitting that special spot inside her, watching as she comes undone in my arms. Her hair falls all over her face, her cheeks are flushed and covered in paint, her eyes are glossy and heavy, and paint is smeared all over her beautiful body.

She looks like a goddamn masterpiece.

She looks like mine.

The sight of her does it for me as I thrust one more time inside her, coming apart with her name on my lips.

"Goddamn." I push her hair away from her face, pressing our foreheads together. Her heaving chest mirrors my own. "That was…"

"Perfect," she finishes for me.

I smile, watching her lips curve up. "Yeah. Perfect." Sliding my hand to her cheek, I caress her skin with my thumb. The color green spreads over her, bringing out the intensity of her eyes I love so much.

She bites her lip, peeking down at herself. "I'm a mess."

"That you are, dirty girl." I rub my nose against hers. "Good thing there's a shower here." My hands cup her ass as I carry her away from the wall toward the bathroom outside of this room.

"Wait!" She shifts in my arms, looking over my shoulder. "We made art."

Turning around, I observe the image on the canvas we created.

A voluptuous ass print of Sarah's, in pink, yellow, and orange, takes up the bottom part of the easel. Her back and head are outlined with almost all the colors we used. And my handprints in green and blue are placed on the side of her head.

If this isn't the most erotic piece of artwork I've ever seen, then I don't know what is.

And I'm already trying to think of where I can hang it where no one else will see it.

"We look good together," I muse.

She smiles, but it doesn't reach her eyes. If anything, it looks somber, and I'm not sure why. She softly presses her lips against my own. "Thank you for bringing color back into my life."

Fifteen

SARAH

My brush dances with a mind of its own across the canvas in various vibrant strokes. The image in front of me is nothing like I've ever painted. It's bright, bold, and colorful.

Something I never thought I'd see again.

"I see you've decided to venture into the land of color." I twist on my seat, finding my professor standing behind me, observing my work with a pleasant smile.

I place my brush in a holder and wipe my hand on my smock. "I have."

"I take it something or someone helped to bring some color back into your world," she muses.

"You could say that." I grin, planting my hands on both sides of my stool.

"Very good." Her smile widens as she nods. "Have you thought about the show I mentioned to you?"

"I have, and I'll be displaying a few pieces." I look at the canvas beside me. "This being one of them."

She claps her hands together. "Marvelous!" A student in the front of the room calls for her attention. "Let me know if you need any assistance with anything. I look forward to seeing all your final pieces at the show," she calls over her shoulder as she steps toward the front of the room.

Grabbing my brush, I hesitantly scan my work.

I actually did it.

For the first time, I painted with color. And it wasn't nearly as scary as I thought it would be.

If anything, it was liberating.

Tilting my head to the side, I can't help but notice that my painting looks similar to someone else's style.

But who...

That's when it hits me.

My mom.

It looks exactly like something she would paint. Maybe all those years of watching her paint for hours are starting to come out in my work. And I couldn't be happier about that.

My phone alarm interrupts me, reminding me I have places to be.

Quickly, I pack up my supplies, glancing one last time over my shoulder at my first painting with color, and I know there's one man responsible for bringing color back into my life, even if he didn't do it intentionally.

He did.

And I can never thank him enough for the gift he's given me.

* * *

"Everything looks good." Dr. Martin enters the room, reviewing the charts in her hand. "Your blood work is excellent, and from the ultrasound results, I can confirm the baby's heartbeat is strong. It's exactly what we want to see at this stage in your pregnancy."

For the first time in weeks, relief hits me. "Thank God." I let out a deep breath. "Looks like I'm not a total failure."

Dr. Martin frowns. "Why would you think that?"

I shrug. "I don't know. I'm just worried I'm going to fu... I mean, mess up." I run my fingers through my hair, pushing it behind my ear. "I wasn't prepared for this and have no idea what I'm doing."

She places her charts on the counter and sits across from me, crossing one leg over the other. "You know, I don't think any woman is ever actually prepared to be a mother. No matter how many books you read, videos you watch, or pieces of advice you receive, something will catch you off guard, and you'll think you're a failure when you're not. Believe me, I have three of my own. They're all adults now, but man, when they were babies..." She shakes her head, laughing. "Let's just say I had my hands full and had no idea what I was doing. But because I gave it my all, night and day, they turned into three beautiful, intelligent young women. And I know the little one inside you will be very lucky to have you as a mom."

"How do you know that?" I ask, the tip of my nose stinging.

"Because you're worried about failing, and that shows how much you care about your baby. You're trying to do everything right when not everything will have clear cookie-cutter instructions for you." She smiles warmly.

I nod. "I guess you're right. There really is no exact manual on how to raise a baby, and I would know. I've spent hours trying to find it online."

She chuckles softly. "Tell me, what have you been doing to prepare?"

I sigh, fidgeting with the hem of my shirt. "I've been taking my pre-natal vitamins and keeping up with my appointments here. I've ordered everything for the nursery, but I'm just waiting for it to be delivered soon, and I just signed up for a birthing class that starts after the holidays." I glance up at her, nervous that I'm forgetting something.

"See, you're doing great," she exclaims. "Have you had any issues with anything? Any side effects?"

"Well," I start. "My back, feet, and even my breasts have started to become sore. Sometimes, certain foods give me heartburn that normally wouldn't. I'm tired...a lot. And then I had that week of nonstop morning sickness. But I haven't been sick since then. All in all, nothing I can't manage."

She smiles. "Certain symptoms will come and go. Others will just become more prominent throughout the pregnancy. Everything you mentioned is normal and nothing to be alarmed over." She purses her lips and then asks, "And I assume you're doing all this yourself?"

I swallow the lump in my throat and nod. "Yes. It's just me."

She gives me a look of pity, making my stomach churn. If she knew I was purposely trying to avoid the father of my baby, she wouldn't be looking at me that way. She would look at me the way I deserve, with disgust in her eyes.

"If you have any questions or concerns, please call the office anytime and ask to speak with me. I'm always here to help," she offers. The corners of her eyes crinkle as her smile widens.

"Thank you," I respond as she picks up her charts and walks out the door.

I slide my arms in my coat sleeves when I feel a vibration in the pocket. Seeing Natalie's name dance across my phone's screen brings me a sense of comfort I desperately need right now.

"Hey, Natalie," I answer, walking out of the office toward my car.

"Hey, Sarah! I just wanted to see if you want to go out on Friday. Vanessa has to work, so it would just be you and me. What do you think?"

I usually would love a chance to go out, but since my bank account is now in the negative, it doesn't seem like a great idea.

"Umm, money is kind of tight right now. Maybe another night," I respond, hating how pathetic I sound. I get inside my old car, turn the key in the ignition, pray it will turn on, and when it does, I blast the heat on my hands.

"Let's stay in! That sounds like a better night to me, anyway. How about we do it at Nathan's house? I'll ask him to pick up some pizzas on his way home from work, and he has a freezer full of ice cream at my request," she adds with a giggle. "Paul probably won't be there because he has an away game that night."

Relief and something else fills me. Is it disappointment?

"Are you sure you're fine with staying in?" I ask. "I don't mean to be a downer or anything."

"Trust me, you're not," she confirms. "I prefer this plan. I just want to see you. We've all been so busy recently, and I don't care what we do as long as I get to see you."

Warmth spreads through my chest. "Okay. Then yeah, that sounds like a fun night to me."

"Perfect! I'll text you on Friday. Bye, Sarah!"

"Bye, Natalie."

I pull out of the lot and head toward campus, which is only ten minutes away. As I drive by the sports arena, I notice a full parking lot and people walking in holding signs. There must be a basketball game tonight. I stop, letting some fans cross in front of me, and that's when I see a sign with the words *Go, Weston!* on it.

Not thinking about it, I turn in the lot and find a vacant spot in the back. I don't have money for a ticket, so I don't even know what I'm doing here, but I feel like I'm being pulled toward the gym like a magnet.

Entering the arena, I begin to walk around when I hear someone yell, "Hey, it's Paul's *friend*."

The way he emphasizes friend has me turning with a smile.

"Hey," I offer, walking up to the familiar face who gave me my ticket the last time I was here. The halls are pretty deserted now, making me think the game must have started.

He looks around his booth and then back at me. "Paul didn't put any tickets aside today. Do you need one?"

I shake my head. "He doesn't know I'm here. I was hoping there might be somewhere I could watch off to the side," I admit with a lift of my shoulders.

He smiles, shaking his head, and motions for me to come behind the booth door. "Come with me." He places a closed sign on the booth window and opens the door. "I could get in trouble for doing this, but if you promise not to say anything, we'll be good."

"I promise." I hesitantly follow him into a back room, where he opens the door to a set of stairs.

I'm fairly certain it's frowned upon to follow men you don't know into back rooms, but...actually, there is no *but*. It is completely frowned upon.

He points up the four flights of stairs. "My knees are too run-down to make it up there, but when you get to the top, you'll have a clear view of the game. And remember, I didn't bring you here." He winks as he shuffles past me, heading back to the booth.

My hand wraps around the old metal railing as I take my first step.

Here goes nothing.

By the time I reach the top, I'm hunched over, out of breath, and reminded that I hate cardio more than anything in the world. But as I look up, seeing the big glass window before me, I straighten and walk over, pressing the palms of my hands to the surface.

Wow.

This room has the perfect view of the entire court, and I have it all to myself. Off to the side, I spot a fold-up metal chair and drag it toward the window, making myself as comfortable as possible.

Gazing down from this height, you'd think I'd have an issue differentiating which player is Paul. But the man stands out like a sore thumb as he controls the ball, dribbling down the court. I'm hypnotized as he runs back and forth, making shot after shot.

My eyes catch on the scoreboard, finding that Linrey University is up by twenty points, all thanks to Paul, who is playing incredibly tonight.

But Paul doesn't play like this occasionally.

This is how he plays all the time.

He's a born leader and a natural talent on the court.

And I'm certain his dad would be proud of him if he were here now, watching him play.

I know he struggles with seeing himself as more than just the last name on his jersey, not feeling worthy enough to wear it, but to me, he's always been more than a name.

He's the guy who has my heart, even if I refuse to admit it out loud.

I reach for my phone in my coat pocket and scroll to the last message I received from Paul after our date almost a week ago.

Paul

> I had a really nice time tonight. I hope you did, too. The offer still stands for a second date, so just let me know, and I'll make that happen for you.

It killed me not to text him back.

That night was the best night of my life. Well, it's tied with our first night together, of course.

But nothing can happen between us. I gave him the one date he asked for, and that's all I could risk giving him.

A tear rolls down my cheek, and I hastily wipe it away.

This is all my fault.

I should have known better.

I internally shake my head, feeling overwhelmed at being here, watching the man I love from afar, knowing that's all...

Hold up. What did I say?

The man I love...

No. No. No.

I can't love him.

Because if I love him, it will only make this hurt even worse. It will make things messy and complicated.

I can't...

I sigh, shaking my head as more tears escape down my cheeks.

But I do.

I love him with everything I have.

My heart thuds in my chest as I place my palm against it, willing myself to breathe in and out.

What am I going to do?

The only thing I can do.

Because I love him, I can't tell him.

And I need to continue the pretense that I want nothing to do with him.

At least until I figure out how to fix everything. How to put everything back together again as it should be.

But every time I rack my brain for an answer, I come up blank, losing myself to frustration beyond measure.

I feel helpless and alone, shackled in a battle against Greyson Black that I'll never be able to win.

I'm not strong enough to beat him.

And I won't risk playing against him only to lose.

The consequences are too dire.

So, for the sake of me, the baby, and Paul, I'll do what I must to keep us all safe.

And as if the universe has a cruel sense of humor, my eyes catch on Greyson, sitting on the bench, scowling. To most, he probably appears immersed in the game, but upon further inspection, I notice his eyes glued to Paul, watching every move he makes. Anger radiates around him, his fingers gripping the edge of his seat in a death grip. The way he's staring at Paul is as though he's ready to murder him right there on the spot.

A shiver runs through me.

Greyson's a deplorable asshole with no soul or conscience, but would he ever go that far?

What has him wound so tight that he appears ready to risk it all?

Could Greyson be jealous of Paul?

Would he let jealousy consume him?

Greyson's words repeat in my mind: *"Paul took something from me, so now I'm taking something from him."*

But what did Paul take from Greyson?

An overwhelming need to leave swarms me as each question rattles off, one right after the other.

Knowing Paul's safe, surrounded by people with no way for Greyson to do any harm to him in the middle of a game, I fold the chair, lean it against the wall, and return down the stairs just as halftime begins.

Opening the door to the booth, I find the man sitting in front of a computer, typing away.

"You know, I never did get your name," I say, walking up to him.

He smiles. "It's William, but you can call me Will."

I extend my hand toward him. "It's nice to officially meet you, Will. Thank you for letting me up there tonight. I needed that."

He shakes my hand. "Don't mention it. Anything for Paul's *friend.*"

Sixteen

PAUL

Today kicked my ass, and that's putting it lightly.

After losing our first game on the road, I got stuck sitting next to Greyson on the plane ride home, who was nothing but a dick, insisting he needed to use the armrest between us. At least I had the aisle seat and could stretch my oversized legs. And to top it off, I still haven't heard from Sarah. Not once.

She completely ignored the text I sent her after our date, and it fucking sucks.

No. I internally shake my head. *It hurts.*

All I know is the minute I walk through my front door, I plan on taking a long, hot shower and collapsing on my bed for the rest of the night—absolutely nothing else.

Opening the front door, I find Natalie watching TV on the living room couch.

"Hey, what's up, Natalie?" I drop my sports bag beside the door, planning to take care of it later.

"Paul!" Her eyes widen. "Don't you have a game tonight?"

I shake my head. "It was this morning. Got switched because of a scheduling conflict."

"Well, it looks like you're just in time then!" she exclaims. "Sarah's on her way over for a movie night."

My brows furrow as I slam the door firmly behind me at the mention of Sarah. "Sarah?"

"Ow!"

I stiffen, feeling heat creep up my neck, realizing who I just shut the door on.

Fuck!

"Sarah, I'm so sorry!" I open the door wide, pressing my hand onto her lower back, leading her inside. "Shit. Are you okay?"

She rubs her forehead. "I'm fine. No big deal."

But it is a big deal. She's so small, and I'm so big. I didn't mean to hurt her. Fuck.

"Wait here." I quickly look between her and the kitchen. "I'm going to get some ice!" I run to the kitchen, pull out the ice tray, and slam it on the counter. Cubes fall everywhere, but I grab most of them and bundle them in a plastic bag. Returning to the living room, I find Sarah sitting on the couch beside Natalie.

I sit on her free side and gently press the ice to her head, where I notice a small purple bruise forming. "Maybe I should take you to the hospital to get checked out for a concussion."

"Paul, I'm fine. I swear. I don't have a concussion." Her hand lands on my thigh, and all the air in my lungs evaporates. "I was looking down at my phone when I walked up the steps. It was my fault. Don't worry."

"I'm sorry." I scrape the palm of my hand down my face.

The front door opens, revealing Nate, who walks inside with a few pizza boxes in his hands.

"Hey, man. You made it in time for movie night." He places the boxes on the coffee table and sits on Natalie's free side.

It's getting tight on this couch, so I stand, still holding the ice against Sarah's head.

"I've got it," Sarah says, placing her hand over mine to take over. I can't help but notice how small and soft her hand is compared to mine.

"Yeah. Sorry again." I squeeze the back of my neck. I can't believe I just fucking did that.

"What did you do to the poor girl?" Nate asks, smirking.

I gesture toward the door. "I shut the door on her face. Completely by accident," I add hastily.

Nate shakes his head, restraining a laugh.

I'm such an idiot. "Well, I better go shower. Enjoy your movie night." I take a step on the stairs when the sound of her voice brings me to a screeching halt.

"Aren't you going to stay for the movie?" Sarah asks.

My eyes lock with hers, and when I internally ask, *Do you want me to stay?* with my brow raised, she nods just the slightest bit.

"Yeah. Sure. Let me shower real quick, and I'll be right down."

She smiles, appearing relieved by my answer.

After I get out of the shower and slip into a pair of grey sweatpants and a black T-shirt, I head downstairs, finding the three of them on the couch, so I take the love seat. Quickly, I hide a small shopping bag on the other side of the chair before anyone sees it.

"So, what are we watching?" I ask.

"The new *Halloween* movie," Nate responds, handing me a slice of pizza on a plate.

"I love scary movies," Sarah notes.

"I don't." Natalie frowns. "You told me we were watching a romantic movie."

"It will be romantic, baby." He lifts his arm, and she instantly cuddles into his side. "Because I'll be here to keep you safe." He kisses the top of her forehead, and she giggles, swatting his chest.

The two of them couldn't be more in love.

"I hope you have the ice cream I like," she murmurs.

Nate laughs as he stands up. "Let me go get everything."

"And the whipped cream and toppings!" Natalie calls out to him.

That boy is whipped. I chuckle to myself, knowing I would do anything to be just as whipped if it meant being with someone I love.

"I can't believe Thanksgiving break is coming up," Natalie mentions, positioning pillows around her. "Are you heading home for Thanksgiving, Sarah?"

Sarah's lips part. "I...umm..." She quickly looks down at her lap and then back at Natalie. "I have so much to do for my art show, so I think I'm just going to stay here."

"Really?" The corners of Natalie's lips turn down. "You can't take a tiny break to spend Thanksgiving with your family?"

Sarah subtly shakes her head. "No." She tries to give a tiny smile, but it looks forced and unnatural.

"What about you, TB?" Natalie asks, cocking her head to the side.

I chuckle at the nickname Natalie has bestowed upon me.

"TB?" Sarah's brows furrow together as she repeats the letters out loud.

"Teddy Bear," Natalie clarifies, sounding proud of herself. "He's a big guy with a soft center. It fits him perfectly. Don't you think?"

Sarah's lips curve up. "It sure does."

"I hope everyone wants ice cream," Nate says, walking in with several flavors, bowls, spoons, and all the toppings you could imagine.

"So, Paul, do you like scary movies?" Sarah asks.

"Like them? I love them," I say matter-of-factly, trying to impress her as I take a scoop from the chocolate ice cream container.

But thirty minutes into the movie, I remember that I, in fact, do not love scary movies. Not one bit.

My eyes flicker to the couch to see if anyone else feels the same way, but I find Natalie sleeping against Nate, who looks to be having difficulty keeping his eyes open. And Sarah, who's watching the movie with wide eyes, shoving popcorn in her mouth. Nate glances at me, then at Sarah, and then back at me with a mischievous grin.

"Well," Nate starts. "I'm going to bring this one to bed. See you guys later." He lifts Natalie in his arms and winks at me as he passes me to go up the stairs.

This is probably the time to say something, but I'm coming up blank. My whole mind is a fucking blank canvas when I'm around her.

"Is there a blanket I could use?" Sarah asks, wrapping her arms around herself.

I reach for the one on my lap, knowing it's the only one down here. "Here. You can use this one."

"Oh no. I don't want to take it from you." She swats the blanket away.

"I promise it's fine." I push the blanket toward her.

She purses her lips and then stands. "I have a better idea." Taking a step, she sits beside me, our thighs touching. "We can share." Her fingers reach for the blanket, pulling it toward her and spreading it over our legs.

"Cool." I clear my throat.

Cool?

What the fuck is wrong with me?

I reach over the side of the chair and grab the hidden bag. "I ah...got you something."

Placing the bag on her lap, she scrunches her face, unsure what she's about to find.

"Why?" she asks.

"Just open it."

She sighs and quickly pulls out the contents, holding the black fabric between her fingers.

"I felt bad about your dress getting ruined the other night, so I went to the store to get you a new one," I tell her.

She rolls in her bottom lip. "That was really sweet of you. Thank you." She folds the dress, placing it neatly back in the bag. "About the other night. I'm sorry I didn't respond to your text after; it's just..."

"I know, Sarah."

She tucks in her chin, glancing down. "I don't think you do," she whispers.

My fingers tilt her chin up to face me. "Then why don't you tell me?"

She shakes her head. "Can we just keep watching the movie?"

I hesitate, knowing I should push her when something is holding her back from me. But reluctantly, I release her chin. "Okay."

She leans back, brushing her arm against mine. "But you don't like this movie, do you?"

"I mean." I shrug. "I wouldn't say it's one of my favorite movies."

"What's your favorite movie?"

"Pshh. That's a tough question. There're so many."

She puts her index finger to her cheek, tilting her head. "On the count of three, name the first movie that comes to mind. One. Two. Three."

"*Star Wars: Episode Four*," I rush out. Shit. Why did I say that? She probably thinks I sound like a weird nerd.

You are a nerd.

"I've never seen any of the *Star Wars* movies. Let's watch it."

My brows crease. "Are you sure? You seemed pretty into this one." Just as I look at the screen, the man has a knife the size of a baseball bat going into some person's stomach—instant regret.

Sarah notices my reaction and giggles. "Yeah, I'm sure."

She steals the remote and types in some words, and soon after, *Stars Wars: A New Hope* is playing on the TV.

"Okay, but if you don't like it, we can shut it off and put the other movie back on," I suggest.

"I always watch scary movies, so I want to watch something different tonight." She pulls the blanket up higher on her waist.

"You do?"

"Yeah." She shrugs her shoulders. "I can't explain it, but those movies are like comfort movies. Like *It, Halloween, Sleepy Hollow*." She looks lost in thought when she says, "It's probably because Halloween was...is my mom's favorite holiday." She gazes over at me. "You think I'm weird. Don't you?"

My lips curve up as I shake my head. She's worried I'm going to think she's weird when I was worried she was going to think I'm weird. "No, not at all." As she turns her eyes toward the screen, I say, "So, my buddy Will told me you were at my game the other night. Heard you had special seats."

She subtly shakes her head, pursing her lips. "Nope. He must have me confused with another girl who wanted to watch you play."

I rub a hand over my face, laughing. "Why can't you just admit you went to my game?"

She sighs, tossing her hands in the air. "Fine. I went to your game. Happy?"

"Why did you go?"

She looks down at the remote in her head. "Honestly, I don't know."

I let out a deep breath. "Can we cut the crap, Sarah?"

Her eyes shoot up to mine, widening.

"We both like each other. Probably more than like each other. And I'm tired of dancing around this thing we have going on."

She bites down hard on her lip, her brows pinching together in concentration. "You shouldn't like me."

"Why the hell not?"

"I don't know, we're just...different." She looks away from me. "You're this gorgeous basketball god that all the girls at this school fawn over, and I'm just...me. I'm nobody."

I reach out for her, gently tilting her chin toward me. "Hey, you're right. I am a gorgeous basketball god," I tease, making her scowl.

"You're a real piece of work." She nudges my arm with her shoulder but eventually lets out a little laugh. She turns to face me. "You seemed kind of tense when you first got home. Bad day?"

I know she's deflecting, hoping I forget what we were just talking about and I'll give her a few seconds to think that.

But only a few seconds.

"Yeah, kind of. Just a lot on my mind." My fingers push back her hair, combing through the silky strands. "But it's a lot better now."

She blushes, easing into my touch.

"So, you going to tell me the real reason why you aren't going home for Thanksgiving break?" I ask. "Because I know you didn't give Natalie the honest one."

She tenses, withdrawing from me. "I don't know what you're talking about."

I wrap my arm around her waist, pulling her against me. "We don't have to talk about it, but I'm not okay with you spending the holiday alone." I twirl a piece of her long, dark hair between my fingers. "You're coming to my house for Thanksgiving."

"W-what?" She laughs nervously. "I am not coming to your house for Thanksgiving."

"And why not?"

"Because..." She fiddles with the blanket on her lap. "Because we barely know each other."

I arch a brow. "You've come multiple times on my cock. I would say you know me much more intimately than most people do."

Her cheeks blaze in a red hue. "You know what I mean."

"All right." I shrug. "My favorite color is green, my favorite season is winter, I have a lightsaber collection, I'm not big about going out and being with crowds, but I do like to read, and I've read every *Harry Potter* book five times. I have two brothers and I'm the middle child, I drink only iced coffee no matter what the temperature outside is, I'd like to get a dog someday, I can't cook for shit but I'm really good at ordering food, I'm basically a Ping-Pong pro, and I like you."

Her eyes widen. "Stop saying you like me."

"Why?"

"Because—"

I press two fingers to her lips.

"You're going to say something to try to push me away. It's a defense mechanism you have. And I'm telling you right now, it won't work anymore."

Her eyes water the slightest bit, revealing how right I am.

"I know you're scared. You've repeatedly told me that you don't do relationships, but that's not true, is it?"

Her eyes close as defeat dances across her features.

"You've never been in a relationship because you keep your guard up. It's not that you don't do them; you don't allow anyone to get close to you. But guess what?"

I remove my fingers from her lips.

"What?" she whispers.

"I'm not just anyone."

Her big green eyes pierce mine.

"I'm the guy who will change that for you."

Her body relaxes beside me as she takes in my words. "Okay," she breathes.

"Okay?" I ask, a little shocked. "Just like that?"

She closes her eyes. "I'm tired of fighting this." Her eyes open, vulnerability flashing across them. "But can we start slow? I just have some things I need to...figure out first." She looks down, her hands fisting the blanket.

I grip her chin lightly, angling her face up toward mine. "We can go as slow as you want. Although we have covered all the bases..."

She shakes her head, but there's a small smile on her face.

"And Sarah, if you ever refer to yourself as less than me again, we're going to have a problem. I never want to hear the words *I'm nobody* coming out of your mouth when you're everything to me. Understood?" My thumb floats over her parted bottom lip.

She swallows and then hesitantly nods. "Yes."

"Good. And you're coming to Thanksgiving at my family's house. It's only a thirty-minute drive from the city in the suburbs."

"That doesn't really feel like starting slowly to me…"

"If I tell them we're just friends, will that make you more comfortable to come over?"

She bites her lower lip and nods.

"Okay. Then that's what I'll do."

"Thank you." She reaches up, placing the palm of her hand against my cheek. Her thumb brushes over my stubble as her eyes fixate on my lips.

I lean down before I can stop myself, pressing my lips to hers. I can feel her body melt against mine until, suddenly, she pulls apart.

She looks down. Anywhere but at me. "What about all those other girls?"

"What other girls?"

"The ones that fawn over you at your games or when you're out in public. When I went to your game, two cheerleaders thought they were going home with you that night. And then, when we all went to that new bar, a group of girls just flocked to you at the table like you were a celebrity."

I sigh. "I won't lie to you and say that doesn't happen because it does—a lot. But I genuinely do not give one shit about those other girls," I state firmly.

"You don't?"

I shake my head. "You're the only girl that's taken up space in my head. Night and day." My lips land on her temple. "Playing basketball professionally and being known for having a famous father will, unfortunately, keep me in the spotlight. Girls will see my name and the dollar bill signs but they don't see *me*. The real me. That guy I reserve only for you."

She studies me momentarily, taking in my confession before simply snuggling beside me, pulling the blanket up around us, and hitting play on the movie.

"Paul?"

"Yeah, baby girl?"

"Do you really have a collection of lightsabers?"

"Yeah, but don't tell Nate. He thinks I only have two."

We both laugh, and it feels like maybe, just maybe, I've broken a piece of the indestructible wall she keeps up around her heavily guarded heart.

Seventeen

SARAH

My clammy palms grip the leather wheel as my stomach twists into a thousand knots. I rest my forehead against the smooth steering wheel, idling in the street out front of Paul's family home, or more like mansion, surrounded by a pristine metal gate and perfectly trimmed bushes slightly covered by last night's dusting of snow.

What am I doing here?

I won't fit in with these people. I know I won't because Paul has two things that I'll never have.

Money.

And a family.

Paul offered to drive me, but I didn't want to risk appearing as more than friends to his family, so I told him I'd meet him here. Besides, I wasn't lying when I told him I wanted to take things slow because I had things to figure out. Things like how to get Greyson to end his blackmailing tirade over me. There has to be a way. I know there is. I just haven't been able to figure it out yet.

But I will.

I just need time.

And once I figure it out, I'll be able to tell Paul everything.

And I mean *everything*—no more lying.

The wrath I'll face from Paul for holding out on this information will be understandable, but I did it for both of us. Actually, make that the three of us. And I hope he'll be able to forgive me.

I internally shake my head, knowing this isn't the time to think about this. Instead, I need to focus on the task at hand: Thanksgiving dinner with Paul's family.

My stomach recoils, nerves eating away at me. I can't even remember the last time I celebrated Thanksgiving.

My mom always taught me never to arrive empty-handed, which is why there is a pathetic-looking pumpkin pie sitting on the seat beside me. It was the only thing I could afford with my bills getting bigger and bigger after each doctor appointment and each new thing I was learning online that I needed to buy to be ready for a baby.

My chest tightens as the daily financial panic plays out in my head, reminding me that I won't be able to do this.

I'm going to fail.

Even with my lists, spreadsheets, and binders, it's inevitable. Because if I can barely afford to take care of myself, how am I going to—

Tap. Tap.

I startle, slamming my hand down on the horn for a split second. *Shit. Shit. Shit.*

Taking a deep breath, I sit up and turn to the window beside me to find Paul taking my breath away in a pair of black slacks and a button-down green shirt with the sleeves rolled up a bit over his muscular forearms. Holy hell.

He smiles, motioning for me to roll down the window, which I do. And yes, I have to crank down the window because my car is an ancient relic.

After the window is down, I face straight ahead as Paul leans in, placing his large hands over the window ledge.

"How's it going?" His deep voice reverberates in the tiny space, sending a shiver across my skin.

I nod. "Good. Really good."

"I see you brought a pie."

"Yup. Pumpkin."

"That's one of my favorites."

"Good. Good." I nod again like a damn idiot.

"Sarah?"

"Yes?"

His hand gently wraps around my chin, turning my head to the side so my eyes lock with his. "Were you planning on coming inside, or did you want to stay out here during dinner?"

I let out a deep breath I hadn't realized I had been holding in. "I'm just...nervous." My eyes fall on my outfit that I'm now completely second-guessing. Maybe I should have used what was left on my emergency credit card to buy something that made me more presentable than this old beige sweater dress. But it was the only thing in my closet that covered my tattoos. "I don't think I'm going to fit in very well," I admit.

"Why?" he asks.

I let out a little chuckle. "No offense, Paul, but your house might be bigger than the White House. And here I am, showing up in a seventeen-year-old car with a dress I've had for as long as I can remember and a pie that, honestly, might have passed its expiration date." I push away from his hand and smooth out my hair. "This was a bad idea. I should probably go. I don't want to hold your family up. They're probably waiting for you."

Paul laughs, shaking his head. "Oh, you stubborn woman." With extreme precision, Paul swiftly opens my door, reaches inside, turns off my car, and unbuckles my seat belt. The warmth from his breath caresses my cheek as he gets right up in my face. "I don't give a fuck what kind of car you're driving or what you're wearing. I don't care if that pie is a day old or two weeks old. I'll still eat every last bite because you brought it. The only thing I care about is that you're here." He grabs the pie and backs away, putting his free hand out for me to take, which I hesitantly do. "And they're not waiting for me. They're waiting for you. My mom, for one, is very excited to meet you."

"But—"

"Don't worry. I told everyone you're *just* a friend." His lips press against my forehead as his hand cups my cheek, his thumb gently stroking back and forth. "Don't ever think for a second that I care how much money you do or don't have. That shit has never mattered to me and never will."

A small smile graces my face from his words. I've never felt like I've had to be anyone but myself when I'm with him, and that's exactly how I feel right now. I feel like me.

I brush down my dress and straighten the black belt around my waist. "Do I look okay?"

"Well, honestly, I would prefer you not wear anything, but I suppose since you're meeting my family, clothes are required."

My cheeks blaze as I lightly smack his chest. "Paul!"

"You look beautiful, Sarah." His fingers push back a piece of my hair. "I love it when you blush. It lets me know that even when you pretend you don't feel this thing between us, you do. And it gives me hope."

My heart hammers in my chest. "Paul, I—"

His eyes look over my head. "We better go inside. We have an audience."

I turn around, finding several pairs of eyes watching from one of the main windows before the curtains quickly close.

We laugh as Paul's hand finds mine, leading me toward the most enormous oak door I have ever seen.

As we step inside, I remove my hand from Paul's and pull down my dress, ensuring it covers everything, even the tattoos on my thighs.

"You can all come out now," Paul announces, walking farther inside.

My eyes dart around the massive space before me. There's a white spiral staircase that looks like a workout to get to the top, crown molding, a chandelier, pristine furniture, and...paintings. Distracted, I approach the painting on the wall closest to me.

Clearly, someone very talented made this piece as they perfectly captured every emotion felt with each color and brushstroke.

Paul's significant presence approaches me from behind. "Do you like it?"

"It's beautiful." I tilt my head to the side, trying to read the signature on the bottom. "Who is the artist?"

Paul reaches out, brushing his finger over the black scribble. "My mom."

I turn to him, my mouth agape. "Your mom's an artist?"

He nods, smiling. "Who did you think let us use their art studio?"

My eyes widen, horror filling me. "We had sex in your mom's art studio?" I whisper-yell, looking around to make sure no one just heard that.

He shrugs.

"And may I ask where you put the evidence of our...*art* session?"

Please don't say in his family's living room.

"Ahh. That is a surprise for another day." He winks with a mischievous grin, tapping my nose.

"Paul!" I scold, running a hand down my face. "If someone sees my ass print, I think I might die of embarrassment."

Paul laughs loudly. "Baby girl." His knuckles stroke my jawline as he looks down at me. "No one gets the privilege of seeing your ass except me."

He kisses the top of my head just as heels clicking against the hardwood floor approach us.

"Well, there you two are!"

Quickly, I take a step away, distancing myself from Paul while setting a clear boundary between us.

A petite woman with perfectly coiffed blonde hair, a warm picturesque smile, and the friendliest pair of light blue eyes I've ever seen approaches. It's not hard to see who Paul did not get his height from.

"Sarah, I'm so glad you could join us. Paul has told me so much about you." Her arms wrap around me, and I freeze, unfamiliar with the gesture from a stranger. Paul smiles, tipping his head toward me, letting me know it's okay to reciprocate. My arms move on their own accord, wrapping around her slender frame.

"It's nice to meet you, Mrs. Weston."

"Oh, please, just call me Kathy." She smiles as she separates, glimpsing up at her son beside me. There's no way I can refer to her by her first name when she looks like she could be a freaking First Lady. It feels inappropriate. "Paul, you didn't tell me she was this beautiful."

"Jesus, Mom." His cheeks redden as he pinches the bridge of his nose.

Suddenly, two guys, equally as tall as Paul, with the same light brown skin color, walk up from behind his mom.

"Hi, I'm Paul's older brother, Ray." Ray pushes up his thick-framed glasses before reaching out his hand toward me. He's lean, just like Paul, with the same short hairstyle faded on the sides, but the most noticeable difference is their eyes. Where Paul's eyes are a deep chocolate brown, Rays are a soft shade of honey. They suit him nicely.

I take his hand, smiling.

A little boy runs up to Ray, stretching his hands in the air, signaling he wants to be picked up.

"And this guy is Lucas, my son."

"Hi, Lucas." I smile at him and wave.

He quickly waves and bashfully hides his face into Ray's chest, giggling.

"He's a bit of a flirt. Takes after his father, if you ask me." A tall, slender woman with a deep tan and long, flowing dark hair that surpasses her waist enters the room, appearing as a picture of elegance. "Hi, I'm Tina,

Ray's wife." I extend my hand toward her, but she swats it aside and wraps me up in a hug.

I guess this family is filled with huggers.

"And I'm Kevin," the second guy says as he scoops me up in his massive arms, bringing me up to a height I've never seen before. It's immediately evident that Kevin likes to go to the gym. His body is muscular and beefy, unlike his two older brothers, who stare at him as he swings me around.

"Put her down, Kevin. She's not a damn doll for you to play with," Paul scolds.

Kevin gracefully places me back on the ground. "Well, someone is a little possessive over his *friend*."

Paul's hand wraps around my waist, pulling me in beside him. "I don't share."

"You never were good with sharing growing up. Guess that's one thing that never changed." Kevin winks at me.

"Now, now, boys," Mrs. Weston admonishes. "Play nice, please. It's Thanksgiving."

"Yes, Mom," all three say in unison, causing me to stifle a laugh.

"Uncle Kevin! Uncle Kevin! Pick me up like that!" Lucas wraps himself around Kevin's leg, begging for his turn in his arms.

"Okay, little man. But no getting sick this time," Kevin remarks as he lifts Lucas.

"I was three when that happened. I'm older now. I'm almost four," Lucas reminds him.

Mrs. Weston laughs at the scene before her. "Well, what are we all waiting for? Let's go stuff our faces!"

"Here! Here!" Ray and Kevin cheer in unison, leading the way into the dining room, everyone else following closely behind.

Paul pulls me aside before entering the room. "Everything okay so far? Is this too much for you?"

I shake my head, smiling. "No. This isn't too much." I give a half shrug. "Your mom wasn't what I expected." Releasing a breath, I confess, "When I got here and saw the size of your home, I envisioned getting ambushed by judgmental snobs, but she was...so warm and welcoming. Your whole family is, and it wasn't what I anticipated." I swallow down my emotions, giving Paul my best attempt at a smile. "They seem really great."

"They are." He smiles. "I'm lucky to have them." Paul's lips press against my temple as his hand finds mine. "Let's go eat. But I'm saving room for dessert."

"Please tell me you're not talking about that horrible pie I brought?"

He shakes his head. "Nah. I'm not talking about the pie. I'm talking about you." He winks as he enters the room, leaving me completely and utterly weak in my damn knees.

Eighteen

PAUL

I stretch my long legs in front of the roaring fire, rubbing one hand over my full stomach and placing my other on the back of the couch behind Sarah, snuggled up alongside me. Gazing out the window to my right, I see snow falling steadily, painting our backyard in a thick coating of pure white.

Life is good.

When I peek down, I find Sarah's eyes closed and her lips faintly parted. The sight of her soundly sleeping against me causes a slight warmth in my chest. I reach for the beige sherpa blanket and pull it up around her, covering her legs tucked in beside her.

"I don't think I can eat another bite," Kevin grumbles, sprawled out on the floor.

"I might have a little room left for one more piece of pie," I admit, patting my stomach.

As if on cue, my mom walks into the room. "Anyone want any more pie before I pack everything up?" Her eyes land on Sarah, glossing over.

"What's wrong?" I ask.

She dismisses me with a hand wave. "Absolutely nothing."

"I could go for a piece of the apple pie," I say. Just the thought of it makes my mouth water.

Thankfully, there's no more pumpkin pie after I roped in Kevin and Ray to help me finish it. The thing tasted like a hard-boiled egg, leaving a horrid aftertaste, and I now owe them both fifty dollars. But seeing Sarah's heart-stopping smile as she watched us pretend to enjoy it made it all worth it.

"Okay." My mom nods, looking between Sarah and me affectionately. Her eyes then dart around to the rest of the group.

"I don't think I'll be able to eat for a week," Tina murmurs as she sits on the couch and snuggles against Ray. She just put Lucas to bed, leaving the adults to relax.

"I'm good," Ray adds with a smile.

"Maybe just one piece of the apple pie," Kevin notes. "And one piece of the chocolate pie. And maybe also—"

"I thought you said you couldn't eat another bite?" I ask, chuckling.

"I'm a growing boy," he counters, stretching. "My appetite is never satisfied."

My mom shakes her head, laughing as she turns toward the kitchen. "Coming right up."

Sarah shifts beside me, her eyes blinking open as she glances up at me. An adorable smile appears until she realizes her proximity to me and sits up, inching away. "I'm sorry. I didn't mean to fall asleep on you. I must have gone into a food coma."

I lean closer to her and whisper, "You can fall asleep on me anytime."

She blushes as I tuck a loose strand of hair behind her ear.

"Get a room," Kevin remarks.

Tina kicks him in the leg, shaking her head.

"I concur," Ray says with a teasing grin.

She swats his arm. "Excuse them." She faces Sarah when she says, "I'm afraid the Weston boys don't know how to be romantic."

"What?" Ray's brows pinch together. "I'm romantic. Just the other day, you said you wanted me to take you out, so I did."

Tina rolls her eyes. "You took me golfing with you so I could drive the golf cart."

"Ouuuu," Sarah and I remark in unison, laughing.

"You said you like to drive!" Ray exclaims.

Tina crosses her arms over her chest with a scowl. "And guess what? I'm going to return the favor. When I go Black Friday shopping tomorrow morning, I'll let you come with me and hold all my shopping bags."

Ray groans, rolling his head against the back of the couch. "I guess I deserve that."

Sarah yawns beside me, standing up. "I think I'm going to head to bed now. It was lovely meeting you all. I had...a really nice time today." She smiles, appearing happy, but a smidge of sadness is shadowing over her features.

"Good night, Sarah. I hope to see you again soon," Tina quips.

"Keep my brother in line, Sarah," Kevin mumbles into the carpet.

Sarah giggles, glancing at me.

"I'll walk you up." I start to rise, but she places a hand on my shoulder, stopping me.

"It's okay. I know how to climb stairs," she says. "Even if your stairs are intimidating as hell."

My lips curve up. "Okay. Well, good night, Sarah."

She smiles and turns, heading down the hall toward the furthest set of stairs leading to the guest room. I showed her the room earlier when I insisted she stay the night because I didn't want her driving in the dark when it was snowing. She was hesitant about staying until I opened the front door, revealing her car hidden in a thick blanket of snow.

The weatherman said this area had already received up to nine inches. Sarah told me it looked like only a few. So, I promised to show her what nine inches looks like later, and I'm a man of my word.

"Man, you have it bad." Kevin sits up, leaning on his elbows as he watches me with an obnoxious grin.

"What?" I ask, shifting in my seat.

"You love herrrrrrrr," Kevin coos.

I roll my eyes. "Are you twelve?"

"Just admit it," Kevin counters.

"Paul, I have your pie here!" Mom yells from the kitchen.

Saved by Mom.

"Well, I would love to answer your question, but Mom's calling me, so..." I jump up from the couch, jogging into the kitchen.

Mom is divvying out slices of pies on plates as I enter, glancing up at me. "Honey, since I have you alone, I wanted to talk to you about something."

"Shoot," I say, taking a seat at the island.

She leans against the counter, crossing her arms over her chest. "I saw Ron, the family's financial advisor, at the bank the other day. He mentioned that you haven't touched your trust fund since it came into your possession four years ago. Why?"

I shrug. "There hasn't been anything I wanted to spend it on."

She tilts her head. "Is that the only reason?"

I purse my lips. "Sometimes, it drives me crazy how well you know me."

"So sue me," she remarks with a smile.

I shake my head. "I don't know. I mean, I have my other accounts I use, but that trust fund, well, I guess I think of it as Dad's money. Nothing has felt good enough to spend it on. I just want to make sure that whatever I use it for, Dad would approve of it."

"Honey, your father would want you to do whatever you want with that money. He left it in his will for all his children for that very reason. He just wanted his kids to be happy."

"I know." I shake my head, looking down. "I just don't want to mess this up. You know?"

She walks over to me, placing her hand on my shoulder. "Your father loved you, Paul. Very much. And know that he would approve of whatever you decide to do with that money." She presses a kiss on my forehead. "Now..." She reaches for a pie in the middle of the counter. "Take this pie."

"Mom, I know I'm a big guy, but there's no room in my stomach for all of this," I joke.

"I just figured your girlfriend might want some too." There's a twinkle in her eyes.

"Mom, I told you we're just friends."

"Mm-hmm." She purses her lips, raising a single brow. "I don't think the two of you know what that word means."

I shake my head. "She just went up to bed anyway."

"Well, go give her some pie before she falls asleep!" My mom pushes me out of the kitchen.

"I know what you're doing," I say, amused.

"I don't know what you're talking about."

"Oh really? Because I think you engrained in me that the way to anyone's heart is through their stomach."

She shrugs. "Well, we'll never know if you don't go give her a piece of the pie. Now, will we?"

When I don't move, she swats me out of the kitchen.

I shake my head, laughing. "Okay. I'm going. I'm going."

"Wait!" She turns around and grabs a can of whipped cream from the fridge. "You can't have apple pie without whipped cream." She places the can in my free hand and gently pushes me toward the end of the hall.

After walking up the stairs, I head toward the guest room and lightly knock on the door. "Hey, Sarah. It's me."

There's no answer.

Maneuvering everything in my hands, I wrap my fingers around the doorknob and nudge it to open the tiniest bit, peeking inside. But the room is empty.

Hmm.

I push the door open and walk inside, heading toward the bathroom. But the door is wide open, and she's not in there. I spin around, seeing her bag on the floor by the closet, but as I inspect the room closer, I notice a blanket and pillow missing from the bed.

My brows furrow. *Where did she go?*

I move out of the guest room and look inside my room, but it comes up empty as well. With the pie and bottle of whipped cream still in my hands, I descend the spiral stairs leading to the basement.

When I walk to the other side of the room, I find Sarah curled up on the sofa, watching TV. She sits up when she sees me, appearing guilty. The only thing she's wearing is one of my oversized T-shirts.

Goddamn.

"Oh, hey..." She tucks a piece of hair behind her ear nervously.

Placing the pie and can of whipped cream on the coffee table, I plop myself on the couch beside her. I rest my elbows on my knees and nudge her with my shoulder. "Want to tell me why you're sleeping here instead of in the guest room?"

She fidgets with the end of the blanket, shaking her head.

"Are you ever going to tell me what happened?" I ask softly.

She slowly nods, her attention solely on the blanket. "I just don't want to ruin today."

I nod, understanding. "Okay. Move over."

She looks up at me. "What?"

"Move over." With one hand, I reach over my shoulder, whip off my shirt, and stand, unbuttoning my pants and letting them fall to the floor. Sarah's eyes graze over my body, appearing in a lustful trance.

God, I love it when she looks at me like that.

I slide in behind her and pull her body on top of mine. "That's better."

She rests her head on my chest. "This can't be comfortable for you."

"Actually, it's very comfortable." I enclose my arms around her, my hand splayed over her back, sliding under the T-shirt she's wearing. I feel a shiver take over her as I glide my hand up and down her smooth skin, warmth seeping through my fingertips. Her tattooed arm on my chest catches my attention, and I can't help but move my other hand to her wrist, tracing every flower.

"What was the first tattoo you got?" I ask.

She points at the white flower on the inside of her wrist. "On my eighteenth birthday, I went and got a lily tattoo. It...was my mom's favorite flower. Mine too." She looks overcome as she says, "This one means the most to me. The rest are just floral designs I liked."

"I love them." Lifting her wrist to my lips, I press a kiss on the lily, feeling a slight tremble spread over her.

She nuzzles her face into the crook of my neck. "Thank you for inviting me today. I honestly can't remember the last time I celebrated Thanksgiving."

"Really? Not even with your family?" I ask carefully. I had a feeling when she told Natalie she wasn't going home for Thanksgiving, it was because of her family. Maybe they don't get along. Or maybe they live far away. But I didn't want to push her into telling me when the last time I tried to force her into telling me something, she ended up in the middle of the woods having a panic attack.

I've realized I just need to tread carefully and be patient with her. Let her come to terms when she's ready to tell me her secrets.

"I...umm..." She clears her throat. Silence fills the room until she says softly, "I don't have any family."

My heart splinters. That's not what I was expecting.

"No one?" I hold her tighter.

She shakes her head.

"It's been just me for a long time now." She sits up, looking down at my chest as she traces a circle on my skin, keeping herself distracted. "When I was seven, my mom was diagnosed with an aggressive form of breast cancer. The doctors told us to prepare for the worst, and, well, that's exactly what happened. She died... She died on my eighth birthday," she whispers.

"Jesus, Sarah. I had no idea."

"How would you when I never told you or anyone?" She tries to smile, but it falters as she shakes her head. "After that, my dad went down a bad spiral of depression. He stopped going to work. He stopped showing interest in everything he once loved. He stopped caring about anything and everyone, including me. And it was on the one-year anniversary of my mom's death, my ninth birthday, that I came home from camp and found a couple of police officers and a service worker waiting for me."

Her fingers pause on my skin as my heart beats rapidly beneath her touch, knowing and fearing where this story is going.

"They were waiting for me because...my dad had an accident. His car veered off the main bridge in our town, and he didn't make it." She shakes her head, drowning in her memories. "I knew. I just knew in my heart it wasn't an accident. I saw the way my mom's death affected him. I saw how it destroyed him. And I knew how much he missed her and wanted to be with her again." She blinks away the fresh tears clinging to her lashes. "I love my dad so much. He was caring and kind, and I know how much he was hurting to have done to himself what he did, but...I've never been able to forgive him for putting me through that. For...leaving me when he was the only person I had left in my life."

I hold her tighter, needing her to know I'm here.

She's not alone anymore.

I catch the tears sliding off her chin, her bottom lip shuddering under my touch.

"I'm so sorry, Sarah." What is the right thing to say to this? She lost both of her parents within a year of each other on her fucking birthday. One from cancer and one from taking their own life.

"I didn't have any family who could take me in, so I was sent to a group foster home, where they tried to help me find my forever home like some sad puppy. But I didn't. I was moved from home to home, but no one wanted the quiet, depressed little girl. Can't say that I blame them." She lifts a shoulder. "But the second I turned eighteen, I came into some money my parents had left for me in their will. It wasn't a lot, but it was enough to help cover what my scholarship wouldn't for LU, and it paid for a roof over my head. I was lucky in that regard," she says quietly. "My mom left me, even without meaning to. My dad left me purposely. And every foster home left me feeling unwanted and a little more broken. They all just...let me go."

Her words leave a gaping hole in my pounding heart, my chest aching unbearably.

Silence fills the air around us, her eyes appearing translucent as she copes with releasing her story out loud for what I assume is the first time.

Her trust in me to share her story causes a rush of protectiveness to swarm within me. "I'm not letting you go, Sarah."

Her eyes hold mine, void of any emotion, as tears continue to trickle down her face.

She doesn't believe me. And why would she when no one has ever stayed?

My fingers glide over her cheeks, wiping away every tear from her face. "So, when we met on your birthday, and you told me to make you forget, you meant—"

"Yeah." A forced half smile appears. "I don't know why. Maybe it was because it was my twenty-first birthday, or maybe it was because..." She shakes her head, lost in thought until her eyes catch mine. "I never did thank you for that night. You were the best distraction I could have ever asked for."

"Sarah, you never have to thank me for that. That night..." I grip her chin. "I don't want to scare you away, but the night I met you was the best night of my life. It's me who should be thanking you."

She looks down, biting her bottom lip as the prettiest shade of pink covers her cheeks.

"I'm so sorry you've had to go through all this alone," I offer. "But thank you for telling me. I can't even imagine how hard life has been for you. How lonely it's been."

I'm starting to wonder if this is maybe why she distances herself from people. She's been alone for so long, taking care of herself, that she doesn't know what it means to have someone take care of her—someone in her corner who wants to be there for her no matter what.

Someone who won't let her go.

She shrugs it off. "I've had over a decade to grieve. You'd think I could talk about this without crying." She rubs a spot on my chest where a few tears landed.

"There's no time limit on grieving. I still miss my dad every damn day."

She nods. "I thought since you lost your dad, you would understand the feeling," she admits in a broken whisper.

I hold her tighter, wishing I could take away her pain and sorrow. "I understand the feeling of losing a parent. But Sarah, I still had my mom and brothers and a roof over my head. What you went through is beyond words. It's nothing I can comprehend, and I don't even know the right thing to say to you because I'm starting to think there isn't a *'right thing'* to say." I let out a rush of air. "Family is the most important thing to me. I don't know what I would do without mine. They have my back every day of the year. They're there for me even when I'm not there for myself. But you lost your whole family, and that's…" I stop myself when I see her suck in her trembling bottom lip. "I'm here, Sarah. You know that, right?"

She nods, lost in thought. "Thank you for listening."

"If you have something to say, I'll always listen to you." I tuck a strand of loose hair behind her ear. "I wish my dad were here to meet you. He would have really liked you."

Her eyes meet mine. "You think so?"

"I know so." The tips of my fingers trail down her spine. "You're smart, ambitious, talented, beautiful… I can keep going if you want."

She suppresses a smile, nuzzling her head against my chest.

We lie in silence for a moment, and I'm pretty sure she's fallen asleep until she says, "Can you do something for me?"

"Anything."

She leans up, slowly gliding her lips over mine.

"Tell me what you want, Sarah, and I'll make it happen."

"I want..." She pauses as my hand slides down her back. "You to distract me."

I hesitate. "Are you sure?"

"Yes. Make me forget," she breathes. "I know I'm an emotional mess right now, and I just laid out some pretty heavy shit, but all I want to do is spend the next five minutes in a bubble with you." She bites her bottom lip. "Distract me, Paul. Please."

I lean toward her, brushing my lips against the shell of her ear. "I'll do anything for you. But I'm going to need a lot more than five minutes." Her eyes sparkle as an understanding passes between us. "Now sit on my face, and I'll make sure my tongue is the only thing you're thinking about."

She lets out a nervous laugh. "You're joking, right?" When I don't say anything, she widens her eyes in horror. "You'll suffocate."

I smirk. "If I die with my head between your thighs, I'll die the happiest man alive, baby girl."

She opens her mouth to protest, but I'm too fast for her. I lift her hips so she's straddling my chest. My fingers trail over the tattoos on her thigh, running my index finger up the inside of her leg. "Have I ever told you how sexy these look on you?"

She clears her throat. "You might have mentioned it before."

I smirk, remembering our first night together and how I spent a lot of time memorizing every image imprinted on her skin with my lips and tongue.

She hasn't moved, and I'm becoming impatient for a taste.

"A little further up, baby girl." I squeeze her thighs and wink as she looks down at me, but she's frozen. "Sarah?"

"Mm-hmm?"

"Everything okay?"

"Yeah. Totally fine." She slides her fingers through her hair and then fans herself. "Is it hot in here?"

"Are you nervous?"

"Nervous? What? No." She adamantly shakes her head. "Sex with you doesn't make me nervous."

"But what we're about to do isn't technically sex, so—"

"No one has ever done this to me before," she admits, staring up at the ceiling.

I'll be her first.

"Sarah, look at me."

Her beautiful green eyes lock on mine.

"Do you trust me?" I ask.

"With my life."

"Then let me take care of you."

One sentence.

Seven words.

That's all it takes for her face to soften and for her hips to lift toward my mouth.

"That's it, baby girl. Just like that."

She hovers over my face, her shaking fingers gripping my shoulders.

"Now what?" she asks breathlessly.

In one swift motion, I rip the underwear off her and grip her hips. "Now, I need you to hold the back of the couch while I enjoy my new favorite dessert."

I yank her down, smothering myself in her pussy, and the second my tongue swipes through her center, I feel her body relax as she lets out a soft moan of approval. My tongue laps up every inch of her, concentrating on her clit where I feel her tremble with each swipe of my tongue and every suck from my lips.

"Fuck. I knew your pussy would taste delicious." I groan, flattening my tongue against her as I take a long, leisurely stroke. "So fucking sweet."

I dreamed of this moment. Tasting her decadent pussy for the very first time, and it's better than I ever could have imagined.

"Oh God. Right there. Right. Right. Oh... Oh... More!" she pleads.

Sarah's pussy starts grinding ravenously against my face.

"That's my girl. Ride my tongue."

Without any warning, I shove two fingers inside her soaking wet pussy, thrusting frantically, feeling her clench around me as she screams out in pleasure.

"Fuck. I'm almost... Oh my God."

My thumb strums across her clit before I replace it with my lips, and I suck hard, still thrusting inside her with my fingers when her whole body shudders, and she screams against the back of the couch, unraveling. As the orgasm begins to fade, I slowly slip my fingers out of her and lift her small body, sitting up to bring her right against my chest that she sags into.

"I got you." I rub her back over the T-shirt, holding her in my arms. "I've always got you."

She looks up at me with her glossed eyes and rosy cheeks, telltale signs that her orgasm was satisfactory, but I still need to know. I need to hear it from her lips for the sake of my own damn pride.

"How was it?" My knuckles stroke her cheek.

"You've ruined me." Her forehead presses against my shoulder. "I think that was the best orgasm of my life."

She places the palm of her hand on my chest, like when we were in the woods. And I watch as she matches her breathing to mine, coming down from her post-orgasmic high, looking serene.

She tilts her head, staring at what's on the coffee table. "Why did you bring a whole pie down here?"

"Thought you might be hungry." I tap the tip of her nose.

"Well, I am a bit hungry now." Her eyes move from the coffee table back to me, with a playful gleam bouncing over them. "But I think just for whipped cream."

My brows raise. "Oh yeah?"

She nods, reaching over for the can. "Do you like whipped cream, Paul?" Her voice is sultry and sweet. Her nails trail down my chest, leading to the edge of my boxer briefs.

I swallow, watching as she gets up from the couch and kneels on the ground between my legs. "Yeah. I ahh...I like whipped cream a lot."

"I was hoping you might." With sensual movements, she removes her T-shirt, giving me the best view of my life.

Sarah, naked between my legs.

My eyes roam over her body, tracing over every delectable curve. Her breasts heave with each inhale and exhale, her nipples hardening under my stare. All I want to do is reach out to her, touch her, taste her, but I sit back, giving her complete control in this moment.

Because this moment is all hers.

The palm of her free hand slides up my bare thigh, right over the hard bulge between the dead center of my legs, eliciting a groan from me.

She bites her bottom lip, her hand rubbing against me. Her fingers tuck under the waistband, pulling the fabric down until my hard cock springs free. I watch as her eyes widen and her tongue comes out, licking her lips, appearing as though my cock is her favorite guilty pleasure.

"You going to show me how much you want my cock, baby girl?" My hand cups her cheek, my thumb brushing over her bottom lip. Her iridescent green eyes connect with mine as she shakes the can in her hand.

"I've wanted to do this for so long," she confesses.

The palm of her hand glides up the inside of my thigh, pushing my legs apart so she can get closer to me.

"Do whatever you want to me. I'm all yours." My cock throbs at the sight before me. Does she know how many times I've envisioned this exact scenario? Well, maybe not with the whipped cream, but that's an added bonus.

She positions the can over her hand, squirting a dollop onto her finger. Her tongue darts out of her mouth as she slides her finger between her lips, sucking off the cream.

Holy fucking fuck.

"Mmm." She releases her finger. "I forgot how much I love whipped cream."

Her free hand grips my cock, stroking me. Providing the perfect amount of pressure to send me over the edge.

"Fuck," I hiss, letting my head roll back but still keeping an eye on her. There's no way I'm missing a single second of this.

She places the palm of her hand underneath my cock to hold it while she takes the can of whipped cream with her other hand, slowly dispensing a line down my hardened length.

"You're so big. I hope there will be enough," she muses.

"You sure know exactly the right thing to say, don't you?" My fingers reach out to her, running through her silky strands of hair as she tosses the bottle to the side.

A devilish little grin appears on her face right before her tongue sneaks out between her lips, and she licks off the whole line of cream as her hand massages my balls.

"Fuck. Fuck. Fuck," I groan uncontrollably.

There's not a second of hesitation as she opens wide and takes almost all of my cock inside her, sucking on it like it's her favorite thing in the whole goddamn world.

Her head bobs up and down like a pro, her fingers gripping my thighs, holding me to her.

My hand rests on her shoulder, stroking her skin. "You're fucking perfect."

The tip of my cock hits the back of her throat, making her eyes water, but she keeps pushing herself, getting as much of me inside her warm mouth.

It doesn't take long for me to feel myself start to lose control, so I gently push on her head before it's too late. "I'm about to come."

She shakes her head. "Swallowing," she mumbles around my cock, picking up the pace.

Well, fuck me.

I let out a groan as I come, my cock pulsing inside her mouth, my eyes not getting enough of her, watching as she swallows every last drop.

She backs away on her knees, looking up at me, licking her lips. "How did I do?"

I let out a breathy chuckle, rolling my head against the back of the couch. "How did you do? Sarah, that was the best fucking blow job of my life." I reach for her, gripping her at her waist, and pull her back onto my lap.

"I've never done that before," she quietly admits, hiding her face in the crook of my neck. Her lips press against my skin over and over again.

That admission fucking does something to me.

My arms hold her closer, possessively against my chest. My lips brush over her forehead. "That was perfect."

We hold each other tightly, neither wanting this moment to end. Eventually, when I look down at Sarah's closed eyes and parted lips, letting me know she's asleep, I glide us down onto the sofa, holding her snugly against my body. My bicep slides under her head as a personal pillow as I fall asleep beside her, wishing we could spend every night like this together.

Nineteen

SARAH

Nerves rattle every square inch of me as I repeatedly tap my pencil on my desk, guilt increasingly eating away at me. Even going out with Natalie and Vanessa last night didn't help much with putting my mind at ease. If anything, it just made me feel guiltier for keeping my pregnancy a secret from them as well.

Not being able to tell Paul that I'm pregnant with his baby is taking a toll on me, both physically and mentally. I haven't been able to sleep more than a few hours, and when I do fall asleep, I wake up drenched in sweat from the same nightmare. Greyson standing over me, laughing menacingly, with his laptop in his hand, pressing upload for the world to see...me.

I cringe, internally shaking my head.

Thanksgiving with Paul's family last week was perfect. I might have been a little overwhelmed at first, being in a home with people I don't know, but that feeling was soon replaced with warmth. Whether by Mrs. Weston, Tina, or even his brothers, they welcomed me into their home as though I were part of their family.

It felt...strange, but in a good way. It was an unfamiliar emotion that I hoped I might be able to feel again someday.

And it was becoming increasingly apparent how much Paul wanted me in his life. I mean, the man has pretty much spelled it out on a billboard for me, but with the ominous blackmail cloud hanging over my head every single day, I haven't opened my eyes to see what being with Paul would mean clearly.

But now I know it would mean being with someone who makes me feel like all the bad days are behind me. Like there is hope and happiness just waiting for me at the end of the tunnel, as long as I take his hand and walk through it with him by my side.

So, enough is enough. It's time to put an end to this blackmail bullshit because I won't stand by and let someone like Greyson Black drag me, Paul, or our baby down with him.

I won't let it happen.

I just need to think harder, and a plan will come. I know it will.

I press my palms to the side of my head and close my eyes. *Think. Think. Think.*

"Are you sure you can get into the professor's computer to change my grade?"

The low, husky voice to my right breaks me from my haze.

"Are you kidding? I doubt he even has a password for that ancient piece of junk. It'll be like taking candy from a baby."

I peek over my shoulder to see a guy I recognize from the basketball team. I'm not sure, but I think his name is Glen.

"How much will it cost me?" the guy in the blue hoody asks quietly.

Glen glimpses around, ensuring no one is eavesdropping. My eyes are glued to the textbook before me, pretending to be skimming the pages.

"Two hundred and fifty. And you need to keep your mouth shut. If I go down, you go down," Glen threatens.

"Yeah. Yeah. I won't say anything. I just really need to pass this class. I won't get into law school if I don't." I notice the guy wearing blue fidgeting nervously with his hair.

"Like I said, it's a piece of cake. There are only five minutes left of class, and I need more time than that to do this. During our next class, I'll be able to access his hard drive as soon as he's hooked up to the Wi-Fi. As long as his device and my device are both using the same Wi-Fi, it'll work. So, don't worry. You'll be passing this class by the end of the week." Glen pats the guy on the shoulder reassuringly.

"Thanks, man."

So Glen is a little computer whiz. Huh. I wish I knew how to hack into computers. It might come in handy, especially with... *That's it!*

"All right, I'll see everyone in the next class. Don't forget to turn in your essays on your way out," the professor announces to the students, eagerly filing out into the halls.

I quickly shove everything in my bag and run out the door, heading straight to work like a girl on a mission.

Greyson Black is about to regret ever threatening me.

* * *

I nibble on my thumbnail, anxiously watching Greyson's office door. He's been in a meeting on the fourth floor for the past hour, and I should have snuck inside his office the second he left, but nerves have been taking over me, leaving me hostage to my desk chair.

But it's now or never.

I pick up the stack of papers in front of me with shaking fingers, clutching them to my chest, and take a deep breath.

I can do this.

Straightening my shoulders, I stroll toward his office, stopping beside Gianna's desk. "Has Greyson come back from his meeting? I have some contracts I need him to sign."

She looks away from her computer and at me with a smile. "No, I don't believe he has. Shouldn't be much longer, though, I would imagine."

I nod. "Would it be okay if I leave these on his desk?"

"Of course." She motions toward his door. "It's unlocked."

"Great." I throw on a smile and quickly enter, shutting the door behind me. My back rests against his door as my eyes rove around the space, my chest blooming with anxiety.

His office is suffocating. Intimidating.

With its bare walls and dark features throughout, it reminds me of a prison cell. There are no personal touches or something that would give anyone a clue as to who the office belongs to. It's isolating. And I'm ready to get the hell out of here.

But first...

My eyes scan over his desk, immediately spotting his laptop, and a sense of hope washes over me at having luck on my side for once. Taking a few steps over to his desk, I drop the stack of papers on the corner and pick up the laptop cautiously. Opening it, I quickly see a password is needed to get in, which I figured, but I'm not worried, now knowing what Glen can do. Tucking the laptop under my arm, I turn to leave, placing my hand on the doorknob when I hear voices on the other side of the door.

Shit. Shit. Shit.

"Oh, Mr. Black. How did the meeting go?" Gianna asks loud enough for me to hear.

Sweat breaks out on my forehead as I bite my bottom lip so hard that a drop of blood hits my tongue. The metallic taste instantly makes my stomach churn.

But I cannot get sick right now. I need to hide. And fast.

Sweat builds on the back of my neck as I look around, immediately realizing there's no closet to hide inside. I reach for the nearest window, trying with all my strength to shove it open, but it's stuck.

Without thinking about it, I place the laptop on his desk, exactly as it was before, then walk to the other side, move the desk chair out of the way, and crouch down before the small space. I crawl under and sit, bringing my knees to my chin, and pull the chair toward me just as the door opens.

Holding my breath for dear life, I hear footsteps entering the room, and then my biggest fear comes true as Greyson pulls out the chair and sits in it, letting out a long sigh. He pushes forward, leaving only an inch of space between me and his body. My eyes stare directly at the center of his knee. A tremble explodes inside me, knowing what this man can do and how bad this will be for me if he finds me here.

Suddenly, the desk above me vibrates.

"Hi, Dad."

He leans back in his chair, kicking his legs to the side.

"Yes, everything is running smoothly. No issues to report." He sighs. "Okay. Goodbye."

My breath hitches as he sits up, slamming his phone to his desk. "Fucking imbecile. If he thinks I'm taking over this miserable place, he has another thing coming."

My heart pounds so loudly beneath my chest that I fear he might hear it.

A soft knock sounds at the door.

"Come in," Greyson says with irritation sharp in his voice.

"Hi, Mr. Black." Gianna's soft voice fills the room. "I don't mean to bother you, but could you help me with some boxes that were delivered? I figured you would have no problem lifting them."

She's helping me.

"Of course. Let me get my things together. I need to be heading out." I see his hand grab his backpack on the floor beside him, hear the zipper being undone, and immediately know he's putting his laptop inside. *All of this was for nothing.* He pushes his chair back, steps around the desk, and walks toward his door.

When his door closes behind him, I feel air fill my lungs as I take my first big breath in too long.

Knowing I need to quickly get out of here, even without his laptop in my hands, I unfold myself from under the desk and stand, straightening my skirt. Just as I pass the side of his desk, my eyes spot his phone. His phone that he must have left behind since he was in such a hurry. His phone, which he'll most likely realize soon enough, is missing, and he'll need to retrieve it.

It looks like this wasn't all for nothing, after all.

My fingers wrap around his phone and swiftly shove it inside the confines of my bra for safekeeping. And then I move out of his office like my ass is on fire as I grab my things from my desk and know exactly where I need to go next.

* * *

"Hey, Glen!" I enthusiastically wave my hand from the corner of the hall where I've been hiding out like a total creep as I spot him approaching the players' only entrance at the arena, and I run up to him, evidently out of breath.

He tilts his head, observing me, eyebrows pinched together. "You're Paul's girl, right?"

"Umm." I smooth out my hair, tucking it behind my ear. "Listen, I don't mean to be rude, and I hope you don't get upset." I motion for him to follow me, away from prying ears that may walk by. "But I heard your conversation in class earlier today with that guy about getting into the teacher's computer."

His brows raise defiantly. "What? You plan on telling or something?"

"Oh. No. No. No." I shake my head adamantly, waving my hands. "I just wanted to see if your services were open for other people, too. I would, of course, pay you," I add.

Even knowing I don't have a single penny to my name after last week's paycheck from work covered my rent and a few groceries, leaving nothing left.

He purses his lips. "What do you need?"

I swallow. "Well, there's something on someone's computer and phone that I need erased. Like completely expunged. Is that something you can do?"

He nods. "Usually. Depends on the security factors and..."

"And?"

"And on whose computer and phone do you want me to hack into?"

"Oh." This could be a slight problem. "I don't know if I can say that without it getting back to him, and if it got back to him, that would create a lot more trouble for me."

He sighs. "Listen, you're Paul's girl, and I'm tight with Paul. So what gets said right now stays between us."

I nod. "I appreciate that." I glance nervously around the empty hall, fearful that the two guys I cannot risk finding me here like this will walk into view any minute.

"Look, I have a game I need to get ready for, so—"

I whip the phone out of my coat pocket and hold it out for him to take, which he does, scrutinizing it.

"Who does this belong to?"

Just say it.

"It's Greyson Black's," I rush out.

His eyes momentarily widen. "How the hell did you get this?"

"I was just in the right place at the right time," I offer with a quick shrug.

He examines the phone in his hand, flipping it over. "Okay, so let me get this straight. You want me to hack into Greyson's computer and phone and delete something off of it?"

"Yes..."

He runs his fingers through his hair, a loud swoosh of air leaving his lungs. "And what do I need to delete?"

I open my mouth but pause, suddenly realizing that in order to delete the video, he'll need to watch it.

This was the worst idea I've ever had.

I swallow the lump in my throat. "You know what, forget I said anything." I start to reach for the phone in Glen's hand, but he stops me, gently pulling the phone from my reach as he places his free hand on my shoulder.

"I can't help you if you don't tell me what I should be looking for on his devices." He looks me dead in the eye, and I realize he's right.

My shoulders slump. "A video," is all I say, looking down at the ground, my cheeks heating up. Maybe this was a stupid idea, but I'm running out of options.

He removes his hand from my shoulder, nodding, knowing exactly what kind of video I'm referring to.

Shame fills me.

His fingers grip the strap of his sports bag. "I'm not sure I'll be able to hack into this."

Dread fills me. "But I thought if I got you his device and you just connected it to the same Wi-Fi..."

He shakes his head. "Greyson has one of the best security systems on his laptop. I can only imagine how difficult it will be to get into his phone. I've never seen someone so paranoid about people getting into his things." He shoves the phone into his pocket. "This isn't the same as hacking into the teacher's ancient computer with no security features. That I can get into no problem. But this is Greyson. He doesn't play around."

My eyes mist over as I nod, defeat weighing down on me. "I understand. It was worth a shot. Thanks anyway." I turn, but Glen gently grabs my elbow to stop me.

"Let me see what I can do tonight, okay? I can try to get into his phone and see if it's also connected to his laptop. It might not work, but I can try."

Optimism suddenly outweighs the defeat taking over my heart.

I give a half smile. "Thank you."

He has us exchange numbers before he walks off and passes through the entrance, leaving me hopeful for the first time in months.

The video may not be erased yet, but with a bit of luck, it shouldn't be long until Glen can hopefully take care of it. And then...then I can finally tell Paul *everything*.

A smile forms on my face as I pull out my phone.

Sarah

Is an offer for a second date still on the table?

Twenty

PAUL

I stare at my phone in my hand, smiling like a goddamn idiot because the moment I saw her text, I knew another piece of that brick wall between us had crumbled, knocking my heart right onto fucking cloud nine.

"Paul!"

My eyes dart to the back of the court to find Glen calling for me, frantically waving me over.

"What's up? And where the hell have you been? I had to warm up with Jamie." I throw my hands in the air dramatically. He knows how much I hate changes because they throw me off my game, and let's just say I don't like feeling off my game.

He rolls his eyes. "I think there is a bigger problem than you having to play nice with Jamie for ten minutes."

I arch a brow. Now, I'm curious.

He glances around, noticing Coach Rivers talking with the officials in the back. "Let's talk in private." He strides toward the locker room, and I willingly follow as a cloud of impending doom hangs above us.

Walking past my teammates, I see them all on the court, warming up smoothly, ready to take on the opposing team. We've been on a consecutive winning streak for the past few weeks and need this win tonight to keep heading in the right direction toward March Madness.

And I won't let anything distract me from getting us all there.

After the door swings shut behind us, Glen turns, dragging a hand over his face before pacing back and forth.

"What's going on, man? You're kind of freaking me out." I cross my arms over my chest, waiting.

He lets out a rush of air, pausing mid-step to look at me. "I figured I should tell you about my conversation with your girl."

My stomach tightens as his words roll over me. "Tell me."

"Well." He drops his sports bag on the ground and takes a seat on a nearby bench, staring up at me. "She heard me telling someone in class today that I could hack into the professor's computer to switch their grade."

"I thought I told you to stop doing that shit," I scold.

"I know. I know. But I need the money." He shrugs his shoulders. "Anyway, she just approached me outside the entrance asking if I could hack into someone's computer and phone for her."

My eyebrows pinch together. "Whose?"

"You're not going to like this…"

"Glen," I grit out.

He reaches into his pocket and removes a phone, holding it out for me to take.

"It's Greyson's," he says as my fingers wrap around the clear plastic case surrounding it.

My stomach plummets. Anything involving Greyson is not good. And the fact that Sarah is entangled just makes me want to strangle him without even knowing what's going on.

"You're sure?" Why the hell would she want Glen to hack into his things?

"Positive. But this is the reason why I'm telling you." He sighs, looking up at the ceiling, squeezing his eyes shut.

"Fucking tell me, Glen."

"She told me she needs me to delete a..."

"A what?" I clench my jaw, agonizing over the anticipation of what will come out of his mouth.

"A video..."

My vision goes blurry as I shake my head, blood pounding in my ears. "I'm sorry. Say that again."

Glen pinches the bridge of his nose, wincing. "A video. She needs a video erased from his things."

Rage boils beneath my skin. There's only one kind of video that comes to mind. And to think that he has a video like that of Sarah causes me to only see red.

Everything. Is. Fucking. Red.

"I'm going to kill him," I say, sounding calm when it's the last thing I feel.

Glen grabs my arm and pulls me on the bench beside him. "Listen, we don't know for sure what kind of video it is."

I glare at him.

"Okay, maybe it is that kind of video." He scrunches his face and reaches into his bag for a sports drink. "You know, shit like this makes me queasy. I can't deal with this stress." He guzzles his drink as he rubs his stomach. "I doubt either of us could get into his computer anyway. It's more secure than the President's."

"He practically sleeps with it," I note. "Doesn't let it out of his sight." I massage my aching temple. "Why didn't she fucking ask me to do this for her? I'm the one who taught you how to do this shit."

"Maybe she's embarrassed and doesn't want you seeing what's on the video." He shrugs his shoulders.

"And like hell, I'll be letting you see what's on the video," I state, tucking the phone under my arm.

He chuckles.

"This isn't funny."

"I know. I know. I laugh when I'm nervous." He crosses his arms over his chest. "Have you ever mentioned to her that you can do this kind of stuff? That you're a badass when it comes to computers."

I shake my head. "No. The one time she saw my computer in my room, she freaked out and—"

Everything around me freezes.

She didn't freak out about my computer.

She freaked out about the tiny camera sitting on top of my computer.

She freaked out because she was worried I filmed her when I would never do something like that.

But someone else might.

Someone like Greyson.

My knuckles ache as I grip the edge of the metal bench. An unfamiliar animalistic roar escapes from my lips as I fight with everything inside me not to go out on that court right now and murder Greyson.

Standing abruptly, I punch the closest thing next to me: a metal locker, splitting the skin on a couple of my knuckles. A few droplets of blood spiral a path down the back of my hand and then onto the floor.

"Shit, man." Glen pulls my arm back. "You'll break a finger and be out for the rest of the season. Is that what you want?"

"I don't care!" My chest heaves as I slam both fists against the wall, panic engulfing me. The pounding of my heart beats erratically beneath my rib cage. My throat goes dry as I gasp for air. "I can't fucking breathe!"

"Paul, take a deep breath." He steps away, giving me space. "Talk to me, man."

I drop my head, closing my eyes.

Inhale. Exhale.

Inhale. Exhale.

"It was him," I say in a cracked whisper.

"What was?"

"Greyson. He fucking filmed her without her knowing. I know it was him. I'm going to kill him, Glen. I'm going to make him pay for what he did to my girl."

"Okay, but how about you take a seat first." Glen guides me back on the bench and hands me a bottle of water. "Listen"—he places his hand on my shoulder—"you're coming up with a scenario in your head when you don't know that's what actually happened."

"But it—"

"Maybe it is," he rushes out. "But you don't know for sure. And I'm not going to let you go out on that court and ruin your career by murdering Greyson."

I hold my head in my hands, focusing on my breathing as I let out a shaky sigh.

"I just need you to spend the next couple of hours out there, getting your head in the game and showing everyone who the fuck Paul Weston is," he demands. "And then, you can go find your girl and find out what the hell is going on."

The buzzer in the arena sounds, making us both look at the door. *It's time.*

I stand, rolling my neck. "This is going to be the longest fucking game of my life."

"That's the spirit!" Glen cheers as he jumps up, wrapping an arm around my shoulder.

"But if I find out it's true, you cannot stop me from killing him." I narrow my eyes on Glen, who only shrugs.

"If it's true, I'll help you." He hands me a small towel to wipe the blood off my hand. "Getting away with first-degree murder is what friends are for."

Twenty-One

SARAH

Slumping against the back of my door, I kick off my flats and enter the kitchen. Opening the fridge, finding bare shelves and rancid leftovers, I close it and stand in front of the cabinet, praying to see something edible inside.

Please. Please. Please.

Swinging open the door, I find one box of instant macaroni and cheese and do a little happy dance.

As I pour the noodles into the pot of boiling water, I hear my phone vibrate on the kitchen island; an unknown number flashes across the screen.

"Hello?" I answer hesitantly.

"Hi, Miss Fleur. This is James down in the lobby."

"Oh." Relief fills me from the sweet man's voice. "Hi, James. How are you?"

"Can't complain. Gotta lay off the sugar per my wife's request, but all things considered, I'm good." I chuckle, stirring the noodles in the water. "We received some heavy deliveries for you, and I was wondering if this would be a good time to bring them up?"

"Yes!" I completely forgot the baby's furniture was scheduled for delivery today. "That would be great. Thank you!"

An hour later, my living room is overrun with boxes.

Was I under the impression the furniture would be delivered fully assembled?

Yes, I absolutely was.

No matter. I can put it together myself. I'm sure it won't be too difficult to do.

Gazing around at what my emergency credit card bought me, I feel good about how it was spent.

And I'm so ready to tell Paul.

I just really hope that after I explain everything to him, he understands why it took me so long to tell him.

I shake my head, catching a glimpse of myself in the window. Instinctively, I raise my T-shirt and observe myself, noting the beginning of an official baby bump. It's small and barely noticeable. Most would probably think I looked like I ate a burrito or two for lunch. I'm sure when Paul saw my body on Thanksgiving, he assumed I was just bloated from all of the food. But I wasn't. I'm just pregnant and so happy as I see the light at the end of the long tunnel.

Everything feels like it's finally coming together.

My eyes water as a smile blooms across my face, and my hand slides protectively over my stomach.

"So soon, I'm telling your daddy everything. He thinks we're going on a normal date tomorrow night, but that's when I plan on telling him all about you right after Glen deletes the video. And everything will be okay. I promise."

Although, I am fully prepared to give Paul an out.

I'll understand if he wants nothing to do with me or the baby. I'll have to.

But I'm not going to lie and say it doesn't hurt to think he might choose to leave...like everyone else in my life has done.

I shake my head, not wanting to go down that road tonight.

There's no use worrying over something that hasn't even happened yet.

After eating every last drop of the macaroni and cheese, I get down to business by opening all the cardboard boxes and removing each piece and tool. Seeing everything laid out leaves me feeling utterly overwhelmed as I still try to convince myself this will be a piece of cake.

I can do this!

But as one hour turns into two and then three, I realize I can't, in fact, do this myself.

Frustrated tears cascade down my cheeks as I throw the mini wrench on the floor. My fists clench by my side as I look around at the disaster site that has taken over my living room. A crib with no side rails stands tilted on one side of the room, a rocking chair that doesn't rock sits in the corner, a baby changing table is in pieces across the floor, and a car seat that I already know I won't understand how to put in my car sits in its box, taunting me.

I failed.

I can't do this.

How will I be a good mom when I can't even read simple directions?

I pinch the bridge of my nose, feeling the beginnings of a headache forming. What am I supposed to—

Knock. Knock. Knock.

My eyes bounce to the closed door. Who the hell could that be?

I grab my phone from my pocket and see it's just after ten p.m.

Tiptoeing to the door, I'm just about to look through the peephole when the deep timbre of his voice stops me in my tracks.

"Hey, Sarah, it's Paul. We need to talk."

I frantically wipe at my tears and push back loose strands of hair that escaped my ponytail. After spending the night trying to assemble a nursery, I look like a hot mess with sweat running down my temple and over my back. Not to mention, my cheeks are probably crimson from heat exhaustion. And as if on cue, my stomach rumbles, alerting me that my baby and I are hungry...again!

The nutrition label on the box of macaroni and cheese was a lie. It wasn't three servings. It was barely even one.

Knock. Knock. "Sarah?"

This can't be happening.

Left with no other option, I walk over to the door. Taking a deep breath, I open the door just a few inches, intending to hide the catastrophe behind me.

"Hey, Paul. What are you doing here?" I forge a smile, hoping he won't see through it.

His eyes examine me, concern etched all over his facial features. "You want to tell me what this is." He holds up Greyson's phone while his eyes look me up and down, observing my appearance. "Are you feeling okay?"

"I...umm." Of course, fucking Glen told him. I was stupid for thinking he wouldn't. "Actually, no. I'm not feeling that great. You should probably go so you don't catch whatever I have."

He watches me silently until he finally says, "What's going on?"

I shake my head. "Nothing. Like I said, I'm just not feeling well."

He lightly pushes on the door, but I keep my foot behind it, not letting it budge while gripping my hands on the edge for backup.

"What are you hiding?"

"Hiding? I'm not hiding any—"

"Is someone in there?" he asks, his eyes darkening.

Okay, now I'm pissed.

"Are you accusing me of hiding someone in here?" I ask, defiantly crossing my arms over my chest and moving my foot to jut out my hip. In hindsight, this is where I made my mistake. Because just as I jut out my hip, removing my foot from behind the door, Paul pushes it open, and there's nothing I can do to make it stop.

"Wait, Paul!"

But it's too late.

He bypasses me as he steps inside, eerily silent, his eyes scanning the room. Every damn piece of baby furniture is on display for him to see.

His silence begins to suffocate me.

"It's not what you think," I say meekly.

"So, you're not pregnant?" he asks.

I yank at the hem of my shirt, eyeing the ground. "Okay, so maybe it's exactly what you think."

Paul spins towards me, his eyes bulging wide and his mouth agape.

I shuffle my foot, biting my bottom lip. I don't know what to say. This wasn't at all how I planned on telling him the news. "Do you want to sit?" I motion toward the couch, where he drops down.

He slides Greyson's phone on the coffee table and rests his elbows on his knees, holding his head between his hands.

After a few minutes of insufferable silence, he asks, "How far along are you?"

"Umm." It's time to tell him the truth. He deserves the whole truth and nothing but the truth. I let out an anxious sigh. "Almost sixteen weeks."

His eyes shoot up to mine. "Am I...the father?"

My shoulders drop as I nod, looking at the floor through a blurry lens.

"And how long have you known?" he stresses through clenched teeth.

I hesitate before softly saying, "Three months."

His eyes blaze with fury as he stands, turns away from me, and walks over to the barely standing crib. He looks down at the baby mattress and slams his fist on it, the whole thing falling to the floor.

Well, there goes at least two hours of my life.

I rub my forehead. The headache increases with each passing second.

"So, were you ever planning to tell me, or were you just going to keep this a secret from me forever?" His voice is lethally low, spiked with...pain...because of me.

"I was going to tell you, I swear. I just—"

He spins around, looking at me as though I'm the last person on Earth he wants to see. And it breaks me.

"You just what? You've known for three months. Three months! And you never said anything to me. Not once. And then I come here to find this"—he waves his hand around the room—"fucking baby furniture." He looks away, running his hand over his head before squeezing his neck. "I have told you everything. Everything. About how important family is to me. About my dad. My fears and insecurities. Trying over and over again to knock down that damn wall you keep up between us. And I thought...I thought I had finally made some progress. I thought the wall was crumbling." His head tilts down, and the dejected look on his face is one I will never be able to forget. "I opened up to you because I trusted you with everything, including my heart." He shakes his head, staring at me like he has no idea who I am.

Tears pour down my cheeks, and I can't rein them in. I sniffle, trying as hard as I can to make them stop, but I fucking can't. And I deserve to feel this way. I deserve every ounce of this viselike grip squeezing my chest because I hurt this man. This amazing man who would part the seas for me if I asked him to is standing before me in agony, all because of me.

But what he says next makes my heart fragment into a thousand tiny, jagged pieces.

"I need to go." He walks around me toward the door, no longer looking at me.

"Wait, Paul! Please don't go. Let's not leave it like this. Can we please talk?" I swipe at the tears on my face with trembling hands. "I can explain everything if you just let me—"

The door slams behind him right in my face.

My knees fall to the floor.

A sob takes over my body.

My chest clenches where my heart resides.

He let me go.

Twenty-Two

PAUL

M y knuckles knock on the door for a third time as I wait for the only person I want to see.

The door creaks open. "Paul, honey. What are you doing home?" my mom asks, her brows furrowed, confusion written all over her face.

Oh, I don't know. I've just been spending the past few days mulling over the fact that I'm going to be a father, and Sarah never bothered to tell me. And the worst part is, I'm not entirely sure she was ever planning on telling me.

"Just needed a change of scenery," I tell her as she opens the door wider for me to enter.

She watches me with skepticism in her eyes. "It's a Friday night, and my twenty-two-year-old son came home because he needed a change of scenery?" she asks. "Yeah, I'm not buying it." She heads toward the kitchen. "Did you eat?"

I hang my coat in the entryway closet, brushing the dusting of snow off my shoulders. "No."

"Go get comfortable in the TV room, and I'll throw together your favorite: chicken parmesan with spaghetti."

A small smile makes its way onto my face for the first time in days. I plop onto the sectional, stretching out my legs, and turn the TV on, scrolling through until I see a familiar title: *It*—one of Sarah's "comfort" movies.

God, what is wrong with that girl? I let out a low chuckle, running a hand over my face. However, something must be wrong with me, too, because I sit back and start watching one of the scariest movies I've ever seen.

Just as the big fucking scary-ass clown torments the kids in the haunted house, and I'm positive I'm going to have nightmares for the rest of my life, the delicious smell of my favorite meal steals my attention.

"Dinner is served!" my mom announces as she enters the room with two plates in her hands and sets them down on the giant accent table in front of me. Her eyes look to the TV screen as she sits beside me. "Interesting movie choice."

"I was just flipping through," I lie, turning it off.

"Mm-hmm…"

I don't hesitate before I shove a fork and knife into the chicken, taking a heaping bite. The familiar, savory flavors instantly put my overworked mind at ease.

Now, this is comfort food.

"You always know how to make me feel better," I mumble through the food in my mouth.

"That I do." She smooths a napkin over her lap. "I always told you the way to anyone's heart is through food, which stands true with my son."

We both eat in comfortable silence, but the second my fork lands on my empty plate, she clears her throat. "So, do you plan on telling me what's bothering you, or will I have to pry it out of you?"

I lean back on the sofa, letting out a frustrated sigh.

This isn't exactly an easy conversation to have with my mom.

"Is it something between you and Sarah?" she asks.

I look at her and nod. "You could say that."

"But when you two were here for Thanksgiving, I could have sworn I heard wedding bells ringing above you." She smiles, placing a comforting hand on my shoulder.

I shake my head. "I don't even know what to say."

"Well, why don't you start by telling me the overall problem."

I stare up at the ceiling. "She kept a secret from me."

A big fucking secret.

My mom nods. "Do you know why she kept the secret from you?"

That's the part that has been bothering me most.

Why didn't she tell me she was pregnant?

We could have been going through all of this together.

I could have been by her side these past few months with every doctor's appointment and buying her whatever she and the baby needed.

"Not a clue," I muse. "I thought we were close enough to tell each other...things. But she never told me, and I kind of found out by accident, and then it just makes me wonder if she ever planned on telling me." I sigh. "That's what I'm upset about. I only found out accidentally when she didn't want me to know."

My mom purses her lips. "Is this secret something you can forgive her for?"

I rub the back of my neck, squeezing my tense muscles. "I don't know. I'm trying to understand why she wouldn't tell me, but I just can't."

"Honey..." She places her hand on my shoulder. "I'm not saying whatever happened between you two is okay, but until you know why she did what she did, I don't think you should write her off just yet. I think there's more to the story. And I think you know that too." She pats my knee reassuringly. "You know I pride myself on being a good judge of character, so truthfully, I like her. I like her a lot. And I especially like her a lot for you."

"I like her a lot too," I admit.

"So, why don't you talk to her? Find out what's going on."

I rub my hand over the top of my head, my hair grazing the palm of my hand. "I don't know if she wants to talk to me. I kind of left in a hurry..."

My mom's eyes narrow at me. "Did I raise you to run from your problems?"

"No." I shake my head. "I think I was so hurt I didn't know what to do. I needed to get away to think." My eyes drift to the ceiling, lost in thought.

I've been so upset, mulling over that moment of anger in her apartment, that I haven't even had a chance to think about Greyson's phone I left with her.

I rub my temple. That's going to be a whole other damn problem to deal with. But Sarah, being pregnant with my baby, takes precedence.

"And what have you been thinking about?"

What have I been spending my time thinking about?

Easy.

I've been thinking about her emerald-green eyes that I want to gaze into for the rest of my life.

I've been thinking about how good she feels in my arms when she lets go of everything in her mind, giving herself entirely over to me for me to take care of.

I've been thinking about how I can be myself with her and how she makes me feel...normal.

I've been thinking about a future with her and our baby. One where they both wear a matching jersey with my last name on it, cheering for me at a game as I run up to them, taking them both in my arms, feeling the happiest I've ever felt in my life.

"About..." I hesitate before saying, "How she's the woman I'm going to marry." I look from the ceiling to my mom. "She's the woman I'm going to marry, Mom."

There's not a hint of doubt in my voice.

She's the one.

"Ahh," my mom muses. "Do you think that's why you were so hurt? Because you love her?" she asks, knowing the answer.

"Possibly," I murmur, hating that she's always right. I shake my head. "I should never have walked out on her."

Mom nudges my shoulder with her own. "So what are you going to do about it?"

I stare at the ceiling, racking my brain for an answer.

What am I going to do?

What does Sarah need me to do to prove I can be there for her and the baby?

I pinch the bridge of my nose, feeling ashamed of how I handled finding out she was pregnant. I want to think there was a valid reason why she didn't tell me, but there's no reason I can believe that would have kept me away from her.

If she had told me she was pregnant, I would have been there for her from day one.

I would have supported her with any and every decision.

But the moment I found out she was pregnant, I did the one thing she may never forgive me for.

I let her go.

I did what everyone else has always done to her.

As I flash back to the disaster I saw at Sarah's apartment, it occurs to me what I need to do to prove I'll always take care of her.

I eye the time on my phone, noting how late it is and knowing I can't do what I need to until Sarah leaves for work tomorrow.

"I think I know what to do, but it's kind of late now. Is it okay if I stay here tonight?" I ask.

"Well, that's a silly question when you have a bedroom here." My mom chuckles.

I stand, stretching, rubbing my full stomach. "I'm going to head to bed. Thanks for talking with me, Mom."

"Of course, honey." She stands, wrapping her arms around my waist quickly before letting go. She pats my chest encouragingly. "Do what you need to do to get your girl back."

I would move mountains and rivers or even set the whole damn world on fire if it meant I could get my girl back.

But I'm hopeful that assembling some baby furniture is a decent start to prove to her that I will always take care of her.

And I am never, ever leaving that stubborn raven-haired, green-eyed beauty again for as long as I live.

* * *

After waking up early and eating an all-you-can-eat breakfast buffet my mom insisted on making, I headed to the local improvement store before driving to Sarah's apartment.

I know she's not home. It's why I purposely chose to come at this time. But just in case, I knock on her door, thankful when she doesn't answer. My fingers reach above the doorframe, where I can see a spare key hiding from people who aren't my height, and I use it to unlock her door.

Walking inside, I'm immediately hit with an overwhelming sense of guilt.

Every piece of disassembled baby furniture is exactly where it was when I was last here, looking like Sarah gave it her all, but it was just too much for her to do by herself.

And I wish she knew she didn't have to do this alone.

I walk around, picking up the instruction manuals flung nearby and the flimsy tools they came with, knowing these only made things more difficult for her than they needed to be. They weren't setting her up for success at all.

Knowing her, it probably made her feel worse that she couldn't put these pieces together herself.

Sitting on her couch, I take in everything as the realization, for the first time, comes crashing down on me.

I was so consumed with the notion that she never told me about being pregnant that I didn't stop to think about what that actually meant...

I'm going to be a dad.

A swoosh of air exits my lungs as I lean back and process that sentence.

I'm. Going. To. Be. A. Dad.

The thudding of my heart echoes in my ears. My hand rests against my chest, where my heart pounds erratically.

But suddenly, a smile takes over my face.

A genuine goddamn smile.

"I'm going to be a dad," I whisper. The reality of the situation should alarm me. It should leave me an anxious, riddled mess. But all I feel is an overwhelming sweeping sensation of happiness from my toes to the top of my head.

Tilting my head up toward the ceiling, I close my eyes and speak words from my heart that I wish I could say to the man who made me who I am today: my dad. "I'm going to do my best to be just like you. To be the best dad, husband, and man. I will make you proud, Dad. I promise."

While wiping away the few tears that managed to escape, I spot the ugly gremlin on the side of the couch beside me, Teddy. Picking it up, I look it over carefully. The poor guy could use some love. Examining it in my hands, I come to the conclusion that throwing him in the wash is out of the question for fear that it might disintegrate. No, I'll leave this to the professionals.

My eyes wander around the apartment as I question what else, besides the baby furniture, Sarah needs help with but hasn't told me.

Getting up from the sofa, I walk into the kitchen, noting the bareness of the counters and shelves. Worry fills me as I open the fridge, finding it practically empty.

"The way to anyone's heart is through food."

My girl and my baby will never know hunger again.

I pull up my notes app on my phone and add "Groceries" as the first item on the to-do list, followed by "Assemble Nursery," "Take Teddy to the dry cleaners," and "Order books on how to take care of a baby."

While tucking my phone in my pocket, my eyes spot a pile of envelopes on the kitchen island, and I immediately gravitate toward it. I know I shouldn't open Sarah's mail. It's illegal and an invasion of her privacy, but the second I recognize the name of a nearby hospital as the return address, my stomach recoils, knowing what it is.

A bill.

Fuck it. I'm opening it.

Swiftly, I pull out the paper and scan the contents, observing the amount due at the bottom and knowing Sarah doesn't have that kind of money. Repeating my actions, I open the next envelope in my hands, knowing that, once again, it's another bill. Except this one is her past-due credit card statement. As my eyes scan over the credit card purchases of baby furniture and necessities, I sink to the counter stool beside me with the same question I've asked myself a hundred times, overpowering my thoughts.

Why didn't she tell me?

She knows I have money.

And knowing she's just scraping by, trying to afford everything for a baby...*our* baby, causes my heart to tighten painfully.

I rub at my chest, a significant ache filling me, knowing that she's been going through all of this alone.

Dropping the bill, I rest my elbows on the counter and hold the sides of my head, my fingers digging into my scalp. None of this makes any sense. But the fear that there might be a legitimate reason why she didn't tell me courses through me.

Without needing to think about it, I place all the bills on the counter, laying them out flat, while I reach for my phone and wallet. Within minutes, I have them all paid off, making me feel slightly better that she won't have to worry about these anymore.

She may be mad at me for doing this, but it doesn't bother me. Because she'll soon learn what it means to be taken care of by me.

212

Twenty-Three

SARAH

"That looks like a monkey's butt!"

Natalie and Vanessa bicker and tease each other like two best friends because that's exactly what they are.

I've never had an easy time making friends, seeing that I bounced around from house to house as a child, grew up used to doing things independently, and learned that I could only rely on myself.

But meeting Natalie was one of the best things that ever happened to me. I not only gained a friendship with her but with Vanessa as well, which is why I was so glad they invited me to go out with them to this *Wine and Paint Night*, even if that meant I would, unfortunately, need to skip the wine portion of the evening.

Let's just say I was in desperate need of a distraction, and I was thankful that these two could provide me with one.

My paintbrush strokes across the canvas as I mirror the sunset image the instructor created, intending for us to duplicate. Scenic images are my favorite to make, so I find myself getting lost in the colors and textures until I arrive at a point where I feel pleased with my work.

"Done!" I announce.

It's not one of the best pieces I've ever created, and I will blame the extra stress in my life for that. But as I tilt my head to the side, gazing at the image before me, I feel…happy. For at least a few seconds, which is more than I've felt since Paul left my apartment in a fury, never once looking back at me.

Immense shame washes over me.

"Sarah, that's beautiful!" Natalie gets up from her seat to stand before my canvas, her wide eyes moving over the image. "Where did you learn to paint like this?"

I shrug nonchalantly. "My mom taught me."

The mention of her causes a tiny ache in the center of my chest as a memory of her in a bright yellow paint-stained smock with the most beautiful smile on her face floats across my eyes.

"I'm surprised you don't do this professionally," Vanessa offers as she stands beside Natalie. "People would pay a lot of money for a beautiful painting like that."

I scoff, suddenly embarrassed by the attention. "Oh, I'm not that good."

My mom was a good artist.

No, my mom was the best artist I ever knew.

Natalie and Vanessa give each other a knowing look before Vanessa says, "You're wrong. You're very talented, and you should be proud of yourself."

I feel tears on the brink of spilling out, but I do everything I can to hold them inside. "Thanks, Vanessa." Glancing between Natalie and Vanessa's painting, I bite my bottom lip, stifling a laugh.

"Go ahead. Let it out," Vanessa suggests, throwing her hands in the air.

"I was just going to say I wish I could return the compliment." A bubble of laughter escapes me, causing my whole body to shake. Vanessa and Natalie's laughter joins mine, and pretty soon, that's the only noise heard in the place.

And fuck, it feels so unbelievably good to laugh.

"Refills, anyone?" A waitress approaches our table with a bottle of wine in her hands.

Vanessa and Natalie don't hesitate to say, "Yes, please."

I wipe the laughing tears from my eyes and lift my glass of sparkling water. "I'm all set."

"Sarah, the place is called *Wine and Paint Night*, not *Water and Paint Night*," Natalie teases.

"I know. Trust me, I wish I could join you guys, but it's just…" It's just that I'm pregnant and haven't been able to enjoy a glass of wine in months. It's straight-up torture, if you ask me. "I have to be up early again for work."

"Hey, don't worry," Vanessa remarks. "Natalie and I will drink enough for the three of us."

I force a small smile, averting eye contact, fearing they'll see right through my lie.

"Everything going okay at work?" Natalie asks, tilting her head. When my eyes meet hers, I'm suddenly afraid she can read my thoughts.

But she can't, right?

"Oh, yeah. Yeah. Everything is fine." I widen my smile, but who am I kidding? It's not fooling anyone.

"And you still like working for a bank?" Natalie asks.

"It's…umm…" My throat tightens at this question. Because no, I don't like working for a fucking bank. I don't like staring at a computer screen all day, advising people with a shit ton of money on how to invest it. And I most certainly don't enjoy being threatened and blackmailed by the boss's son. But I have no choice and need to remain working here, especially after Paul made his feelings clear on where he stands with me.

And with our baby.

He left.

"I opened up to you because I trusted you with everything, including my heart."

Oh fuck. My eyes begin watering, and there's not a damn thing I can do to stop them as both girls watch me, appearing concerned. "It pays the bills," I softly say, clearing my throat.

"Oh, Sarah." Vanessa wraps her arms around me. "What is it?"

"It's nothing," I answer, trying to brush off the subject. Without realizing it, my arms tighten around Vanessa. Clearly, my body is begging to be comforted even if my head isn't strong enough to admit it's what I need.

To not feel alone in all of this bullshit for just one day.

That's what I really need.

Vanessa pulls away just the slightest bit to look at me.

Taking a deep breath, I admit, "It's just some asshole at my office." I wipe the tears from my cheeks, hating that I appear weak in front of them. "Nothing I can't handle."

"Is there anyone in your office you can talk to about this?" she asks.

"It's a company filled with rich, old, powerful men. It's also the boss's son. They wouldn't care or do anything about it. I would quit, but...I really need the money right now."

And it's true. I would quit in a heartbeat if I didn't desperately rely on every paycheck to survive.

Vanessa hesitates, looking between me and Natalie. "I know you don't know him very well, but if you ever need help, I know Paul would take care of things for you. He's a really great guy. He'd give you the coat off his back on the coldest day of the year."

Sucker punched right in the gut.

That's the only way to describe how I feel at this very moment.

Clearing my throat, I shake my head. "No. I got this. Really. Please don't say anything to him." I reveal a smile, trying my hardest to appear okay. The last thing I need is for them to mention this moment to Paul.

"I won't," Vanessa confirms. "But if there is anything Natalie and I can do to help, you'll let us know, right?"

Oh, how I wish they could help me.

I nod as more tears begin to run down my face.

Damn hormones.

"I'm sorry. I don't know why I'm so emotional," I lie.

Vanessa wipes the tears from my face, throwing her arm around my shoulder. "It's Natalie's painting. It's so ugly it just makes you want to cry."

"Hey! At least mine doesn't look like a monkey's ass!"

"Touché," Vanessa replies.

Natalie's slender arms wrap around me. "We girls have to stick together."

"I'm seriously so glad I met you guys." My voice comes out small as I try to rein in my sobs. God, how pathetic am I? "I don't know what I would do without you."

Natalie squeezes my hand as the three of us share a moment I'll never forget.

* * *

Feeling completely worn out, I lean against the elevator wall, my whole body ready to soak in a warm bubble bath.

Spending a girls' night with Natalie and Vanessa after a long day at work was exactly what I needed, but it was also draining. And I have sore feet and an aching back to prove it.

Rubbing my temple as a headache forms, I close my eyes, picturing the one person I wish I could see.

Paul.

It's been days since I've seen or heard from him. And the thought of never seeing him again is scaring the fuck out of me.

But it wouldn't surprise me if he left for good.

Everyone always leaves.

Not to mention, I deserve it this time.

I kept one of the biggest secrets of my life from him—one that will impact his life significantly. That is if he decides to be a part of our baby's life.

But I'm guessing from how he left and hasn't returned that that was his answer.

And it's okay. I'll figure everything out, just like I have been doing since I was nine.

One damn day at a time.

Alone.

The metal doors slide open, and I head down the hall directly toward my apartment door, searching my bag for my key.

Emotions grip me at the thought of opening this door and having to stare at the disassembled baby furniture for another night.

All I want to do is cry, but I think I'm even too tired to do that.

I pop the door open, stepping inside, just as my stomach rumbles.

I know, pretty baby. My hand rubs my stomach. *As soon as I take a bath, I'll make us something to eat, and then—*

My bag drops to the floor.

Where is all the half-assed assembled baby furniture?

My eyes fly to the lock on my door, but it doesn't appear damaged, as though someone broke in.

Glancing around, I notice everything else appears where it belongs—nothing except the baby furniture is missing.

Did some asshole come in here just to steal my baby's furniture? What the actual fu—

"Ow!"

A loud groan comes from the spare room, aka the baby's future nursery, causing my eyes to widen in alarm as my heart rate accelerates. My hand reaches into my purse on the floor for my bottle of pepper spray. I slowly flick the cap and quietly walk toward the room, tiptoeing one step at a time. I hear shuffling and movement coming from the other side of the door, and my heart pounds so loud beneath my chest that I can barely hear anything else.

Maybe I should call the police...

"Fuck yeah! I did it!"

I freeze in front of the door. *Did what?*

The door is cracked open only an inch, hiding the man from my view. My shaking palm lightly pushes the door open as I take a deep breath.

One... Two... Three!

"You messed with the wrong crazy bitch motherfucker!" I scream, jumping inside the room, holding the pepper spray in front of me with my thumb hovering over the switch as I aim at...

Paul?

"Holy shit, Sarah!" Paul presses his hand to his chest, startled.

"Paul?" I blink a few times. "What are you..." My throat goes parched as my eyes take in the room. Every piece of baby furniture is assembled. Every screw is fastened. Every bolt is tightened. And every damn knob is precisely where it belongs. Confusion fills me as I take in the completed nursery, my mouth agape. "Why did you do this?"

My eyes drift to Paul, meeting his. And I notice hurt flash across his chocolate brown eyes.

"Well..." He tugs on the silver chain around his neck. "I guess I can understand why you would ask me that, seeing how I left things with you the last time I was here."

I tuck the pepper spray in my back pocket. "Yeah. I, umm, didn't think I was going to be seeing you again," I voice steadily, trying to appear strong when I'm ready to crumble inside.

He shakes his head. "You know I'm not that kind of person. I just needed to think about things. I needed to cool down." His eyes narrow the slightest bit. "It's not like I was given a heads-up about this."

I look down at the floor, guilt eating away at me.

"I know." I wrap my arms around myself.

"Do you think we can talk?" Paul asks quietly.

I nod, staring at the plush beige carpet.

"Sarah?"

I shake my head.

"Look at me."

A tear escapes, cascading down my cheek.

"I can't," I whisper.

He takes a couple of steps until he's standing directly in front of me, his shoes coming into my line of sight. Two of his fingers slide under my chin, lifting my face so I have no choice but to meet his eyes with my own.

"Talk to me."

I swallow hard, closing my eyes. "I thought you left," I admit in a whisper. "Like everyone else."

"Sarah…" His thumb caresses my skin. "I'm not going anywhere. And I'm sorry that I made you think that I was. But I'm here and I'm always going to be here."

I nod, opening my eyes, feeling tears spill down my face.

"You don't believe me, do you?" he asks.

I shake my head. "I watched you leave, and I didn't think I'd ever see you—"

His lips press against my temple. "I'll spend every day proving to you that I'm not going anywhere. You're stuck with me, Sarah. Whether you like it or not, you're stuck with me."

I let out a shaky sigh. "Being stuck with you sounds pretty nice."

"Yeah?" He wraps his arms around me, pulling me against his body. My eyes close as my head rests against his chest, and I melt into him, cherishing his embrace.

And it feels…perfect.

"I can't believe you put everything together." My eyelids flutter open as I turn my head to the side, focusing on the baby crib, perfectly standing against the side of the room. The changing table appears assembled beside the far wall, and the matching rocking chair sits in the corner of the room with...

I step away, tilting my head to the side. "Is that Teddy?"

Paul strides toward the chair, picking up the unrecognizable teddy bear. "I took Teddy to the dry cleaners. They cleaned his fur, sewed his eye back on, and gave him a new pink bow." He hands him over to me. "What do you think?"

I clutch the bear to my chest, sobbing like a baby. "He...looks...perfect."

He took my ratty old teddy bear to the dry cleaners.

He did that for me.

"Don't cry, baby girl." His fingers slide against my cheek, his knuckles running against my jawline. "I'm here."

"I can't help it. Everything makes me cry now because my hormones are all over the place, and I hate it so much," I confess. "I saw one of those ASPCA commercials the other day. The one with the Sarah McLachlan song, and I cried for almost two hours straight."

Paul rolls in his bottom lip, stifling a laugh.

I swat at his chest. "It's not funny!"

He clears his throat, shaking his head, trying to appear serious. "Definitely not funny."

I purse my lips, considering, and take a step away to place Teddy on the changing table. "I guess it's a little funny."

His lips curve up the tiniest bit as he bundles his arm around my waist and pulls me into him.

I clasp my arms around him, gripping his shirt in my fingers. "I'm so sorry. I should have told you everything. I shouldn't have lied to you. I was just so scared. I didn't know what to do. I didn't want to—"

"Breathe, Sarah." He rubs my back. "Just breathe. Everything will be okay."

No, it won't. Not until I tell him about Greyson.

"Paul, I...I want...no, I need to tell you everything."

His hand runs over the back of my head and down my spine in a soothing, gentle motion. "Have you eaten tonight?"

I shake my head.

"Why don't we order some delivery, and then you can tell me everything?" His cheek rests on the top of my head as his arms wrap tighter around me, making me feel safe, protected, and...loved.

"Okay." I let out a deep breath. "But can we stand like this for one more minute?"

He kisses the top of my head. "Of course."

After a few minutes, I slowly unwrap myself from around him and look up into his eyes. "I'm ready."

He takes my hand and leads me to the living room, but as we walk out the door, I take one last look over my shoulder at the room that, thanks to Paul, now looks like an actual nursery.

Seeing everything put together makes this all feel more real.

"What are you in the mood for?" Paul plops down on the sofa, pulling me down beside him. He pulls up his phone, scrolling through his food delivery app. "There's Chinese, pizza, Mexican—"

"Mexican!" I exclaim.

"Mexican it is, then." He presses a few buttons and then places his phone beside him. "It'll be here soon."

"How did you even know what I wanted?"

He smirks. "I didn't, so I ordered a bit of everything."

"A man who buys his woman food is a good man," I tease.

"His woman, huh?"

I shake my head. "I'm sorry, I didn't mean to insinuate—"

He presses his lips to mine, instantly shutting me up as his hand cups the back of my neck, pushing me into him.

God, this man can kiss.

He pulls away, resting his forehead on mine. "You're mine, Sarah Fleur. Don't ever forget that."

I smile at his words. No one's ever claimed me before. I'm all for feminism, but damn, hearing those words come out of his mouth just ignited a spark in the center of my core.

"Tell me I'm yours," he whispers against my lips.

I playfully brush my lips against his. "You're mine, Paul Weston."

Thirty minutes later, Paul greets the delivery guy at the door while I change into an oversized T-shirt. When I come out of my room, I see bags and bags of food.

"Paul, what did you do?" I laugh, holding my hand over my mouth.

He shrugs. "I just wanted to make sure you and our baby have a good meal."

Our baby.

My eyes water, but I blink a few times to stop them.

He brings all the food to the coffee table, and I get comfortable on the couch, gliding a blanket over my legs. I reach for a piece of a quesadilla and take an unladylike bite.

"Mmm. This is so good," I mumble through a mouthful of food.

He smiles. "You might want to wash that down with something." He spins around, walking into the kitchen.

Shit. I never went grocery shopping today. Not that I would be able to afford much...

"I'm sorry." I quickly get up, following him. "I never went grocery shopping. I'm afraid there's nothing in the fridge. I can only offer you tap water."

"I went grocery shopping," he says casually.

I pause mid-step. "You did?"

"Yeah. I noticed you had nothing in your fridge or cabinets, so I went to the store and got some essentials."

I open the fridge to look inside, and my mouth falls open. "You stocked my fridge."

"Well, I wasn't sure—"

My arms enclose around him tightly. "Thank you."

His arms wrap around me. "You're welcome."

I peek into the open fridge beside us and spot a bottle of whipped cream. "Paul?"

"Mm-hmm?"

"Does whipped cream count as an essential item?"

"When it comes to you and me, yes, it absolutely does."

We both laugh as he grabs me a sparkling water from the fridge and then clutches my hand to lead me back into the living room, but I stop when I notice my Mt. Everest pile of bills on the center of the island is missing.

"Paul, did you move my bills?"

"No." He shakes his head. "I took care of them and then threw them out."

My mouth opens wide. "Come again?"

"I took care of your bills." He shrugs and then sits on the couch.

"You...you can't just go around paying people's bills. Those were my bills. I was going to...eventually pay them. Someday," I add, trying to sound pissed about this when really, all I feel is relief as an invisible weight lifts from my shoulders.

"And now you don't have to."

"I don't understand." I shake my head, taking a few steps until I stand between his legs. "Why?"

His hand gently grips my wrist, pulling me onto his lap. "Why would I take care of bills pertaining to you and our baby? It seems kind of obvious to me."

I shake my head. "I'm just not used to this."

"Used to what?"

"Being taken care of," I whisper. "It's a lot to wrap my head around."

He ghosts his lips over my ear, sending a chill down my spine. "I'm always going to take care of you and our baby, whether financially, mentally, or physically, so I suggest you get used to it."

"I'll try," I murmur, picking up another piece of a quesadilla.

After eating all the food I can fit in my stomach, I curl up against the couch, facing Paul.

He leans back, placing his arm on the back of the couch, and, with his other hand, pats the top of his thighs. "Let me see your feet."

I cock my brow. "You got some weird foot fetish I don't know about?"

He chuckles, shaking his head. "Give me your damn feet, woman."

I stretch my legs out, placing my feet on his lap as he reaches for one of them. The moment his thumbs dig into the sole of my foot, I can't help but moan out in pleasure.

"Oh my God." I tilt my head back. "This is amazing. Can you do this every night?" I ask, completely teasing.

"How about I let you choose every night how I'll make you moan? Deal?" He grins with a wink, sending a blush over my cheeks.

"Deal," I breathe.

We sit like this for a few minutes in silence as he continues massaging my feet. It feels very domestic and natural. But above all, it feels right.

When he finishes, I pull my feet back, tucking my knees against my chest.

Paul's fingers reach out, tenderly brushing against the hem of my shirt. "So, are you ready to tell me why you kept your pregnancy a secret from me?"

I swallow the lump in my throat, anxiety trying to strangle me from the inside out.

"You promise you won't be mad?" I ask timidly.

"I won't be mad."

"And...you won't leave?" I whisper.

His hand stills. "I'm not leaving, baby girl. Not today, not tomorrow, and not ever."

I nod, glancing down at my hands on my lap. "Greyson Black."

Paul's body tenses. "What about Greyson Black?"

"He's the reason I couldn't tell you," I breathe, pinching my eyes shut for only a moment.

"I don't understand…"

I clear my throat, my eyes watering. "Growing up in foster care, moving from house to house, made it difficult for me to make friends. Actually…it was impossible for me to make friends." I rest my cheek against the back of the couch. "So, when I started my freshman year at Linrey University, I thought it was my chance to try. And I did that by going to parties." I close my eyes and take a deep breath, hating how much I remember every part of the night that has haunted me for years. "One party in particular was at the Kappa Alpha house. A couple of girls who I recognized from classes were there, and they called me over to sit with them. We were laughing and drinking, and it just felt so good."

I'm still too nervous to make eye contact with Paul, so I tell my story to the side of his shirt, where my fingers clutch onto the fabric.

"A group of guys came over. And one of them was Greyson. He had his eyes on me the whole night, making me feel so…special." I internally cringe. "When he asked me to go upstairs with him…" I shake my head, so ashamed of myself. "I was drunk, and I didn't say no when I should have because I didn't want those girls to think less of me. To think I was some pathetic loser. And I thought I would impress them if I went upstairs with him, so I did. I took his hand and let him lead me up the stairs to his room."

Paul's fingers swipe across my cheek, wiping away a single tear. He places his hand on top of mine, squeezing it for encouragement.

Reminding me he's here and he's not going anywhere.

"Nothing about that night felt right. I should have turned around. I should have run. But when we entered his room, he shut the door behind us, and I felt trapped. I was naïve thinking that maybe we would just talk or…do other things, but he didn't waste any time getting what he wanted." Paul's body turns into me as he pulls my body against him. "When I woke up the next morning alone in his bed, I didn't remember much of what happened. I was naked with bruises all over my body. I couldn't think straight, so I just grabbed my clothes and got out of that house as fast as I could, feeling so stupid and used. I told myself I would forget that night like it had never happened. But later that day, I got a text from an unknown number. It was…a video…of me and Greyson."

This time, I can't fight the sob that overtakes me. I press my face into Paul's side, hiding it. His hand finds my back, rubbing slowly in a gentle circular motion.

"He sent a text that said, 'I own you.' I was so scared, but there was nothing I could do. No one I could go to for help. So, I spent the next couple of years trying everything I could to stay out of his sight. And as evident from the panic attack I had while running out of your room, I never stayed over at any man's house for fear the same thing would happen again. I…never slept with anyone after Greyson until you."

Suddenly, a thick blanket wraps around my shoulders, cocooning me in warmth. A shiver wracks through me as I continue.

"That night at the bar, on my twenty-first birthday, I think everything just hit me really hard. I couldn't stop thinking about my parents or Greyson; all I wanted was a distraction. Just one night where I felt in control of my life again," I say softly. "Four weeks later, I found out I was pregnant. But I had no idea who you were, and I know that was my fault."

"Sarah—"

"No, it's okay. I was the one insistent on not exchanging names." I shake my head. "I met you at Natalie and Vanessa's a week later when you tried acting all smooth." My lips curve up at the memory, and Paul's arm tightens around me. "Anyway, when I started my internship at LH United, I found out that Greyson is my boss's son. And well, he…" My voice cracks when I say, "He made it perfectly clear that he's still holding the video over my head to do with whatever he chooses." My hand reaches for my neck, absently running my fingers along my skin.

Paul tenses. "Did he hurt you?"

I subtly nod, closing my eyes, tears dropping from my lashes.

"I'm going to kill him," Paul grits out, his chest heaving. "I'm going to fucking kill him."

I swallow hard, sniffling, trying to calm my racing heart. "I had planned on telling you everything. I swear I did. After you invited me to that game, I thought I would tell you over dinner. I hoped we would figure everything out together. And I optimistically thought that maybe I wouldn't have to go through all this alone anymore. But while I was waiting for you outside the locker room, Greyson found me. And he told me that I needed to stay away from you or...he was going to release the video, and he was going to make it look like it was you who released it. He said it would ruin your career in the NBA. It would ruin your life." I bite my bottom, trembling lip. "He told me that you took something from him, so he was taking something from you. I have no idea what he was referring to, but he was so mad, Paul. There was nothing but fury in his eyes, which scared me so much."

Finally, I look up into Paul's eyes. "I'm so sorry, Paul. I didn't know what to do. And I couldn't risk it. I couldn't risk him destroying your career because of me. And I tried so hard to stay away from you in fear of what Greyson would do, but eventually, I couldn't fight it anymore, and I was trying to figure out how to fix everything. I was working on a plan, and I thought I could finally tell you I was pregnant once I got the video erased, but I never planned on you finding out the way you did. Everything just became too much for me and..."

A violent sob escapes me, overwhelmed at the feeling of finally telling him everything.

Absolutely everything.

Paul's hand rubs up and down my back, but he doesn't say anything until...

Twenty-Four

PAUL

"He filmed you without your knowledge?"

She nods against my shirt.

"And then blackmailed you?"

She nods again.

"Which is why you asked Glen to hack into his devices?"

"Yes. I'm so—"

My arms wrap around her tightly, moving her body so she's straddling my legs while my hand cups the back of her head. She buries her face into the crook of my neck, trembling, and I feel like I might do something that I'll regret.

Something like killing Greyson Black with my bare hands this very instant.

"I need to hold you, Sarah, or I'm going to get up and go kill that motherfucker."

She holds me tighter, gripping the back of my shirt.

"Please don't leave me," she whispers.

"I'm never leaving you." My lips press against her temple over and over again. "I'm so fucking sorry."

"You didn't know."

"I don't care. The moment I knew you were pregnant, I should never have walked out. I should never have left you and will never do that again."

A beat of silence passes before she asks, "What are we going to do?"

We.

It's about damn time she realizes she doesn't have to do this alone anymore.

"Well, now that I know the full story, I think I know who we can contact for help." I let out a frustrated sigh. One I had been holding in for far too long. "I can hack into computers, but just simple things. Nothing fancy. I was a bit of a loner when I was a kid and preferred to spend my time with my computer instead of people."

She looks up at me, her brows furrowing.

"I didn't mention it to you because you freaked out when you saw my computer setup in my room," I offer.

She looks down. "I should have told you everything sooner."

"You didn't know, baby girl." I push back a few pieces of hair behind her ear. "The problem is, I don't think I'm going to be able to break into Greyson's computer without help. I tried to get into his phone before I came here the other day, but even that was impossible to break into, and usually, it's a simple process."

Her worried eyes widen.

"It's okay, though. My brother, Ray, can help us. He'll take care of this for us."

"How do you know he'll be able to?"

I scrape a hand against my stubble. "I can't really talk about his job, but all I can say is he works for the government, and hacking into someone's devices to delete a video is probably one of the easiest things he'll ever do."

I also don't actually know my brother's job title or the specific details of what the hell he does for the government, but from the size of his house, I'd say it's pretty lucrative.

She freezes in my hands. "But...does that mean...he'll have to watch it?" A red tint spreads from her cheeks to her neck.

"He won't watch it. He'll know what it is as soon as he finds the video and will take care of it." She anxiously chews her bottom lip. "I trust him with my life. And if there were even a doubt in my mind he would watch it, I wouldn't ask him to help us."

"Okay," she says softly.

"Besides, no one gets to see this body but me." My hands slide over her waist. Feeling her in my grip, beneath my touch, is helping to simmer the rage within me, knowing that Greyson has a fucking sex tape of her that she didn't consent to... *Deep breath. Deep fucking breath.* "I will never let that video get released. Do you understand?"

She doesn't hesitate when she says, "I do."

I do. It has a nice ring to it.

I look at the time on my phone, knowing it's too late to call Ray. He's probably sound asleep in his recliner, snoring away as a basketball game plays in the background on his TV. "I'll contact my brother first thing in the morning to see what we need to do. I don't want that video on Greyson's devices any longer. He probably already got a new phone, but he'll likely have all his files saved on the cloud or a hard drive."

She looks down, disappointment evident in her features. "I thought if I got his phone, I would be that much closer to getting rid of the video. I didn't think of the possibility that it would be stored everywhere."

A single tear slides down her porcelain cheek as she leans away, reaching inside her coffee table drawer to pull out Greyson's phone. She holds it before her, waiting for me to take it.

"I will take care of this, Sarah. You won't need to worry about this for much longer. I promise."

I brush the tear away, studying her carefully.

I can't even wrap my head around everything she's been through, and my heart aches for her.

"So...I know I just threw a lot at you," she says. "But there's one thing I need to make clear." She sits up, looking me dead in the eye, clearing her throat before she continues. "When I found out I was pregnant, I didn't know what to do. I wasn't even sure I was going to keep the baby because I was scared I wouldn't be able to do this alone. But when I thought about my childhood, going from house to house, I realized I could never live with myself if I put my child through that, too." She shakes her head. "I want this child. I want to be a mom and love this baby the way they deserve to be loved." A small smile forms on her face until it abruptly falls. "But I don't want you to feel trapped. I know you're going into the NBA next year, and I don't want to ruin your dreams. So, if you don't want to be a part of this, I understand and am ready to do this myself."

I can't help the instantaneous laugh that rumbles in my chest and bursts from between my lips.

She smacks my shoulder, appearing mildly irritated. "What's so funny?"

"You," I manage to say. "Sarah, why the hell would you think I'm leaving you or the baby?"

"I just wanted to give you a way out if—"

"I don't want a way out."

"You don't?"

"No." I run my hands up and down her back. "I want to be a part of your and the baby's life if you let me. I want to be at every doctor's appointment and every baby class. I want to rub your feet and buy you whatever weird food cravings you have. I want to hold your hand in the delivery room, cheering you on. I want to be the one who wakes up in the middle of the night to feed the baby so you can sleep. I want a life with both of you. I don't want it to be a part-time job when I'm fully ready for this. I'm all in."

She purses her lips, tears pouring out of her eyes.

"You've spent almost your entire life taking care of yourself, but now it's my turn to take care of you." I brush my lips across hers. "Let me take care of you, Sarah."

She hesitantly nods.

My lips press against hers slowly, savoring the warmth and taste of her, never wanting it to end.

But she slowly pulls back. "So we're really doing this? We're having a baby...together?"

"Looks like it." I look down at her stomach. "Can I?"

A gentle, breathtaking smile appears on her face.

I slide my hand under her shirt, placing it on her bare stomach, noting the small bump. Something I would never have noticed previously. "Have you felt any kicks yet?"

She shakes her head. "Not yet. But the doctor said I'll probably start feeling something in a few weeks." She places her hand over mine. "I thought I would be showing a lot more than I am, but the doctor assured me that sometimes, with your first one, you don't start showing until sixteen to twenty weeks. So I guess this is just the beginning."

"I never even noticed," I murmur, moving my hand to her thigh. "When is your next appointment?"

She reaches for her phone on the coffee table. Looking at her screen, she says, "I have a follow-up appointment in a few days, and then I have the next ultrasound appointment on New Year's Day for the twenty-week appointment to find out the baby's sex and to make sure the baby is developing as expected."

"I'll be there for both of them," I confirm.

Her smile widens, becoming brighter and more beautiful than anything I've ever seen.

I rest my head against the back of the couch, my fingers still holding her securely to me. "There are a few things I think we should discuss."

"Like what?"

My eyes hold hers. "Like how I don't like the fact that you're living alone while pregnant or with an asshole like Greyson out there."

Her shoulders drop. "There's nothing I can do about that, though."

My hand reaches her face, and I trace her jawline back and forth. "How would you feel if I moved in with you?"

Her eyes widen slightly, but they don't look disturbed by the idea. Maybe a bit intrigued.

"I don't want anything to happen to you," I start. "If there's any reason you need to get to a hospital, I want to make sure I'm here so I can get you there as fast as possible. And if Greyson has any fucked-up plans about coming here, I want to make sure I'm here to beat the ever-living shit out of him."

A content sigh leaves her lungs. "I think it would make me feel safer having you here. So, yes. I think you should move in."

"Good." I kiss her temple, reach for my wallet in my pocket, and then take out one of my credit cards. "This is for you."

She stares at my credit card before moving away from it, like it has an infectious disease, but my hold keeps her in place. "You're having our baby. Which means if you're hungry, you order food. If you're cold, you buy a new coat. If you're feeling run-down, schedule a massage. If you're not sleeping well, buy the most expensive mattress you can find. And baby girl, if you ever feel like replacing that tin can on wheels, be my guest because there's no limit on this card... This is for whatever you need. Are we clear?"

Her lips press together in a thin line, but she reluctantly nods. "I don't want you thinking I did this on purpose to trap you or something. I'm not a gold digger. I've taken care of myself for as long as I can remember, and usually, I can keep up with everything, but with the baby, things have become pretty tight."

She appears ashamed of herself when she has no reason to be.

I brush her hair back from her face. "I would never think that, baby girl. I was there with you that night. I remember quite well how good it felt when your soft hands rolled the condom on my cock."

She blushes, shaking her head.

"Now, about Greyson." I pinch the bridge of my nose. "I don't want to incentivize him to release the tape. So, until my brother takes care of it, we have to be careful about being seen in public together."

"Yeah. I understand."

"But I don't think you should continue to work at the bank either."

She shakes her head. "I don't have a choice. I need to finish my internship with LH United, or I'll lose my credits. I'm already taking extra classes to graduate before the baby is born. I need these credits." She restlessly twirls a piece of her hair. "I was hoping they'd offer me a job at the end of the internship, but I guess that's out of the question now." She blows out a whoosh of air. "I'll need to start looking for another job soon."

I tip her chin up. "How much longer do you have for the internship?"

"Just one week. Only two more shifts."

I nod. At least I know that we have a good amount of away games this upcoming week, which means less of a chance for Greyson to be at the office while she's working. "I would never tell you what to do, but after your internship, I don't want you anywhere near that bank again."

She scrunches her face, focusing on the front of my shirt. "It will be hard to find a job when I'm pregnant. No one will hire me."

"Then don't work."

She lets out a humorless laugh. "Good joke."

"I'm not joking."

"I have bills to pay and things to buy for the baby."

"Sarah, I have more money than I know what to do with. Let me take care of things financially right now, and after you have the baby, if you want, and only if you want, you can look for a job if that'll make you happy."

She rolls her lips from side to side, debating something inside her head—something she wants to say but doesn't know if she should.

"What's going on inside that head?" I ask.

"I want to paint," she blurts out.

"Then paint."

"I mean like as a job."

"I know what you mean." I grin in amusement.

"Do you...do you think I can do it?" she nervously asks.

"I do. And I think if that's what you want to do, then go for it. Listen to your heart." I press my hand against her chest, over her heart. "And do what makes you happy. Do whatever it is that brings the light back into your eyes."

She smiles, grinning from ear to ear. "Okay. I'm going to do it. Or at least try to."

"That's my girl!" I encourage.

She chuckles and then yawns, her eyes drooping. This has been one long hell of a day for the both of us, and I think it's time to bring it to an end.

"Let's get to bed, baby girl."

Without waiting for a response, I lift her in my arms and carry her to her room, or, I guess, our room now. Laying her down, I reach for the blankets and bring them up to her chest before I get in beside her, pulling her small body right up against me.

I think she's fallen asleep until I hear her soft voice.

"Paul?"

"Yeah?"

"Did you mean it when you said the night you met me was the best night of your life?"

I smile, kissing the top of her head. "I did." My hand brushes down her back as she curls into me. "Go to sleep, Sarah. You're safe now. I will never let anyone hurt you again."

Gazing down at the woman in my arms who stole my heart, I think about how one night completely changed my life in more ways than I can ever thank her for.

The night that I will always remember as the *best night of my life.*

SARAH'S 21ST BIRTHDAY

Goddamn, those eyes.

Those beautiful, vibrant green eyes.

I can't stop gazing into them. They're the most brilliant shade of green I've ever seen. Big too. Making her appear like a damn Disney Princess.

She has me hypnotized to the point where I can't even remember why I came here tonight.

Oh, that's right, because Glen dragged my ass here with some of the guys from the team.

Guess I'll have to thank him later.

My eyes travel down her body where my hand rests on her hip. She leans into me, her hand relaxing against my chest, her long, black nails curling into my shirt.

"Make me forget," she whispers, her eyes pleading with me to take her away from here.

She's itching to get out of here.

And so am I.

"Your place or mine?" I ask, bending down to brush my lips across the shell of her ear.

She peeks up at me under those thick lashes. "Neither."

My brows furrow. "Then where would you like to go, birthday girl?"

She glances around, her breathing increasing.

"Hey." I cup her cheek, my thumb gliding against her soft skin. "If you've changed your mind, it's not a big deal. We can sit here and—"

"No." She pushes her long, dark hair over her shoulder. "I was just thinking, maybe we could get a room upstairs."

I smirk. "You in a hurry?"

She nods, rising on her tiptoes. "You have no idea."

Her soft lips ghost over mine, giving me a tiny taste of what's to come, igniting an inferno within me.

"Let's get out of here." I straighten, leave a bill on the counter to cover the drinks, take her hand in mine, and lead us directly to the lobby. "One room," I request, quickly placing my card on the counter for the man standing behind it. He takes it and types on his computer before suddenly freezing. His eyes widen, recognition crossing his face from the name on my credit card.

Fuck.

"Hey, you're—"

"We're in a bit of a hurry." I hold the girl's hand, keeping her against my side. She has no idea who I am, and I intend to keep it that way.

The man nods, thankfully taking my hint, then tells us our room number, dropping a key card in my hand.

Walking into the room, we both look around. It's nothing special. There's a bed, a bathroom, and a TV.

I find myself wishing I had taken her somewhere nicer for her birthday.

"Well, it's not the Taj Mahal, but I like it." She shrugs and walks up to the wall-sized window overlooking the city. "Wow," she admires. "Okay, I really like it."

The moon outlines her features in a subtle glow.

She's the epitome of beauty.

And she's mine. For tonight, anyway.

I snake my arm around her waist, and my large hand splays out over her stomach, holding her flush to my chest. She molds into my body like she was made for me. And me alone.

"What do you say we make this a birthday you never forget?" I ask.

"I like the way you think, big guy."

I smirk at the nickname. "Oh, baby girl, just wait until you see how big I am." My lips glide over her shoulder, sending shivers down her spine.

"Promises. Promises," she whispers, tilting her head over her shoulder.

Our eyes connect, neither of us looking away.

The electricity pulses in the air between us.

I want her so fucking badly, I can't wait another second.

So I don't.

My lips crash with hers in a hungry, ravenous kiss.

She lets out a whimper that goes straight to my cock like a bolt of lightning. Her body begins shifting around to face me, but I stop her, placing my hands firmly on her hips.

"Hands on the window."

Her breath catches as she looks at me with those damn big eyes, but then quickly obeys my demand.

I grip her hips to pull her into me and press my hard cock against her ass, which she wiggles beside impatiently.

"Patience." I let my hand travel down her stomach. "I need to get you ready for me first."

My fingers pop the button of her jeans and slowly glide down the zipper. I hear her breathing pick up, anticipation building between us.

God, I need this tonight.

I need her.

"Just remember, if you want me to stop, say the word. Okay?"

She nods, pushing her ass against me. "Keep going."

My fingers loop in the belt rings before I slide her pants down over her luscious curves, letting them rest against her thighs.

I let out a breath, admiring the ass in front of me in nothing but a black lace thong. "This ass is sinful." My hand skims over her skin, squeezing before I bring it to her front, cupping her pussy. The thin piece of lace is the only barrier between us.

My fingers trace her center back and forth, noting the damp fabric. "Wet already." I push the fabric aside, swirling one finger above her entrance. "Let's see how much wetter I can make you." In one go, I thrust knuckles deep inside her.

The prettiest moan fills the room as I slide in and out of her, prepping her carefully.

I wasn't lying about how big I am.

And I definitely don't want to hurt her.

"More," she breathes, her breath fogging the glass.

I shove two fingers inside her, feeling her core clench with desire. My thumb gently rubs circles over her clit, round and round, as I watch and listen to what she needs.

"Oh my God... Just like... Right there." Her pussy grinds relentlessly onto my hand. "I'm so...so..." She lets out a scream as she comes apart on my fingers, panting rapidly. Her trembling body eases into my hold, her hands gripping my forearms for support. She turns her head over her shoulder, bites her bottom lip, and says, "If that's what you can do with just your fingers, then I'm dying to see what you can do with your cock."

God, this girl has a mouth. And I love it.

I press soft kisses across her jawline, enjoying the whimpers she produces with each one. "And how does the birthday girl want my cock?" My hand travels up her stomach and under her shirt, where my index finger circles her belly button. "Slow and gentle? Or fast and hard?"

"Fast and hard." Her voice comes out breathy.

"Your wish is my command." I spin her around to face me and drop to my knees, my face almost level with her breasts. My fingers grip her pants and underwear, sliding them to the ground. She carefully steps out of them and then brazenly removes her top and bra, standing before me in nothing but her birthday suit.

My eyes graze over every inch of her gorgeous body, unable to get my fill of her. And then I notice them. All the floral tattoos covering her arms and thighs. *She's a fucking work of art.* "You're exquisite," I whisper, tenderly kissing her porcelain skin repeatedly.

And even in the dark, with the moon as our only light source, I can just make out the faint shade of pink covering her cheeks.

"Thank you." Her soft voice fills me with yearning. A need to satisfy this woman overtakes me.

Standing before her, I play with a soft piece of raven-black hair cascading down her chest.

"This is by far the best birthday I've ever had," she admits. Her hands press into my chest, running down my torso until she gets to the hem of my shirt, lifting it for me to remove. As I toss my shirt to the floor, her eyes widen, and her head tilts to the side as she takes me in. "Someone works out."

I chuckle. Little does she know that's pretty much all I do. Well, that and gaming, but she doesn't need to know about that. Don't want her knowing the truth about me, which is I'm a certified nerd.

Yeah, we definitely don't want her to know that.

"I think you forgot something," I note, stepping back to give her space. She smirks, dropping down to her knees. The sight alone is enough to make me come, but I fill my head with thoughts of smelly locker rooms, old gym socks, and broccoli to keep it together.

Her hand flattens against the rather large bulge in my pants, rubbing her palm from top to bottom, causing me to groan as pleasure takes over.

There's a desperate need to be inside this woman like I've never felt before.

"Stop teasing me." My fingers comb through her hair, brushing it out of her face. My hand reaches into my back pocket for my wallet, pulling out the condom.

She unbuttons and then unzips my pants, sliding them down my long legs, leaving me in only my underwear. The state of my erection does not go unnoticed as she comes face to face with it. The only thing separating me from her lips is a measly piece of fabric. Her fingers loop under the waistband, slowly sliding down my briefs.

"Well, shit. Looks like you weren't lying," she breathes, shaking her head. "There's no way that's going to fit."

I laugh, taking the final step out of my underwear. Her eyes look up at me with a mixture of yearning and lust. Giving her the condom, I watch as she first strokes my entire length in a firm grip before rolling the latex on. My thumb floats over her bottom lip. "We'll make it fit, baby girl."

She stands in front of me. "Promise?"

I fill the space between us, pressing her body against the glass. "Promise."

Our mouths collide as we devour the hell out of each other.

She wraps her hands around my neck, pulling me in as she nips on my bottom lip hard.

A groan leaves me as I lift her in my arms, pushing her against the window. If I thought anyone could see inside, I would have the curtains closed and her beautiful naked body in the bed with me. But as it is, we're so high up with no lights on that I'm certain no one can see her.

Her legs wrap around my torso, the heels of her feet digging into my ass.

Reaching between us, I position my cock at her entrance, swiping it through her wet center.

"Please," she begs, deliciously scratching her nails across my back.

And because I can't wait one more second, I thrust inside her, but only a few inches, giving her body a chance to acclimate to my size. Her head rolls back as her lips part in a silent moan.

"Are you okay?" I ask, stroking her cheek.

"M-more. I can take it." She looks up, locking eyes with me as I continue sliding inside her.

"That's a good girl," I praise, pushing more of myself inside her tight entrance. *Fuck. Fuck. Fuck.*

She bites her bottom lip until I'm all the way in, and she finally releases a gasp. "I've never felt this full before."

"Is that a good thing?"

She nods, her lips curving up. "A very good thing." She nips at my lip. "Now move before I scream."

My lips brush against her neck. "Oh, I plan on making you scream, baby girl, but not until you come all over my cock."

My cock slides in and out, slowly at first, until I pick up the pace, going hard and rough like she asked for.

"Yes," she moans, clutching onto me, rolling her hips as she grinds her clit over me.

I grip her ass, pounding into her. But it isn't enough. Looking over at the bed, I make a last-minute decision and carry her over, laying her on her back.

"What was wrong with the...ohhhhh," she moans as my thrusts reach deeper inside her, hitting that special spot as I clutch her left leg behind her knee, bringing it over my shoulder, plunging inside her at a maddening pace.

"Oh my God... I'm going to..." she pants, her body tensing as her back starts to arch off the bed.

"Me too," I say, feeling my balls tighten painfully, waiting for her to find her release first.

And she does.

The second that sweet sound of her crescendo scream echoes in the room, I spill into the condom, coming right along with her until I'm completely spent.

That was the best fucking orgasm of my life.

I hold myself over her, hovering as I catch my breath. She's beautiful beneath me. The afterglow of her orgasm shows in her flushed cheeks and glazed green eyes, staring up at me with a look I've never seen before. "That was—"

A pounding on the wall behind the bed makes us both glance up. "Keep it down in there! Some of us are trying to sleep!"

We look at each other, trying but failing to hold in a laugh. She loses it first, bubbling over in a fit of laughter as I remove myself from her, rolling over to toss the condom in the trash and then rolling back toward her to pull her body against mine.

She wipes away the tears from her eyes, giggling. Her smile might be my second favorite thing about her. The first is those beautiful eyes I'm trying to engrave in my memory at this very moment.

"I'm sorry. I don't mean to be loud," she whispers.

I brush the palm of my hand down her back. "You never have to apologize for being loud in the bedroom. In fact, I don't think you were loud enough. Want me to really give you something to scream about?"

She bites her bottom lip, her hand cupping my cheek. There's no awkwardness between us or weird after-sex tension. Just a feeling of calm. A comfortable sensation as though we've known each other for years.

But that can't be true.

Because I would recognize these eyes in a crowded room.

I'm sure of it.

"Where have you been all my life?" she asks softly.

I press my lips to hers, savoring the sweetness. "Waiting for you."

Twenty-Five

SARAH

My trembling hands rub the denim covering my thighs over and over again as my legs bounce in anticipation, my eyes glued to the frosted-glass door at the front of the room.

The second we woke up this morning, Paul sent his brother, Ray, a text message asking for his help. It only took thirty seconds for Paul's phone to ring and for Ray to tell us where to meet him.

So, that's where we find ourselves now.

Waiting in a secluded café in the Seaport district, overlooking the ocean.

My eyes wander to the large window, where I see big fluffy snowflakes falling gracefully outside. It's a picturesque view that would make for a lovely painting. One that would surely put anyone's anxious mind at ease.

But my mind isn't just anxious.

It's a riddled mess that I can't shut off.

It's racing with worries and dread, overthinking everything that could go wrong with asking Ray for help.

Like what if Paul's wrong, and Ray does have to watch the video?

What will he think of me?

Will I ever be able to face him again?

What if there's nothing Ray can do to completely destroy the video?

What if—

Paul's hand rests on my bouncing knee, his thumb brushing the inside of my leg.

"Everything is going to be okay," he notes reassuringly, placing a muffin and tea in front of me.

I nod, restlessly running my fingers through my hair before shoving them into my coat pockets. "You're right. I know you are. It's just, what if—"

Ding.

The bell above the frosted-glass door chimes, and my eyes shoot over to find Ray walking inside. He spots us quickly in the back of the café and advances toward us, brushing snow off his jacket and removing his knitted beanie.

"Hey, Ray." Paul stands to greet his older brother, gripping his shoulder in a manly half hug.

"Have you grown since I last saw you a few weeks ago?" Ray jokes. They both laugh and as they part, Ray's eyes meet mine. "Sarah." He holds his arms out wide, and without thinking about it, I stand and walk into him, hugging him back.

"Thank you for meeting us here," I murmur.

"Of course."

We part and take our seats. Ray immediately pulls out a laptop from his bag and sets it up. He wipes the lenses of his glasses with his shirt, looking between the both of us.

"Okay. So who's going to tell me what's going on?"

I glance up at Paul, who looks down at me.

Paul only gave Ray vague details over the phone, letting him know there was something he needed immediately erased from someone's devices.

He failed to mention that it was a sex tape.

And that the sex tape is mine.

Paul's hand finds mine on the table and squeezes it lightly in encouragement.

"I will," I say in a slight whisper. Clearing my throat, I look at Ray and tell him everything. Everything except the part about me currently being pregnant with Paul's baby, since we decided this morning that Paul's mom should be the first one we give the news to. But throughout the whole story, Ray remains neutral and attentive, only once letting his feelings show by clenching his jaw and closing his eyes after I admit to being blackmailed for the past few months. "Well." I study the table before me, wrapping my arms around myself. "I think that was everything."

Paul's arm skates around the back of my chair, scooting me closer to his side.

"Sarah." I glance up to find Ray staring directly at me with...pity? No, not pity. More like a deep sympathy in his golden brown eyes. "As Paul probably told you, I can't talk about the specifics of my job. But I can say that I work in a special part of the government that, unfortunately, deals with things like this all of the time, and it's my job to make things disappear. I've seen things that, well..." He hesitates before saying, "What I'm trying to say is, I want to make sure you know that what happened to you is not your fault."

His words sucker punch me right in my gut.

I didn't admit this to Paul, but ever since that night with Greyson, I've believed it was my fault.

That I should have known better.

Been more careful about who I slept with and where.

"It's just sometimes I can't help but wonder if I didn't—"

"No." Ray shakes his head. "It's *not* your fault."

I nod, unable to speak, because I can feel my throat beginning to burn and tighten as I hold back the sting of tears forcing themselves upon me. These are words I've needed to hear for so long. I've blamed myself for that night when Greyson was the only person to blame.

He filmed me.

He blackmailed me.

He threatened Paul and me.

He controlled me.

But when I look at Paul, studying me cautiously, all those realizations come crashing down, and I break.

Silently, I begin to sob into my hands as Paul pulls me against his side, running his hand up and down my back, soothing me. His lips kiss the top of my head.

"Let it out," he whispers.

I nuzzle my face into his shirt. "He t-taped me w-without me knowing," I stutter.

Paul's grip on me tightens. "I know. And he will pay for doing that to you. But right now, we are going to take care of the video so he can't cause any more harm to you, okay?"

I take a deep breath, staring into Paul's eyes.

I should have told this man everything from day one.

But I didn't know... I didn't know what it meant to be with someone who would turn the world upside down to take care of you.

"If this is too much, I can bring you home so Ray and I can sort the rest of everything else out," he offers.

I shake my head. "No." I push my hair back behind my ear. "I'm okay. I am. Really. It just hit me all of a sudden. Holding this in for so long and telling two people in less than twenty-four hours is just taking a toll on me. But in a good way, if that makes sense."

Paul kisses my temple. "It does."

I turn to Ray, who has been quietly watching us. "I'm sorry, Ray. I swear I'm not usually emotional."

Ray displays a gentle smile. "There's nothing to be sorry for." And then, he starts typing into his computer. "I would suggest we keep the video and turn it into the authorities—"

"No," I cut him off, adamantly shaking my head before focusing on Paul. There's a reason I never went to the authorities about this in the first place. And I won't be doing that now. "Please don't make me go through that. If that's the only evidence we have against him, then so many more eyes will watch that video. They'll see me at my most vulnerable... I can't go through that...I...just want the video erased. It's his word against mine. I won't win. It's what so many girls have to go through all the time, fighting for control over their own lives. And I'm not..." I lower my head. "I'm not strong enough to endure that process." A tear rolls down my cheek. "Please don't make me."

"Baby girl, we won't make you do anything." Paul's eyes meet Ray's, having a silent conversation before they go back to mine. "It's your choice. Whatever you want to do, we support you and will make it happen. Letting the law punish Greyson for what he did is good in theory, but we all know how that might go. He comes from a wealthy family with plenty of connections. He'll get off and face a community service sentence at most while you'll have to relive that nightmare." He shakes his head, anger in his darkening eyes. But the second they land on me, they soften. "If you don't want the authorities to handle things, I'll take care of him myself."

I shake my head. "No. I don't want him to hurt you."

His lips curve upward. "Don't you have any faith in your man?"

I open my mouth to speak, but he cuts me off.

"I won't let anyone hurt you. And what Greyson has been doing to you..." He shakes his head as his jaw clenches. "He will suffer. I promise you that."

I let out a shaky sigh, knowing I won't win this one. As much as I don't want Paul to risk getting hurt on my behalf, I know he won't. And I know he'll keep his promise. "Thank you."

Ray clears his throat, bringing our attention back to him. "Okay, so his name is Greyson Black, age twenty-two, Caucasian male, who attends Linrey University. Is all of that correct?"

"Yes," Paul answers.

I lean into Paul, feeling completely drained. But looking between these two, I've never felt safer.

I've never had people in my life who would fight my demons for me. Not since my parents died. And it feels really fucking good.

Ray continues typing until suddenly, his fingers lift from the keys. "Found him."

"That quickly?" Paul asks.

Ray furrows his brows. "Why do you think the government pays me the big bucks? I'm the best of the best."

"And I was starting to wonder if it was just you in the family with the big ego," I mutter to Paul, making him smirk.

"Now," Ray starts. "Because of the firewalls and security surrounding his system, I'm going to need to, unfortunately, take this one step further. But it should work if you're willing to try, Paul."

"Whatever you need me to do," Paul responds.

"Good. Because I need you to put this chip"—he reaches into his pocket, revealing a tiny black chip—"into his computer. Do you think you can do that?"

"I thought you could access his devices from your computer? Like right now?" Paul asks, concern laced in his voice.

"Deleting things from the internet and completely erasing files from a person's computer are two entirely different things." Ray tilts his head. "It's not impossible for me to eradicate everything from his computer without using this chip, but if you can insert it into his computer, it will make things much easier and smoother and save us a lot of time."

Paul taps the table with his index finger. "Okay. We have an away game in a couple of days that we leave tomorrow for. I can try to get his computer when he's not in his room. But then what?"

"Well, once you insert the chip, I'll have access to everything on Greyson's hard drive and cloud, including his phone. Any piece of technology he's ever used will be at my fingertips."

"But how will you know when you've found the right...video?" I ask fearfully, dread filling me.

Ray regards me and immediately understands my concern. "I won't watch the video, Sarah." His eyes move between me and Paul. "Although I will need someone to confirm it's the right video. Would you be comfortable if it was Paul who confirmed for me?"

I swallow the lump in my throat. "Y-yes."

"Think you can do that, Paul?"

Paul hesitantly nods, letting out a deep breath. "Whatever you need me to do, I'll do it."

I can feel his body tense beside me, so I reach for his face, turning his chin toward me. "You're the only person I trust to help me with this."

He sighs, mixed emotions filling his eyes.

"It's just..." He runs his hand over the top of his head, appearing so overwhelmed. "It's going to kill me to watch it. To have to watch what that asshole did to you." He looks off to the side, appearing lost in his thoughts.

"I only need you to watch for a second or two," Ray states. "Once Sarah is in the picture, you can shut it off and confirm with me that it's the right file. And then, once you do, I'll trace it to every location it's stored in and completely erase it from existence. Greyson will never be able to get his hands on that video again." His fingers start typing away as his eyes narrow in on his screen.

Paul nods. "I can do it." His lips brush against my ear, and he whispers only loud enough for me to hear, "For the mother of my child, I will do anything."

I look up, tears forming in my eyes for an entirely different reason than five minutes ago.

The mother of my child.

"All right." Ray closes his laptop and shoves it in his bag. "It's settled." He focuses on Paul. "Call me when you get his computer, and I'll walk you through the process. It should only take a matter of minutes."

Paul nods. "Okay."

Ray's attention slides to me. "We will take care of this, Sarah. I promise." He reaches across the table, squeezing my hand.

"I know you will. Thank you."

Ray stands, adjusting his coat. "Guess the next time I'll see you guys will be in a few weeks on Christmas."

I open my mouth, not sure how to respond to that. I don't want to intrude on their family Christmas, and Paul hasn't mentioned anything to me. "I'm—"

"We'll be there," Paul affirms, sending warmth through my chest.

Ray smiles as he turns around and walks out of the café and into the snow that appears to be falling harder since we arrived here.

My shoulders slump as I relax into my chair, picking a piece from the muffin. It's been a rough few days, and I'm mentally hitting a wall. "What should we do now?"

Paul tosses his head to the side, contemplating. "What would you like to do? I don't have basketball, and I already finished my assignments for the week, so I'm free all day."

"Hmm..." I mull a few ideas over but say, "Nothing. I want to do absolutely nothing with you."

Paul's lips curve up. "And what does nothing entail?"

"Blankets. Lots and lots of blankets on the couch with movies and food. Yes, definitely food. And maybe ice cream. Possibly sex." I purse my lips, deep in thought, tapping my chin. "Definitely sex. And naps. That's what a day of nothing means to me."

He laughs. "That sounds like my kind of day." He rotates his shoulders, stretching his arms. "And what movies should we watch?"

I know I will regret these words the second they leave my mouth, but after everything Paul has done for me, it's the least I can do for him.

"I was thinking we could have a...*Harry Potter* marathon," I mumble the ending, hoping he missed it.

"I'm sorry..." He positions his hand around his ear as a shit-eating grin appears on his face. "What was that?"

I sigh, closing my eyes as I pinch the bridge of my nose. "I said we could have a *Harry Potter* marathon."

I open my eyes, finding Paul suppressing a smile.

"Unless, of course, you don't want to—"

"Oh, there's no way I'm passing this up." He rubs his hands together gleefully.

I roll my eyes. "Yeah, I figured."

He stands up, buttoning his coat. "Please tell me you've at least seen the first one."

I shrug, standing beside him. "I think I've seen it. It's the one with the hobbits and the special ring, right?"

His mouth parts in horrified shock.

I nudge him with my shoulder. "Kidding. I've seen the first two."

"Well, I guess that's better than nothing." He pulls my hat down over my ears. "You know, if we have a boy, we could—"

"Nope. No. Definitely not. We are not naming our baby Harry," I state matter-of-factly. "It's not happening."

"Fine." His glove-covered fingers intertwine with mine, leading me to the door. "What about—"

"If you say a character's name from *Star Wars*, then we're skipping the sex part of today's activities."

Paul quickly pretends to zip his mouth shut and throw away the key, making me laugh.

He looks down at me, his eyes gleaming. "You know me too well, baby girl."

I shrug nonchalantly, pretending I don't feel butterflies in my stomach from how he looks at me. "I think we just get each other."

He opens the door for me, and I walk out into a winter wonderland. Big fluffy snowflakes fall all around us, sticking to the ends of my hair. I look up to the sky, spinning in a circle as I stick my tongue out, catching a few flakes. And when I become still, breathless from all the spinning and laughing, with the biggest smile I've ever worn, I glimpse at Paul, and the indescribable feeling hits me like a ton of bricks.

This is happiness.

And I know it's all because of him—that ten-foot-tall, amazingly kind, and gentle man who would do anything to keep me safe. To make me feel cared for. To make me happy.

My arms move on their own accord, wrapping around his waist as I burrow my head into his chest.

Paul rests his chin on my head, his hands securing me to his body. "I think we do, too."

Twenty-Six

PAUL

"You sure you don't want to head down to the hotel bar with us?" Glen asks while buttoning his shirt and then spritzing too much cologne over himself. He smooths his hair on the top of his head, admiring himself in the mirror.

"Yeah. Haven't been sleeping great, so I'll be heading to bed early. Need to be ready for tomorrow's game." Truthfully, I haven't been sleeping great, but that's because I can't stop thinking about what Greyson did to Sarah. And every time I start thinking about it, I feel ready to hit the closest object near me.

The anger that I've been feeling radiating inside my body these past few days takes over me like an unyielding hurricane ready to destroy anything in its path.

And the only thing I envision at the end of that path is Greyson fucking Black.

"Suit yourself. I won't be back too late. And…" He pauses as he opens the door. "Tell Sarah I say hi while you two have sexy time over FaceTime." He does a poor job of winking.

"Get the fuck out of here." I laugh as I throw a pillow at him that hits the now-closed door.

I couldn't risk telling Glen about the plan I'm currently partaking in because that would mean risking his involvement with this whole thing, which I'm unwilling to do. So he's under the impression that I took care of the video myself, and that's all I said of it.

I reach for my phone, ready to call my brother, but he beats me to it.

"Are you ready?" he asks as I press the phone to my ear.

"I am." I jump out of bed and reach into my bag, grabbing the chip from the pocket. "You're sure this is going to work? I don't want this to backfire and cause Sarah any more issues."

"Relax. This is what I do," Ray says confidently. "The bastard won't know what he had coming until it's too late."

"Okay. Okay." I let out a deep breath. "Now, how the fuck am I supposed to get into his room without getting caught?"

Knowing Greyson, the second we checked into the hotel, he threw his stuff inside his room and wandered to the hotel bar to find the night's entertainment. So I'm not too worried he'll be in his room; I'm more concerned that this whole mission will be unsuccessful.

I can't fail Sarah.

"I checked the hotel camera footage and saw Greyson leave his room ten minutes ago. So stop being a pussy and open the email I just sent you," he says matter-of-factly.

"You're the pussy," I murmur under my breath as I open the email and scroll to the QR code.

"I'm the one currently sitting in a multibillion-dollar facility with access to any camera in the world."

I roll my eyes. "Now what?"

"Now, walk over to Greyson's room across the hall and hold that code in front of the door scanner."

"This better fucking work." I walk out into the hallway, checking both sides.

Seeing the coast is clear, I step toward Greyson's room. Holding the QR code before the scanner, I wait until a green light flashes and the door unlocks.

"I'm in." My hand clutches the door handle, pushing it open, and I step inside, quickly closing the door behind me. I bolt the top metal lock in place in case Greyson decides to make an early appearance.

"Okay, now find his laptop," Ray directs. His fingers are heard in the background typing away, preparing for his upcoming task.

I hit the speakerphone option and place the phone on the nightstand. After a few minutes, I find his laptop in a case at the bottom of his suitcase.

"It has a fucking lock on it," I groan, pulling at the lock that won't budge.

"Jeez, this kid really is paranoid."

I look around the room, searching for anything to take this lock off with, when I spot stationery sitting on the nearby desk. A paper clip on the stack of note cards grabs my attention. Quickly, I unbind it, transforming it into a straight line, and shove it in the lock, playing with it until I feel the abrupt snap of the lock releasing.

I carefully unzip the case and then pull out the laptop. "I got it." I hit the power button, watching the screen wake, and a box appears, asking for a password.

"All right, insert the chip."

I pick up the laptop and turn it over, but I can't find a hole big enough to fit the chip into. "I can't find the hole."

I regret the words the second they leave my mouth because as soon as they do, Ray says, "That's what he said."

I shake my head. "Really. Right now?"

"Sorry, but it was the perfect setup." He coughs, holding in his laugh. "It's on the left side, closest to the screen.

I find it and do as he says, and then wait. And wait. And wait. "How long is this going to take?" I glance over at the door, anticipating Greyson storming inside.

"Relax. I'm almost…" A box displays on the screen asking me to approve the user. "Okay, approve the access for me."

The second I do, my stomach drops, fearful of what my brother is about to find.

He lets out a heavy breath, alerting me that something isn't right.

"What? What?" I squeeze the back of my neck, trying to remain calm. But I fucking can't.

"I'm going to need you to take a deep breath, man," he says calmly.

"Ray, if you don't tell me what the fuck is—"

"He has a whole folder of videos."

I drop the laptop on the bed. "What do you mean a whole folder."

My brother clears his throat. "Apparently, Sarah isn't the only one he has done this to, which might explain why he's so paranoid about people getting into his computer." He pauses before saying, "He's labeled all his folders by their names: Jessica, Christina, Kristen, Alison…"

My heart rate accelerates. "He's done this to others. He's filmed them all?"

My brother hesitates before saying, "Yes."

I pace in the room; the anger I feel at this moment is unfathomable. There's a beast inside me, clawing at the walls of my skin, itching for release from its confines.

"Listen," Ray starts, "I know we told Sarah we wouldn't, but I'm starting to think we need to inform—"

"No," I cut him off, my voice authoritative. "I'm not putting her through that. You know as well as I do that a guy in his financial status will get off without so much as a scratch on his record." I pull at the silver chain around my neck, my fingers tightening around the cold metal. "I will take care of him myself."

Ray sighs. "I get it, I do. I would be losing my mind if this was Tina. But don't you want the authorities to—"

"I said I will take care of him," I grit out. I won't make Sarah go through that horrible process or let anyone else see this video. She's trusting me to take care of this for her. To take care of her. And that's exactly what I'm going to do. "Did you find Sarah's video?"

"Yes. There's a file here labeled 'Sarah.' I'm assuming this is it. When I asked you to confirm her video for me, I didn't think he would be stupid enough to label the video with her name, so you no longer need to confirm. I'm deleting it—"

"Send it to me."

"What?"

"Fucking send me the video! I need to see what he fucking did to my Sarah!" My fingers dig into the back of my neck. "I need to confirm it's the right one. I promised her I would!"

"Paul. I don't think—"

"Ray." The pure venom in my voice doesn't go unnoticed by either of us.

"All right. Don't say I didn't warn you."

A ping on my phone alerts me to the message from my brother.

"Delete every single fucking video, Ray. Delete them all."

"I'm almost done," he says assertively. "The system is just processing the request."

I press play on the video, watching a timid Sarah enter the room, unknowingly being taped from a camera, most likely sitting on his computer, appearing like any ordinary gaming system.

No wonder she fucking ran out of my room that day.

Pure, unfiltered rage fills me.

She looks so frightened as he towers over her, shutting the door behind him. She sways a little on her feet, losing her balance and appearing way too drunk to be having sex.

But the motherfucker doesn't care.

He throws her on the bed like a monster who has just caught its prey.

But this monster is no match for me.

I delete the video, knowing I've seen all I can handle.

"Paul, are you—"

"Did you finish?"

"Yes. They're all gone. I'm sending a virus to his computer to destroy his hard drive as a warning. I'll keep tabs on him to ensure this doesn't happen to anyone else. Are you—"

"I need to go."

"Wait! Paul, don't do anything—"

I end the call before I can hear my brother tell me not to do anything stupid. To not do anything I'll regret.

But I'm not going to regret what I'm about to do.

Not a single second of it.

With trembling fingers, I remove the chip from the laptop and shove the computer back into the bag, securing the lock. Looking around, I ensure everything is exactly how I found it, exit his room, and head straight down to the bar with fury penetrating every inch of my skin.

Begging to be released.

Begging to come out and play.

Begging to make Greyson suffer.

The second I walk into the bar, my eyes scan the room for Greyson, and the moment they latch onto him, I feel a force within me that no one will be able to stop.

My feet move swiftly toward the stool that Greyson is perched on, talking to a blonde beside him. As though he can sense me behind him, he turns at the last second, looking right at me with wide eyes as my fist connects with his nose, sending blood spraying everywhere.

Greyson tumbles to the floor, but I don't give him a chance to get up as I crouch over his body. I straddle his chest, keeping one hand clutched onto the fabric of his shirt, pressing him down as my other hand turns into a fist, connecting over and over again with his face.

His bloody fucking face.

I don't hear the scream beside me.

Or the people around me yelling for me to stop.

At this moment, I don't recognize myself.

I only think about Sarah and what he did to her.

What he's done to every single one of those girls.

Eventually, two pairs of hands grip me from behind, pulling me off of Greyson. My chest heaves, adrenaline coursing through me as I'm pushed away from him, feeling like I've barely scratched the surface of the amount of pain I want to cause him.

"Paul, you need to fucking calm down. Everyone's watching," Glen whisper-shouts beside me. He grips one arm behind my back while another player from the team grips my other one, firmly keeping me in place.

I'm going to fucking kill him!

"What the fuck is wrong with you?" Greyson spits blood onto the floor as someone helps him to a standing position. One of his eyes is swollen shut, his lip is split open, and blood smears down his already bruising skin.

"You fucking touch her again, and I will kill you. I will fucking destroy you," I roar, sending gasps throughout the crowd gathered around us.

It takes Greyson only a split second before he smirks, shaking his head as he understands why I just beat the living shit out of him. He knows Sarah told me about the video.

"You fucked up, Paul. Big time," Greyson proclaims, wiping the blood from his face with his shirt. He clutches the back of the chair closest to him for support, appearing unsteady.

But I don't miss the innuendo in Greyson's words. He thinks he still holds power over Sarah with the video. He thinks he can now follow through on his threat and release the tape for the world to see. And he thinks he can make me appear as the bad guy in this story by making me look like I'm the one who released it.

But he can't.

And he'll never be able to hold any power over Sarah again.

I'll make sure of it.

Greyson shoves through the crowd, pushing his way toward the exit, blood still coating his face.

After he disappears, the hands around me release, and Glen stands in my direct line of vision, scraping a frustrated hand over his face, a beer in his free hand. He lets out a low whistle. "I'm sure it was well deserved, but you know that Coach will not like this. Nor will your agent."

I drop onto the stool, breathing hard. "No, they won't." I swipe the beer from Glen's hand and take a gulp. "Not one goddamn bit."

* * *

"Take a seat." Coach Rivers motions to the empty chair in his tiny hotel room, displeasure written all over his face—well, that and exhaustion.

I never thought I would have to endure the sight of him wearing flannel pajamas.

But here we are.

"Care to tell me why I got a call at one in the morning, alerting me that my two captains were fighting in the bar downstairs?" His voice is calm, with an undercurrent of anger tucked beneath.

"Sir, I'm sorry. I just…" I can't tell him about the tape because no one is ever going to see that tape again. "I snapped." I squeeze the back of my neck. "It won't happen again."

He sighs, rubbing his hands over his face. "Please tell me this wasn't over a girl."

I clear my throat. "I mean…"

His hand goes up. "Save it. I don't want to hear it." He shakes his head; disappointment is evident. "I like you, Paul. I really do." He straightens, rolling his neck. "But behavior like this is not tolerated under any circumstance. And especially not under my watch. I understand quite well that Greyson is not the easiest to get along with. Hell, one of the reasons why we were so eager to make you co-captain is because we needed to find a way to balance things on the team. You both play one hell of a game. However, Greyson likes to use intimidation to motivate his teammates, whereas you encourage and uplift. You're someone that your teammates look up to and respect." He pinches the bridge of his nose and then rubs at his temple. "I'm a man who needs a solid eight hours of sleep." He lets out a resigned sigh, glancing at the clock on his nightstand. "I need you to give me your word you won't pull a stunt like this again."

"I promise, sir. Never again."

Continuing the season with Greyson is going to be miserable. Fucking miserable. But I know this is his one warning to me, and I won't ruin my chance of getting into the NBA because it's no longer just myself I have to take care of and provide for, but both Sarah and our baby.

And a career in the NBA will mean they will always be provided for.

He subtly shakes his head. "All right. Knowing you, I'm sure there was a valid reason for the fight, and I could bet some good money that Greyson deserved what he got."

My brows shoot up, surprised by his omission.

"Be that as it may, I still have to set an example for the team. Half of your teammates were in that bar, witnessing the ordeal, and I'm sure the other half have already heard about it, which means you will not be playing in the next three games. No exceptions. I'll leave it to you to explain to your agent why you'll be absent."

Fuck. Dan is not going to be happy about this.

But it was worth it.

Every second of my fist pounding into Greyson's face was worth it.

Because I will always protect Sarah and our baby.

Repercussions be damned.

"Yes, sir." I grasp the arms of my chair in a firm grip. This feels pretty lenient, given the circumstances, so I'll take it with no complaints. "I understand."

He slowly leans back in his chair, his shoulders dropping.

"I think it might be best if you return home early. Take some time to clear your head and think about things. Get some distance from certain members of the team," he advises. "But I expect to see you when we return on Monday for practice."

"I'll be there."

"Good." He motions toward the door. "You may leave."

I nod, getting up from my seat, my feet reaching the door in only a few strides.

"And Paul?"

I look over my shoulder. "Yes, sir?"

"I hope this girl was worth it."

I don't hold back the smile when I say, "She's worth everything, sir."

Twenty-Seven

SARAH

Racing into my apartment, I slam the door behind me and lean against it, pressing my palms against the smooth surface, gasping for air.

I've never been this horny in my life.

What is wrong with me?

I know there was a part in one of the baby books that said there could be an increase in your libido, but I didn't think that meant me.

I kick off my heels and struggle to unzip my dress fast enough, darting toward my room. As the fabric of my dress falls around my legs, brushing against my overly sensitive skin, it sends shivers down every square inch of my body. I don't bother turning the light on as I throw my phone on my nightstand and, in record time, reach behind me to unclasp my bra, letting it drop to the floor.

Freedom.

Jumping on my bed, I shimmy out of my panties as I squirm and moan against the satin sheets. Reaching beside me, I grab Teddy and toss him inside the nightstand drawer.

This is not something he should see.

The aroma of man surrounds me as I turn my head to the side and inhale the scent from Paul's pillow. Fuck, he smells so damn delicious.

My whole body feels alive. Every nerve ending is zapping with a lustful need that overwhelms me. It's too much.

And all I need is Paul.

The man who is fifteen hundred miles away from me currently playing a basketball game as we speak.

The man who called me last night to tell me everything was taken care of. That I was free. No longer shackled with that video being held over my head.

Because Paul took care of me.

Like he's always done.

I just wish he were here to take care of me now.

But alas, I'm going to have to do it myself.

Closing my eyes, my hand glides across my skin over my breasts and hardened nipples down my stomach until finally reaching its destination. I spread my legs as wide as they'll go and swipe a finger through my wet center, enjoying the slight pressure my body is craving. Needing. Wanting.

I slide a finger inside me, pretending it's Paul who is making me feel good as he thrusts in and out, kissing every part of my body.

"Mmm, Paul," I moan.

He always knows exactly what to do to pull an orgasm out of me over and over again, and he doesn't stop until he knows I'm completely satisfied. Until I'm spent, collapsing into his arms for support.

My finger doesn't feel like enough, so I add another one, feeling that familiar stretch as I push in and out, but it's still not satisfying. I groan in frustration and pound faster inside myself, begging my body to give me the release I need.

Think of Paul's tongue swiping over you.

Think of Paul's lips sucking on you.

Think of Paul's hard cock pumping in and out of you.

It feels like forever passes as a bead of sweat rolls down my forehead and my chest heaves up and down.

Why can't I make myself come?

I need this. I need the release. I need to be pushed over the edge by an orgasmic avalanche of pleasure.

But it's not working.

I withdraw my fingers and stare up at the ceiling, breathless.

"Fuck."

My eyes water as frustration takes over me. I need Paul to take care of me. A single tear slides down my cheek and onto my pillow.

Turning my head to the side, I reach for my phone and scroll until I see Paul's name.

Sarah

I wish you were here.

As I put my phone back on my nightstand, I hear a quiet ping. Only I know the ping didn't come from my phone because I always keep my phone on silent.

My heart stops as every muscle in my body freezes, realizing *he's* here.

The area between my legs suddenly purrs back to life with a pulsing need, knowing he has a dead-center view of *me*. And after quickly grasping what he just witnessed, heat rushes over my entire body in embarrassment.

I hesitantly look up to find Paul leaning back with his legs spread out as he sits in the corner of the room with a bouquet of lilies, my favorite flowers, in his hands.

He's not supposed to be here.

But he is because he's somehow always here when I need him.

Anticipation fills me as he appears downright ready to dominate me in the best way possible, his darkened eyes scanning over my naked body spread eagle before him. I can't help but notice the prominent bulge between his legs, straining against his pants, begging to come out and play. My mouth waters as images of me on my knees before him flash through my mind.

Fuck, I want it.

I want him.

"P-Paul?" He doesn't say anything. He simply licks his lips and moves his eyes to mine, jump-starting that familiar throbbing sensation in my core.

He casually stands, placing the flowers on the dresser, still watching me as he begins to unbutton his shirt, one button at a damn time, revealing his chiseled chest.

"I thought you had a game tonight." My voice comes out breathless, sultry. I start to close my legs, but he shakes his head with disapproval, so I keep them open, feeling wetness drip down the inside of my thighs.

"I came home early to surprise you," he says with a deep, husky voice. The shirt stretches over his broad shoulders as he slides it down his arms and off his body. He takes a few steps, bringing him to the edge of the bed beside me, towering over me. His hand reaches out, gently stroking my cheek as his eyes trail down my body in appreciation.

I've never felt so exposed in my life.

So wanted.

So loved.

"You definitely surprised me," I breathe.

A tiny smirk appears on his face until his eyes meet mine, darkening. He bends down, bringing his face before me, his lips ghosting over mine. "Although that was the best show my eyes have ever seen, it seemed like you were having some trouble with things. Want me to take care of you, baby girl?"

Oh God. Yes, I do. I really do.

I shake my head, biting my bottom lip. "Please."

"Always such a good girl," he whispers before gently kissing my lips. He stands up straight and walks away, leaving me confused as he walks to the end of the bed.

"What are you—"

Suddenly, he grabs my ankles and pulls me to the end of the mattress, leaving my ass hanging over the edge. Kneeling on the floor, he places my legs over his shoulders, gazing between my legs with a ravenous hunger in his eyes. "I'm going to eat this pretty pussy until you come all over my tongue, screaming my name," he warns.

"Promises. Promises," I whisper.

A low chuckle leaves him before he swiftly takes one long, leisurely swipe of my center with his tongue.

"Oh, yes," I moan.

"Sarah?"

"Mm-hmm?" I grip the sheets in anticipation of what's to come. Newsflash. It's me. I'm about to come.

"I'll always be here for you." And with that, he buries his head between my legs, devouring me like a starved man.

"Oh my God." My back arches off the bed as he thrusts two fingers into me, pounding away, giving me exactly what I need. His free hand reaches up, pinching a nipple between his fingers, mimicking what his mouth does to me that drives me over the edge. It doesn't take long for my legs to shake and the fire in my core to erupt, seeing that I've been on edge most of the day. But the second his lips wrap around my clit and suck, I lose it. "Paul!" I scream out for him, my core fiercely clenching as he continues thrusting and sucking, never letting up until he's pulled every last ounce of an orgasm out of me.

As I collapse onto the bed, he removes his fingers from me, observing me. Leisurely, he sucks his fingers clean, closing his eyes. "So fucking sweet."

He gently moves my legs from his shoulders and stands, quickly taking his belt, pants, and underwear off, appearing before me as the basketball god that he is.

I crawl back on the bed, resting my head on the pillow, and when I peek up, my eyes immediately notice his thick cock, looking very pleased to see me. Paul starts to prowl on top of me like a hungry lion, ready to ravage me as he kisses his way up my body. The taut muscles over his back and shoulders flex with every lethal move he makes. His hard cock glides against my leg, igniting a thundering pulse between my thighs.

I inhale a shaky breath. "Paul?"

"Mm-hmm?" He continues his trail of kisses, nipping and licking his way up my body.

"I want to ride you."

He freezes above me, his lips pressed down between my breasts. His eyes look up at me, and a devilish grin appears.

"Whatever my baby girl wants, she gets."

Before I can comprehend what is happening, Paul flips us over. I land on top of him, gripping his shoulders as he leans back against the headboard.

"Let me see what my girl can do." His eyes sparkle with lust, watching me as I lift my hips, positioning myself above him.

I feel the head of his cock near my entrance and drop myself down only an inch, enjoying the stretch.

Paul releases a low groan, gripping my hips. I sit like that for a few seconds, teasing his tip as I lift myself just slightly up and down. His fingers dig into my ass as I finally slam down on his thighs.

"Oh God," I cry, rolling my head back as I remain frozen, adjusting to the overwhelming but completely satisfying fullness he provides me.

Pain meets pleasure.

"Fuck, you feel so good. So fucking perfect," Paul groans as his head rolls back and his grip tightens.

The room falls silent, like the calm before a powerful storm.

We both look at each other at the exact moment with nothing but unbridled need in our eyes.

This man has ruined me for anyone else.

He's all I will ever want or need.

And he knows it, too. His eyes soften before me as he cups my cheek in his hand. I close my eyes while he brings our foreheads together, kissing my lips softly.

It's soft. Sweet. Perfect.

I open my eyes, staring into two pools of chocolate brown with tiny golden flecks. Unspoken words travel between us, whispered in the silence around us—three little words that hold more meaning in the English dictionary than any three words combined.

I love you.

Straightening my back, I clutch Paul's shoulders for support as I roll my hips sensually and slowly, feeling every inch of him inside me. Paul leans forward, taking one of my breasts in his hand while he begins sucking on my hardened nipple on the other one. He teases, sucks, and licks each nipple back and forth, turning me into a breathless, panting mess.

Eventually, his hands move up to my waist, gliding smoothly over my skin before splaying out over my back, securing me to him as I begin to lift my hips up and down, riding my man. I don't let up even as my thighs start to shake and my body tenses, readying for an orgasm that I just know will put all others to shame.

"That's it, baby girl," Paul whispers. "I want you to come all over my cock like you own it because you do. You own all of me."

Paul sneaks a hand between us, encircling my clit with just the right amount of pressure to send me over the edge, free-falling into his arms, collapsing against his chest. He takes over, thrusting into me wildly before tensing beneath me with a guttural groan as his warmth spills inside me.

I'm shaking from head to toe. Every part of my body tingles in pleasure as a heavy weight of exhaustion sinks over me like a cozy blanket.

Resting my head on his shoulder, I place my hand on his chest, feeling the mirroring beat of his heart to my own. His hand clasps mine, intertwining our fingers as his other hand slides around my body, protectively holding me.

Once we both have our breathing regulated and our hearts pumping at an acceptable speed, I let my eyelashes flutter open.

"So, are you going to tell me why you aren't playing in your game right now?" I ask, trailing a finger over his collarbone.

He takes a deep breath, his finger tracing over the tattoos on my thigh.

"Yeah, I am." He kisses my temple, holding me tighter to his body. "I told you everything with the video was taken care of, and that part was true. But when Ray got into his computer, he discovered that you weren't the only one Greyson did this to."

I sit up in shock.

"You mean…"

He nods. "Yes. There were others." He pushes my wild sex hair behind my ear. "Ray saw a file labeled 'Sarah' and assumed it was yours. He didn't need me to confirm anymore, but it wasn't good enough for me. I couldn't risk it. So I told Ray to send me your video."

My lips part in shock. He had my permission to watch it, and I knew that was the plan, but hearing him confirm that he did is entirely different. "You saw it?"

His eyes travel up to the ceiling. "I only watched the first minute." He looks back at me. "I saw you walk into the room with him, and then I saw him push you onto the bed, and that was all I could stomach."

I bite my bottom lip, remembering how scared I was then.

"I wanted to kill him, Sarah. I wanted to kill him with my own two hands, and I've never felt that way about anyone in my life. I wanted to see with my own eyes what he did to you so I wouldn't feel an ounce of remorse for what I was about to do to him." He reaches for the comforter, bringing it up around us. "So, after I saw what I needed to see and confirmed with Ray that every single video was erased, I went down to the bar where a few guys from the team were, including Greyson and I… I beat the shit out of him. All I saw was red. I couldn't stop. But it's not enough. It'll never be enough after what he put you through." He runs a trembling hand over his face, going silent.

I pull his hand away, kissing each knuckle. "You wanted to protect me. You wanted to make me feel safe, and you did. It's over now. And I can't thank you enough for what you and your brother have done for me."

He shakes his head. "Don't thank me, Sarah. Not for that. Not for something that never should have happened to you." He wraps his arm around me. "Coach got wind of what occurred, and although he assumes something bad had to have happened for me to act out of character, I didn't tell him what caused me to lose my cool. So he suspended me from playing in my next three games as a warning to me and the rest of the team that behavior like that is not tolerated."

I reach up to his face. "I'm so sorry."

He smiles. "There's nothing for you to be sorry about, Sarah. I will do whatever I need to do to take care of you." He places his palm over my stomach. "And our baby."

I swallow every ounce of emotion in my throat.

"I'm really glad you walked into that bar on my birthday," I whisper, holding back my tears.

"Me too, baby girl." He pulls me down with him, wrapping the blanket around us as he spoons me from behind, keeping his hand on my stomach while kissing the top of my head. "Me too."

* * *

Blues and greens. Smooth lines and textured waves. Past, present, and future.

My brush strokes feverishly across the smooth surface, the image in my mind jumping onto the white canvas. My knuckles tense, my neck stiffens, and my bottom lip aches from biting down hard while lost in concentration.

Painting is not what one would call a physically demanding activity, but with me, somehow, it ends up that way.

My wrist attempts to give out on me as I reach for the top of the board, touching up a blue corner. But I can't stop. Not until I've perfected this piece.

A piece that means so much to me.

A piece that is essentially a part of my heart laid before me in a flurry of colors and shapes.

Just one more...

Done.

I sit back on my stool, rolling my neck and shoulders.

I didn't realize when I decided to submit some pieces for the art show how much of myself I would be displaying for others to see. Vulnerability used to be something I viewed as a weakness until recently. Until I realized how much is required of a person to be vulnerable before others.

It takes strength. It takes courage. It takes perseverance.

With each image I've created for this show, I'm feeling ready to be inevitably vulnerable in front of strangers, but it's even scarier to think of presenting my pieces to those closest to me.

Like Paul.

My work could be shown worldwide, and the only person whose opinion I would care about is his.

Shaking my head, I murmur, "I hope he likes these—"

"Who are you talking to?"

Paint spills on the floor as I jump from my seat, spinning toward the door where I see Natalie standing with widened eyes and her hands apologetically in the air. My chest heaves as I slap my hand over my heart.

"Sorry! I didn't mean to scare you," she rushes out.

Waving a hand around dismissively, I reply, "It's fine. I was just lost in the zone." I bend down to pick up the brushes and grab some paper towels to clean up the paint on the floor. "What are you doing here?"

She steps inside, examining the room. "I was on my way back from therapy and saw your car in the lot. Figured I would find you here." She leans against one of the tables, her hands clutching the edge. "Want some company back to our apartments?" Natalie's eyes take in my artist apparel of paint-splattered clothing and... *Shit!*

I suddenly realize I'm not wearing one of the oversized T-shirts or sweatshirts I use to hide my small baby bump because I knew no one would be here tonight. But as I casually glance down at myself, relief is felt when I see my apron completely concealing my stomach.

Thank fucking God.

"Definitely." I turn my easel toward the window, not ready for her to see the image, and head for the closet to get my winter coat, which I manage to put on while removing my apron.

"Are you ever going to let me see your work?" she teases, smiling.

"You will. But not until the show," I respond, zipping my coat. "I'm...I'm just not ready yet."

She nods in understanding. "I've got the date marked on my calendar. I'll be there." Her smile widens.

My fingers dig into the tender spot between my shoulder and neck. "Fuck, this is the one part about painting I can't stand."

"How long have you been here?" Natalie walks beside me as I shut off the lights, stretching my neck from side to side.

Reaching for my phone in my pocket, I wince when I see the time. "Shit. Five hours."

Natalie's eyes widen. "Have you eaten?"

I shake my head, hating myself for not taking a break to eat.

Natalie interlocks her elbow with mine. "I know just the place we can go!"

"Please tell me they serve fries."

She nods. "Fries, burgers, milkshakes. All the fast food your heart desires." She laughs. "It's a diner near campus called Turn Back the

Clock. Jason took me there a few weeks ago, and I've been dying to go back for another milkshake."

I smile. "Sounds like my type of food."

Pulling out my phone, I text Paul to let him know.

Sarah

I'm going to be home late. Going out with Natalie for some food.

Paul

I'll be waiting in bed for you...

Sarah

Good. Because I think I may need a full-body massage.

Paul

Hmm. Pretty sure there's some special oil in the bathroom we can use for this problem...

Sarah

Have you been snooping in my bathroom?

Paul

Seeing that it is currently our bathroom, I wouldn't call it snooping. Just researching.

Sarah

Researching what?

Paul

Like, what toys and goodies you like to use.

Thirty seconds later

My cheeks heat up just thinking about him in bed…waiting for me with my special toy in his hand…

God, this man.

My man.

"Who's making you smile like that?" Natalie asks, eyebrows waggling.

I shove my phone in my pocket, shaking my head. "No one. I was just checking my emails."

"Sureeeeee," Natalie purrs as we approach my car.

Guilt hits me. I know she's teasing. I know she doesn't actually care who I'm texting. But I'm filled with regret for not telling her anything. For keeping so many secrets from her, when she has been my first friend in… Well, damn, I guess she is my first friend.

"Natalie." I press my hand on the top of my car door, steadying myself, feeling words ready to break free from within me.

She tilts her head, watching me from the other side of the car. "Yeah?"

I clear my throat. "I just... It wasn't easy for me to make friends as a kid. And I don't have much experience with the whole friends thing in general. I've been a loner for as long as I can remember, pretending it didn't bother me and that that was how I wanted things. It's just not easy for me to connect with people. To form lasting relationships. And even last year, when I would go out, it was just to..." *To try to feel in control of my life. To make the thoughts stop. To not feel so alone all the time.* I shake my head, feeling a sting at the tip of my nose. "Some things are going on in my life right now that I'm not ready to talk about, but I just want you to know the day I met you was one of the best days I've ever had. Your friendship...means a lot to me, and I don't want to lose you," I choke out.

Natalie sprints around the front of the car, tackling me in a giant bear hug. She doesn't say anything, but I hear the occasional sniffle as she holds me tight, saying everything she needs to without words.

She parts from me to look at me, gripping my shoulders. A few tears trickle down her face, and I can't help but wipe them away.

"You'll never lose me. Whatever is going on, I'm here for you." She smooths out my hair, smiling. "When you're ready to talk, I'll be ready to listen. Deal?"

"Deal." I let out a relieved sigh, thankful for her understanding.

Thankful for the first friend I ever made.

Twenty-Eight

PAUL

"Relax," I coax Sarah as we walk up the front steps to my house. "She's going to be over the moon from the news."

"You say that, but all your mom will be thinking is that I'm the broke girl who got knocked up by her fabulously rich son on purpose when that wasn't the case at all. We used a condom!" She stops, bringing her hand to her forehead, looking ready to burst into tears.

"You're never going to forgive the condom industry for this, are you?" I tease.

She swats at my chest. "It's not funny! She's going to hate me. Your whole family is going to hate me. They're going to think I'm a gold digger that used you."

I gently lift her trembling chin. "Is that what you think? That my family will look at you like you're a gold digger?"

"Well, won't they?" she asks, vulnerability mixed in her words.

"No, Sarah." I shake my head, wrapping my free arm around her while balancing a pie in my other. "They all fell in love with you at Thanksgiving. Ray and Kevin both won't shut up about you. Tina called me the other day just to ask about you. And I'm not proud to say it, but a small part of me thinks my mom might like you more than me." I chuckle. "If anything, they're going to be happy for us."

"How? How can they be happy for us when your mom probably thinks this will mess up your future? That...I ruined your future."

I hesitate, watching her carefully when it occurs to me. "Baby girl, is that what my mom will think or what you think?"

Her eyes close as she admits, "It's what I think."

"Oh, Sarah." What am I going to do with her? "You've done the complete opposite of ruining my future. You've turned it into something worth living for." Her eyes flutter open. "Basketball is my career, and it's what I've done my whole life. It's what I enjoy being a part of. And yeah, having a baby as a rookie isn't going to be easy at all, but having a kid... Sarah, that's on a whole other level of being happy. You're giving me the best gift I could have ever asked for."

"Really?" she asks, sounding unsure.

"Really." I push back her hair and run my thumb under her eye, where one solo tear streams down. "You have a lot to offer the world, Sarah Fleur. And I'm going to make sure someday soon that you know it with everything inside you."

After pressing a kiss to her temple, I take her hand in mine and walk through the front door.

"Hey, Mom," I yell as we walk inside.

Footsteps are heard quickly approaching. "Paul? I didn't know you were... Oh my God, Sarah!" My mom pushes past me, circling her arms around Sarah. "I didn't know you were coming! Why didn't you tell me, Paul?" She lightly punches my arm.

"Ow." I rub my bicep. "Don't damage the money maker."

She shakes her head, laughing. "Well, I am so glad to see you, Sarah." I arch my brow as she says, "The both of you."

"Don't worry. I know I'm still your favorite," I add.

She takes the pie from my hand. "I don't have favorites, but if I did, it would be Sarah." I see her wink over her shoulder at Sarah, who laughs.

"I'm insulted," I say, grabbing Sarah's hand and leading her into the kitchen behind Mom.

I pull out a stool for Sarah and sit on the one beside hers.

My mom places the pie in the fridge and then turns around, smiling. "I didn't expect you until later. So what brought you here early, sweetheart?"

I squeeze Sarah's trembling hand. "Well, actually, Mom..." I sit up straighter. "Sarah and I have something to tell you."

"I knew it!" My mom claps her hands together.

"You knew what?" I ask cautiously.

"If you didn't come here on Christmas Eve to tell me I'm going to be a grandma, then I'm sending back your gifts." She places a hand on her hip, glaring between us.

"Well, technically, you already are a grandma..." I murmur, noting her genuine happiness. Her reaction was precisely what I had expected because nothing makes my mom happier than her family, especially a growing one.

"You really did know," Sarah murmurs softly, her shoulders relaxing.

"Of course I did! Call it a mother's intuition, but I just knew it in my gut." She squeals, making her way around the counter so that she can wrap her arms around Sarah. "I am so happy for the both of you."

Sarah's eyes close as a smile shows on her beautiful face, looking at peace.

I didn't realize how much my mom's approval weighed down on her. But I hope she's ready for the day this baby is born. Because she's not just gaining a child, but also a whole damn family who will love her like she's always deserved to be loved.

* * *

Sarah's white-gloved fingers intertwine with mine as we walk out the house's front door. Her deep breath leaves her lungs in a white puff of smoke as the tip of her nose turns rosy-pink, making her look adorable.

She'd kill me if I ever called her that, though.

"Sooooo…" I tenderly squeeze her hand. "Didn't go as badly as you thought it would, now did it?"

She smiles. "No, it didn't. Your mom is pretty cool."

"What can I say? She takes after me." I shrug.

She laughs. "You wish you were that cool."

"Pshh." I lead us down the street lit up with Christmas lights as far as the eye can see, enjoying the feel of the holiday magic in the air. Snow falls around us in big white flakes.

And everything about this moment with her right now is…peaceful.

After the rest of the family came over for Christmas Eve, it was nothing but chaos, noise, bickering, and laughter for the next few hours. Followed up with a dinner feast ready to serve an entire army. I watched as Sarah fit in with my family so naturally. She and Mom talked about some of their favorite paintings, Kevin teased her like she was his little sister, and Sarah made me proud by giving it right back to him. And Ray plated Sarah's food and made her laugh a few times with some dumb dad jokes, looking out for her like a big brother would.

God, when she laughs, it makes everything around me disappear. The way her eyes squint as her smile grows, it's nothing short of enchanting.

And when the time came for dessert, we broke the good news to everyone. Sarah was hugged so many times I started to get jealous, and that's when I decided we should get some fresh air and take a walk.

She places her free hand on her stomach over her black coat. "This baby will have so many people who love them." She looks up at me, smiling.

"They sure will." I lean down to kiss her temple.

"It feels good telling people," she admits.

I rub the back of my neck. "Yeah, about that…"

"What?"

I laugh nervously. "So don't get mad." She stops walking, narrowing her eyes on me. "I was doing some research about babies. Just preparing myself. And I accidentally left some books in the living room at my house, and, well, Nate came home and saw them."

Her eyes widen. "And what did you say?"

"I mean." I scratch the top of my head, suddenly feeling fidgety. "I blurted out the truth. I didn't want to lie to him. I told him you and I are together and that we're having a baby. But he's not going to tell anyone, including Natalie. He just asked that we tell the group as soon as possible because he doesn't keep anything from Natalie, and not saying anything will kill him."

She blinks a couple of times. "You told him that we're together?"

My brows furrow. "Yes. Was I not supposed to?"

She shakes her head. "No. No. It's not that. I just...we haven't...I don't know...I just thought we were supposed to have a conversation about that. I don't know. I've never done this before. I mean, am I your girlfriend? Was I supposed to assume we're together because we're having a baby? Or was I supposed to wait until you asked me? Oh God, just tell me to shut up, please." She covers her face with her hands, turning a faint shade of pink.

"Sarah?"

"Mm-hmm?"

"Can you look at me?"

"No, I don't think I can right now."

I chuckle, removing her hands from her face. "I didn't officially ask you because I thought you knew how I feel about you."

She bites her bottom lip. "I mean, I do. It just would be kind of nice to hear it. I'm not good with this, and it might help to reaffirm things for me." Her big green eyes look up at me, vulnerability like I've never seen before flashing in them.

My hands brace both of her cheeks. "Sarah Fleur?"

"Yes?"

"Will you be my girlfriend?"

"God, what are you twelve or something, Paul?" She flips her hair over her shoulder and takes a step to start walking away, leaving my mouth agape as she wears a shit-eating grin.

"Oh, no, you don't!" I scoop her up in my arms, spinning her in the air.

"Ahhh, put me down!" She's giggling uncontrollably. "It's so high up here!"

I place her in front of me, resting my hands on her rosy cheeks. The corners of her lips tug up when she says, "Yes, Paul. I'll be your girl-friend."

"You're mine, Sarah." I rub the tip of my nose over hers. "Don't ever forget that."

"Does that mean you're mine?" she asks.

"Always."

"Did you just quote *Harry Potter*?"

I stand straight, scrubbing a hand over my face. "Just because I say the word *always* does not mean I quoted *Harry Potter*." I take her hand in mine. "But is it one of the best scenes of all time? Absolutely."

She giggles beside me, shaking her head. "Oh, Paul. I love how much of a nerd you are."

"You do?"

"Yeah. It's a complete turn-on."

"Well, in that case, I would never be opposed to some role—"

"Nope." She shoots her hand in the air before me. "I'm going to stop you right there, big guy. There's no way I'm dressing up as Princess Leia."

I shake my head, chuckling. "We'll save this conversation for another time."

She laughs beside me, squeezing my hand.

"So," I start. "We find out next week what the baby's sex is. Are you nervous?"

She shakes her head. "No. I don't care if it's a boy or a girl. Just as long as they're healthy." She looks up at me. "What about you?"

"It doesn't matter to me if they're a boy or a girl. Just as long as they have your big, beautiful green eyes." I glance down at her and wink.

A hint of a blush stains her cheeks. "I hate when you say nice things like that."

"Why?" I ask, amused.

"Because it does this to me." She points to her bright red cheeks.

I laugh, bringing her hand to my lips, and kiss the back of it over the glove. "But that's exactly why I do it."

She shakes her head, giggling. But as soon as her eyes meet mine, that beautiful smile falters.

"What is it?" I ask.

"It's just..." She hesitates, tilting her face toward the night sky. Snowflakes fall on her face, but she doesn't seem to care one bit. Something's worrying her. I can see it in those eyes I love so much. Letting out a puff of air, she looks at me. "Do you think it's weird that there's been no retaliation from Greyson?"

My brows furrow as I gaze off.

The thought of Greyson taking revenge has crossed my mind once or twice. But there's no way he can prove that Ray and I broke into his computer.

It's not possible.

"He's not going to hurt you ever again, Sarah." I brush a few snowflakes from her cheek. "You're safe now, and I sure as hell will never let anything happen to you."

She has no idea the lengths I would go to keep her safe.

"I know you won't. I always feel safe when I'm with you." She sighs, tucking her head against my side. "I think it's just going to take a little bit for me to get used to not having that video hanging over my head. I mean, I was expecting to run into him at work my last week, but he was never there. It's been a few weeks and we haven't heard anything from him." She shrugs. "Something just feels off. Has he been weird when you see him at basketball?"

I shake my head. "He missed a couple of practices, and he's been avoiding me at games, as he should. But there was nothing out of the ordinary." I brush my lips across her temple. "I don't want you to worry about him."

She looks up at me, the corners of her lips turning up. "I'm sure it's nothing." Her arm loops with mine. "Let's keep walking. I want to make room for another piece of apple pie."

We walk around the neighborhood for a few more minutes until Sarah stops with a gasp.

"What's wrong?" My eyes rake over her, but I notice nothing out of the ordinary. My hands push back her hair. "Is it the baby?"

She shakes her head. "Sorry." Her eyes peek around me at the view I'm now blocking. "It's just so beautiful."

"What is?" I turn, finally realizing what has captured her attention. An old colonial house that appears as though it's seen better days. Large columns stand in the front, and a barely surviving deck wraps around the house. It's the only house in this area that sits on a lake with woods surrounding it, keeping it hidden from prying eyes. No one has lived in it for years.

"You like that?" I ask, confusion evident.

She nods. "It reminds me of the house I grew up in with my parents when I was a little girl. My mom always took me outside on nice days to paint on the porch, and my dad would sit in an old rocking chair, waiting to see what we created. Those are some of my favorite memories."

Her eyes glisten, and I find myself wrapping my arm around her, pressing my cheek against the top of her head.

"Is that who taught you how to paint? Your mom?" I ask.

"Yeah." She stares off. "As I get older, I feel like I remember less and less from my childhood. But I remember all the times I spent with her in her art studio. Or at her art shows. She was amazing. So unbelievably talented. I wanted to grow up to be just like her."

"She would be so proud of the woman you've become, Sarah."

She swallows, her eyes misting. "My dad couldn't paint for shit." A slight bubble of laughter escapes her. "But he was the best dad. He would stay up late with me if I had a nightmare. He taught me how to ride a bike. He would pick me up from school early to take me out for ice cream on special occasions like my birthday. He..." She pauses, lost in her memories. "That's why I never understood why he did what he did... Why did he leave me?" She looks up at me, hurt glimmering in her eyes.

"I can only imagine he wasn't in his right mind." I hold her tighter, needing to remind her I'm right here. "I'm not saying what he did was right, but he probably felt alone and scared. He needed help. And unfortunately, it probably got so bad in his head that he only saw one answer to solve his problems. But that doesn't mean he ever stopped loving you. He most likely convinced himself that what he was doing was best for both of you when it wasn't."

She sniffles. "I know. When I think of him, I try really hard to only think of the good memories. Because I know the man I saw toward the end of his life wasn't my dad. He was just a shell of a person by that time, consumed by depression." She shakes her head. "When my mom died, I think that's when my dad truly died, too. He lost his other half. His reason for living." She lets out a deep breath. "I miss them all the time. Especially around the holidays."

"I bet they miss you too, baby girl. All the damn time."

She wipes some tears from her cheek and shakes her head, throwing a little grin on her face, her eyes memorizing the old house before us. "Someday," she starts, "I want a house just like this with twinkling lights hanging everywhere. I want it painted white with black trim and shutters. I want a stone pathway that leads up to the house with lilies potted on each side. I want a large eastern redbud tree smack in the front yard."

"An eastern redbud?"

"Yes," she confirms. "It's a beautiful tree that blooms in an abundance of pink flowers."

"I didn't take you for a pink kind of girl…"

"I have my moments." She waves me off with her hand. "But most importantly, I want a small art studio next to the water where I can paint any time of the year. It'll have twinkling lights surrounding it, looking straight out of a fairy tale. And inside, I'll have plenty of room for my supplies and paintings." She sighs, her eyes roaming over the whole property. "I could see myself painting here."

Hmm. That's not such a bad idea…

But also, speaking of painting…

"How are your pieces for your show coming along?"

"I think okay." She shrugs, sounding unsure. "I've never done something like this before, so I'm not entirely sure what to expect, but so far, I'm happy with what I've created."

"Well, I can't wait to see what you've made." I spin her out, watching the smile bloom across her face. "I'm going to point at every painting and say, 'My girl made that.'"

She spins into my arms, placing her palms on my chest. "Do you think anyone will actually buy one?"

An optimistic light glows around her like an eternal flame, and I don't want to see it ever doused out.

"They'll probably hold a bidding war," I affirm, tucking her under my arm as a shiver runs through her. I tug on her hat, making sure it covers her rosy ears. "Let's get back home and warm you up."

"I think I know a few ways you can warm me up," she offers with a mischievous sparkle in her iridescent green eyes.

"Oh yeah?" As we begin to walk in the direction of my house, I ask, "Should I warm you up with my tongue, fingers, or cock?"

"Hmm…" She taps her chin. "I think all three."

"All three?" I chuckle. "My girlfriend is pretty damn greedy."

She pulls on my coat, gripping the fabric with her fingers, bringing my face before her. "Damn straight I am." Her lips press against mine in an all-consuming kiss before she parts and whispers, "When it comes to you, I want it all."

* * *

Coffee roasting first thing in the morning is one of my favorite scents. It brings back memories of times when I was a kid. Times when both of my parents were here on Christmas morning.

Following the aroma into the kitchen, I find my mom in her flannel pajamas.

"Merry Christmas, Mom." I wrap her up in a bear hug.

"Merry Christmas, sweetie." She turns around, brows furrowed. "Why are you up so early?"

I take a seat at the counter. "Couldn't really sleep."

She pours a mug of coffee for me and slides it my way. "Everything okay?"

"Yeah." I nod but then shake my head. "Actually, I don't know. Do you ever feel like things are too good? Like something will happen to ruin how perfect everything has been going."

"Is that what you're worried about?"

"I just can't help but feel like something is going to take away this happiness from me." I shrug, bringing the coffee mug to my lips.

"Oh, Paul, sweetheart, you're allowed to be happy." She wraps her arms around my shoulders. "Happiness is not something that can be taken from you. It's what you make of it. And right now, you've got a lot of things going on to make you feel overwhelmed, but that doesn't mean it's bad."

"Why are you always right?"

"Because I'm your mother." She steps away to put her mug in the dishwasher.

"I didn't get a chance to talk to you alone last night," I say. "How do you feel about...being a grandma?"

She beams. "Oh, I'm just..." Her eyes water. "I'm just so thrilled. But I also wish your father were here because I know how proud he would be of you and how much he would love his grandchild." A sad smile forms on her face.

"I miss him all the time." I hold in the tears, fighting the urge to cry like it's my only job in life. "And it bothers me that I'll never be able to introduce him to Sarah. I think..." I clear my throat. "I think he would have really liked her. And knowing he won't be here to meet his grandchild hurts, Mom." I pinch the bridge of my nose, letting out a deep breath. "It hurts so much."

"He would have loved Sarah, sweetie. I know because I do." She reaches across the counter and squeezes my hand. "Your father is always watching over us. Day and night. And you better believe that he will watch over your child like it's his sole purpose."

She's right.

He may not be with us today, but I've always known he watches over his family.

"I take it that this is what the big secret was about?" my mom asks.

I let out a deep sigh. "Yeah." My hands cup around the warm mug. "But it was all a...misunderstanding," I offer.

"And how do you feel?"

"Feel about what?"

She smiles. "About becoming a dad?"

I rub at my chest. "I know I'm young, but I feel...excited. Ready. I feel like the void inside me has been filled for the first time in my life." I rest my forearms on the counter. "Growing up with a famous dad and then having people compare me to him was always a lot. It's not that I wasn't proud to wear our last name on my jersey because I was and always will be. But sometimes it's overwhelming because I feel the pressure that comes with it, and I don't feel good enough to continue the legacy." She gives me a slight frown, disagreeing with me. "And even though sometimes it feels like I have all eyes on me while surrounded by people, I still feel...lonely." I shrug.

"Paul, I had no idea you—"

"I didn't tell you," I interject, shaking my head. "But ever since I met Sarah, I haven't felt lonely. And gaining not just her but also a child in my life... I feel lucky. I feel damn lucky. But above all, I feel whole."

My mom sucks in her bottom lip, her eyes glimmering with unshed tears.

"Mom, please don't cry," I plead, feeling horrible that I've made her cry on Christmas morning.

She waves her hand dismissively. "These aren't sad tears; they're happy tears. And I'm just... I'm so happy that you're happy, honey."

I look over at the stairs, ensuring no one is coming down. "Sarah was worried about telling you. She didn't want you not to like her and thought you would think she did this on purpose to trap me like some gold digger."

She gasps, bringing her hand to her chest. "No, she didn't."

I nod. "She hasn't had a family in a very long time, and she gets scared to connect with people because she thinks everyone will leave her. So I think she was afraid to tell you because she likes you and was scared telling you would push you away. She didn't want to disappoint you."

She shakes her head. "I'll make sure she knows that is not the case when she's like a daughter to me."

"I think she'd like to hear that." I trace my finger around the edge of the mug, clearing my throat. "There was one more thing I wanted to talk to you about before everyone gets down here and the mayhem begins."

"Let me hear it."

"I know what I want to do with my trust fund."

She arches a single brow. "And what would that be?"

"I want to buy the old, abandoned house at the end of the neighborhood. The one that sits on the lake."

"The one that needs some major loving?" she asks. "Probably a whole new foundation, for the yard to be leveled, the deck to be reattached, the shutters to be hung straight, a fresh coat of paint, and I can only imagine how much work needs to be done to the inside... That one?"

I smile. "Yeah. That one."

Her lips curve up as her eyes water. "I think your father would very much approve of that."

"I thought so, too," I add, blinking back tears.

I won't let you down, Dad.

Twenty-Nine

SARAH

We walk inside a familiar old building—a building I never thought my eyes would lay upon again.

Feelings I've pushed away, deep down inside me, scratch at the surface, threatening to expose my true emotions.

Anguish. Pain. Sadness.

"Are you okay?" Paul asks, eyeing me as he helps remove my coat.

I force a smile and reach for his hand. "I'm fine."

But the truth is, I'm not.

Because how are you supposed to feel entering the group foster home where you spent your first Christmas without your parents?

Paul pulls me into his side, leading me behind his family as we head toward the back of the building, where a giant, fully decorated Christmas tree stands. Children run through the halls, giggling and screaming in excitement.

"Wow! Look at all those toys," one boy admires, watching Paul and his brothers as they place the abundance of bags filled with toys around the tree.

"Kathy." A woman, appearing in her mid-forties, approaches, extending her hand toward Mrs. Weston. "Always so nice to see you and your family. We can't thank you enough for everything."

"Deloris, you know we would never miss this," she replies warmly, shaking her hand.

"Well, let me gather the children, and then we can start. The caterers you sent over have begun prepping this afternoon's feast. The kitchen smells amazing!" She beams before walking away.

"Has your family done this before?" I ask Paul.

"We do this every year." He shrugs. "My dad was adopted when he was a kid, and it was always important to him to give back. So we've been participating in this yearly tradition for as long as I can remember." He wraps his arm around my shoulder. "My mom hires a team of caterers to prepare food for all the children and employees here. And then Kevin, Ray, and I get all the presents that Tina wraps for us. Every child writes down one thing they want, and we get it for them." My stomach drops, remembering when I had to write down what I wanted from Santa. "Although, we always end up getting way too much stuff. I guess we go a little overboard, but we just want to make sure that every child here has a present from Santa."

My heart.

It stills beneath my chest.

This guy really is a goddamn teddy bear.

And he's all mine.

I wrap my arms around him, nuzzling my face into his chest. "I can't get over how lucky I am that I found you."

His arms around me tighten as he kisses the top of my head. "It's me who's the lucky one."

"All right, everyone." Deloris walks into the room with a line of children behind her, eagerly peering around at all the bags of toys. Excitement flashes in their little eyes as a buzz of anticipation floats in the air. "Who is ready to see what Santa brought for them?"

"I am!"

"Me!"

"Me! Me! Me!"

Deloris laughs. "Okay. Take a seat around the tree, and we'll get started."

The children quickly sit on the floor, bouncing in anticipation. A few of them find it impossible to sit still and try peeking in the bags, but they're each secured shut with a ribbon.

Kevin sits on the closest chair and pulls one of the bags beside him. "Santa told me you were all good this year. But I don't believe him. Is it true?"

"Yes!" the children all squeal, giggling.

"Well, I guess we'll find out." He reaches inside the bag, pulling out the first toy. "Do we have a Henry?"

A little boy no older than five jumps up, happiness evident all over his adorable chubby cheeks as he rushes up to Kevin, smiling brightly at the box in his hands. "Is that the train set I asked Santa for?"

Kevin hands it over to him. "Guess you'll have to open it to find out."

Henry starts ripping the red glossed wrapping paper in a hurry, and as his eyes catch on the blue train set, he looks up to Kevin and says, "Thank you!"

Kevin nudges the top of his head. "No problem, little man."

My eyes wander around the room, taking in the chaotic but heartwarming scene.

There must be at least fifteen children.

Fifteen children with no families or a place to call home.

My eyes water and my throat begins to constrict, remembering being here like it was yesterday.

"Still okay?" Paul whispers beside me.

I nod, trying to rein in my emotions, but it's becoming impossible.

I clear my throat. "I'll be right back. I just need to use the restroom."

"Want me to come with you?"

Shaking my head, I say, "No. I'll be quick."

I walk through the entryway out of view, exploring the halls, remembering every room, window, and piece of furniture. It doesn't appear much has changed since I was last here.

My hand runs along the wall, old memories running rampant through my touch until I approach the sitting room, where another beautiful Christmas tree adorns the corner. There's a window bench I know very well, bringing a slight smile to my face. It was where I spent many nights curled up, refusing to sleep in the room assigned to me.

I wanted to see the sky.

I wanted to feel close to my parents.

Sitting on the bench, I pick up the photo album resting beside the wall. Carefully, I flip through, seeing photos of children who lived here over the years. Children who had their whole lives turned upside down were brought here to feel any semblance of everyday life.

My eyes immediately stop on an image.

Squinting, I take the photo out of the sleeve and bring it up for a closer inspection.

It's me.

I run my hand over the picture.

A frightened girl with jet-black hair, pale as the moon, sits with a teddy bear clutched to her chest, showing just the tiniest smile.

It was the first time in months I had smiled, thanks to the man sitting next to me, beaming at the camera. He's the man who gave me Teddy all those years ago.

I don't know who this man is. But I hope he knows what that teddy bear means to me.

I hope he knows that because of him, I never gave up.

TWELVE YEARS AGO

I wrap the blanket around my scrawny body, tucking myself into the corner of the window seat bench, watching the snow fall outside. The glass is cold, each pane frosted, but I'd rather be here than anywhere else in this unfamiliar place.

Children are laughing in the other room, opening their Christmas presents. But I don't understand how they can be happy when we're here because we don't have parents.

And nobody wants us.

Tears gather in my eyes, slowly falling down my cheeks, and I let them, not worrying about wiping them away since no one is here to witness them.

"Somebody told me you might be in here."

Whipping my head to the side, I spot a very tall man leaning against the doorframe. He takes a few steps, approaching me, causing me to withdraw further into the corner.

He raises his hands. "It's okay. I'm just here to give you your present from Santa." He dangles a bag in front of him, trying to lure me with the promise of a toy.

The only problem is there's no toy I want.

And when they asked me to fill out my letter for Santa, there was only one thing I could think of that I desperately wanted and needed.

And there's no way it's in that bag.

It's not possible.

I turn my head to glare out the window. "I didn't want anything."

"Hmm. That's not what Santa told me." He shakes his head. "No, he told me your gift was the most special of all the gifts today."

"He did?" I ask suspiciously.

He crosses his heart. "On my honor."

I purse my lips, sitting up straight.

He points to the other side of the bench. "Is it okay if I sit here?"

I nod, watching as he sits, stretching his long legs before him.

"How tall are you?" I ask.

He scratches his head. "Last I checked, I was six foot seven. But my wife keeps telling me she thinks I'll never stop growing." He laughs, placing the bag between us.

I try to peek inside, but there's tissue paper on top, covering whatever hides beneath.

"So, why aren't you out there with all the other kids?" he asks.

"I prefer being alone."

I wrap the blanket tighter around my shoulders, suddenly feeling colder than I was just a minute ago.

"Santa told me you've had a tough couple of years." He frowns, leaning back. "Is that true?"

"I...I lost both of my parents." I wipe my eyes. "And I don't have anyone else." I shrug, trying to feign indifference and act brave in front of this stranger when I feel ready to fall to pieces.

"I'm sorry." He looks up at the ceiling. "I have three sons running around here somewhere, and they're the joy of my life. I can't imagine how I would feel if I lost one of them."

I look down at my lap. "It's my first Christmas without them," I whisper. Glancing at the bag, I shake my head. "There's nothing in that bag that will make things better."

He pushes the bag a little closer toward me.

"Doesn't hurt to see," he adds with a slight shrug.

"I don't believe in Santa, anyway."

"Don't believe?" he ponders. "Hmm, that's interesting."

"What's interesting about that?"

"Well, if he's not real, how would I know what you asked for in your letter to him?"

My lips part in shock. "He told you?"

"Think of me as one of his elves."

"You're too tall to be one of his elves."

He chuckles. "Santa doesn't discriminate. Besides, he needs someone to reach all the high places on his Christmas tree and change the light bulbs."

An unfamiliar sound slips from my lips: laughter. Quickly, I cover my mouth with my hand, alarmed by my reaction.

I can't remember the last time I laughed.

The man watches me, tilting his head to the side. "It's okay to laugh, sweet girl."

I shake my head. "I don't think it is."

He turns, facing me. "Without laughter, we only have silence." He picks up the bag, handing it to me. "We need laughter to make the days better. No matter how hard things may be, we must remember never to give up. And laughter, well, it keeps us going. It gives us something to live for."

I hesitantly take the bag from his hand and reach inside, beneath the tissue paper. My fingers grip something soft and pull it out, tissue paper falling around me, revealing a teddy bear.

"When Santa told me that all you wanted for Christmas was a hug, well..." He clears his throat. "We just knew this guy would be perfect for you."

I brush my fingers over the bear's beige face, admiring the big, round brown eyes. He's smiling, wearing a big pink bow around his neck.

"He's perfect," I admit softly, admiring him.

Cautiously, I bring him to my chest, and then, as though everything has snapped into place, I clutch him in my arms, closing my eyes. Tears run down my cheeks like rampant rivers. It's the first time I've hugged anyone, well, anything, since my parents' deaths.

"Oh, sweet girl." I look up, finding the man with a tear flowing down his cheek, making no move to wipe it away. "Is it okay if I hug you?"

I nod because this man seems to need a hug as much as I do. And as his arms gently wrap around me, I find myself leaping into his embrace, burying my face into his chest, crying harder than I have in my entire life.

His hand softly brushes over the top of my head. "Let it out."

And I do.

Minutes go by, the man not saying anything as I break down in his arms, missing my parents so unbelievably much.

I don't know how I'll ever get over losing the two most important people in my life.

I don't know if I'll ever fully be okay again.

Eventually, when all the tears have fallen and my breathing evens out, I release the man from my grip, wiping my eyes.

"Thank you," I murmur. The teddy bear sits on my lap, and I bring it to my chest, hugging him tightly, holding on to him like he's my lifeline.

The man smiles, wiping his tears. "What are you going to name him?"

I think it over before, confidently saying, "Teddy."

He mulls it over, tossing his head from side to side. "I like it."

"Oh, there you are!" Valerie, the woman who runs this place, walks into the room. "We were looking for you." Her eyes spot the bear in my hands. "And who do we have here?"

I peek at the man beside me before I reply, "Teddy."

"Well, it's very nice to meet you, Teddy," Valerie says. "We were just getting the afternoon lunch set up. Do you want to come out and join the other children?"

I shake my head. "I'm not really hungry. Is it okay if I come out later?"

She gives a small smile. "Of course." Looking between me and the man, she asks, "Would you mind taking a picture together? The snow in the background is just so beautiful."

"Absolutely," the man responds. "If it's okay with this sweet girl."

I smile and nod, leaning in toward him.

I face Valerie, who pulls out a camera and snaps a quick shot. "Perfect!" She pockets the camera into her green dress. "Join us when you're ready,

Sarah. I don't want you missing out on all the good food," she says warmly before turning and leaving the room.

"It really is good food," the man adds, rubbing his stomach. "I think I should join them before it's all gone. Want me to get you a plate?"

I shake my head. "Can you do something for me instead?"

"Of course."

"Can you tell Santa I say thank you for sending you to me?"

He sucks in his bottom lip, appearing like he might cry again. But instead, he clears his throat and says, "I'll pass the message along." He stands, looking down at me. "Don't give up, sweet girl. Things will get better. And one day, everything will fall into place as it was meant to be. I promise."

I smile, watching as he walks away and turns the corner out of view, wondering if we'll ever meet again.

* * *

"What's wrong, baby girl?"

I shake my head as my memory fades away. Wetness coats my cheeks as I look up to find Paul watching me from the doorway.

"Oh, nothing." I wipe hastily at my face.

Paul walks over to me, sits beside me, and wraps his arm around my waist. "Talk to me."

I let out a deep breath. "This is where I spent my first Christmas without my parents." I shrug. "It was just bringing up a lot of emotions. And I needed to walk out of that room before I started crying in front of the kids. Fucking hormones." I attempt to fake a smile, but I know Paul will see right through it, so I stop myself, letting my true emotions show.

Paul's hand finds mine. "This was the foster home you lived in?"

"Yeah. I grew up just a few towns over from here, so this was where I was first sent for a couple of years before I started my journey through the foster care system. I spent a lot of time on this bench." I pat the space beside me. "I was just flipping through this photo album when I found a picture of me." I hold out the photo for Paul to see. "It just brought back a memory. Hence the tears." I smile, looking up at Paul, but his face appears paralyzed.

"Paul?" I try to remove the picture from his sight, but he grips my wrist. "What's wrong?"

He clears his throat, taking the photo from my hands. "Sarah…" His free hand rubs the back of his neck. "Do you know who the man in this photo is?"

I shake my head, eyeing the image. "No. He's the one who gave me Teddy, though. He made my first Christmas here bearable. He even gave me my first real hug in forever. I hadn't let anyone touch me after my parents' deaths. But something about this guy made me feel comfortable and seen. And I just jumped in his arms like a freaking koala and bawled my eyes out for a while. He just sat there and let me, not saying anything. It was exactly what I needed, and then—"

Gazing up at Paul, I find a tear cascading down his cheek.

"What's wrong?" I turn to him, cupping his cheek, worried.

"Sarah, the man in that photo is…my dad. That was…" He sniffles, clearing his throat. "That was the last Christmas I had with him. He died a few days after this picture was taken."

"Wh-what?" I grab the photo from him again and look closer.

The big chocolate brown eyes.

The light brown skin.

The height.

The chiseled jaw.

The smile.

It's Paul's doppelganger.

I was so lost in the memory that I didn't clearly see him.

But now I do.

I turn to Paul, trying to wrap my head around this. "I met your dad?"

"Yeah, baby girl." He nods, brushing his lips over my temple. "You did. You met my dad."

And the most breathtakingly beautiful smile I have ever seen appears on Paul's face.

Thirty

PAUL

The house is thumping with music, the drinks are flowing, and the excitement in the air is palpable as people fill every nook and cranny of the downstairs. It's a typical New Year's Eve night for college students, and this year, Lord help us, Nate and I decided to play hosts to the partygoers.

Out of the corner of my eye, I see Natalie and Vanessa walk inside, brushing snow off of themselves as they greet Nate by the front door. Sarah's not with them because she's coming straight from the art studio on campus after working on her pieces for her show, but I thought she would have been here by now.

Squeezing the back of my neck, I pull out my phone to check my message chain with her and find she still hasn't responded.

Paul

Let me know when you're here.

Unease fills me, but I'm sure she's okay.
Inhale.
Everything is okay.

But it's snowing heavily outside. What if she got in an accident on her way here?

She has to be okay.

Exhale.

What if Greyson found her?

But I haven't heard a peep from Greyson. If anything, he's been keeping his distance from me during basketball games and practices.

I guess after almost being beaten to a pulp, he understood my message loud and clear.

Stay. The. Fuck. Away. From. Sarah.

With a deep breath, I take a large swig from my drink and observe my friends.

Tonight's the night Sarah and I will tell them about us. We decided a few days ago that it was time. Well, more so me because I'm finding it impossible to keep my hands to myself when I'm around her, and it's only a matter of time before someone notices.

So yeah, call me selfish, but I'm ready to let the whole damn world know that she's mine.

Not to mention, Sarah's baby bump is developing as she's in her *second trimester*—a word I learned from one of the baby books I purchased—and it won't be long until it's apparent that a baby is growing inside her. There might even come a point when the oversized sweatshirts aren't enough to keep our secret anymore.

So, it's time.

And I'm good with that because, on top of wanting everyone to know that this woman is mine, I want everyone to know that this woman is having my baby.

I quickly put another drink together and stride toward the group to find Nate kissing Natalie as though it were their last night on Earth together. These two can't keep their hands off of each other. And I'm pretty sure I used to be jealous about that, but now that I have someone I can't seem to keep my hands off of, I understand the feeling.

It's love.

And goddammit, I love Sarah more than life itself.

The word has been bubbling inside me for weeks, months, no… If I'm being honest with myself, it's been bubbling inside me since the moment I first laid eyes on her.

That was the moment I fell in love with her.

I've been overthinking when I should tell her—wanting everything to be perfect for her. Wanting to be sure she feels the same way. But is there ever a right moment to say those three words? Or is it something you just rush out because you can't hold it inside you for another damn second?

Either way, it's time to let her know how I feel.

To let her know how I've always felt.

And always will feel.

Reaching the group, I hold out the red solo cup for Vanessa. "Hey, Vanessa. Want a drink? It's your favorite."

She takes it from me, notices the red liquid, and smiles. "Thank you, Paul. Always such a gentleman."

I take a sip from my cup. "Anything for you, ladies." Nate and Natalie are locked in a staring contest, having a private conversation with their eyes. "Hey, love birds. You're supposed to wait until midnight."

Natalie giggles, pulling away from Nate. "I tried telling him that, but he wouldn't listen to me."

"How do you put up with them?" I ask Vanessa.

"Aw, I think it's cute." Vanessa smiles, but it doesn't reach her eyes as sorrow overpowers her features. I would bet money it has to do with Jason, who is currently on his way to California for the Rose Bowl game tomorrow.

"Hey, guys!" I hear her voice and immediately feel a lightness in my chest.

She's here. She's safe. She's okay.

Still drinking from my cup, I let my eyes rove over Sarah as she approaches, loving the short silver dress she's wearing that pushes away from her waist, hiding her baby bump and showing off those sexy tattoos on her body. She pushes her jet-black hair over her shoulder, and I'm already counting down the minutes until I can fist it as I shove my cock in her pretty pussy.

Fucking hell, I wish everyone would leave right now so I could take her upstairs and devour every goddamn beautiful inch of her.

"Oh my God, Sarah, this dress is everything." Vanessa twirls her finger, waiting for Sarah to give a spin for her, which she does. The light catching on her dress makes her sparkle, and the smile that flashes on her face makes her shine.

Is it possible to think a disco ball is sexy? Because that's what she looks like, a fucking sexy disco ball.

"Don't you think she looks hot, Paul?" Vanessa lightly shoves her elbow into my stomach, catching me out of my trance.

"Yeah. Yes. Yes. Definitely. You...umm, you look really beautiful, Sarah," I respond, clearing my throat.

A lovely shade of pink spreads over her cheeks. "Thanks, Paul."

"So, Sarah, who'd you come here with?" Nate asks, looking between the two of us. *The fucker.* He's dying for us to tell everyone so he doesn't have to keep the secret any longer.

All in good time, my friend.

Sarah plays it cool, shaking her head. "Oh, no one."

"Really? What a coincidence because Paul's not here with anyone either. Right, Paul?" Nate raises his brows with a smirk that I wish I could wipe from his face.

A bit of my drink goes down the wrong pipe, so I bang my chest as I glare at Nate and say, "Right."

"Hey, Paul. It looks like Sarah could use a refill," Vanessa points out, and I'm thankful for the distraction.

"Yeah, of course. I can get you whatever you want."

Knowing she couldn't have any alcohol, I put a bottle of sparkling cider aside in the fridge so she could still feel like she was having a normal

New Year's Eve night with everyone. I motion for her to follow me, and she walks closely behind me. I let my hand hang behind my back, and once we're out of the group's eyesight, her fingers intertwine with mine as I lead her through the crowded house and into the kitchen, which is a little quieter.

"Do you think they know?" she asks. "Well, we know Nate does, but do you think the others do?" She throws her hands in the air and then rubs her temple. "God, I'm so nervous to tell them."

I shake my head, laughing. "No way. But they will soon enough." She leans against the counter, and I place my hand on her hip, my fingers trailing over the fabric of her dress. "How did everything go at the studio?"

She smiles. "Good. I just had one last painting to work on, but I'm pretty much finished with the others. Maybe just a few last-minute touch-ups." She lets out a deep breath. "I think...I'm as ready as I'll ever be for the show in a few weeks."

Knowing she's nervous when she has not a damn thing to be nervous about, I kiss her temple and say, "I'm sure they're beautiful, and I can't wait to see them." Reaching into the fridge, I pull out the sparkling cider.

"I can't have champagne."

"I know, so I went to the store today to get you this." I turn the bottle around so she can see the label, and I watch as a grateful smile appears on her face.

"You did that for me?"

"Don't even act like this is a big gesture, baby girl. This is just a man making sure his woman is taken care of."

She pulls on my shirt, bringing her face closer to mine. The intoxicating scent of her apple honey shampoo fills my nostrils. "I really do love it when you sound like a caveman and act all possessive of me."

I place the cider on the counter and lean down, brushing my lips across her ear. "Well, I hope you're ready. Because as soon as the secret is out, everyone, and I mean everyone, will know that you're mine."

She bites her bottom lip. "Keep talking like that."

"Like what?" My hand grips her chin, forcing her lips dangerously close to mine. "Like how all I want to do is fuck you in that closet." My eyes linger on the small closet door down the hall before landing back on her, watching her lips part. "I want to thrust my cock so hard into you that you'll feel me for days, thinking only of me." I back her against the counter, caging her in as I brush my erection against her stomach. The whimper coming from her luscious lips drives me wild with need. "And I want to feel your pretty pussy coming apart on my cock harder than you ever have before." She subtly starts to grind against me, searching for friction. And I can't wait to find out how wet she is for me. "Do you think you can do that for me?"

"There's only one way to find out," she whispers, half in a lust state.

Hastily, I take her hand and look around, ensuring no one notices us before pulling us into the cramped closet stuffed with jackets and who knows what else. Turning the dim light on, I observe Sarah being the good girl she is as she braces herself against the wall, legs apart, scrunching up the hem of her dress, revealing her black lace panties as she sticks her ass out and waits for me.

"Don't make me wait," she says in a breathless plea.

I stand directly behind her, my cock practically rubbing itself on its own against her voluptuous ass. My hand reaches down between her legs, slowly tracing a single finger across the middle of her underwear, back and forth.

"You're soaking wet." I spread a trail of kisses across her shoulders. "Does the thought of getting caught turn you on, baby girl?"

"Paul..."

"I think it does." I tear her panties off in one go, loving the gasp that escapes her, and then release my painfully hard cock from my pants, rubbing just the tip between her wet center. "I think the idea of someone seeing you being claimed by me makes you wetter every second. Would you agree?"

She nods eagerly. But she takes me by surprise, taking one of my hands and placing it over her mouth.

I chuckle. "Scared you're going to be too loud?"

She looks over her shoulder at me and, against the palm of my hand, remarks, "Make me scream, big guy."

Locking eyes with her, there's no hesitation as I thrust inside her in one go. I feel her clench around me as she moans into my hand, bracing the wall for support as her head falls back against my chest.

My free hand wraps around her waist, seizing her against my body as I quicken my pace, slamming into her in a frenzy.

"Mmm, yes," she moans into my hand.

"You take my cock like such a good fucking girl." My lips brush against her neck before I bite down, sucking on her skin. I reach into the top of her dress, finding one of her hardened nipples ready for me to twist and pinch over and over again before eventually doing the same to the other one.

She's panting persistently, chest heaving, by the time I remove my hand.

I wonder if I could make her come from nipple play alone. I'll find out another day, though. That's for damn sure.

I reach around her, sliding my hand down her dress and beneath the fabric to get where I want to be. Steadily, with the palm of my hand, I begin to circle her clit faster and harder, giving her the pressure she needs to send her body over the edge.

Her body molds against mine, shuddering beneath my touch. I can feel her legs shaking as she pushes her ass against me as hard as she can, keeping pace with me. "That's my girl." She continues picking up speed. "Fuck, Sarah, you feel so damn good. Your sweet pussy was made for me and only me."

The praise is all she needs to come undone. Her back arches into me as she screams into my hand, biting down on my skin. My release quickly follows her own as my balls tighten almost painfully before spilling inside her.

My forehead rests against her shoulder as I continue holding her up for support, listening to her panting breaths matching my own.

"I've got you."

"You always do," she breathes.

I press a kiss on her cheek. "We should get out of here before someone comes looking for us. I would have to kill anyone who saw you like this." I slide out of her, tucking myself back inside my pants, wishing we had more time for another round.

She laughs softly.

"You think I'm joking?"

"No, I know you're not. That's why I'm laughing. You're crazy."

"Only for you."

Reaching for the hem of her dress, I pull down the fabric, confirming it fully covers her ass. I watch as she smooths out her hair and fixes her lipstick, her cheeks holding a rosy sheen.

She looks like she was thoroughly fucked.

But most importantly, she looks like she's mine.

Taking her hand, I open the door and walk out casually. A few people nearby turn their attention toward us, but I keep walking until we get back to the kitchen to get Sarah some water and then continue our journey to the front room couch so she can get off her feet.

I know she's perfectly healthy, as stated by her doctor at every appointment, but after the workout I just gave her, I want to ensure she's hydrated and rested.

We're sitting for only a few minutes when I hear a blood-curdling scream and instinctively jump up, blocking Sarah from whatever threat is nearby. However, when my eyes catch on the bottom of the stairs, where the sound came from, my heart plummets with a harsh force.

Vanessa is lying unconscious on the last step as Natalie hovers over her, frantically trying to wake her up.

"What's going on?" Sarah asks, unable to see around me.

I turn toward her. "Stay here. Don't move."

"But—"

"Don't move," I warn.

She hesitates before pursing her lips and then nods, crossing her arms.

Within seconds, I'm over by Vanessa and Natalie, with Nate reaching down for Vanessa.

"I've already called for an ambulance," Nate states, bending over Vanessa. "Vanessa, can you hear me?"

She mumbles inaudibly.

"Fuck. Fuck. Fuck!" Nate runs a hand through his hair and then slides a nearby couch pillow under her head. And that's when I see it.

Blood.

Lots and lots of blood.

"What the fuck happened?" I ask.

"She...she was gone for a while. S-so I went to look for her and...all of a sudden, she crashed down in front of me as though she was thrown." Natalie can barely control her sobs. She brushes the hair away from Vanessa's eyes. "When I looked up, I saw...a guy around our age. I didn't recognize him. But he disappeared down the hall."

Without thinking, I race up the stairs, looking between all the rooms, but come up empty. Walking down the stairs, I say, "There's no one up here."

"He probably took the fire escape out," Nate responds, sounding calm when I know he's anything but that. He wraps an arm around Natalie. "Do you remember what he looked like?"

She shrugs, wiping tears from her eyes. "He just seemed average and...wait." She stops, lost in thought, before saying, "He had this weird skull tattoo on his neck. Yeah. I'm sure of that. I remember seeing it."

"Okay, we'll find him." Nate kisses the top of her head as his hand finds Vanessa. "She's going to be okay."

The next hour is spent talking with the police and getting Vanessa on a stretcher and on her way to the hospital. Nate and Natalie went with her so I could stay here and try to find out what I could about who may have been at the top of the stairs. And after getting some information that might be useful, I kick everyone out of the house.

"Is she going to be okay?" Sarah approaches me hesitantly. Tears stream down her cheeks as she wraps her arms around her stomach.

"Yes." I slide my arms around her waist, holding her close to me. "She's going to be okay. They'll take good care of her at the hospital."

She shakes her head, sniffling against my chest. "Why would someone do that to her?"

"I don't know, but we'll find him." I glimpse at the time on my phone. It's just after midnight. "I should get you home. I need to go to the hospital. Nate just texted me to let me know that Jason's flight was delayed for California, so he left to go to the hospital, and I have some information I need to give him in person."

She nods. "Would it be easier for you if I stay here?"

The answer is yes. Her apartment is in the opposite direction of the hospital, not to mention there's a freaking blizzard going on outside, but I know how she feels about staying in other people's rooms.

Not that I would ever blame her for feeling that way.

"I mean, yes, it would be. But I know you're uncomfortable with it, so I'll take you to your place."

She shakes her head. "No. I...want to stay here."

I arch a brow. "Are you sure?"

"Yes," she says confidently.

I mull over her decision. "Okay, let me get you set up."

Taking her hand, I lead her up the stairs to my room. Pointing to the special lock I had installed on my door a few weeks ago, I state, "The code is 0801. Only Nate and I know it, and well, now you." I smile, pushing open the door, wondering if she caught on to her birthday passcode. I wave a hand around the room. "Every piece of technology, besides the

TV, has been packed up and placed in the closet. There's no video game cameras or speakers or anything."

"Why would—"

"Why would I do that? Simple. To make you feel comfortable if you ever wanted to spend the night here." I lift a shoulder nonchalantly.

Staring down into her glimmering eyes, I see awe. She bites her bottom lip, holding her emotions inside like always. Something that she's quite good at and something that I wish she would stop doing.

She doesn't need to hide her feelings from me. I want her to let me in. I want her to know she no longer needs to go through anything alone.

Never again.

The protectiveness I feel over both Sarah and our unborn baby fiercely surrounds me. Maybe it's not a good idea to leave her here without me. We don't even know where this guy is, for sure. And if anything happens to her, I would never forgive—

"I'll be fine." She reaches up, gliding her hand over my stubble, her thumb stroking my cheek. "Don't worry about me."

"That's easier said than done." I run a hand over my head, a nagging feeling that the last thing I should be doing is leaving her. "Promise me you'll stay in here. And if anything happens, you'll call me."

She nods. "I promise."

Her eyes catch on something behind me, and I turn to see what's got her lips twisting up into an adorable smile.

"You really did keep it," she mutters softly, admiring the piece of priceless artwork.

Our piece of art hangs on the opposite wall of my bed and provides some much-needed color to my dreary room.

"I told you no one was ever seeing that perfect ass except me."

She blushes. "You should go. I'm just going to shower and head to bed, anyway."

"Okay." I turn to the dresser and take out one of my shirts for her to wear. Leaning down, I caress my lips against hers softly before devouring her, giving her a kiss that tells her everything I need her to know at this moment.

I love you so goddamn much, baby girl.

I pull back, knowing I won't be able to stop if I continue. "I'll be back as soon as I can. Keep the bed warm for me. And enjoy the art." I wink as I close the door and wait for the lock to activate. Heading toward the stairs, I walk away with an impending doom that I shouldn't leave her alone.

That I should never leave her alone again.

Thirty-One

SARAH

I'm safe.

Paul's safe.

I'm safe.

Paul's safe.

The words keep repeating in my head like a broken record as I clutch the blankets tightly to my chest, waiting for the door to burst open, revealing Paul in one piece.

I keep checking my phone for updates from Natalie, but the last one was from two hours ago, just letting me know that Vanessa is doing okay and that they're just running some tests, which is a relief. But I won't be able to sleep until Paul returns.

I know how protective he is of people he cares about, and when he saw Vanessa at the bottom of the stairs, I witnessed unrelenting anger simmer in his dark eyes.

A turn-on? Absolutely.

But I'm worried something has happened to him, and I can't bear the dread building inside me.

I thought I could do this alone, but I can't. I need him.

Because...I love him.

"I love him," I whisper, a weight lifting off my chest at the release of these words. A smile spreads on my face.

It feels...overwhelming. Maybe even a little strange to say.

But it also feels so damn good.

And not knowing where the hell he is or what is going on is bringing that weight right back down on my chest, making it impossible to breathe.

I sit up, leaning against the headboard, biting my black-painted thumbnail before placing my hand against my chest, focusing on each breath I take.

Everything is going to be okay.

Nothing is going to happen to Paul.

I'm sure he just—

The bedroom door swings open, bouncing off the wall, and my eyes widen as I see Paul standing before it, his eyes traveling over me, ensuring I'm safe.

"Sarah," he breathes, his shoulders relaxing at the sight of me. His eyes set on me as he paces urgently toward the bed.

"What happened? Is everyone—"

My words get cut off as Paul swoops me up in his arms, holding me securely against his chest. I wrap my legs around his waist, grabbing onto him with all my strength. His hand cups the back of my head as I nuzzle my face into the crook of his neck, inhaling his scent. His heart races under the palm of my hand before I slide it around the back of his neck.

"I was so worried about you," he says, his fingers trembling against my neck. "If anything ever happened to you, Sarah..."

"I'm right here." I dig my fingers into his shirt, anchoring myself to him. "I'm right here. With you."

He kisses my forehead and then brushes his lips over my cheek. I pull away to look at him, letting our eyes lock.

His eyes pinch shut as his face scrunches with dread. "I can't lose you, Sarah." His voice is barely above a whisper.

"You won't." I press my cheek onto his shoulder, my hand massaging the back of his tense neck. "What's going on inside your head? Talk to me."

He lets out a deep breath and then sits on the bed, still holding me against his body, still needing to feel that I'm here with him and I'm okay.

"When I saw Vanessa in the hospital tonight, all I could think about was you." He flexes his jaw. "What if something like that happened to you? I would lose my mind, Sarah. I would murder the man who did that to you." His hand slides between us, gently pressing against my stomach. "If anything happened to our baby…"

I feel his heartbeat roar under his chest, his breaths coming out shaky. He's panicking.

"Hey." I cup his cheek, watching as he closes his eyes, relaxing into my touch. "I'm good, and so is our baby. Everything is okay." I slide my hand down to the center of his chest. "Breathe for me, Paul." With my other hand, I wrap my fingers around his wrist and place the palm of his hand on the center of my chest. His eyes open, so many emotions flying through them. "Breathe," I encourage.

I feel his chest slowly rise as he inhales, holds it, and then releases it in a long breath.

"Good. One more time," I request.

He does, the whole time keeping his eyes on mine.

My lips press against his cheek and then the other one. I take my time, gliding them across his lips, and finish by placing one last kiss on the tip of his nose.

He clears his throat. "I wanted to turn around and come back to you. It took everything in me not to because I needed to help Jason find the guy."

"Did you find him?"

He nods. "Jason took care of him. It was some guy that Vanessa had issues with before. But he won't be coming near her ever again. Especially after what I saw Jason do to him." He pushes a loose piece of hair behind my ear. "After I dropped him and Nate back off at the hospital, I came straight here because I needed to tell you something."

I freeze in his hold, anticipation building as my heart thunders beneath my rib cage. "Wh-what did you need to tell me?"

His eyes pierce mine, stealing all the air from my lungs. "I love you, Sarah. So goddamn much. So much that, to be honest, it feels..."

"Overwhelming?"

His lips curve up. "How'd you know?"

"Because I feel the same way."

Taking his face between my palms, closing my eyes, I brush the tip of my nose against his and take a steadying breath.

"I love you, Paul," I confess with confidence, dropping my hands to his chest. Opening my eyes, I see his lips split into a wide grin. Tears of joy pool in my eyes as I bite my trembling lower lip. "I just...I just want to make sure you're sure and that you're not just saying those three words because we're having a baby together. Because if that's the case, Paul, please don't feel obligated to love me."

It's been my biggest fear: Paul only wants to be with me because we're having a baby, and he wants to do the right thing out of obligation. It's not because he actually loves me. But can he blame me for thinking that when everyone in my life has either left me or pushed me away to be the next person's problem?

Never good enough for anyone to stay.

Only good enough to make them leave.

He lets out a low chuckle, shaking his head. "I can read you like my favorite book, Sarah. You think I only love you because we're having a baby together, but you're wrong. You think we made our baby *before I loved you*, but the thing is, baby girl, I've loved you ever since my eyes landed on you in that bar and got lost in those big, beautiful green eyes. I've loved you from the moment I saw you, and I will love you for the rest of my life. Making a baby that night was just the cherry on top."

Fresh tears cascade down my cheeks as I take in his confession. "You really love me?"

He grins. "With every beat of my heart and every breath that I take."

Emotions I've never experienced swirl through me like a tidal wave, washing away every trace of loneliness my heart has ever felt. "I don't know what I did to deserve you, but please promise me one thing," I request. He arches a brow as he brushes away the tears on my face with the pad of his thumb. "Promise me you'll never let me go." I place the palms of my hands on his cheeks, my voice trembling with the weight of my words. "No matter what happens, I need to know..." I let out a shaky breath. "I need to know that if I give you my heart...that if I give you...myself...you won't let me go. Because you're the one person in this world, I can't live without."

He shakes his head adamantly. "I will never let you go." His lips meet mine in a tender kiss. "I promise, Sarah. I will love you every day, holding on to you with all that I have. You're not alone anymore. And you never will be again... We have each other now. You, me, and our beautiful baby." He presses our foreheads together. "But I need you to promise me one thing in return."

"Anything," I breathlessly respond, my heart beating out of my chest.

"Promise me you'll always let me take care of you."

I suck in my bottom lip, looking down at the bed. "I'm just not used to it."

"I know." He strokes his knuckles across my cheek. "But I'm making a vow to you right now. I will always take care of you and our baby. No matter what you two need, I will provide for you and be the best man I can be in both of your lives. Always, baby girl."

"Thank you," I breathe, wiping each tear from my skin with trembling fingers.

He places his hands on my cheeks, his thumbs gently stroking my skin. "I love you." He drops one hand, moving it between us, tenderly rubbing my stomach. "And you, little one. I love you, too."

Wrapping my hands around his neck, I say, "I promise I will always let you take care of me and our baby."

A satisfied smile appears on his face. "Then it looks like we have a deal." His lips land on mine, kissing me with all the love we've kept inside ourselves these past five months.

All the love that will only be growing stronger and harder between us with every passing day.

Gently, he lays me down, his body covering mine as he rests on his elbows, holding himself above me.

His fingers comb through my hair, his palm resting against the side of my head. "I love you so goddamn much."

I bite my bottom lip, bringing my hips up to meet his. "Then show me."

He grins, brushing his lips against the shell of my ear. "I'm going to worship every goddamn inch of your body, and only after I'm done will I let you come."

His words ignite my whole body on fire as he reaches down and lets his palm slide up the inside of my thigh, grazing my sensitive skin. "Promises. Promises," I whisper. His fingers reach the apex of my thighs, expecting a barrier of cotton between us, but he appears pleasantly surprised at my lack of underwear tonight.

A low groan escapes him as he slides his finger back and forth through my center. "Always so wet for me." He twirls his finger above my entrance, teasing me.

I inhale a shaky breath, ripping my shirt off my body. "Please, Paul."

He trails kisses down my neck, his warm breath caressing my skin. "I love it when you ask nicely." Two fingers shove inside me, filling me as I arch off the bed, my breasts offering themselves to him. His lips surround a hardened nipple, sucking and nipping as his fingers reach deeper, hitting that special spot.

The one that only he can find.

"More," I beg.

His lips produce a smacking sound as he pulls away from my nipple, watching me with hungry eyes. I grip at his shirt, tugging it over his head, needing to see every inch of him.

Needing to feel his skin on mine.

The palm of his hand presses down, grinding against the most sensitive part of my body as I close my eyes, crying out in pleasure.

"Who does this pussy belong to?" His voice is lethal. Dominant. Sending me so close to the edge.

"Y-you!" I scream as he quickens the pace of his fingers working inside me with just the right touch my body needs.

I'm so close. So unbelievably close. But this isn't how I want to come.

My eyes flutter open to find Paul watching me with lustful eyes. The large bulge in his pants rubs up against my thigh, searching for release, and I can't take it anymore.

I can't take one more goddamn second of him not being inside me.

My fingers impatiently unbutton his pants and carefully pull down the zipper. "Please, God, fuck me, Paul. I'm begging you."

The smile that spreads across his face is beautifully sinful.

His lips ghost over the shell of my ear. "You own my cock, baby girl, and I'll give you whatever you want, which means I'm going to fuck you fast and hard, just the way you like it until you're screaming my name. But you need to do one thing for me."

"Anything," I pant, pushing his pants and boxers down his legs.

"Keep your eyes open. I need to see those beautiful green eyes when you come on my cock."

A shudder runs through me as I nod, teetering on the edge of insanity with his fingers still pumping in and out of me. My fingers clutch the sheet beneath me as my thighs begin to shake.

Pulling his fingers out of me, Paul positions himself on top of me and swiftly thrusts his cock inside me, sending me over the beautiful edge of madness.

And I do as he says, keeping my eyes open until the very end.

* * *

"Sarah Fleur?"

Paul and I jump up from our seats in the waiting room at the doctor's office.

After visiting Vanessa so I could see for my own eyes that she was okay, we went out to breakfast to kill some time and then returned to the hospital for my appointment.

The big twenty-week appointment.

Deep breath, Sarah. Everything will be okay.

"Here," I declare, walking toward the woman with the clipboard in one hand as she motions for us to follow her with her other.

Paul's hand falls on my lower back as he walks beside me. "Are you nervous?" he asks in a hushed whisper.

I start to shake my head but stop. "Maybe a little," I admit. "Not about the baby's sex but about the baby's health. As long as our baby is healthy, that's all that matters to me."

"I'm sure everything will be fine." He smiles at me as the woman ushers us inside. She takes some quick blood samples, hands me a dressing gown, and tells us the doctor will arrive soon before she leaves us.

After changing, Paul lifts me onto the table with ease. "No matter what, Sarah, you're not alone anymore. We're in this together, okay?"

I nod, letting the corners of my lips lift. "Together," I repeat.

Knock. Knock. The door opens, revealing Dr. Martin, who walks in, reading over the papers on her clipboard. "All right, Sarah, are you ready—" She stops speaking when her eyes widen at the sight of Paul. She looks between the two of us, her lips curving upward. I forgot she wasn't here when Paul came with me for the last appointment. "I take it you're the father."

Paul extends his hand, smiling. "That's me. Paul."

"Well, it's very nice to meet you." She places her clipboard on the counter. "Are you two ready to find out the sex of your baby?" she asks with a bright smile.

I lie on my back, lifting the dressing gown to give her plenty of access to my stomach. "Let's do this."

Dr. Martin chuckles. "Someone's eager."

"I just want to make sure our baby is healthy. I read somewhere that the twenty-week ultrasound checks for the development of the baby's bones, heart, brain, kidneys..." I flutter my hand around anxiously. "Well, you know what it does since you're the doctor." I bite back a nervous smile as Paul intertwines his fingers with mine. "And once we know the sex, we can start deciding on a name."

Paul nods in agreement, looking lost in thought.

"It's going to be a little cold," Dr. Martin warns as she begins to lather some gel over my skin.

"Jesus, you weren't kidding." I squeeze Paul's hand.

She places a handheld wand on my skin, moving it around until she finally says, "There you are." She points to the screen beside her and looks between me and Paul. "That's your baby."

I stare at the screen, eyes widening in astonishment. There really is a baby inside me. This is happening.

I look over at Paul, finding his mouth hanging open, and I'm positive the same thoughts are running through his mind. His eyes meet mine when he quietly whispers, "Wow."

"Wow," I repeat with glossy eyes.

"It's no bigger than a banana," Paul observes, staring at the screen.

"That's correct," Dr. Martin confirms. She continues moving the wand and taking notes while she clicks on her screen, pinpointing certain spots on the baby. "I can confirm with certainty that you have a perfectly healthy baby growing inside you, Mom."

Mom. My chest squeezes painfully tight at the word.

"Thank you," I choke out.

Paul's thumb traces over the lily tattoo on my wrist, his eyes welling up as he stands beside me, swallowing down his emotions.

"Now, let's see if we can determine the sex." Dr. Martin moves the wand around but quickly asks, "Are you two ready for me to say?"

We both look at her, nodding eagerly.

"It's a girl," she answers with a gentle smile.

Goose bumps spread over my body, a smile blooming across my face. *It's a girl.*

I quickly glance at Paul to make sure he's happy with this piece of information, but of course, he is. Because when my eyes land on him, I find a breathtaking smile on his face, which tells me everything I need to know.

"We're having a girl," I murmur, peeking down at my stomach.

Dr. Martin clears her throat. "I'll give you two a few minutes and be right back." After she wipes the gel from my skin, she walks out, closing the door behind her.

Paul lifts my hand to his lips, kissing the back of it. "I was hoping for a girl."

"Really?" I ask, surprised. "I would have thought you wanted a little NBA player like yourself," I tease.

He shakes his head, laughing. "I was hoping for a girl because, if it's okay with you, Sarah, I think I know what we should name her."

"What?" I ask hesitantly.

"Lily," he says matter-of-factly. "After your mom's favorite flower."

My throat tightens, my heart hammers, and my eyes water involuntarily. Of course, he would suggest this. There's not one thing this man won't do for me.

Including naming our baby after my mom's favorite flower.

"I love it," I whisper through tears.

"Me too." His thumb rubs over the back of my hand.

Suddenly, I feel a jolt inside me. "Oh my God." I place my hands on my stomach, tilting my head to the side for a better view.

"What?" Paul asks, alarmed. "Should I get the doctor?"

I shake my head. "No. I think the baby…" It happens again, causing the corners of my lips to tilt up. "The baby just kicked."

"Really?" Paul asks, eyes widening.

I grab his wrist and place his palm over the exact spot I felt it before. He stands there for a minute, patiently waiting, when suddenly he jumps back. Laughter erupts from me.

"The baby just kicked…" he mutters to himself, stunned. "I felt our baby kick." His hand runs over his face as he walks back to my side and, once again, places his hand on my stomach. The second he does, the baby kicks again.

A tear travels down Paul's cheek as he shakes his head. "We're having a baby girl."

"We are," I reply with a soft smile. "And she's going to have her daddy wrapped around her little finger."

He chuckles, wiping his eyes. "I can't disagree with that."

I sit up on the table, placing my hands on his chest. "I'm really glad I'm going through all of this with you," I admit. "You've taken a huge weight off my shoulders by being by my side. And I don't just mean here, right now, but I mean with everything."

He tucks a piece of hair behind my ear. "There's nowhere else I would be but by your side, baby girl. Absolutely nowhere else."

* * *

Paul holds my hand firmly, still wearing the biggest smile since we left my doctor's office. He really is so happy that our baby is a girl.

And so am I.

We walk down the hallway toward Jason's apartment, where we know the group is meeting for Chinese food, and I start feeling nervous about what they'll think. We haven't even told them that Paul and I are together, and now we're just going to spring on them that we're also having a baby.

This should go over well...

"Don't be nervous," Paul coaxes.

"I'm not."

"Your hand is trembling." He turns to face me as we stand in front of the door. "They're going to be so happy for us. You know they will be. And I hate to be the one to tell you this, but we might as well tell them now because eventually, it might be kind of noticeable that you are pregnant..." He pulls on the collar of his shirt, appearing uncomfortable.

"What's that supposed to mean?" I cross my arms over my chest, trying to seem insulted when I'm just giving him a hard time.

"Nothing. Not a thing. I just meant...well, umm, shit. This is one of those times when I'm just going to shut my mouth now." He tightens his lips together, putting his hands up in surrender.

I laugh. "I'm just teasing, Paul." I look down at the oversized sweatshirt I'm wearing that originally belonged to Paul but now belongs to me. He doesn't know that yet, though. "I know my sweatshirt isn't going to hide my baby bump for much longer."

"Your sweatshirt?" His brows pinch together.

"You just called me fat, so yes, my sweatshirt." I raise my brows, widening my eyes, waiting for him to counter as I place a hand on my hip.

But he just keenly nods. "It's all yours."

"Good." I grin, but the second I face the door, it falters. "Okay. Let's get this over with."

Paul knocks on the door and then opens it, poking his head inside. "Do I smell Chinese food?"

"Yeah, man. Come grab a plate," I hear Jason say from inside.

"Is it okay if I grab two plates?" Paul walks in, and I step closely behind him, feeling the uptick of my heartbeat.

Surveying the room, I notice Nate, who observes the ceiling, looking anywhere but at Paul and me. I know it's been torture for him to keep this secret, but it won't be much longer now.

"Sarah!" Vanessa and Natalie say in unison. I spot Vanessa on the couch with Jason, sporting a small bandage on her head, but other than that, she looks well, and it makes me feel relieved after what happened to her. And the sight of Jason being so protective of her warms my heart. They're in love, and I couldn't be happier for them.

"Is it okay that I'm here?" I ask, looking between everyone. "I don't want to interrupt if—"

"You're always welcome here," Vanessa adds reassuringly.

I follow Paul into the kitchen, where he starts plating food for us.

"Hey, Sarah?" Vanessa shouts. "I love your shoes. Where did you get them?"

"These?" I look down at my feet, examining my old pair of black Converse with paint splatters. "I've had them forever."

"Oh my God, Vanessa," Natalie gasps, her eyes widening as she looks between Jason and Vanessa. "I just realized that when you guys get married, we'll be actual sisters!"

Jason chokes on his food, initiating Vanessa to pat his back a few times.

"Easy, Natalie. Don't want to kill your brother before he graduates." Nate places an arm around Natalie's shoulder, laughing as he brings his drink to his lips.

"Keep laughing, my friend," Jason mutters. "Especially because I heard Mom tell Dad that she can't wait to see how cute Natalie and Nate's babies will be."

Nate spits out his drink, his face going pale.

"Yeah, that's what I thought," Jason responds with mocking laughter.

"Well." Paul moves into the living room and sits on the arm of the chair across from the group, holding our plates. I sit in the chair, feeling riddled with anxiety about where this conversation is about to go. But it's now or never. "Speaking of babies..." He looks down at me as I nervously bite my thumbnail. I nod in approval for him to continue. "We're having one!"

"Having what?" Natalie asks, scanning between the two of us.

"A...baby," I say, taking a deep breath, looking uncertainly around the room at everyone who has gone into a state of stunned silence.

Maybe this was a bad idea.

"Looks like that answers my question," Vanessa says casually, shrugging her shoulders.

"What was your question?" Paul asks.

A huge grin spreads over her face. "I was wondering if you two were fucking."

The silence is taken over by laughter from all of us. I hide my cherry-tomato face behind my hands, my shoulders shaking from how hard I'm laughing.

"Holy shit, Vanessa." Paul wipes a tear from his face, smiling.

Jason looks at Nate. "You knew, didn't you?"

He lifts his shoulders. "He left some baby books lying around our place. I had my suspicions."

Natalie stands first, followed by Vanessa, who both come over to hug and congratulate me.

"How far along are you?" Vanessa asks, her eyes sliding to my completely hidden stomach under Paul's sweatshirt. I mean, my sweatshirt.

I glimpse up at Paul first before saying, "Five months."

Everyone looks at each other, most likely doing math in their heads and probably now realizing the day we introduced ourselves to each other, we were already *very* familiar with one another.

"Wait, so that means..." Natalie begins to say.

"It's a long story." Paul wraps his arms around me and pulls me in for a kiss, taking me by surprise in front of the group.

But I don't even care.

Not one bit.

Because as my eyes close and my hands grip Paul's shirt, I feel the happiest I've ever felt in my entire life.

Thirty-Two

PAUL

"Has anyone seen Greyson?" Coach Rivers yells into the locker room, letting the door swing shut behind him as we prepare for our game.

Everyone looks around, shaking their heads.

It's unlike Greyson to be late for a game, or even a no-show, for that matter, and immediately something feels off.

"I'll call him." Glen picks up his phone and places it against his ear, but after a few seconds, he lowers it, glancing at the screen. "It went straight to voicemail."

Coach runs a frustrated hand through his hair, shaking his head. "We have five minutes until we're supposed to be out there." Placing his hands on his hips, he stares down the entire room. Every teammate straightens their shoulders, holding their heads high. "I expect everyone to give it their all tonight—no sloppy passes. Stand your ground when you're on defense. I want to see powerful blocks and well-executed shots." Every player in the room intently listens when he says, "Now, let's go kick some ass!"

Whooping and hollering resounds in the room as everyone closes their lockers and begins walking through the doors, heading into the arena.

Glen pats me on the back. "You coming?"

"Yeah." I nod, momentarily distracted by the news of Greyson.

"You don't think…" Glen's brows raise as he scratches his head. He's the only person I told about what we found on Greyson's computer and how we erased it all. Every single last one. Figured he deserved an explanation after I lost my shit in front of the team.

"No. I'm sure it's nothing," I state, trying to convince myself more than him as fear mounts within me. "There's no way he knows it was me. Ray hid all traces of everything."

He lets out a breath. "I hope so. The last thing you want is for him to find out it was you. He already hates your guts as it is."

"Thanks for the reminder, but he won't. I'm sure of it." I unzip my warm-up jacket and throw it in my locker. "I need to finish putting my stuff away, and then I'll meet you out there."

Glen stretches his arm over his opposite shoulder, pushing on his bicep. "I'll be the one scoring all those threes tonight," he declares confidently.

"Yeah. And Earth orbits around the moon," I say, amused.

Glen pauses. "Wait, it does, right?"

"No, you idiot. The moon orbits around Earth." I place a towel over my shoulder before applying gym chalk to the palms of my hands, rubbing them together to help enhance my grip.

"Jesus, you really are a nerd." He snorts as he bends over laughing.

"Get the hell out of here." I whip my towel at him, but he runs out of the room right before it strikes him. His hyena laughter echoes down the hall.

With Glen gone, I reach into my locker and grab my phone, finding a new text from Sarah waiting for me.

Sarah

> No pressure, but if you win, I'll let you do whatever you want tonight…

I smirk, knowing the trap she just set for herself.

I laugh, wiping the chalk dust from my phone, and then shut it off. Turning toward the door, I leave the locker room and head down the hallway into the arena. The place is packed with overzealous fans tonight, more so than usual, as we get closer and closer to the finals, aka March Madness. A buzzing energy in the air takes over me as I step onto the court, catching a basketball from my teammate nearby, and begin to dribble casually, glancing around the gym as I search for my favorite pair of eyes.

Relief fills me as I lock eyes with Sarah.

My green-eyed goddess is front and center, sitting beside my mom, waving at me as her eyes catch mine. Her whole goddamn beautiful face lights up in a smile so big that it produces one on my own. But it's the sight of that stunning baby bump beneath my jersey that makes my chest tighten.

Damn, she looks good in my jersey.

Sometimes, I have to pinch myself to be sure I'm not dreaming. To be sure that this girl in front of me, having my baby, is the girl I will spend the rest of my life with.

And knowing that we're having a beautiful baby girl, who I'm hoping is blessed with her mamma's eyes, spreads a tender warmth through my chest.

I jog over to them, dribbling in between my legs. A giant smile tugs at my lips at the sight of the two of them together, and I make a mental note to ask the team photographer to try to get a picture of them at some point tonight.

"Show-off," Sarah murmurs as I approach, watching me gracefully handle the ball like I was born with it in my hands.

"He gets that from his father," Mom tosses out, laughing.

"Hey." I hold my hand up, examining my fingers, looking right at Sarah when I say, "I thought you said you loved what my hands can do?"

The blush that spreads over Sarah's face is priceless.

"Paul!" She covers her face in embarrassment, and I enjoy seeing that pretty pink shade that covers her cheeks.

"What?" I feign innocence. "It's not like my mom doesn't know we've had sex. I mean, you are preg—"

"I'm begging you to please stop talking!" Her hands fly down to the tops of her thighs as she stomps her foot.

She's so adorable when she's embarrassed.

I chuckle. "Anything you say, baby girl."

My mom laughs, watching the two of us. "I'm so glad to have another girl in the family." She places her arm over Sarah's shoulder. "Not to mention, another one will be joining us soon enough." She bends toward Sarah's slightly protruding stomach. "We girls have to stick together," my mom whisper-yells as though the baby can hear her.

"Paul!" I look over my shoulder, finding Glen calling me to the team huddled together.

"That's my cue to get my ass over there. I'll see you guys after the game." Leaning down, I kiss Sarah.

"Good luck," she whispers.

"I don't need luck." I shake my head. "I only need you."

Jogging over to the team, I find every set of eyes on me, ready for tonight's speech.

Gripping Glen's shoulder, I scan the faces of my teammates. These men look up to me, not because of the last name on my jersey, but because of what I've brought to the table with my skills and talent to every game we've had so far. "I'm not going to sugarcoat things for you. Detroit is tough, and they won't back down tonight without a fight. They're ruthless with an unstoppable winning streak, but that ends tonight! They're on our home court! These are our fans! And we are going to show them tonight what Boston does best." Everyone waits for me to say the magic words. "What is Boston going to do?" I roar.

"Win!" they all chant back.

"We're going to show them whose house this is, boys!" Hollers erupt around me as I place my fist in the middle, waiting for everyone to join. "Let's get out there and give them a night they'll never forget! Linrey University on three. One... Two... Three!"

"Linrey University!" we all roar before separating, making our way to our prospective spots on the court or the bench.

As I walk toward the center of the court, Coach Rivers shouts, "No word from Greyson?"

I shake my head. Fuck, this isn't good.

Coach nods and puts his phone to his ear, appearing distressed.

Pushing down the unease creeping up inside me, I stride to the half-court line and wait in the center circle. The opposing player has to look up at me as he draws near, and I already know this will be an easy tip-off. The ball will be ours in a matter of seconds.

The referee approaches, standing beside us with a whistle in his mouth. I crouch down slightly, ready to spring upwards when the ref blows the whistle, releasing the ball into the air so I'm the first one to reach it.

And that's precisely what I do.

* * *

Fifteen minutes into the game, I glance over at Sarah's empty seat. I don't think much of it until a few more minutes go by, and she's still not there. With the ball in my hands, I dribble toward my mom, passing it off to Glen, and then quickly face my mom and mouth, *Where's Sarah?*

She mouths, *bathroom*, but something doesn't feel right.

Glen scores, running a lay-up to the backboard, and then runs past me, brows furrowed as he asks, "What's wrong?"

I shake my head, eyes glued to Sarah's empty seat. "Something doesn't feel right."

As one of my teammates blocks a shot and steals the ball, he passes it to me, probably expecting me to pass it to our point guard, but instead, I slowly pace up the court, dribbling the ball leisurely beside me. My eyes move to the scoreboard, viewing our leading score by twenty points. We've been on a back-and-forth nonstop sprint, and I shouldn't slow down the pace of the game, not yet, anyway. But I can't help my gut instinct that overrides every logical part of me as I approach the center line and call timeout, catching my team by surprise.

Tossing the ball to Glen, I jog backward.

"Where are you going?" he yells, his arms in the air.

"I'll be right back. Stall for me!"

"How?"

I shrug. "You'll think of something."

Spinning around, I dart down the hallway toward the locker room. Every instinct tells me, no, demands me to head this way. And the second I barge through the locker room doors and come to a complete stop from the sight before me, I understand why.

My stomach plummets from pure, unfiltered terror. My heart pounds violently beneath my rib cage. And my fists clench painfully by my sides.

Sarah.

My Sarah is on her knees, shaking, with tears pouring down her cheeks and trembling hands bound before her. A piece of silver duct tape is placed over her mouth, preventing her from saying anything as her eyes plead for me...to what?

To leave?

Does she really think I would ever leave her?

Has she not been listening to me this whole time?

To the words, I promised her.

"I will never let you go."

And right now, there is no exception to my promise.

The gun that Greyson holds against Sarah's temple clicks as he pulls back the safety, his cold blue eyes narrowing in on me as he coolly utters five words that ignite a raging inferno inside me.

"We've been waiting for you."

Thirty-Three

SARAH

Exiting the women's restroom, I take a left while looking down at my phone, scrolling aimlessly, when I clumsily walk right into someone.

"Oh, I'm so sorry—"

"Don't scream." Greyson grips my upper arm as his free hand pushes something into my side. Something cold, hard, and deadly. I swallow the lump in my throat, immediately knowing what it is.

All the air leaves my lungs as I'm discreetly dragged away from the crowd, with Greyson's fingers digging into my skin, holding me hostage. My eyes take in his worse-for-wear appearance, deranged and unhinged. His hair is askew, deep purple bags appear under his eyes, a dark five-o'clock shadow covers his usual smooth skin, and a slight tremor vibrates in his touch.

"G-Greyson, please don't—"

"Just keep your mouth shut and come with me." He doesn't give me a chance to say anything more as he forces me down the long hallway, eventually pushing open a large wooden door and yanking me into the team's locker room.

"On your knees," he grits out, shoving me down. I catch myself on my hands and knees before my stomach touches the ground.

"Please don't—"

"I said, on your fucking knees! If you make me repeat myself, we're going to have a problem," he sneers.

He pushes the gun harder into my side, and before he can do any harm to my baby, I immediately prop myself up on my knees. The overflowing jersey covers any sign of a baby bump, and I hope to keep it that way.

I won't let him harm my baby.

"I really don't like being made to look like a fool, Sarah." He shakes his head. "You thought you would get away with it. You thought I wouldn't know that you erased everything from my hard drives. You have no idea how much you and your precious boyfriend fucked up."

"I didn't—"

The cold metal of the gun smacks me across the cheek, sending my face flying to the side as I catch myself with shaking hands.

"Don't lie to me!" he shouts, fury lacing his words.

I push myself up, kneeling before him, as I taste the metallic flavor of blood from my split lip.

Placing the gun in the back of his pants, he takes out a roll of duct tape.

"Hold out your hands."

My fingers tremble as I hold them before me, deciding it's in my baby's best interest to do whatever he tells me to do.

The tape digs into my skin as he wraps it around my wrist over and over again, ensuring I can't move.

Furiously, he rips a piece off and then slams it across my mouth, smacking it onto my skin before tapping my cheek like his little plaything. Tears slowly dribble across the tape, falling onto my chest.

"I like you better when you're quiet." His jaw clenches as he looks down at me, proud of his hasty tape work. "Much better." He removes the gun from his waistband, places it on the bench, and then sits beside it, resting against the wall. "And now we wait."

My head rotates, facing him. Every part of me is a shaking mess, but his words have confused me.

Wait for what?

"Ah, let me explain." He rests his forearms on his thighs, leaning forward, becoming insufferably too close for my liking. "You're just the bait."

I don't understand. Why would he need me as—

My eyes widen, understanding jolting through me.

"You're a smart girl. Knew you'd connect the dots." An evil grin appears as he watches me. "Paul will notice you're missing soon enough. It will be impossible for him not to since he's been watching you like a hawk these past few months. And when he comes running in here, ready to be the hero who saves you, well…" He shrugs his shoulders, leisurely picking up the gun beside him and waving it in my face.

I shake my head furiously, murmuring an inaudible plea into the tape. There's no way in hell I'm letting him touch a hair on Paul's head. Even if I am entirely immobile, there has to be some way for me to stop this. Moving my eyes around the room, I search for anything.

Something that will make this nightmare end.

"You see, it took me a little while to figure out how you got into my computer in the first place. Or, more accurately, how Paul did. I had to think long and hard about it, and that's when it—"

But his words are cut off as we both hear feet running down the hallway. My breathing rushes out of me in panted exhales through my nose, leaving me lightheaded as though I'm about to pass out. When Greyson stands beside me, smiling triumphantly, reminding me of the monster I've feared, I know only one thing.

It's too late.

"It's showtime." Greyson presses the barrel of the gun into my temple, eliciting a whimper of pain from me.

The door slams open, and Paul emerges before me, suddenly stopping as he sees the scene in front of him.

His eyes darken, narrowing in on me, observing everything Greyson has just put me through.

I widen my eyes, waiting for his eyes to lock onto mine, and they finally do as I silently beg for him to leave.

Please leave. Please leave. Please leave.

It's the first and only time in my life that I want someone to leave me. To let me go. To get the fuck out of here as fast as he can.

But he won't.

I know he won't.

Because of what I stupidly made him promise me.

More tears fall silently down my cheeks, knowing he won't leave.

He never will.

Thunder roars in my ears from my vigorously pounding heartbeat as Greyson clicks the gun's safety off and says, "We've been waiting for you."

Paul's eyes move to Greyson, staring him down. I see a slight tremble in his fist, tightening by his side. His jaw furiously clenches as tension builds in his shoulders. "What the fuck do you think you're doing, Greyson?"

Greyson casually waves the gun in the air as though it's a toy. "Well, you made a mistake when you once again took something that was mine. And I decided I'm not letting you get away with it this time."

"Greyson," Paul grits out, his chest heaving. "Just put the gun down, and we can talk about this."

"There's nothing to talk about." He points the gun back at me. "As I was just telling Sarah before you rudely interrupted, I know it was you who hacked into my computer. I had to piece together everything, but it finally clicked. That night you stormed into the bar, trying to beat me to a bloody pulp, was when you found my collection of videos, including hers." He laughs manically. "It was my favorite video, too. God, I would watch it on repeat. Couldn't get my fill of her." He strokes the end of the gun over my cheek, and tears gather in my eyes, blurring my vision.

My eyes latch onto Paul as his whole body vibrates in rage. I'm desperately trying to get his attention with whimpers and head shakes, but no matter what I do, he won't look at me.

And I can feel him falling deeper into Greyson's trap.

Greyson's riling him up, waiting for the right moment to strike.

"Don't fucking touch her." The deep tenor of Paul's voice sends an icy chill in the air.

"Or what? I don't think you're the one in this room who can make demands right now," Greyson responds, sliding the gun down my head to the side of my neck.

"What do you want?"

"What do I want?"

"Yes!" Paul roars. "Fucking name it, and it's yours. Just don't fucking hurt her!"

Greyson's hauntingly eerie laugh echoes around me. "I want things to go back to how they were before you came to this school. Before Paul fucking Weston graced Linrey University with his presence, everything was perfect. But then you had to fucking come and ruin everything. Because of you, I was demoted to co-captain. Because of you, the scout from Boston who used to be interested in me gravitated toward you. And how can anyone fucking notice me when all eyes are on you?" Greyson's free hand wraps around the ends of my hair, tugging my head against his leg. "I'm fucking tired of you taking things from me!"

His body trembles beside me, rage engulfing him. "You don't deserve your position on this team. You're only here because of your last name. You know it. I know it. The whole fucking team knows it. But now, because of you, I've lost any shot with Boston. My chances of getting into the NBA are gone. And it's because of you. You fucked everything up for me!" Greyson snarls, shoving the gun harder into my skin.

"That's what this is about?" Paul asks incredulously. "Take my fucking position in the draft. I don't fucking care about any of it. The only thing that matters to me is her!" Paul's unrecognizable voice bellows in the room, pure terror laced between every word.

"Don't you think I know that?" Greyson coolly answers, a frightful calm overtaking him.

Paul's eyes narrow in on Greyson as he suddenly realizes his mistake.

He just revealed his greatest weakness.

The only thing in the world he cares most about.

The one thing he would jump in front of a bullet for.

Me.

I pinch my eyes closed, feeling the gun slide up the side of my head and then push into my scalp.

"And that's why I'm taking her away from you just like you took everything away from me."

Those are the last words I hear before I'm knocked onto the ground, headfirst into the floor, as the loudest bang I've ever heard in my life fills the room, quickly followed by a second one.

Just as I try to turn my body over, something heavy lands on my back, keeping me in place.

Peeking to my right, through blurry eyes, I see Greyson's body lying lifeless on the floor just a few feet away from me, bright crimson blood coating the checker tile floor around him. Realizing it's Paul who fell on me, I maneuver my body, twisting until I come face to face with him.

"Are you okay, baby girl?" His breaths come out shallow, his face paling.

I nod, unable to say anything with the duct tape on. He reaches up, his unsteady fingers quickly removing it from my face.

Sucking in a deep breath, I stutter, "P-Paul. Are y-you okay? What happened?"

His lips curve up the tiniest bit. "I'm okay because you're okay, Sarah. You and our baby. That's all that matters to me."

Something warm and wet drips on my exposed stomach, and when I glance down between me and Paul, I see blood.

Lots and lots of blood.

But I know it's not coming from me.

It's coming from Paul, who rolls off of me, landing on his back beside me with a thump.

"Paul? No. No. No!" His eyes are half closed as he tries to focus on me.

"I love you, Sarah. Promise me...you'll let Lily know her daddy loves her so much." His lips start turning blue as he gasps like a fish out of water, searching for any ounce of oxygen in the room.

Shaking my head, I choke out, "You can tell her that yourself!"

He smiles softly. "I don't...think I can." His hand quivers as he touches my cheek, ghosting his fingers across my skin.

"You promised me you'd never let me go," I sob, bringing my face down onto his chest, not caring about any of the blood soaking my skin and hair. "You can't fucking leave me, Paul. You promised me."

Using my bound hands, I lift Paul's shirt, revealing my worst fear. The bullet hole is directly in the center of his chest.

I bring my wrists up to my mouth and start tearing at the tape with my teeth like a ravenous animal, acting off of a pure adrenaline rush. The sting of my raw, bruised flesh is nothing in comparison to the pain circulating in my chest right now.

But I can't get the tape fucking off.

I try to stand on my shaky legs but immediately fall, tremors wracking throughout my body.

"Help!" I scream through a sob. "Somebody help us!" I place my head on his shoulder. "Please. Anybody," I beg again, feeling his chest slow with each last breath he takes.

"Please don't leave me." I kiss him softly. His beautiful brown eyes, appearing distant and withdrawn, close right after I whisper, "I love you."

Thirty-Four

PAUL

An obnoxiously loud beep wakes me from my nightmare.

My eyes flutter open against a bright light, and I immediately notice pristine white walls and an overpowering antiseptic smell that fills my lungs.

Where the fuck am I?

Panicked, I try to sit up but am immediately met with pain radiating throughout my chest, eliciting a bear-like groan.

"Paul?"

Turning my head to my side, I see her.

The love of my life.

The mother of my child.

The woman I would jump in front of a bullet for.

And did.

Holding my hand, sitting beside me, Sarah instantly stands, gently resting her shaking hand on my cheek. Her exquisite green eyes lock with mine as tears threaten to spill over and pour down her purple bruised cheeks. She inhales a deep, resigned breath, closing her eyes. "I knew you'd never let me go."

And with a single blink, everything flashes before me.

Sarah kneeled before Greyson with duct tape on her hands and mouth. Tears fell from her eyes over a fresh purple bruise forming on her cheek.

Greyson pressed a gun into Sarah's head.

I lunged in front of Sarah, knocking her to the ground.

Greyson pulled the trigger.

A pain spread in my chest that I fought against with everything I had as Greyson attempted to pull the trigger again, but I twisted his wrist, watching as he mistakenly pulled it on himself.

Greyson fell to the floor, lifeless. Blood was pouring out of his neck.

I fell on top of Sarah, trying to keep her safe.

And that's where my memory stops.

"Sarah," I croak, my throat dry and tender.

She sucks in her bottom lip, trembling from head to toe. "I thought I lost you."

"I'm here, baby girl." I squeeze her hand reassuringly. All I want to do is kiss her. Kiss her with everything in me. But seeing that I can barely sit up, I can't do that. "I'm going to need you to do something for me."

"Anything."

"Kiss me, Sarah," I beg tenderly.

She offers a half smile before gently kissing my lips, and I cherish every second of it.

As she slightly pulls away, letting out a shuddering breath, my eyes land on her stomach, and fear sets in. "Are you okay? Is Lily okay?" I examine her, panicking that something might have happened to her or our baby.

But this time, her smile grows. "I'm fine." Her hands rest against her stomach. "And Lily is doing great. The doctors checked me over while you were in surgery and found nothing wrong."

I smile, relief filling me as I slump back against my pillow. "Thank God." Sarah holds a plastic cup of water before me, guiding the straw between my lips for a few small sips. "How long have I been here?"

"Five days." She looks down, clasping her hand around mine. "Do you remember anything that happened?"

I nod. "I remember finding you with Greyson. And I remember the shots going off and falling on top of you. But that's the last thing I can recall."

She remains quiet, not looking away from our hands.

"Sarah?"

Her bottom lip trembles. "I was so scared."

My thumb brushes the back of her hand. "I was, too." I pat the spot beside me. "Come up here. I need you next to me."

She shakes her head. "I'll hurt you. Besides, I should probably go get one of the nurses."

"Not yet." I try to squeeze her hand, but my grip is weak. "I just want to be with you right now." I look down at the bed. "Is it just me, or does this bed seem bigger than a normal hospital bed?"

"It's bigger. They had to give you one of their special beds because of your height."

"Then that means there is plenty of room for you to get up here," I add. "I need you in my arms, baby girl. Please."

She purses her lips, looking over the free space, before finally giving in. Ever so gently, she slides in beside me, being cautious not to touch me as she lays on her side.

"That's better," I note, wrapping my arm over her waist.

She shows a slight smile that quickly fades. Taking a deep breath, she rests her head on the pillow.

"The security team at the arena heard the gunshots and then me screaming for help in the locker room. They ran inside and quickly got the paramedics, who took you to the hospital and brought you in for emergency surgery. I was with you every step of the way, refusing to leave your side, but the second you went in for surgery, your mom took me to get both myself and the baby checked out. Everything was fine, but...there was so much...blood on me. Your blood. Ray and Tina brought some things for me to shower with in your hospital room so I wouldn't have to leave, and Kevin even brought me a change of clothes from your room." She gazes down at the oversized sweatshirt and sweatpants on her body.

My clothes.

"Your surgery was a little more complicated than expected and took a little longer than they anticipated because the bullet…" She sucks in a deep breath, fresh tears spilling down her cheeks. "The bullet missed your heart by only one centimeter." Her eyes meet mine. "One fucking centimeter, Paul," she whispers.

The truth of her words rattle me. I almost didn't make it. I almost died in front of her, never being able to meet our baby. But I don't want her to know how freaked out I am by this.

"Baby girl, I'm here. I'm not going anywhere," I say softly.

"You don't know that," she quietly sobs.

"Hey…" I reach for her chin. "I made you a promise, didn't I? I'm never letting you go, Sarah." My thumb runs across her cheek, wiping her tears away.

Her chin wobbles. "I love you…so damn much. You did something for me that no one has ever been able to do. You brought color back into my life, and I can never thank you enough for that." She reaches for my hand, intertwining our fingers. "I need you… Lily needs you. So, please don't ever put me through this again, Paul. I thought…"

"I know." I press my lips to her temple. "Because I thought the same thing when I saw him pressing the gun into the side of your head."

I thought I lost her.

I thought I lost my whole world.

I thought I lost the love of my life.

But she's here, lying beside me, looking like the angel of my dreams.

"Where's my family?" I ask, looking around the spacious room and seeing their coats and things flung across different chairs.

"Oh." She wipes her eyes. "Tina took Lucas home to get some sleep, but the rest of them just went to the cafeteria a few minutes before you woke up. They'll be back any second. They've..."

"What?"

She smiles when she says, "They've been here for me. I mean, well, they were obviously here for you. But I just felt like they were my..."

"Family?"

Her eyes tear up for an entirely different reason, making me smile.

"They are your family." I brush a loose strand of hair behind her ear.

She sniffles, nodding. "The police came by yesterday. But it was mostly just a formality. Ray handled everything with them and stood by my side when they needed to talk to me. They told me that the security cameras captured Greyson forcing me down the hall into the locker room, and then you running in during the game. And the only fingerprints on the gun is Greyson's. Your coach told the police that he got a call from Greyson's dad, Mr. Black, right before the game because he wanted to know if Greyson was at the game. He told him he was missing for days and wasn't responding to any messages." Her eyes meet mine when she says, "The police will need to speak with you eventually to get your side of things."

She gently squeezes my hand, her thumb caressing my skin. "Nate, Natalie, Jason, Vanessa, and Glen have been in and out of here the past few days. It's been really nice having everyone here." She yawns. And for the first time, I notice the deep, dark circles under her eyes.

"Have you gotten any sleep?" I ask.

She shakes her head. "Not much." Her slender finger points over to the small couch on the opposite side of the room. "Ray insisted that I take that couch as my bed, and I did, but it felt so far away from you. I kept getting up occasionally to ensure you were still breathing." She slowly rubs her stomach. "You...you saved my life. Our lives." Looking up at me with a glimmer in her eyes, she says, "Ever since my parents passed...no one...no one has ever loved me or cared for me as much as you have."

I cup her cheek, bringing our foreheads together. "I would do it all over again, knowing you and our baby are safe."

She takes a deep breath, her fingers tugging gently on my hospital gown. Her eyes connect with mine, and I find myself getting lost in a deep sea of green.

"Look who finally decided to wake up."

Kevin's voice breaks us from the trance. Glancing toward the door, I find my family entering the room with food trays.

My mom quickly scurries over to my free side, dropping her tray on the closest table. "Oh, Paul!" she wails, hugging my head against her shoulder.

I wrap my arm around her back. "I'm okay, Mom. Promise."

"As much as I want to tell you to never do something like that again, I know why you did." She looks over at Sarah with a smile, wiping away her tears. "Your father..." She clears her throat before saying, "Your father would be damn proud of the man you've become."

My eyes water as I suck in my lower lip and nod, her words piercing me directly in my aching chest. "Thanks, Mom."

"Thought we lost you there for a second," Kevin comments, walking up to the side of the bed with bloodshot eyes.

"You definitely gave us a good scare," Ray adds, wiping his eyes.

"I'm okay," I tell them, meaning every word. *I'm okay.*

Ray grips my shoulder. "Guess we'll have to take it easy on you for the next few months."

I let out a deep sigh. "Do I even want to know the expected recovery time?"

"Probably not," Kevin answers. "But this just means you'll have more time for video games with me." He smiles, his eyes watering.

"You know I'll just kick your ass," I joke, trying to ease the somber mood.

"You're delusional. It must be all the pain meds you're on," he quips, wiping his face with his arm. "I'm really glad you're okay, man."

"We all are," Mom affirms with watering eyes, wrapping an arm around Kevin and kissing the top of my head, Sarah's head, and then Ray's. "We're a family. A damn strong one, I must say. And there's nothing we can't get through without each other." Her eyes land on Sarah, softening.

Sarah clears her throat, sitting up. "I just want to thank you for welcoming me into your family and making me feel...loved. I had a pretty lonely childhood, and I spent a lot of time wondering if I would ever be a part of a family again." She swallows, closing her eyes. "But twelve years later, you guys have made that possible for me." She opens her eyes, a tear rolling down her cheek. "And it means a lot to me, so thank you."

I gently clutch her hand, knowing it took a lot for her to be vulnerable in front of my family. To open up a hidden part of herself for them to see.

"One of the best things that's happened to our family was adding you and this new baby to it, Sarah," my mom says, fighting back tears. My mom glances at me quickly before looking at Sarah and saying, "This is your family."

And I can't wait for the day I can finally make it official by giving her my last name.

Thirty-Five

SARAH

TWO WEEKS LATER

Today's the day.

For the first time in my life, I'll show my artwork for others to see and judge. It's exciting but also...terrifying.

Putting myself out there and being vulnerable is not something I would normally do. It was something my mom used to do all the time, though. And I remember attending a few of her shows as a kid, wandering around in awe at everything she created, hoping to be like her someday. And that's why I'm doing this today.

Because I want Lily to know that she can be or do whatever she sets her mind to do. I want to be an example for her, but most importantly, I want to be a goddamn good mom to her.

Just like my mom was to me.

"Are you sure you're okay to come tonight?" I ask Paul, who's sitting beside me in the back seat of the SUV. "I don't want you ripping your stitches or making things worse on yourself just to see my paintings."

The poor man has been bedridden for the past two weeks, itching to get out of the house and do something. Anything.

His hand envelops mine, resting on my thigh. "I wouldn't miss your first show for the world. Not even a gunshot wound to my chest will stop me." He winks.

I roll my eyes, chuckling.

"Besides, the fold-up wheelchair is in the trunk, so I won't have to do anything except sit and be pushed around by my chauffeur for the night, Ray."

Ray does a salute in the rearview mirror, making me laugh.

"Nate and Natalie will be showing up at the opening, and Jason and Vanessa will be heading over right after she gets out of work," Paul confirms, checking his phone. "Mom is devastated she couldn't make it, but she had to get Kevin back to school today. His school was ready to kick him out if he didn't return." He shakes his head, but he and I both know that the only reason Kevin didn't return to school on time was because he wanted to stay by Paul's side, ensuring he was okay. "She'd like to take us both to dinner tomorrow night to celebrate, though."

I smile in understanding. "Your mom sent me a gorgeous bouquet of some of the most beautiful flowers I've ever seen this morning. I don't ever want to know how much she spent on them. And Kevin left me a gift bag filled with art supplies before he left for school." I shrug. "I think your family kind of likes me."

He chuckles. "They don't like you. They love you. And don't forget, they're your family now, too."

"My family," I repeat softly.

The sight of the art gallery appears to my right, and my stomach plummets.

"We're here," Ray announces, pulling up before the entrance where several people stand, bundled up as snow falls around them, waiting to be let inside.

A shaky sigh escapes me as I reach for my door handle, but Paul's grip on my other hand stops me. My hair sways over my shoulder as I quickly turn to face him.

"No matter what happens tonight, I'm so proud of you, baby girl. You did it." He smiles, lifting my hand to his lips, and presses a kiss.

The tip of my nose tingles. Tears try to escape, but I won't let them. Not tonight. Hormones be damned. "Thank you, Paul."

We all leave the car and enter the ample but quaint space. It's dimly lit, with individual spotlights on each piece throughout the room. Servers walk around offering refreshments and appetizers.

It's a bit surreal.

"What do you think so far?" Paul asks.

I nod. "It feels weird."

"A good weird?"

"Yeah." I glance down at him, something I'm not used to having to do while he sits in the wheelchair beside me. "A good weird."

"Ah, Sarah!" Mrs. Blossom strides toward me, looking elegant in a deep blue chiffon wrap dress. "They just finished setting up your pieces." She smiles proudly. "They are stunning. Would you like to come see them before we get started?"

I inhale a deep breath and nod.

As we follow Mrs. Blossom down a hall, nerves start gnawing at my insides.

What if Paul doesn't like my pieces?
What if no one likes my pieces?
What if the reviews are horrible?
What if—

"Sarah," Paul breathes, his lips parted and eyes misting. "You made these?"

I was so lost inside my head that I didn't realize we had come to a stop. When I look before me, I see *my paintings.*

My painting of my mom and dad beside me as translucent shadows watching over me.

My painting of my new family: Paul, Mrs. Weston, Ray, Kevin, Tina, and Lucas.

My painting of my hand and Paul's hand clasped together with a lily on top representing our Lily.

My painting of a field of vibrant flowers, which I used every color possible to create.

And finally, my painting of the photo I found of me, Paul's dad, and Teddy.

That one is my favorite.

Anxiety overwhelms me as everyone remains silent.

"Well..." I fidget with a piece of my hair. "What...do you think?'

Ray stares at the pieces, blinking a few times while appearing in shock.

"Are they that bad?" I ask, wrapping my arms around my stomach as I curl in on myself. Paul grunts, struggling to stand from his chair. "Paul, what are you doing? You shouldn't—"

My words cut off as his lips land hard on mine in an all-consuming kiss, stealing the breath from my lungs. His hands embrace the sides of my jaw in a possessive hold while my fingers clutch onto his black button-down shirt so I don't drop to the floor from my weak knees.

His lips brush against mine as he pulls away, pressing our foreheads together. "They are truly breathtaking, Sarah. Absolutely beautiful."

"Really?" I ask, unsure.

He smiles, wiping a tear from his cheek. "Really."

"These are magnificent, Sarah," Ray murmurs as I help Paul back onto his seat.

"Thank you, Ray."

"And just look at all that color," Mrs. Blossom remarks behind me. "To think this girl wouldn't use anything but black and white paint on the first day of class."

"I guess I just needed some inspiration," I say, gazing at Paul.

She looks between us with a warm smile. "I'd say you found it." A woman at the front of the gallery calls for her, so she excuses herself, leaving the three of us.

"Ray, can you take a picture of me and Sarah in front of her work?"

"Sure." Ray takes Paul's phone and waits for us to position ourselves. One minute, I'm standing next to Paul, and the next minute, Paul pulls me down on his lap.

"Paul, you'll hurt yourself!" I try to get up, twisting and rotating, but he grips me in place.

"I was shot in my chest, not my legs," he counters. "Now sit still; you're making things *very hard* for me if you know what I'm saying."

"I'm going to pretend I didn't hear that." Ray pinches the bridge of his nose.

We both look at Ray and break out into a fit of laughter as he takes our photo. After, he hands Paul his phone and tells him he'll be right back.

"Which one is your favorite?" I ask. Paul spins his chair, so we both face the pieces.

"I honestly couldn't pick. They each represent something so important. They're each a piece of you, which means I love them all equally." He kisses me softly, stroking the inside of my thigh with his thumb, his fingers on my lower back moving in leisurely circles, sending shivers down my back.

"I should probably get up before someone sees us like this. They'll be opening the doors any minute," I breathe, not making any effort to move.

"Let them see us," he whispers. "Besides, we haven't had sex in weeks; let me enjoy touching you."

"The doctor said you shouldn't do anything that makes you too excited," I pant as his fingers inch up my leg and under my dress.

"Is that why you've been wearing pants to bed?" he asks, his nose tracing across my jaw.

"I didn't want to tempt you," I reply, my fingers gripping his shoulder as his thumb slowly drags across the center of my underwear.

Oh God. Oh God. Oh God.

"Baby girl, you could wear ten winter coats, and I would still find you tempting." His gaze is smoldering, focusing on where his hand resides under my dress.

A familiar voice rings out behind us. "There you two are! We've been looking for you."

Paul promptly removes his hand, pulling on the hem of my dress as I straighten my spine and throw on a smile.

"Natalie!" I jump up from Paul's lap to embrace Natalie. "Thank you for coming."

"This is so exciting! I've never been to an art show before. There are so many people here," she exclaims. We part as her eyes turn, taking in my artwork. "Are these your pieces?"

I nod, biting my bottom lip.

"They're beautiful!" She wraps her arms around me again.

Nate walks up beside Paul, lightly grabbing his shoulder. "These are amazing, Sarah."

I thank them both, observing all the people who are coming this way.

Looking down at Paul, I say, "Do you think we could wait in the main room? I don't want to be standing here while people judge them."

"I think you'd be pleasantly surprised by what people have to say," he replies. "But I understand. Let's go get some food."

Nate begins to push Paul's chair, and as we walk out of the room, passing a group of people, Paul points to the paintings and announces, "My girl made that."

My cheeks heat up as he winks at me, Nate continuing to roll him down the hallway.

Natalie playfully bumps my shoulder with hers. "You found a good one, Sarah."

Yes, I definitely did.

As we sit at a corner table, I look around the room. "Where'd Ray go?" I ask Paul.

He glances around. "He should be back any minute. He just, umm, had to make a call."

Just as I place a piece of bruschetta in my mouth, I hear my name called.

"Ms. Fleur!"

I spin in my seat, seeing a young woman quickly striding toward the table. "I have amazing news for you! An anonymous buyer just bought all of your pieces!" she exclaims, holding paperwork in her hand.

I nearly choke on my food. "W-what?"

She nods enthusiastically. "He said he's having a house built for his family and thought these pieces would be the finishing touches needed."

I blink a couple of times, taking in her words.

Someone bought all of my pieces.

"Once the show is finished, the pieces will be sent to the buyer, so if you need any last-minute photos of them, I would suggest doing it before then. But your pieces have been all everyone has been talking about. They love them!" She flashes a beautiful smile, handing me a business card and the receipt for my work. "We would love to have you back, so if you ever have any more pieces you'd like to show, please don't hesitate to call. Congratulations!" She walks away, leaving me reeling from the news.

"Wow...I can't believe..." I'm at a loss for words.

"That's incredible!" Natalie squeezes an arm around my shoulders. "Your first sale!"

"Congratulations, Sarah!" Nate lifts his drink in the air.

While in a haze, Paul lifts me off my seat and pulls me onto his lap. "Congratulations, baby girl."

"People like my pieces," I murmur.

"No." He shakes his head, gripping my chin. "They *love* your pieces."

A smile blooms on my face. "I did it. I actually did it."

"You did." He pushes a piece of hair behind my ear, letting his fingers linger. "There's nothing you can't do, Sarah."

I rest my hand on my stomach, thinking about how drastically my life has changed in the past six months.

How beautifully colorful my life has become.

"He was right," I murmur.

Paul arches a brow. "Who was right?"

"Your dad." I smile. "He said to me, 'One day, everything will fall into place as it was meant to be.'" I gaze into Paul's chocolate brown eyes, softening before me. "When I found out I was pregnant, I thought my life was over when it was only just beginning. Because of one night, I gained so much more than I could have ever imagined." My chest squeezes as warmth spreads through me when I say, "Everything fell into place as it was meant to be."

EPILOGUE

SARAH

ONE AND A HALF YEARS LATER

"Put your hands together for the Boston Celtics!"

The lights dance around the arena as the players run out onto the basketball court, jumping right into their warm-ups. "Welcome to the Jungle" by Guns N' Roses vibrates throughout the stadium as it does at the beginning of every home game.

"Look, Lily, there's your daddy!" I point at Paul, running toward the middle of the court. With no surprise to any, he was the NBA's number-one draft pick and has proven his worth the entire season.

He's all serious. Ready and focused for the first game of the NBA finals. That is until he sees his little girl wearing a baby-sized jersey with his last name on it, and that heartbreaking, beautiful smile appears on his face as he waves to his little princess, jogging over.

"Daddy loves you," he coos as he scoops Lily into his arms, holding her high above his head. Her beautiful, big green eyes widen in excitement. She squeals, making the most adorable baby giggle as he spins her around before bringing her down to his chest. He looks at me and winks. "Daddy loves you too, baby girl."

I shake my head, feeling my cheeks heat up, thankful that Paul's mom is getting food now.

"You know I love making you blush," he teases.

I push my hair behind my ear. "So, are you going to finally tell me what the big surprise is?"

Paul woke me up this morning by whispering in my ear, "I have a surprise for you, baby girl." But now that I know I have a surprise coming my way when I don't like surprises, I've been on the edge of my seat all day, ready to get this surprise over with.

I swear to God, it better not be the Princess Leia costume he tried to get me to wear last Halloween.

Even Princess Leia didn't want to wear that costume.

He taps the tip of my nose. "Nope. You have to be patient."

I roll my eyes.

"Your mommy is so impatient," he tells Lily, who bubbles with laughter. "But I think she'll like our surprise. Don't you?"

Lily places her hand on Paul's cheek, giggling, and my heart melts into a big sappy puddle.

"Okay, you two." I gently take Lily from Paul, adjusting the little pink bow in her hair. "Don't you have a game to warm up for?"

He peers over his shoulder. "I'm going to win this game for you. And after, we'll go straight home so I can give you your surprise." He winks, bends down to kiss me, and then races toward his team on the court, where he spends the next couple of hours making good on his promise, winning his game with a buzzer-beater shot.

* * *

"Hey, Mom, do you mind taking Lily for the night?"

My head whips to Paul with parted lips. We haven't spent a night away from Lily, and I don't know if I'm ready for that yet.

Is that the surprise? Our first night away together since having her?

My stomach coils as I anxiously bite on my thumbnail.

He looks at me, smiling, taking my hand over the center console. "She'll only be just down the street."

I raise a brow in confusion as I look back at Mrs. Weston, who smiles and replies, "Of course."

"This was planned?" I ask, watching Paul, who shrugs his shoulders nonchalantly.

"Maybe," he responds.

After dropping Lily and his mom off at her house, Paul turns in the driver's seat to face me.

"What if she wakes up and needs me?" I ask. "What if she's out of formula? Or diapers?"

Paul laughs, his fingers running through my hair, pushing it back. "We've been living with my mom for a year now. You know perfectly well that the basement is stocked with everything and anything she might need for Lily."

I sigh. "I know. You're right. She'll be fine. Your mom has been nothing but amazing. I don't know what I would have done without her."

After we had Lily, we took up Mrs. Weston's offer to have us live with her. Initially, I was hesitant, not wanting to invade her space, but she assured me that having family in her home was exactly what she needed. And while Paul was away for games, she was always by my side, helping me navigate the enduring trials of motherhood.

God, I was so exhausted the first few months that it all seems like a distant blur now.

"Although..." He hesitates before saying, "There is a slight chance Lily will forget who you are—"

I swat his arm. "That's not funny!"

He chuckles. "She's going to be fine. I promise. It's just one night." He holds a small piece of black fabric before me. "Now, I need you to wear this."

"A blindfold?"

He nods, smiling.

"Really, Paul?"

"Really."

I let out a sigh as I take the damn blindfold and wrap it around my head so I can't see anything. "Now what?"

"Now, I'm taking you to your surprise."

The car starts up again as I feel it slowly drive down the road, but after only a minute or two, Paul brings the SUV to a stop. I hear his car door open and close, and only seconds later, he's opening my door.

"Is this the part of our relationship where you take me into the woods and chop me up into tiny pieces?" I ask, turning toward him but unable to see anything.

He laughs. "We really need to get you off of those damn scary movies." He reaches across me, unbuckling my seat belt.

"Never. They're my comfort movies." I place my hand over the blindfold, ready to tear it from my face. "Can I take this off now?"

"Not yet, baby girl."

I sigh in frustration.

His large hands slide around me, lifting me from my seat. He carries me bridal style, his shoes crunching on...gravel?

Where the hell are we?

"Nervous?" he asks.

"Should I be?" I respond, clutching his shirt. But as my fingers dust along his collarbone, I feel his heart beating rapidly beneath my touch. "Are you nervous?"

"Yes." I can feel him nod. "But it's a good kind of nervous. The kind of nervous I get before a big game." His lips land gently on my forehead, and I bite my bottom lip.

Finally, he sets me down and spins me away from him so that my back touches his chest. His arms wrap around my waist as his lips brush over my exposed neck.

"Okay, now you can look." He slides the blindfold off of my face, my eyes blinking open.

"It's a house…" It's a really lovely house if I say so myself. "Whose house is this?"

It has a wraparound porch with two rocking chairs sitting in the front.

It has fairy lights positioned all over the yard.

It's painted white with black trim and shutters.

A large eastern redbud tree stands in the front.

There's a stone pathway leading up to the house.

And lilies are potted, sitting on every step of the…

Oh. My. God.

My eyes move around the area, realizing where we are.

This was the abandoned house at the end of Paul's neighborhood, hidden in the woods.

The one that I told Paul I loved.

He bought it. No, he didn't just buy it. He transformed it into my dream home.

My mouth parts, all words in the English dictionary erasing from my mind as I'm rendered speechless.

"You…you…" I point at the beautiful house, now seeing it for what it is.

Our new home.

He wraps his arms around my waist, pressing my back to his chest. "I told you I would always take care of you and Lily." His lips brush across my ear, sending goose bumps over my skin.

"Paul, this is more than that." I turn around, clutching his shirt. "You built us a home."

He smiles. "Do you like it?"

Tears gather in the corners of my eyes. "I don't even know what to say except that I love it."

He presses his lips to my temple. "Want to look inside?"

I beam, eagerly nodding my head.

He intertwines our fingers, leading us up the pathway to the front door. Slipping a key into the deadbolt, he unlocks it and suddenly lifts me in his arms.

"What are you doing?" I giggle.

"I have to carry you over the threshold. I'm a sucker for tradition."

"Tell that to the baby we have together…" I tease.

He laughs, bringing me inside and placing me gently on the floor into a massive open space, the breath leaving my lungs as I see what's hanging on the walls. My heart hammers beneath my chest at the sight before me. Placing my hand right over my heart, I whisper, "You were the anonymous buyer."

The first paintings I ever sold hang front and center in the room.

I face him. "How?"

He takes a step toward me, reaching his hand out to trace the tattoos covering my shoulder. "These pictures were too important not to be in our home. They're our family." He smiles. "So, before I asked Ray to take our picture that day, I texted him to call the gallery and purchase all of them with my card." I roll in my bottom lip, shaking my head. "Are you mad?" he asks nervously.

"No," I admit, swallowing every emotion inside me. "I'm so thankful for you. I'm so thankful for this life."

His arms surround me as I do the same, holding him tightly. His lips press against my temple. "Do you want a tour?"

I lift my head. "I would love one."

He takes my hand, guiding me through the massively beautiful house. *Our home.*

The tour starts downstairs, going through the living room, the dining room, the elegant kitchen that overlooks the lake, and his office. And when we make it upstairs, he says, "There are five bedrooms. A master bedroom for us with an en-suite bathroom, a bedroom for Lily, and rooms for guests or future siblings for Lily." I blush, shaking my head.

This man.

He thought of everything.

Absolutely everything.

"Did I do good?" he asks.

"You did really good, big guy." I rise on my tiptoes, pressing my lips to his.

"And I was thinking," he starts. "We could fit some of your art supplies in the dining room. It has a nice view of the lake."

"That works for me—"

He shakes his head, laughing.

"What's so funny?"

"You really think I had a whole damn house built for us, and I wasn't going to include a space for you to paint?"

"What do you mean?"

He holds his hand out for me to take. "Come with me."

I intertwine our fingers, letting him lead us outside to the edge of the giant deck, where my eyes catch on the most beautiful thing I've ever seen.

"It's all yours," he whispers.

My heart bellows beneath my chest as I gaze at the mini cottage before me, knowing what it is. My very own art studio. One that overlooks the lake with beautiful fairy lights surrounding it.

"Paul..." My lips tremble, emotions taking over me like I've never felt before as I bring my shaking hand to my heart.

"Go take a look," he coaxes.

I want to. I really fucking do. But my damn feet are frozen in place. And as if Paul knows this, he intertwines his fingers with my free one and leads us toward my very own art studio.

"When you first saw this house, you told me you could see yourself painting here. You said someday I want a space built by the water where I can create art any time of the year. You were glowing with happiness at the thought of it." He smiles down at me as his hand wraps around the doorknob. "And Sarah, there isn't a single thing I wouldn't do to make you happy. I hope this proves that."

He pushes the door open, directing me inside, and I can no longer contain the small sob that escapes me.

Because I find myself standing in an artist's paradise.

There are easels and paints on one side, a whole wall made of glass that slides open, giving me the most beautiful view of the lake—our lake. And in the back, there's a family portrait of Paul, me, and Lily. Walking up to it, I immediately recognize the brushstrokes and techniques from Paul's mom's collection.

"I don't even know what to say. I'm so overwhelmed. No one has ever done—"

My words cut off as I turn around, stilling at the sight in front of me. My eyes, which usually have to look up at Paul, are currently looking down.

Love overwhelms me as I stare at the man who has my whole damn heart in a chokehold, down on one knee with a small blue box in his hands. His shaking fingers open the tiny box, revealing the most gorgeous ring I've ever seen.

An extravagantly round emerald stone sits on a white gold infinity band surrounded by white elongated diamonds, making it appear like a lily.

"Sarah Fleur." Paul's voice trembles as he says, "I will never be able to put into words what you mean to me. You are not only the mother of my child but the missing piece to my life. You are the reason my heart beats every day, and you are, without a doubt, the love of my life." I can barely see Paul through the rainfall of tears pouring down my cheeks. He gingerly takes the ring out of the box, holding it closer toward me, his eyes glistening against the twinkling lights around us. "My baby girl, will you make me the happiest man in the world and marry me?"

"Yes!" There's no hesitation in my voice. There's no reason for me to take a second to think about my answer. This man has unknowingly given me a life worth living again, and I want to spend every single day I have left with him by my side. "God, yes, Paul." I jump into his arms, wrapping my own around his neck as I greedily devour his lips, never wanting this moment to end.

Parting from me, he takes my hand, slipping the ring on my finger, which fits like a glove. My eyes look from the ring to him, my lips parting with no words spoken, completely too stunned to speak.

"Congratulations!"

"Hell yeah!

"Do you know how long we've been waiting out here?"

I gasp as I turn my head to find an audience. But as soon as I see who it is, I can't help the smile that spreads across my face.

They're here. Natalie, Nate, Vanessa, and Jason.

I clasp my hands on Paul's cheeks, greedily seeking one more kiss before I stand and run over to Natalie and Vanessa with open arms.

"We're so unbelievably happy for you!" Natalie exclaims through tears.

"I've already booked you a couple of appointments to look for a dress. We're going to make a whole weekend of it!" Vanessa squeezes me before wiping the tears from her cheeks.

"I can't wait." I look between them, cherishing this moment I get to share with them.

"Congratulations, you guys." Nate hugs me and then pats Paul, who stands behind me, on the shoulder. Paul's hand lands on my waist, pulling me toward him.

"I think some champagne is in order." Jason lifts a large bottle in the air and then quickly pops the cork off as Vanessa holds some plastic flutes out for him to pour into.

We all lift our glasses in the air.

"To friends that I'm lucky enough to call family." My eyes dance across the room, taking in everything about this moment before landing on Paul, the man who never let me go.

My fiancé.

My soon-to-be husband.

"And to the unwritten chapters of our lives." Paul leans down, kissing the top of my head. "May our stories only get better with time."

"Cheers," we all say in unison, laughing as we take a healthy sip of champagne, knowing our stories are far from over.

Because the best is yet to come.

The End.

THANK YOU!

Thank you for reading Before I Loved You!

If you enjoyed this love story, I would be forever grateful if you could leave a review on the platform of your choice. Your support means so much to me and helps spread the word to other readers!

ACKNOWLEDGEMENTS

To you, the person who decided to give my book a chance—Thank you! I am an extremely new author and hope to learn and grow with each book release, so thank you for your support.

To my twin sister, Amanda—Thank you for everything. I love you.

To my mom and dad—I appreciate your love and support, but please don't read any of my books.

To my beta reader, Ashley—Thank you for your continued support and encouraging words with every book I push your way. I hope you know that you're now stuck being my official beta reader for life.

To my beta reader, Lauren—Thank you for your support and for showing my books so much love!

To my editor, Erica Russikoff—Thank you for your keen eye and attention to detail! It was an absolute pleasure working with you.

To my cover artist, Kate from Y'all. That Graphic—Thank you for creating such stunning covers for my very first series!

Thank you to all my readers who share their love for my books on social media! Your kind words help spread the word to more readers, and I am forever grateful for your support.

ABOUT THE AUTHOR

Ashley Elizabeth is an author of steamy contemporary romance. Her books will always tell a love story with just the right amount of spice and, most importantly, end with a happily ever after. When she's not reading a romance novel or overthinking everything, you can find her at Starbucks, keeping them in business, or watching Jurassic Park for the thousandth time with her fur baby, Bailey.

Keep in touch with Ashley Elizabeth

WEBSITE: ashleyelizabethauthor.com
INSTAGRAM: @ashleyelizabethauthor
TIKTOK: @ashleyelizabethauthor
GOODREADS: goodreads.com/ashleyelizabeth